Face the Music

*To the Simmons
Thanks for
sharing in my
special day.*

Kevin Mallory

Bedside Books
An imprint of American Book Publishing
P.O. Box 65624
Salt Lake City, UT 84165
www.american-book.com
Printed in the United States of America on acid-free paper.

Face the Music

Designed by Dawn Eyestone, design@american-book.com

Publisher's Note: *This is a work of fiction. Names, characters, places, and incidents either are the product of the author's imagination or, are used fictitiously, and any resemblance to actual persons, living or dead, events, or locales is entirely coincidental.*

Library of Congress Cataloging-in-Publication Data is available upon request.

ISBN 1-58982-070-3

Malloy, Kerri, Face the Music

Special Sales

These books are available at special discounts for bulk purchases. Special editions, including personalized covers, excerpts of existing books, and corporate imprints, can be created in large quantities for special needs. For more information e-mail orders@american-book.com or call 801-486-8639.

Face the Music

Kerri Malloy

Dedication

I am indebted to my good friend Laida, who worked many late nights with me, listening to my ideas and providing me many of her own. It's said that good friends are hard to find. Fortunately, I've found a good one in Laida.

Kerri

Chapter One

Lana was surprised when her secretary handed her a pink message slip saying that Dr. Judith Montgomery wanted to schedule a meeting that morning. The word "schedule" caught her eye before any of the other words registered in her mind. The insignificant piece of paper somehow seemed so formal and foreign to the relationship she'd built with Judy over the past several years.

They'd had dinner together the night before and nothing out of the ordinary had come up. An uneasy feeling washed over Lana. Knowing she wouldn't be able to concentrate on a budget proposal she'd planned to work on that day, Lana forced her fingers to dial Judy's extension.

Judy's assistant, Ellie, answered on the first ring as if she'd sat diligently awaiting her call.

"Hi, Ellie. It's Lana. I received Judy's message saying she wanted to see me. Do you know anything about this?"

"No, she didn't mention anything to me. Do you want me to tell her you're on the line?"

"No, that's okay. Do you think it'd be all right if I came down now?"

"Let me check," Ellie offered.

The thirty or so seconds it took before Ellie came back on the line seemed to last forever.

After Ellie told her Judy was available, Lana quickly hung up the phone, announced to her staff of three that she'd be meeting with Dr. Montgomery, and was gone before anyone had the time to respond.

Lana's heart was beating faster than normal as she hurried down the stairwell, taking two stairs at a time. Reaching the bottom step, she slowed her pace, trying to stave off a panic attack by taking deep long breaths, a trick she'd learned in yoga class years before. Concentrating on her breathing stilled her body but did not prevent her thoughts from veering off in a hundred different directions.

What does Judy want to see me about? Why didn't she just call instead of scheduling a meeting? Did something happen to someone? Why didn't Judy mention it over dinner last night?

By the time Lana reached Judy's office, she felt emotionally drained. Ellie was nowhere in sight, and, since Judy's door was ajar, Lana poked her head in. "Hi, Judy. What's up?" she asked, surprised at the smooth sound of her voice.

Judy was sitting at her desk, her head buried in a case folder. The office was in its usual messy state, or, as Judy liked to call it, "organized chaos." Manila folders with color-coded tabs coated the top of the antique desk. The beveled-edged piece of glass sitting atop the mahogany side table was strewn with medical books and magazines, some appearing as if they were about to fall to the ground.

The three rows of shelves taking up the entire wall opposite Judy's desk seemed barely able to hold the treasures Judy's patients had so generously given up. The moss-colored walls, a welcome change from the starkness of the hospital corridors, housed prints of original works of art one would expect to find in a museum. The pastel-colored landscapes, impressionistic in style, along with all the other knickknacks Judy had collected, gave more of a living room feel rather than that of a doctor's office.

Judy looked up as soon as she heard her friend's voice. "Hi, Lana. I'm so glad you could fit me in. Please sit down." She motioned toward one of the floral-patterned chairs facing her desk.

Several seconds went by before Judy broke the silence and confessed she had something very important to discuss. "I've thought about this for awhile," she admitted, "and was waiting for the right moment to bring up the subject. Before I begin, I want you to do two things for me." She momentarily paused to give Lana a chance to respond. When she didn't, Judy continued. "One, promise me you will keep an open mind and listen to all I have to say. I don't expect an answer today. In fact, I would prefer you leave our meeting saying you will give it some thought. Can you do that for me?"

Lana nodded uneasily.

Judy watched in sympathy, aware from her many years of treating Lana on a professional basis that the request she was about to make of her friend might cause her pain. As strong as Lana seemed, Judy knew that on the inside she was still fragile.

"Secondly," Judy continued, "know that I love you like a sister and only have your best interest at heart."

After another moment of silence, Judy proceeded with her request.

Before Judy could get the last word past her lips, Lana vaulted from her chair and began pacing across the spacious office.

Her mind reeling, Lana couldn't believe what she'd just heard. Dr. Judy Montgomery, a noted psychiatrist at Mt. Sinai Hospital and her most trusted friend, wanted her to take a leave of absence and venture to Vermont to help Judy's nephew deal with a recent tragedy. Judy didn't go into too much detail about the situation, but the mention of a four-year-old child's involvement was more than she could handle.

Lana couldn't understand why Judy, who knew her better than anyone else, could believe she was ready to deal with something that hit so close to home. One thing was certain: she would never allow herself to delve into memories that had long ago been buried. Opening old wounds would be like taking the lid off Pandora's box; where she would run the risk of no return.

Lana was bewildered that Judy would even think that she'd want to get involved in this kind of situation. Judy had been her savior over the last few years, and, try as she might, Lana couldn't hold back the feelings of hurt and betrayal running through her.

Finally, when Lana's pacing had slowed almost to a standstill, and Judy was sure her friend had fully digested the information, she broke the silence. "Talk to me, Lana. Tell me what you're feeling."

When no response came, she continued. "In my heart I know you can do this. You know that I would never do anything to hurt you."

Judy studied Lana closely, trying to gauge her friend's silence. When it became clear that Lana wasn't going to respond, Judy tried again to make Lana understand. "You're looking at me with such pain—pain that I remember seeing on your face three years ago. Even seeing the wounded look on your face, I still believe much can be gained from this. Can you at least see that?"

But Lana could only see red. "I can't believe this," Lana scoffed angrily. "This isn't something I can handle and I don't understand how you could even ask this of me!"

"I think if you give it some thought and allow your mind to open to the possibility you might think differently. I am asking you to do this not only as a friend but also as a professional. My nephew needs help with what he's going through, and I haven't been able to breach the wall he's erected."

Shaking her head, Judy conceded, "Maybe I'm too close to the situation. Every time I'm with him or talk to him on the phone I find myself bleeding inside. My usual magic isn't working. In all the years I've been helping people, I've never felt so inadequate." Raising her hands in surrender, she muttered, "I'm at my wit's end." She stood then and walked around to the front of her desk. She wanted to get closer to Lana, yet still give her room to breathe.

Lana only stared, still having trouble digesting the whole thing.

When the silence had hung in the air a little too long, Judy once again broke through the dead air. "This situation is delicate, and my broaching this subject with you is one I have spent many nights contemplating. My nephew Trevor is an extremely private person and had the same reaction to my idea. Eventually, he came around."

She moved forward and placed her hand on Lana's trembling shoulder. "Trust me when I tell you I have exhausted all other possibilities and nothing has worked. There's so much more I wish I could share, which might help you make up your mind, but I can't. You see, Trevor feels the need to protect certain facts, and while I'm not sure I agree with him, I'll do anything to resurrect the person he once was."

Judy tried to intercept Lana's stare, searching for any sign that she'd at least softened to the idea. But all she saw was pain and anger. In a final attempt to get Lana to see reason, she professed, "I ask this favor of you for a couple reasons. First, I want to make sure Trevor and Lily get the help they need, and second, I think it's time—no, I *know* it's time—for you to allow yourself to be a whole person again."

A whole person again? Lana couldn't believe that her best friend could utter those words. "I didn't know I wasn't a whole person!" Staring icily at the woman who now seemed a stranger, Lana added, "This half of a person needs to get some air." Abruptly, she turned and walked out the door.

Tears streaming down her face, Lana took the stairwell to her office, avoiding the usually crowded elevators. By now it was lunchtime and she was thankful her staff would be eating in the cafeteria, leaving her alone to deal with her anguish.

Why was she so angry? Judy hadn't demanded that she accept; she had only asked that she consider the idea. Why was she reacting this way?

The small office with a door, one of the perks she'd received when she was promoted to assistant administrator just a year after starting in the department, suddenly felt claustrophobic. The modest haven usually provided a place where she could lose herself in business matters—sometimes up to twelve hours a day—keeping at bay the dark thoughts that constantly threatened to destroy her hard-earned resolve.

Today that was not the case.

The short walk up the stairs and the deep sadness enveloping her left Lana exhausted, inducing a flood of tears she had long ago thought dried up. Sitting at her desk, her face in her hands and feeling very alone, she began reflecting on her current life.

Over the last few years, the person everyone thought of as Lana had really been an illusion. She vaguely remembered reciting the nursery rhyme "Humpty Dumpty" to her daughter, and she thought of herself as Humpty. She was glued back together but the cracks had never disappeared.

When her life shattered into a million pieces several years ago, she'd worked hard with Judy to put herself back together again. She was now a functional egg! Her career was her life. Working ten- to twelve-hour days was her normal routine. When meetings didn't go too late, an hour-and-a-half workout at the gym was common. Then straight home to a light supper, a quick shower, and off to bed. Occasionally, she squeezed in a late dinner with Judy or her parents. These were the constants in her life, and she depended on her routine as a means of maintaining a sense of sanity.

Most of Lana's coworkers admired her business acumen and tenacious nature. Prior to her arrival, the department's reputation had been in shambles. Now it was considered one of the most efficient in the hospital.

She dressed impeccably, never wavering from her Talbots attire. Many of the clothes she wore were purchased by mail order. Where once she loved to shop for hours with friends, she now preferred perusing catalogues. Malls were totally out of the question—too many people and too much noise.

Working out five days a week helped Lana maintain a trim figure. At thirty-six years old, she was in the best physical shape she'd ever been in. Men and women alike turned their heads when she walked into a room. Her tall, five-feet-nine-inch frame, dark blond, shoulder-length hair, and cerulean blue eyes captured attention, but her standoffish nature said "stay away."

With the exception of those she worked with, Lana rarely looked people in the eyes. At one time, she had been friendly and outgoing. Now she was considered introverted. She never mingled with hospital personnel, other than Judy, and hardly ever associated with old friends.

The hospital staff was aware of Lana's tragic past and maintained a friendly distance from her. New hires at the hospital learned quickly that one didn't get too close to Lana Turnwell. Her aloofness was a badge she wore constantly, never letting her guard down for one minute. She enjoyed her solitude and reveled in the fact that her career was not only life encompassing but lucrative as well. She had become very accustomed to her life and, at times, truly believed things were as normal as they were ever going to be.

Why did Judy have to go and upset the balance she'd fought so hard to achieve? She couldn't believe Judy could ask her this favor. The Judy she thought she knew and loved would never do anything to cause her such pain.

Lana had begun seeing Judy on a professional basis three years ago. When they first met, Lana was just a shell of a person, the result of losing her husband and one-year-old child in a car accident. When her depression refused to subside several months after the accident, she agreed to seek professional help.

Kate Webber had offered to move in with her daughter right after the accident, and Lana had gladly accepted. What originally was supposed to last for a few weeks turned into months.

Watching her daughter's sanity slowly slip away made Mrs. Webber feel as helpless as her child. She pleaded with Lana to at least see her physician in the hopes that a prescription antidepressant would help ease some of the terrible sadness. Lana finally acquiesced, fearing that if she didn't get help soon she might never be able to climb out of the dark tunnel she had mentally dug.

Lana would never forget that particular visit to her doctor. She hadn't showered that morning or donned one of her usual coordinated outfits. Wearing the same sweatpants she'd been living in for days, her hair barely combed and her face devoid of makeup, she let her mother guide her through the waiting room as she'd done when she was a child.

As soon as they reached the front desk, Rose, the middle-aged nurse standing at the reception area, knew immediately who they were. Earlier that morning she'd received a phone call from Lana's mother and had promised she would personally see to it that they would not have long to wait. True to her words, she led the pair directly into the doctor's office. If it seemed strange that she hadn't chosen one of the examining rooms, no one seemed to have noticed.

After their phone call, Rose had made it a point to give the doctor a briefing on Lana's visit. Months before, he'd heard about a nurse who had lost her family in a car accident but hadn't made the connection until Rose mentioned her name. He happened to be walking out of examining room number two when he spotted the woman he vaguely remembered treating some time ago. He was supposed to look in on a patient in room three but instead headed for his office. There he stood in the doorway, watching the young woman's mother guide her daughter into the chair across from his desk. He waited until both were seated before he entered the room.

He barely recognized the frail woman crouched low in the chair. "I'm glad you came in, Lana. I'm very sorry about what happened," Dr. Stevens said, sounding genuinely concerned. "I want to do whatever I can to help."

No reaction. No eye contact. Nothing.

Mrs. Webber waited a moment for Lana to speak. When that didn't happen, she took the lead. "Lana's been having some trouble sleeping and I think if we can get her to at least sleep through the night she'd be…well… physically better."

Dr. Stevens knew that prescribing a sleeping pill was not going to bring this woman out of her deep depression. He had to break through her shell and find out what was going on inside her head. Did she want to get better? Was she suicidal?

He tried a different tack. "Lana, please look at me. I can't help you unless you talk to me. Tell me what you're feeling."

Still nothing.

Intent on breaking through, he looked into her blank eyes and, in a tone laced with heartfelt sincerity, began talking about an excellent grief-counseling program at the hospital.

Hearing the word *counseling* immediately conjured up an image of old widows and widowers sitting in a semicircle talking about the woes of being alone. No way was Lana about to share her innermost thoughts with a group of people she didn't know. She shook her head, and for the first time since entering the medical building, voiced a response. "*No!*"

Her adamant refusal didn't stop Dr. Stevens from trying to steer her toward some sort of professional help. "Lana, if group therapy isn't right for you then at least consider some kind of counseling. What you've gone through is something far too painful for a mind to handle on its own. When the brain becomes too overloaded it shuts down and…"

Lana sat there half hearing what he was saying, focusing more on how sterile the office looked and felt. The wall directly across from her was covered with a variety of frames showcasing the degrees the doctor had earned. Papers, folders, and magazines were neatly placed in piles covering the mahogany desk. The green leather wingback chairs facing the front of the escritoire were stiff, uncomfortable, and cold to the touch. The chrome-framed pictures decorating the remaining walls were the kind one would find on display in any furniture store and in no way gave a glimpse of who this doctor was as a person.

The doctor Lana had been seeing for the last fifteen years had retired a few years ago and recommended she stay on with the physician taking over his practice. She could count on one hand the number of times she'd visited the office since—strep throat, a bad case of the flu, and a major sinus infection were the causes. Consequently, she hadn't developed a relationship with this new doctor and wasn't in the mood to share her life with him. She just wanted drugs to make the pain go away.

As a private person, Lana knew that group therapy was out of the question. She felt incapable of sharing her grief with a room full of strangers. And then there was the feeling that if the accident wasn't mentioned aloud, she would someday wake up from the terrible nightmare and it would all be over.

After finishing his long sermon on the positive effects of counseling, Dr. Stevens saw that nothing had penetrated Lana's despair and walked around his desk. He proceeded to take Lana's blood pressure in hopes that human contact might get her to open up and share her feelings, releasing some of the tension so noticeable around her eyes and mouth.

Feeling her bone-thin arm and slightly trembling body, he talked soothingly to her, hoping she would voice what was going through her head. He asked if she'd been eating, had ventured out of the house, or had returned to her job.

The only response she was capable of was the stream of tears cascading down her face.

Lana was slightly disappointed that she wasn't able to connect with this man, but her current state of mind probably wouldn't have let anyone break through the wall she'd built. She'd agreed to come here for one reason and one reason only. Drugs! She didn't want to waste anyone's time talking about grief counseling or one-on-one therapy. Feeling very agitated, she spoke in a tone edged with sarcasm and told the doctor she didn't want therapy, was in perfect health, and just needed some antidepressant drugs to take off some of the edge.

She softened her tone a bit when she noticed the defeated look on his face. "Look. I promise that if the drugs don't have any effect, I'll go down a different path."

She wasn't a woman to be reasoned with, and the best he could do for now was to follow her lead. He knew that the drugs alone wouldn't solve anything but had faith in her as a nurse that she'd keep her word.

The drugs would at least raise her mood level a bit and hopefully allow her to consider other choices.

Dr. Stevens then walked over to a file cabinet and pulled out several packets. Lana knew what they were the instant she saw them: Prozac. For just a moment she pictured herself addicted to this little pill, the wonder drug that would make everything go away. But she knew better. Nothing could ever make this pain go completely away.

While writing a prescription for the medication, Dr. Stevens once again mentioned counseling, jotting down several programs at the local hospital and a few names of psychologists she might be interested in seeing.

Lana abruptly grabbed the packets and the prescription slip, leaving the other information on the desk, and stood up. Without saying a word, she left the office, hearing in the distance her mother apologizing for her behavior. When she'd had a chance to think about it later, she felt a little embarrassed by her abruptness but rationalized that she wasn't in control of her mind or her body. It was as if a poltergeist had taken control and her actions were no longer hers but those of someone else.

During the ensuing months, Lana felt more despair with every waking day. The antidepressant drug wasn't working as she had expected. It was as if her body was rejecting any substance or sensation that would lift her out of this darkness.

Getting out of bed was a chore, looking in the mirror was too painful, and dark thoughts had taken control of her mind and actions. She couldn't cut food for fear she would turn the knife on herself. Hanging laundry was out of the question too, lest she give in to the impulse to wrap the dangling rope around her neck. Nor could she cry anymore, fearing that any display of emotion would trigger a domino effect, causing her to sink deeper into the abyss she was struggling to break out of.

She felt at peace only when she was asleep, and that was rare these days. Everyday tasks such as taking a shower, blow-drying her hair, or applying makeup had become exhausting, requiring far more motivation than she was able to muster.

Lana's will to live had ended on the day she'd lost the two people dearest to her. Etched in her memory was the call informing her that her husband and baby daughter had been in a car accident.

It was a dark rainy night. She had just finished a long shift at the hospital and was looking forward to spending the remainder of the evening with her husband and daughter.

The part-time schedule she'd chosen after Jessica was born required her to be away from her child only two twelve-hour days a week. Her in-laws and parents split the days watching Jessica, saving Tom and Lana the expense of daycare.

Coming up the drive that evening, Lana noticed that Tom and Jessica were not home yet, which meant they had stayed on to have dinner at Tom's parents' house. Feeling a little disappointed that her family wasn't around, she decided to take a hot bath to perk up her mood. The day had been long and arduous and her aching muscles and weary mind needed a little R and R before the demands of a one-year-old took over.

Placing the key in the lock, anxious to slink into steamy, rose-scented bathwater, she heard her phone ringing, forcing her to quicken her movements so she wouldn't miss the call. She ran into the kitchen to grab the shrilling phone. *It must be Tom calling to say he would be late*, she thought.

But it wasn't.

When the man on the other end asked if this was the home of Thomas Turnwell, she answered "yes" and waited for the usual sales pitch to follow.

Calls like this were not uncommon, as she'd quickly learned after Jessica was born when she'd spent the first six weeks, and subsequently three days a week, at home during the day. It seemed like everyone these days was trying to sell packaged meat, a cheaper phone service, or a new credit card.

But the sales pitch never came.

When the caller asked if she was Thomas Turnwell's wife, she sensed something was wrong. As fear began to creep up her spine, she responded, "Y…yes, this is his wife. Has something happened?" The second she heard the caller say yes, her body collapsed against the partial wall between the kitchen and family room. She was no longer in control of her body—her hands and knees began to shake, her bottom lip started quivering, and tears blurred her vision. She continued to listen as this stranger told her there had been an accident. When the voice on the other end asked if there was anyone who could drive her to Hartford Hospital, the only response he heard was the sound of the receiver hitting the hardwood floor.

Anxious to be with her husband and daughter, Lana wiped the tears from her eyes, straightened her body, and raced to the car she'd just moments ago vacated. Chanting, "Everything's going to be all right," she drove like a woman possessed, running red lights and weaving in and out of traffic.

When she arrived at the emergency room entrance, she raced through the large glass doors. She quickly spotted two men in blue standing at the front desk. Running to them and announcing her name, somehow knowing they were there because of her, she asked if her daughter and husband were all right.

Searching their solemn faces for the truth, she immediately knew something was very wrong.

Just then, an older nurse appeared by her side and gently interlocked her arm around the one that had clung to the policeman. "Please come with me," the nurse said softly as she began guiding Lana away.

Lana knew where they were headed. This nurse was leading her toward the area where individual rooms were used to allow families the solitude needed for crisis situations. Death rooms, as they were commonly referred to by several of her peers.

Panic overtook her like never before. Her body began to shake uncontrollably. She stopped dead in her tracks and refused to move any farther until someone explained what had happened to her husband and daughter. Maybe, she thought, if she didn't go into the room, the news would somehow change.

No one spoke for several seconds. Lana tried to read their faces but only saw pain and sadness. The older of the policemen began explaining what had happened. The only words she heard were "accident" and "killed instantly." Then blackness overtook her.

In the distance, Lana could hear a soothing voice as she slowly regained consciousness. She tried to sit up but felt a hand lightly press her back down. A soft voice whispered that she should stay where she was until she felt strong enough to stand. A pillow had been placed behind her head and her body had shifted into a fetal position, instinctively protecting itself. She asked if both her husband and daughter were dead. When she heard the word *yes*, bile immediately rose in her throat and she insisted they get her to a bathroom. Helping her rise, the nurse quickly ushered her through the door with the bright blue female stick figure painted on its center.

Lana never felt the coldness of this room with its glaring chalk-colored paint, hard ceramic tile, and white porcelain toilet. All she could do was vomit until it felt like everything good and innocent from her life had been expunged. With the last convulsion, her body felt like it would collapse from exhaustion and despair. The nurse, not far behind, quickly grabbed her shoulders before she sank to the ground.

The nurse then gently toweled off her ravaged face and walked her to the room she'd avoided from the start. As they entered, Lana came face to face with a female doctor, a stethoscope adorning her neck, and knew this was the person who had the task of explaining the grisly details. The nurse walked her past the young doctor and helped her lower her body into the metal straight-backed chair. She didn't want to look anyone in the eyes, so she kept her head down as she listened to phrases she herself had used in the past: "nothing could have been done...died instantly...never felt a thing..."

When the doctor asked who they could call to be with her, Lana responded without thinking, giving the names and phone numbers of both sets of parents. She was handed a paper cup filled with ginger ale by the same nurse who had watched her retch her past away. She drank greedily from the cup, her body needing the fortification more than her broken spirit.

She'd sat in her zombie state for some time before she heard footsteps enter the room behind her. Her mother and father rushed to embrace the woman who was still very much their child. Her dad stood over her while her mom got down on both knees and held her tight, nearly squeezing the air out of her lungs.

A flood of tears began their descent down her face, and as much as she tried, she wasn't able to control the river that flowed. A few minutes later she heard the voices of her in-laws and looked up to see her mother-in-law's tearstained face. Both men stood at the far end of the room, talking to the police. Her father-in-law stood as erect as a statue. Lana had always admired his strength and today was no exception. She didn't need anyone falling apart; that she wanted to do alone.

For the first few months following the accident, Lana's mother never left her side. Kate Webber had raised Lana to be strong and independent and was surprised when a few months had gone by and her daughter was still not accepting the deaths. As distraught as she was over the loss of her granddaughter and son-in-law, she set aside her own anguish to focus on the tasks that needed to be done.

Witnessing her daughter mentally slipping away, she knew something had to be done to lift Lana out of the dark hole she'd buried herself in. Kate had moved back home but made it a point to stop by every day to check in on her daughter. Normally, she would let herself into the house, call to her daughter to announce her arrival, and immediately busy herself with laundry, dishes, or any other task that would occupy her time.

While her mom chatted endlessly about mundane topics that were of no interest to her, Lana would sit in silence, ignoring everything but the despair that plagued her every waking moment.

Kate soon realized that her tactics weren't working and began studying Lana's behavior more closely. Reminders of her son-in-law, Tom, and granddaughter, Jessica, seemed to play a major role in Lana's moods. When Lana walked by Jessica's room or picked up something of Tom's, she would stand transfixed for several minutes—sometimes for several hours.

It was not unusual to find Lana sitting in the hallway outside Jessica's room, knees pulled up to her chest, rocking back and forth and crying softly, or sitting in the middle of her walk-in closet clutching pieces of Tom's clothing and staring into space. When Kate saw Lana behaving this way, she would lift her up and bring her to the kitchen, offering favorite foods to help ease the pain. After each of these episodes the results were the same—Lana would spiral into a deeper depression.

Realizing that anything related to Tom and Jessica made Lana cling to the past, Kate decided to remove all reminders of the family her daughter had lost. She tried unsuccessfully to enlist Lana's help in accomplishing the task. Although she had convinced her daughter it was the right thing to do, all Lana could do was sit back and watch her mom carefully pack away all that remained to remind her of her husband and child.

When all of the tangible reminders of Tom and Jessica had been stored or removed, Kate went on to handle the necessary legal and insurance documents. Occasionally, Lana would have some paperwork to sign, but for the most part, her mom handled everything. "Taking care of business" was one Kate Webber's greatest strengths.

Married for forty years, Kate and Ted Webber were deeply rooted to family traditions. Both had found great pleasure in raising their two children, Lana and Todd. Working at a large insurance company in Hartford, Connecticut, provided Ted a promising career, allowing Kate to stay home with their two children. Kate considered herself the CEO of the Webber clan, taking charge of all the household necessities.

During her children's early years, Kate was active volunteering at the elementary school, and later, when both children were in high school, she served as PTO president for three years. Kate's ability to maintain a solid household enabled Ted to concentrate on his career, thus earning him the title of Director of Small Case Underwriting within ten years. Theirs was considered a traditional marriage by the standards of the nineties, and both Ted and Kate were satisfied with how their life had turned out.

Before the tragedy, life had been going well for the Webbers. Lana was a pediatric nurse at the children's hospital. She was married to a wonderful, caring man and was the mother of a healthy one-year-old daughter. Todd was a successful businessman in Chicago. He had married his college sweetheart and was the father of two children.

Ted was gearing up for an early retirement, looking forward to a life of playing golf and traveling the world with Kate. In anticipation of her husband's upcoming retirement, Kate had resigned from all of the committees that had so captivated her while raising her family and was now taking golf and tennis lessons at the country club. Still a member of the garden club, she spent many of her days working with her plants. Her favorite times, however, were when she was babysitting her granddaughter, Jessica.

The shattering news of the accident had a devastating effect not only on Lana, but also on Ted and Kate. The prospect of retirement didn't seem so rosy to Ted anymore. Not being able to stand his own grief, he actually looked forward to the routine of working five days a week. The constant tightness in his chest was temporarily forgotten when he was able to delve into work. Not being a particularly demonstrative man, Ted had difficulty dealing with his emotionally spent daughter. Looking back over the years, Ted realized that he had never involved himself with matters of the heart with either of his children. He had left that task to Kate, who so aptly handled such situations. Therefore, he could only watch as his wife dealt with their daughter's shattered emotions.

After everything of Tom's and Jessica's had been moved or stored away, it didn't take long for Lana to come to the realization that this tragedy was in fact real and that she couldn't continue on this dark journey much longer.

It was also difficult for Lana to witness the transformation in her mother since the accident. Kate had aged ten years in just a short time. She tried to sound cheery and bright during her visits, but Lana noticed that her once clear blue eyes were now encircled by darkness, her usual radiant smile now seemed forced, and her formerly graceful movements were stiff and deliberate. Lana also realized that her dad didn't come around as often as he used to, and when he did he kept himself busy repairing things, whether they needed it or not.

One morning as Kate was letting herself into Lana's house she was surprised to see her daughter sitting at the kitchen table. Usually when she stopped by this early, Lana would be lying on the sofa in the living room, catching up on missed sleep from the night before.

Kate immediately sensed that something was different about her daughter this morning, but before she could ask, Lana announced, "I can't do this anymore, Mom."

As Kate started to speak, Lana held up her hand. "You and Dad have been very supportive. I couldn't have gotten through this without your help. But I'm still feeling empty and desperate inside, so this morning I called Dr. Montgomery, a therapist I knew from the hospital. I am seeing her this afternoon."

Chapter One

Kate stared in disbelief. Over the past few months, she'd tried several times to convince Lana to seek help. Lana, though, had turned a deaf ear to suggestions of any kind of therapy.

Seeing her mother's stunned expression, Lana explained, "I'm not sure why I waited so long to admit I needed help, but it's like a lightning bolt hit me this morning and caused my mind and body to fight against each other. My body is screaming for exercise and aches with boredom, whereas my mind wants to crawl into a hole and hibernate. This war has been raging for some time and I can't explain why, today of all days, I finally decided to break out of this battle zone."

Kate listened carefully as Lana shared what she'd been holding in for so long. For the first time since the night of the accident, Kate could almost feel Lana's pain start to ebb. "I'm so proud of you, darling," she said as she took her daughter in her arms.

As she held her daughter tightly, Kate mouthed a thank-you to the God who'd been missing from her life for the past few months.

As a pediatric nurse, Lana had had the opportunity to work with Judy Montgomery a few times and knew immediately that there was something very special about this woman.

Judy had surfaced one day when a teenage boy had been seriously injured in a car accident. The boy was paralyzed from the waist down and screamed day in and day out that he wanted to die. Judy worked with him tirelessly, even though the boy usually yelled for her to get out of his room and leave him alone. His parents would visit as often as possible, sometimes coming two or three times a day, and leave—more often than not—in tears.

With the exception of Judy, everyone was beginning to wonder if this boy was ever going to mentally heal. But she never gave up, and over time her magic, as those around her had called it, finally worked. Judy and the teen actually became good friends and by the time the boy left for the rehab hospital he was telling all the nurses he'd be back to visit in his souped-up wheelchair.

Tragedies were Dr. Montgomery's specialty. As a member of a psychological trauma consultation group, she became well known in this very specialized field. In addition, she volunteered at a few homeless shelters, offering counseling to anyone seeking help or guidance.

The way she dealt with family tragedies was heartwarming, and the nurses on the floor likened Dr. Montgomery to an angel. Looking at her pale, clear skin, one hardly noticed the small wrinkles around her eyes and mouth. None of her coworkers knew her age, but rumor had it that she was close to sixty. Her salt-and-pepper hair was always tightly pulled back, but you could count on unruly wisps to form a crown around her face. The colorful caftans that doubled as her uniform were a welcome change from the stiff white coats generally associated with hospital attire. The only sound one heard when she approached was the clinking of the bracelets adorning both her wrists.

Remembering the day of their first visit brought a smile to Lana's face. It was springtime and the flowers were just starting to bloom. Tulips were popping up around the elm trees in the front yard, and a splattering of flowers was coloring the ground around the mailbox. The bright red flowering azalea bushes in front of her house were a splendid contrast to the lush green grass. She knelt down to feel its softness and realized it needed to be cut. She felt a bit of a twinge, realizing she hadn't noticed before today that the seasons had once again changed.

The sun's brightness caused her to squint, so she turned back to fetch her sunglasses. Inside, she shed her heavy sweater and pulled a lightweight jacket out of the closet.

Walking to her car, Lana noticed that children were out on the sidewalk jumping rope and riding bikes. The sight put a lump in her throat and she had to look away to fight back the tears. As she turned her head, she saw a neighbor washing his car with the radio blaring and a group of boys shooting baskets next door.

She stood paralyzed on the brick walkway, feeling overwhelmed by all the activity, until the roar of a lawnmower snapped her out of her trance. Suddenly she began to experience a strange feeling of wonder. For the first time in a long time, she actually noticed things going on around her, a sign that possibly her heart and soul were mending.

Even though Lana knew that going to meet with Judy was the right thing to do, she still felt a great deal of trepidation. She hadn't driven since the accident and wondered if she still remembered how. Kate had driven her home from the hospital that awful night and her dad had followed behind them. The car had sat motionless in the driveway since then.

Chapter One

After sliding into the four-door sedan, bought specifically because of the newborn baby, Lana spent a few minutes adjusting the mirror and drivers seat and manually rolling down the window—anything to delay the inevitable. She sat there for several minutes before taking a deep, long breath and finally turned the key in the ignition. The strong sound of the engine coupled with the vibration of the idling car prompted her to place the shift in reverse and back out of the driveway.

While in the middle of the street, with no one approaching, she turned on the radio, scanned for one of her favorite songs, and shifted into drive. The music had a settling effect on her frazzled nerves and provided just the right distraction from the task at hand.

Lana noticed Judy standing on the sidewalk outside the building as she pulled into the parking lot. Nervously looking at her watch, she realized the drive over had taken twice as long as usual because of the two stops she had made to calm her nerves.

Before she'd stepped out of the car she began her apology. "I'm sorry for being so late, but I didn't realize how hard this drive was going to be. I should've left myself more time."

Judy couldn't help but notice Lana's sad eyes, quivering lips, and frail body. Without saying a word, Judy helped her out of the car and immediately gave her a hug. Cupping her hands around Lana's drawn face, she looked directly into her downcast eyes and said gently, "I understand how difficult this trip was for you. I'm just glad you made it."

Judy had a way of making even the worst of circumstances seem in some way manageable. That morning, as they walked arm in arm toward the entrance of the medical building, she talked of spring and rebirth, indirectly showing Lana that anything was possible. Their brief conversation had put Lana at ease, and when they finally reached Judy's private domain, Lana was pleasantly surprised that it in no way resembled a doctor's office, but rather a sitting room. Lana instantly felt comfortable in these surroundings, and when both women were seated in the overstuffed chairs by the window, conversation flowed like a river that had been dammed far too long.

Lana couldn't have stopped herself even if she'd wanted to. She talked at length about the accident, her deepening depression, and her parents.

Tears streamed down her face as she tried to accurately relay her innermost feelings and guilt about the accident—thoughts she hadn't mentioned aloud to anyone.

Judy had heard through the office grapevine about Lana's loss and immediately felt deep sorrow for the nurse she'd respected so much. She remembered the first time that she'd had the pleasure of meeting Lana. It was while she was visiting a young male patient who had been paralyzed in a car accident. After leaving the boy's room one evening, Lana introduced herself as one his nurses and confided that she was genuinely concerned about the boy's state of mind.

Judy knew most of the nurses were fed up with the teen's antics and was surprised that Lana hadn't been affected in the same way as her peers. Instantly, she recognized that Lana was a special person and felt an immediate kinship to this nurse who had cared so deeply for the errant teen.

Working different shifts hadn't allowed a friendship to develop between the two women, but a deep appreciation had been felt on both sides.

Over the next three years, the doctor-patient relationship slowly evolved into a deep friendship between the two women, and once or twice a month, when their schedules would allow, they'd share a peaceful dinner at one of their favorite restaurants.

After Lana had begun to accept the deaths of her husband and daughter, and the depression had lessened somewhat, the next step was to become a productive member of society again. That needed to be accomplished fairly quickly, as Tom's death benefit, received shortly after Kate filed all the necessary paperwork, was dwindling.

When Lana and Tom had purchased their three-bedroom Cape Cod style house three-and-a-half years earlier, they had used most of their savings. The constant repairs and the remodeling of a bedroom into a nursery quickly depleted what little money remained. After Jessica was born, Lana reduced her hours at work to part-time status and proudly accepted the trade-off of spending more time with Jessica rather than building up a savings account.

Now she had neither.

Her mother saw the bills piling up and offered financial assistance, but Lana politely refused, worrying more about her parents' retirement plans than her own financial affairs. Even though she'd come very far, emotionally speaking, she still couldn't fathom the idea of working. Feelings of emptiness and loneliness overshadowed any desire to become productive again.

Life was going on around her, though, and all the self-pity in the world wasn't changing the fact that shut-off notices for the phone, electricity, and cable were filtering in. Eventually this reality penetrated Lana's lethargy. Money was an integral part of life and if she wanted to keep her house and consequently her sanity, she'd have to reenter the working world.

It was hard for Lana to hide her growing concern about money during her sessions with Judy, and when Judy brought up the subject one day about a return to work, Lana told her flat out that nursing was not part of her life anymore. Although Judy disagreed with that decision, she let the matter slide, knowing that in time the bug that had bitten Lana in the first place would again bite.

By this time, Judy had grown very fond of Lana and didn't want the hospital to lose such a unique employee. She'd heard about an opening in administration and personally sought out the director of the department in the hope that maybe a few strings could be pulled. It was easier than she'd expected; he gladly accepted her recommendation and hired Lana a week later.

The position in administration proved to be a welcome change for Lana. Going to work every day gave her life some purpose. The plethora of tasks that needed attention enabled her to bury herself in work and ignore any reminders that threatened to send her over the edge again.

The hospital staff began noticing a change in the administration department. Budgets were finalized and accepted by all department heads, state regulations were posted regularly for all to follow, and patient files were completely transferred on-line. Lana's medical background and superb organizational skills were just the right combination to successfully meet both medical and administrative needs.

This career change was so different from anything Lana had ever done; it totally engrossed her, leaving little time for a personal life. Initially, friends and neighbors called offering help or just a friendly ear, but Lana kept a cool distance from anything or anyone connected to her old life. Her longtime friends hadn't given up entirely and occasionally checked in to make sure she knew they were waiting in the wings.

The one disappointment that she couldn't seem to overcome was her aversion to seeing her in-laws. Just hearing her father-in-law's voice brought back memories of her husband, remembrances still too painful to face.

On several occasions following the accident, her in-laws tried to get in touch, but she always found an excuse not to see or talk to them. After a while they stopped calling Lana directly, resorting instead to gaining any information they could from her parents. Lana couldn't reconcile in her own mind why she was so reluctant to see them and decided during one of her sessions with Judy to broach the subject. After Lana had explained her dilemma, Judy suggested she write them a letter. She pointed out that if Lana allowed herself to empathize with her in-laws and help them deal with their pain, she would benefit from the experience as well.

Initially, Lana was taken aback by this suggestion. Being totally absorbed with her own recovery, she couldn't understand why Judy felt she could in any way help someone else. She mulled over the suggestion for a few days, but sheer fear prolonged the dreaded task of writing the letter.

One night when she was home alone and feeling low she remembered Judy's suggestion. Thinking that writing this letter might somehow be therapeutic, she sat down at the roll-top desk in her room and began to write.

Dear Mom and Pop,

It is has been almost two years since we last saw each other and I am sorry that it has taken me so long to get in touch. My only excuse is that a part of me died that night we lost our family and for the last few years I have been trying desperately to resuscitate my life. I am deeply sorry that I have not been there for you both. I needed time to heal, and unfortunately, every time I heard your voices I was reminded of the two people dearest to me I had lost. For several months after the accident, a cloud of darkness settled around me, rendering me virtually incapa-

ble of rational thought. Feelings of anger, despair, and bitterness plagued my existence until, with the encouragement of my mother, I decided to seek professional help. Through therapy I've been able to put the tragedy behind me and cope with life without Tom and Jessica. This metamorphosis has been the most painful in my life, and even though my face is the same, the person inside me has not yet become the butterfly.

Someday, I promise you we will again meet, and by then I hope we can reminisce about life before. I yearn for that day!

Love,
Lana

Lana set down the pen, reflecting on the words she had finally put on paper. Her mood began to lift considerably, just as Judy had said it would. Over the years, Judy had proven again and again her talent for knowing what was right. Baby steps, she'd called them. This was just one in a series of many.

Chapter Two

Judy still hadn't heard from Lana several days following their meeting. She'd gone to pick up the phone many times but had thought better of it knowing her friend needed time.

This morning, unable to concentrate on work, Judy sat staring out the window, mesmerized by the signs of spring. Variegated tulips formed a ring around the old oak tree, light green buds speckled the colliding branches, and various shades of green painted the grass. The orchestra of chirping birds could barely be heard over the muffled sound of a leaf-blower removing the remnants of autumn's fallen leaves.

Spring was Judy's favorite time of year, showcasing all that was reborn and bringing life to new wonders. It was this time three years ago that Lana had come to her for help. Remembering the frail, broken-spirited person emerging from the car that day still made her heart ache. Judy had been overcome by an immediate need to take this person under her wing and nurse her back to health. In all of her years of practice, this burning desire to help a patient had never been so strong or commanding.

Always believing that analyzing people and their problems was the reason she had been put on this earth, Judy led a very contented existence. She'd never had a burning desire to have a significant other, nor did she possess the maternal instinct to have children of her own, but she spent a great deal of time working with patients in the pediatric ward. She felt triumphant when she watched people open up, sometimes for the first time in their lives, and blossom like flowers that have just been kissed by the sun.

The rewards of her job were never-ending, and she often joked with her patients about how she planned to remain in practice until she was laid to rest.

Snapping out of her reverie, Judy pondered, as she'd done over and over during the last few days, whether or not she'd made the right decision to involve Lana in this most complex situation.

The two people she had grown to love most in the world were silently suffering, and she couldn't get either of them to open up their hearts enough to see that their lives were not whole.

Lana, a truly beautiful person both inside and out, lived a robotic existence. Always on a schedule, she filled her life with work and other mundane tasks that kept her from forming lasting relationships with either men or women. Amazed by her lack of interest in anything but work, Judy had tried repeatedly to convince Lana to search for the person she'd once been and let her emerge through the shell that had enveloped her. Lana had become the productive member of society everyone wished for. But in the process, she'd sealed off the part that made her human. Even though Judy thoroughly enjoyed her newest friend, dismay filled her heart at the thought of Lana living this existence for the rest of her life.

The other lost soul in Judy's life was her nephew, Trevor Collins. Trevor was the offspring of a brief marriage her sister Carol had in her early twenties. Judy could still picture the grief-stricken look on her parents' face when their firstborn daughter broke the news of her impending divorce. Not having approved of her marriage in the first place, the family wasn't surprised when Carol and child were moved back in two years later.

Trevor's dad, Rory Collins, was a handsome, smooth-talking salesman, always searching for the best deal on everything. Rumors of cheating and gambling circled around town for several months before Carol confronted her husband with the hurtful gossip she'd been reluctant to believe. Vehemently denying any wrongdoing, Rory tap-danced around the truth and convinced Carol the rumors were lies.

Unable to stand the lonely nights, the neglect of her husband, and the lack of trust in their short marriage, Carol filed for divorce shortly after Trevor was born and moved back home. Furious that his wife had divorced him, Rory moved out West to open up a new sales territory in Southern California. Without so much as a phone call or note, he disappeared out of Carol and Trevor's lives shortly after the divorce was final.

Judy was living at home and attending the local university when Carol and Trevor moved in. Although it was going to be a hardship sharing a room with her older sister, she was glad to do it for her nephew. Trevor was the cutest baby she had ever known, and she loved the idea of seeing him whenever the mood struck.

Not particularly fond of Trevor's dad, she was delighted when the news came that he was moving to the West Coast. Judy and Rory had been like oil and water, constantly disagreeing on every imaginable topic. Rory's main goal in life was to score the big deal and make millions, whereas Judy didn't care much about money and yearned to help the less fortunate.

Although Carol and Judy had never been close, they made the best of the somewhat cramped situation. The five-year age difference was part of the reason they'd never developed a close relationship, but mostly it was disparate personalities that caused the gap.

Carol was the pretty one—tall, slender, and feminine in every way. During her high school years, the phone was like a permanent part of her anatomy. As captain of the cheerleading squad and playing the lead in the school's productions of *Oklahoma* and *Romeo and Juliet*, she won the title of most popular girl in high school. The oversized letterman sweater from the captain of the sports team du jour was part of her daily attire.

Judy never envied her sister for what she believed was a rather shallow existence. Even though she was several years Carol's junior, she had the brains and mindset of one far beyond her age. Judy dealt with issues of substance, such as race, equality, and women's rights—unlike her sister, who was more enamored of boys and social status. Because she was far ahead of her time, people had trouble understanding where Judy was coming from when she lamented about society's ills.

Years went by, and when not so much as a word or a red cent was received from Rory, the Montgomerys continued on as if he'd never even existed. Carol had taken a low-paying job as a secretary at a local manufacturing company, which kept her and Trevor mostly dependent on her parents' generosity. Although the extra hands were a godsend when it came to caring for Trevor, the need to spread her wings and live on her own with her child prompted Carol to take night classes at the local university to complete the degree program she'd left years before to marry Rory.

This decision was met with mixed emotions by her parents. They were from the old school and couldn't fathom why a young woman with a child would ever dream of living on her own. They did, however, understand Carol's need to better her life and graciously offered whatever assistance they could while she attended evening classes.

During his early years, Trevor flourished with all the attention he received from his grandparents and Aunt Judy. His grandfather had taken great pride in teaching him the art of fly fishing, and his grandmother, an avid baker, had taught him how to make chocolate-chip cookies and knead dough for homemade bread. Aunt Judy, when she wasn't busy with schoolwork, took him to Red Sox baseball games, the soda shop, and the movies. His mom was mostly absent during much of his young life, as she was working ten-hour days at the plant and attending school at night, so the only time he spent with her was on the weekends.

Talk of Trevor's dad had long since ceased in the Montgomery household. Early in his life, when Trevor would ask about his father, nobody really knew what to say. His grandparents' usual response was that his dad loved him very much but had to live in California because of his job. Aunt Judy's mouth would turn downward as she tried to explain how Rory couldn't come home for visits because California was very far away. As for Carol, she had refused to discuss the subject with anyone, including her only son. As young as he was, Trevor could feel her pain and learned to keep his feelings to himself when it came to his dad.

The teen years were not as kind to Trevor. His mom had long since graduated from college and was rapidly moving up the corporate ladder. The four-bedroom colonial house they'd moved into years earlier, located halfway between his grandparents' house and Aunt Judy's in the next town, was a dismal place for the boy, who found himself alone most of the time. Although his mom tried to be home every night at a reasonable hour, most of her evenings were spent preparing for the next day.

The wonderful times he'd spent with Aunt Judy and his grandparents had sorely diminished over the years. Aunt Judy was busy with her flourishing practice and his grandparents had become snowbirds, living in Florida during the long dark days of winter.

Feeling left out and lonely, Trevor started acting up in school and began hanging around with kids—as his mother repeatedly reminded him—from the wrong side of the tracks.

Jamie, his newest best friend, was from a family of six children, and, like Trevor, was being raised by a single mother. It didn't take long before the two boys became inseparable, pretending not to care about the absence of a father figure and earning the reputation of troublemakers. Trevor began cutting classes, earning C's and D's where once he wouldn't have accepted a B.

Aware of her son's changing attitude, Carol instituted tougher rules in the household with respect to homework, grades, and curfews. The one thing she didn't change was the limited amount of time she spent with her only son.

Watching from a distance as the relationship between her sister and nephew slipped further and further into an abyss, Judy decided to intervene and counsel her nephew before more damage was done.

Judy was shocked to hear how her nephew had developed such negative views on life when it seemed like they'd agreed on just about everything such a short time ago. What had happened to this once positive-thinking individual? From then on, she made it a point to have dinner with him at least once a week to try to reestablish the connection they'd once shared and to offer whatever support she could.

Over time, Judy came to realize that Trevor had never made peace with his father's abandonment and behaved badly as a means of getting his mother's attention. He felt abandoned not only by his father but also by his mother, grandparents, and her, when they all went on with their lives, leaving him alone to face the difficulties of adolescence.

Hearing this, Judy felt partly responsible for her nephew's crumbling life and sought to change his views. She had better luck talking to her nephew than she'd had with her sister, who politely asked her to mind her own business. They'd never seen eye to eye on anything, so Carol's remark came as no surprise.

Over the years, Trevor had developed a passion for music and playing the guitar. Judy had helped nurture what she thought was just a hobby. Where once she'd taken him to baseball games, she now found herself buying tickets to concerts. She gladly paid for guitar lessons and welcomed the idea of Trevor forming a band.

By his senior year, Trevor's grades were back up to a respectable status. And he and his best friend, Jamie, had stuck with the band for more than a year—busy most weekends playing gigs at local birthday parties, bar mitzvahs, and school dances.

It came as no surprise to either his mom or his aunt when he announced a few days before graduation that he was going to pursue rock and roll stardom in Los Angeles instead of attending college. Carol and Judy tried desperately to change his mind but nothing they said had any effect.

Life seemed to fly by after Trevor moved out West. Carol was promoted to vice president of operations and spent most of her time on the road, while Judy was stretched to the limit with her busy practice and speaking engagements. The elder Montgomerys were spending more and more time in Florida and had recently made it their permanent residence.

Judy and Carol would get together occasionally when both were in town and compare notes on news from Trevor. Having virtually nothing in common with her sister, Judy was glad they were able to connect on some level. She'd resigned herself years ago to the fact that she and Carol would never be close and learned to cope with the emptiness that existed when more than miles distanced families.

In the beginning, Judy could expect a couple of letters a month from Trevor. The thread that ran through most of those early letters was the difficulty of making it on one's own. Forming a band was the easy part—dealing with personality conflicts, prima donna attitudes, and the hours of rehearsals constituted more reality than these two small-town Easterners had bargained for. Both were gifted musicians and Judy believed that if they stuck it out success would come.

Chapter Two

Whenever she received a letter from Trevor, she was quick to respond, including in the envelope a check for a few hundred dollars. She always referred to the donation as a down payment on his success so it wouldn't appear like charity.

Three years almost to the day of the big move out West, Trevor wrote that a record deal was in the works for his band. Although the letter was brief, Judy could feel his excitement jumping off the page. Apologizing for the recent gaps between his letters, Trevor explained that working twelve to fifteen hours a day didn't leave enough time for eating and sleeping, never mind letter writing.

Thrilled for her nephew, Judy could hardly wait to discuss this latest development with her sister. Over the last few years, she'd come to look forward to her visits with Carol and actually enjoyed the light and funny conversations they shared over dinner.

The album was cut six months later and Judy immediately went out and bought dozens of copies. She gave them to all of her patients and associates, playing the proud aunt to the hilt.

When concert dates were set, she and her sister declined the offer of a flight to California and elected instead to attend the concert at Foxboro Stadium in Massachusetts. The two women planned on making a weekend of it, and actually looked forward to doing some catching up. A week before the big night, they talked endlessly about what they would wear, where they would be sitting, and their excitement about seeing Trevor again.

They reminisced about the day Trevor had packed up the old Volkswagen van he and Jamie had purchased with the money they'd saved from their gigs. Judy had never forgotten the look on her sister's face when her only son had driven off in the beat-up jalopy, filled almost to bursting with everything he and his best friend owned. She watched her sister that day with a new set of eyes. She actually admired the courage Carol possessed—first in leaving the father of this remarkable boy and now in offering her son the same freedom to pursue his dream.

The night of the concert was by far one of the most exciting times of Judy's life. Preparing for the big event was exhilarating but in no way came close to the feelings the two women experienced when they arrived at the stadium and were escorted to a roped-off area reserved for band members and VIPs.

Seeing Trevor in the distance, giving what appeared to be an interview, Judy experienced an overwhelming sense of love for and pride in the boy she had helped raise. He was as handsome as ever. His dark wavy hair was longer than she'd remembered and it seemed like he'd grown even taller.

Feeling a desperate need to break through the crowd and take him into her arms, she forced herself to keep back and wait for the interview to end.

As soon as Trevor spotted the pair he motioned for them to join him. After the hugging, kissing, and crying subsided, Trevor extracted himself from their loving embrace and explained that it was time for them to find their seats, promising he'd see them after the show.

Even though the music was far too loud and the crowd beyond boisterous, both women thoroughly enjoyed themselves. The only disappointment was the limited time they were able to spend with Trevor. The band was leaving first thing in the morning for another city and it was already past midnight before the last encore was finished. It was obvious Trevor was overtired and both Judy and Carol reluctantly said tearful good-byes after giving him a dose of parental advice. The women stayed up most of the night, reliving the evening's events before finally falling into an exhausted sleep.

Trevor's career took off once the tour ended; the band's album topped the charts shortly thereafter. As the letters home became fewer and farther between, Judy resorted to reading *Rolling Stone* and other magazines for news of her famous nephew.

Judy and her sister tried to stay close, but the catalyst that had brought them together was now off in the distance, preventing them once again from having much in common. Finding comfort in her work and considering many of her colleagues as extended family, Judy was able to live an enriched life over the next two decades.

During this time, almost a decade ago, Judy and Carol lost both parents, one right after the other. Agnes Montgomery had died instantly of a heart attack after spending fourteen glorious days aboard a luxury cruise liner exploring the Alaskan coastline. As she disembarked from the ship, her husband by her side, she dropped to the ground and never regained consciousness.

Three months later, Judy stood next to her mother's gravesite staring down the empty hole where her father would be laid to rest. Both Judy and Carol believed their dad had died of a broken heart, his mind willing his body to stop living so he could once again be united with his lost love.

Touring abroad prevented Trevor from attending either funeral. Although the two sisters were heartsick over the deaths of their parents, the emptiness caused by Trevor's absence was a pain neither woman mentioned aloud.

Judy often thought of Trevor's success with mixed emotions. She was proud and genuinely happy he was living his dream and receiving the accolades he so deserved. Deep inside, though, she worried about the cost of giving up one's anonymity. Of not being able to take a pleasurable walk through the park, shop in the local grocery store, or dine at any place one's stomach desired.

The latest letters she'd received from her nephew were quite different from the earlier ones. He wasn't comfortable with people constantly touching him or pretending to know what he was all about. He talked about the pathetic way commercialism dictated music, and how he often thought about dropping out of sight to give his mind and body a chance to rejuvenate. More often than not, he seemed distressed by the music industry and troubled with band members who he thought were giving in to the demands of the music henchmen.

When Judy received one of these disturbing letters, she would immediately try to phone Trevor, hoping to help him resolve the battle raging in his head. By the time it took for them to hook up, Trevor had always managed to minimize his inner conflict and involve himself in another project—a method of survival that, she knew, would come back to haunt him. With Trevor on an emotional high during these project start-ups, her words basically went in one ear and out the other, frustrating her completely.

Five years ago, after receiving another of Trevor's "the world has gone to hell" letters, she booked a flight to Los Angeles to surprise her nephew. Her fear of flying had kept her on the East Coast most of her life, but she was willing to put her disquietude aside and white-knuckle it out to L.A. to be with her nephew.

That particular trip was one Judy would never forget. Not being able to sleep the night before, she arrived at the airport several hours early in hopes that watching successful takeoffs and landings would ease her mind about her own flight. Sitting by herself at the gate, she became mesmerized watching the small dashes of silver in the sky transform into monstrous birdlike figures, then land within a mile or so from where she sat. Somehow hearing the powerful booms of the jet engines eased her anxious mind.

More and more people began filing in as the time neared for her own flight. Feeling confident after watching dozens of planes success-fully take off and land, Judy boarded the plane without much trepidation. As the plane moved slowly toward the runway, she fidgeted a bit, trying to steer her thoughts in another direction. She shut the blind next to her seat, closed her eyes, and pictured the garden outside her house. Within minutes, the flight attendant was performing her perfunctory routine, pointing to exit signs, placing an oxygen mask up to her mouth, and talking about the seat cushions doubling as a floatation device in the event of an emergency water landing. Refusing to think about any kind of disaster, Judy pulled from her carrying case the novel she'd started a few nights ago and immersed herself in the story of a young woman's struggle in a male-dominated society.

After about an hour of flight, she put her book aside and readied herself for the light fare being handed out by the flight attendant. Open-ing the blind, she shielded her eyes from the bright sun stealing through the window by her side. The minute her eyes adjusted to the brightness, she looked down and noticed the matchbox-sized houses and cars, far-stretching roads, and clustered buildings representing the area's major city.

She stared in amazement at how neat and tidy the world looked from above. A smile formed on her face as she was reminded of when she was a teenager baby-sitting for the boy next door. Whenever she arrived, the little boy would pull her hand and lead her to the backyard where he had built a small town out of dirt mounds, miniature cars and trucks, and houses made of Popsicle sticks. They would play for hours in this make-believe world, stopping only when it became too dark to see anything. Leaning her head against the window, she wondered why the world couldn't be that simple.

The layover in Chicago was brief and uneventful, and she was thankful she didn't need to change planes. Landing at Los Angeles International Airport was painless, like the takeoff. Judy breathed a sigh of relief when she'd stepped off the plane and walked through the gate. She selected the first cab in a long row of yellow and handed the address to the driver. She then rested her head against the back seat, closed her eyes, and enjoyed the feel of the hard earth beneath her.

Feeling the tension of the flight start to leave her body, Judy allowed the music and the vibration of the moving vehicle to lull her into a light sleep. As the cab slowed almost to a halt, she opened her eyes and stared in disbelief at the sight before her. Large black iron gates separated her from a palatial estate.

At that moment, the driver turned his head and said this was the address she had given him. Judy told him her name and watched as he pressed the intercom button located just outside his door and announced her arrival. Several days earlier, Judy had left a cryptic message on Trevor's answering machine, saying she would be flying out within the next week and hoped he would be in town so they could get together. She asked him to call if he was not going to be around and, since she hadn't heard from him, she assumed he was home this week. She was relieved when the large gates slowly opened and the cabby carefully negotiated the winding drive.

Never one to swoon over money and power, Judy was nevertheless shocked when she gazed upon the place Trevor now called home.

The house was situated in the Hollywood Hills and sat kitty-cornered on the edge of what appeared to be mile-high cliff. The white stucco house boasted one of the grandest entrances she had ever seen. Tall Doric pillars, marble steps, intricately carved doors, and an exquisite crystal chandelier, seen through the large Paladin window above the entrance, adorned the front of the house.

The circular driveway was hardly noticeable amidst the trees, bushes, and flowers surrounding the concrete drive. Spiny cacti, softened by the delicate rose-like bushes surrounding them, caught her eye almost immediately. Innumerable hues of green from the different types of plants provided a splendid contrast to flowers bordering the walkway in shades of magenta, yellow, and red. In the center of the drive, a bed of lavender-colored pansies encircled a magnificent fountain spouting clear water, reminding her of how hot and thirsty she was feeling in the back of the cab.

Judy almost stumbled as she stepped out of the taxi and didn't notice her nephew emerge from the front portico. Trevor had been home working in the studio when the announcement came that Aunt Judy was at the gate. Not believing that she was truly here, he abandoned the sheet music he'd been staring at all morning, ran through the house and out the front door, and stared in amazement at the visitor. His aunt was gathering her luggage when he ran toward her and lifted her off the ground, spinning her round and round.

Taking Trevor's face in her hands, Judy stared into those familiar eyes and whispered how much she loved and missed the man she still thought of as a boy. Watching him mouth the same loving words, she held his hand while tears of joy spilled onto her cheeks. Arm and arm they walked into the house, leaving the luggage standing in the middle of the driveway.

The minute she walked into the elegant foyer, Judy's eyes widened in wonder. The chandelier she'd noticed from outside seemed to come alive, its massive array of crystals shooting out rays of light to illuminate the most magnificent artwork and Persian rugs her eyes had ever seen.

"I can't believe this place!" she burst out as she stepped down into the living room. The ebony grand piano in the far corner of the room was first to capture her attention. Even though this room was twice the size of her own living room, it gave off the same cozy feeling she'd worked hard to achieve. The seating area in the middle of the room exuded the warmth of a much-lived-in house. A pair of comfortable upholstered chairs in a coordinating plaid print complemented the sage-colored chenille fabric on the overstuffed sofa. Tables and other occasional chairs were spread around the rest of the room. Everything was so cleverly matched that nothing seemed out of place.

"Trevor, this is so beautiful."

He was proud of his house. But it was the view he couldn't wait to share.

"I really love it here. But wait till you see this," he said as he pulled back the ivory-colored sheer curtains, sounding much like the young man she'd missed over the years. The entire posterior wall was glass paneled, offering a panorama of rolling hills.

Judy's eyes glazed over as she stared at the most breathtaking view she'd ever seen. "Trevor," she gasped, "it takes my breath away. No wonder you love it here so much."

Trevor had worked long and hard with the architect and builder, and then with the interior designer, and was anxious to show his aunt the rest of the house. But after a brief tour, he could tell she was becoming a little weary.

"Would you like to lie down for awhile?" Trevor offered.

"And possibly miss something?" Judy answered. "No way!"

He laughed then—something she hadn't heard from him in a long time.

"So, you like what I've done with the place?"

"I'm still in a state of shock," Judy admitted. "I never dreamed anything could be this beautiful."

"I needed a place to call home and I wanted it to be really special."

"It is that," Judy agreed, still taking it all in. Then her eyes focused on Trevor and she heard something in his voice that had been absent of late. "It's nice to hear the passion in your voice when you talk about your home. Having a place to call your own is very important."

Trevor nodded. "Being on the road as much as I am really takes its toll, and it's important for my home to be a place where I can totally immerse myself. Some nights I just sit in the living room and get lost in the view."

"I can understand that," Judy said, gazing through the wall of glass. "It reminds me of flying, being this high up—minus the fear of takeoffs and landings. I'm not sure I could live here, though."

"Why not?"

"I'd never want to leave," Judy said, laughing.

Trevor knew exactly what she meant. In the past year, he'd spent many days within these walls, not caring if he ever ventured out. "Some days it's hard for me to leave this place."

"I hope you're not becoming the Howard Hughes of the music industry," Judy joked.

"I don't think you have to worry about that," Trevor assured her.

She didn't want to get into anything too heavy, but refused to let the opportunity pass without at least mentioning her concerns stemming from his letter. "I do worry about you sometimes."

"What's there to worry about? I have everything I've always wanted and more."

"Is this," she asked, motioning toward all of the fineries surrounding them, "enough for you?"

Trevor knew his aunt didn't have a materialistic bone in her body. Yes, she enjoyed fine art, comfortable surroundings, and an expensive bottle of wine every now and then. But for the most part, she'd always worked for the good of mankind.

"For now, yes," Trevor said evenly. "I'm very content with my life. Sure, I wish some things were different. Once in awhile it would be nice to go out without people hounding me for an autograph, or to have the paparazzi take a short walk off a long pier. But then again, I knew what I was getting into and it's a small price to pay for everything I've attained."

Judy wasn't so sure about that but she didn't want to spoil the weekend by mentally doing battle. She'd left her analyst hat at home this weekend and looked forward to just being his aunt. "I think I'll take you up on your offer to rest a bit," she told him. "I didn't realize how tired I was until now."

For the first time since she'd arrived, Trevor noticed that the young, spry woman he'd grown up loving had turned the corner. Where had the time gone? She was still one of the most spirited people he'd ever met, but it was hard not to notice the graying hair, her slightly slowed gait, and the light wrinkles sprinkled around her face.

Trevor led the way up the beautiful staircase and pointed along the hall. "Yours is the last one on the right. There's an intercom if you need anything. I'll be in the studio."

Judy entered her room and knew it was the right one when she spotted her bags in the corner. The view from this room, similar to what she'd experienced in the living room, left her breathless. But what caught her attention was the luxurious bed that stood in the middle of the room. Soft off-white tulle fabric draped around the four-poster bed gently softened the sleek lines of the light-colored wrought-iron frame.

Large overstuffed pillows stood behind ten or so smaller versions in various white-on-white textured fabrics. The neutral-toned area rug in front of the bed blended perfectly atop the bleached oak floor.

A wicker fainting couch, covered with heavy brocade pillows matching in color the ones on the bed, sat in the corner. It looked so inviting she wanted nothing more than to just sink down in the middle of it and grab a quick nap. She decided to unpack first and place her toiletries in the bathroom, after which she could take a short nap. Her eyes refused to cooperate, detailing instead every item in this fabulously furnished haven.

The only infusion of color was the hand-painted armoire on the opposite side of the room. A sea of flowers and vines colored in light shades of purple, yellow, pink, and green bejeweled the doors of the armoire. This pastel-colored piece had been artfully placed alongside a doorway which led to the most spectacular bathroom she'd ever had the pleasure of seeing. Pictures of flowers similar to those painted on the armoire hung in gilded frames, across from the oversized ornately carved mirror above the cream-colored porcelain sink. Hand-painted around the frames were vines appearing as if they were living, snaking their way between the frames and windows and around the doorway. Thick, fluffy towels boasting the same floral patterns hung from several racks just below the border of paintings. Painted tiles, matching the garden of flowers in the picture frames, encircled the oversized Jacuzzi, giving one the feel of bathing in a garden.

If it weren't for the overwhelming need to be with her nephew, Judy thought she could easily lose herself in this guest suite for days before the desire to be with others came her way.

The next few days passed in the blink of an eye. Trevor, anxious to give his aunt a taste of his world, set a demanding schedule for her. Going to the downtown studio was a real treat for her. Watching her nephew come alive as he played the guitar gave her a glimpse of the person he'd become over the last decade and a half.

Like his mother, Trevor was a perfectionist, refusing to allow time or anyone to dictate when a song or sound reached optimum status. The amount of work involved in producing a song overwhelmed Judy. She didn't think she had the stamina to endure all that was involved in making an album.

Just one song took days to complete, not to mention the time spent before it was even brought to the studio. All the starting, stopping, changing notes, trying different instruments, and shuffling the hundreds of buttons on the panel in the control booth confused her. She didn't understand why the person in the booth kept halting play when she herself thought it sounded fine.

After spending time in the studio each day, Trevor had taken her to all the tourist sites she'd heard so much about—the homes in Malibu, the Santa Monica pier, the famous shops along Rodeo Drive, and the finest restaurants in Brentwood.

Trevor was recognized at most of the places they went, but for the most part, people left them alone. Judy was proud of the way he handled himself when people started circling. He calmly took her hand and led her away, never once letting the throng of people get under his skin.

Jamie had accompanied them on a few of their excursions and she was glad their friendship had withstood the test of time and fame. Trevor seemed happy and secure in this environment and she was pleased she'd been able to witness it firsthand. She agreed that there was a downside to all this, as Trevor had written in his letters, but for the most part it seemed he was leading a charmed life.

On Judy's last night in town, Trevor suggested an early dinner and a quiet evening at home since they'd been going nonstop since she'd arrived.

They were sitting on the sofa in the living room enjoying each other's company when the front door opened and in walked Jamie with a beautiful young woman on his arm. They'd seen Jamie earlier and he'd mentioned that he might stop by to say good-bye since she would be leaving first thing in the morning.

Just as Judy was about to stand, the young lady shuffled over, a bit unsteadily, and introduced herself. "Hi. I'm Cindy."

Judy put her hand out to exchange the customary handshake when she noticed the young woman was tipsy. She quickly looked toward Trevor, but his eyes were busy spitting fire at his best friend.

It only took a minute before Jamie was quickly escorting Cindy out the door.

"Bye-bye. Nicccccccce to meet you," Cindy slurred as Jamie practically dragged her from the house.

As soon as the door shut behind the couple and Trevor had taken a few moments to calm down, he apologized. "I'm really sorry about that."

"Why should you be sorry?" Judy asked.

"Maybe sorry is the wrong word. I just didn't want anything to spoil our visit."

"Well, it didn't," Judy assured him. "Don't worry."

But it had. Trevor seemed so preoccupied after that, and Judy wanted desperately to change his mood so their fabulous visit would end on the high note it deserved.

"Don't let a thing like that taint this evening," Judy urged.

"How can I not when it's been tainting my life?"

"Okay then, tell me about her."

"About who?"

"Cindy," Judy answered.

"Not much to tell," he shrugged. "She's Jamie's girlfriend."

"Don't you like her?"

"Not particularly," Trevor answered nonchalantly.

"Why not?"

Trevor was becoming agitated. "Do we have to ruin the remainder of the night by talking about her?"

"No. But if something's troubling you maybe I can help," Judy offered, wanting to ease some of the tension.

Trevor thought for a while before he committed to saying anything more. He was afraid that if he started he'd spill everything he'd kept inside for so long. His aunt didn't deserve this on her last night.

"Does Jamie know how you feel?"

"Oh, yeah! I've made it quite clear. But he's oblivious to Cindy's faults and I don't know what to do."

"What do you know about her?"

"Besides being a drunk, not much."

"Have you tried to talk to her?"

Trevor shook his head. "I wouldn't waste my time."

"Why do you think it would be a waste?"

"Because I run into users like her every day. She's young and stupid, as far as I'm concerned. I just don't understand what Jamie sees in her."

"Maybe he's in love," Judy said easily.

"Love, my ass!" Trevor exploded. "How can anyone love a person like that? She's a mindless parasite who's latched on to the gravy train. I can't understand why Jamie stays with her. You're the expert. Why does he put up with her?"

"I'm not sure. There are many reasons why people stay with one another. Maybe Jamie likes being needed. Or maybe he's tired of being alone. I don't know either of them well enough to make a judgment."

"Well, I think he's gone temporarily insane. I can't even talk to him about her. He's totally shut me out."

"He does that because he doesn't like what he's hearing," Judy pointed out.

"What he's hearing is the truth," Trevor corrected.

"Maybe so, but he's not ready to hear that right now. Don't worry, though; he'll eventually come around and realize he's been walking around with blinders on." Judy waited a moment for that to sink in, then added, "And you? Is there anyone special in your life?"

Trevor gazed at his aunt, somewhat surprised that she'd changed the focus of the conversation to him. "You know the answer to that. I'm married to my music, much like you and my mother are to your careers."

"Touché."

Trevor was immediately contrite. "I didn't mean to sound so harsh. Jamie's got me all tied up in knots."

"I can see that," Judy said to him. "I know you're his best friend, but you've got to let go a little. He'll come around."

Trevor didn't respond. Instead he turned away, wanting this conversation to end.

But Judy wasn't ready to let his last comment slide. "Now, about what you said…you know, about being married to our work. Don't use our lives, your mother's and mine, as a template for your own. I never married because…well, frankly, I never met the right person. I never set out to be alone; it just happened that way. I'm lucky, though. My patients fill up most of my heart and you fill the rest."

As Trevor heard those words, he turned back to face the one person he could always count on.

"Now, your mother," Judy grumbled, "she's a different story. I think she would be much better off if she'd unfreeze her heart and let someone in. But sometimes the hurt goes so deep that without the proper help it's almost impossible to heal."

"And me, what do you think happened to me?" Trevor asked her.

"Do you want me to be honest?"

"I don't know. Will it hurt much, Doc?" He tried to sound light-hearted but she could tell their introspective chat had touched a chord.

"It may sting a little but I'm sure you can handle it," Judy assured him. "I think you're probably a little gun-shy when it comes to commitment and trust. But I also believe you haven't met the right woman. When you do you'll be able to get past that hurdle and let someone into your life."

"What makes you think this woman exists?"

"Call it a hunch. I just do."

"I don't know if I agree with you. I like my life the way it is, thank you."

She patted his shoulder and teased, "We'll see about that." She turned then and started for the stairs. "It's late and I'd better head on up before it gets too late and you have to carry these old bones to bed."

Chuckling, he came up behind her and lifted her off the ground. "It would be my pleasure to carry those old bones to bed."

The next morning came too soon. As Judy stood at the gate waiting to board her plane, she watched as Trevor walked away. She felt the same empty feeling she'd had so many years ago when he'd gone in search of his dream. She hadn't realized until this moment how much she'd missed him over the years.

Chapter Three

A knock sounded at the door, rousing Judy out of her daydream state. "Come in," she called out.

Lana walked through the door looking as if she hadn't slept in days. Dark circles shadowed her usually bright eyes, her ordinarily erect posture appeared slightly hunched, and the white blouse under her suit jacket looked as if it had come directly from a wash load that had sat in the dryer too long.

Lana quietly closed the door and in a low voice began, "Judy, I have gone over your request a million times, trying to find the answer I know you want to hear."

When Judy started to mouth a heartfelt apology, Lana stopped her dead in her tracks.

"Please let me finish."

Judy nodded her head, realizing that Lana had probably rehearsed this speech and any deviation from the script would set her off course.

"I can't convince myself this would be good for either your nephew or me. We don't even know each other. I can't help but feel that I would be intruding on something so personal and private. Plus, I'm not sure I'm strong enough to deal with what he's going through. It wasn't so long ago that I was on the brink of a breakdown, and I'm worried that if I get too personally involved I'll open myself up to a possible setback. I can't risk it right now and I'm truly sorry! You've been my guardian angel and have asked nothing of me over the last three years. I want to help you so badly…I just don't know if I'm the right person."

Tears streaming down her face, Lana finished, "I haven't slept for days and all I can concentrate on is what you've asked, and why I can't help you."

Judy could see the pain etched on Lana's face and wished she'd never mentioned the situation at all. Lana's trembling body and quivering voice reinforced just how wrong Judy had been. She couldn't stop the flow of her own tears and had to search her drawers to find a fresh box of tissues.

Why had she done it? She'd thought this question over a thousand times and guessed her overwhelming need to help her nephew had caused her to break all the rules.

Judy's reaction startled Lana. Judy had always been focused and ready to share her infinite wisdom whenever Lana needed it. Sometimes Lana would call her late at night when insomnia threatened her sanity, or first thing in the morning when getting out of bed was like scaling a mountain. If Judy had minded she'd never let on.

Lana walked around the desk then, forgetting all the reasons she'd carefully scripted as to why she couldn't help this woman, and embraced the person she'd held on a pedestal for the last few years—the woman who had been instrumental in rebuilding her life. She hadn't anticipated this reaction from the person she idolized most in this world, and for the first time since the request, she understood the desperation Judy must have felt.

"I'm so sorry I've hurt you," Lana murmured.

Judy couldn't believe what she'd just heard. Lana deserved to be angry and instead she was the one doing the apologizing. "No, it's me who should be saying I'm sorry," Judy insisted. "I never should have asked this of you. I went against my better judgment and followed my heart. I only hope you'll be able to forgive me."

Six months earlier, Judy had answered a call from a very distraught Trevor. His voice shook as he told her Jamie had been in a plane crash. The plane carrying Jamie and a few other friends had gone down in a storm, killing the pilot and all six passengers. Tears flooded her own face as Judy listened to him sob for several minutes before announcing he had better go and make more calls. She had begged him to come home and be with his family, but he declined, saying he had too much going on to even consider leaving California.

Without thinking, Judy grabbed an overnight bag and stuffed in enough clothes for a few days' stay. She never gave any thought to her fear of flying; she just drove to the airport in hopes of securing a seat on the next flight out to Los Angeles.

Later that Saturday, when Judy walked up the marble steps of her nephew's mansion, she was disappointed as a housekeeper emerged instead of Trevor. In broken English, the housekeeper explained that Trevor was not at home and probably wouldn't be back until later that night. Judy silently chastised herself, wishing she had informed Trevor of her plans.

Fortunately, the housekeeper trusted her instincts and welcomed Judy into her employer's home, showing her to the guest suite she remembered so vividly. Sitting astride the fainting couch, she asked if the housekeeper had a phone number where she could reach Trevor.

By the time the housekeeper returned, Judy had already hung her two lightweight dresses in the spacious closet, placed her toiletries in the bathroom, and had her assistant rearrange her schedule for the beginning of the week. Then Judy called Trevor's cell phone.

Just hearing his aunt's voice brought forth a flood of emotions he'd been holding back during the past twenty-four hours. The familiar sound reminded him of home, something he needed more than ever right now.

"Trevor, where are you?"

"I'm on my way to the studio. Why?" Trevor asked, rather perplexed.

"Would you mind turning around and picking me up?"

"What?" Trevor gasped, his breath catching in his throat.

"I caught the last plane out and your housekeeper was kind enough to let me in."

When he had called Judy with the news, he'd known the minute he'd hung up the phone that she'd come. He just hadn't counted on her getting here this soon. He'd never bothered to call his mother. Aunt Judy had always been there for him, and she was the only person he wanted to be near right now.

Over the next few days, Judy never left Trevor's side. Jamie's mother had flown out with a few of his brothers and sisters, and together they made the funeral arrangements. The media swarmed over the entire affair, causing Trevor once more to wish this music circus he'd joined when he was only a teen would somehow dissipate.

He was edgy and solemn during the few days following the funeral, and Judy did everything in her power to lift his spirits. She hated seeing her nephew suffer so much and prayed he would be able to work through his grief in a relatively short time. Three days after the funeral, Jamie's family had packed their things and left Trevor's home, still somewhat in shock that Jamie was truly gone but content with the trust fund he'd set up for each of them.

This was the first time Judy had been alone with her nephew since the accident, and she desperately needed him to talk about his grief.

Trevor sat at the piano, stroking the keys. The sound emanating from the piano gave her a glimpse into the way he was feeling—sad and lonely, with a touch of anger. The tune was far from melodious and was beginning to get on her nerves.

This past week had not been easy for her nephew, and her heart went out to him. He'd taken control of everything—the funeral arrangements, selecting the plot, opening his home up for the brunch after the burial, and filling in the details of Jamie's life for his somewhat estranged family. With so much going on, he hadn't had the time to really feel the impact of his best friend's passing.

That time had come.

Judy walked up behind Trevor, put her arms around his upper torso, and held him tightly, somehow trying to squeeze out the pain from his hunched body.

He turned then into his aunt's open arms and let forth the anguish he'd been holding onto since the call came that Jamie had been killed.

Judy held on tight for so long her arms began to ache, and when she shifted slightly to alleviate some of the pressure, Trevor took the opportunity to ease from her embrace. Feeling ashamed of his outburst, he got up from the piano bench, walked toward the glass wall, and stared out into the blackness of the night.

Watching her nephew's reaction, Judy wanted to crawl into his mind, hear all that haunted him, and assure him that all would be well in time. Her nephew had a habit of minimizing the most meaningful situations, always finding something to take his mind off the real issues, and she wasn't about to let him hide this time. He had to face this head on and deal with what was in front of him. She wasn't leaving until that had been accomplished.

Standing pat on what she believed in, Judy said in a somewhat harsh tone, "Talk to me, Trevor. Tell me what you're feeling. Let me help you work through this."

If only it was that easy, he thought. "I can't talk about it."

Judy wasn't about to let up. "I know it's pretty raw right now but you really need to get it out."

"There's so much more to this than you know," Trevor said, shaking his head. "Stuff that I can't deal with right now."

Her gut feeling over the last few days told her something more than Jamie's death was bothering him.

"What is it? Is it the band? Some deal you're in the middle of? What? I'm here for you, but I can't help you if you don't talk to me."

"Don't push me on this," Trevor insisted, turning away from her.

That wasn't good enough for her. To Trevor, not pushing issues meant not dealing with them at all. She couldn't let that happen.

"Trevor, listen to me," Judy demanded, then softened her tone. "I want to help you and I can't do that unless you allow me to. I need to know what the hell you're talking about and I am not leaving until you spell out what it is you can't deal with. I suspected it was more than just grief for your best friend, but, although I'm good at my job, I'm no mind reader. Talk to me!"

Trevor saw the pity in her face fade, and in its place frustration took over. Somehow, seeing this transformation gave him the strength to talk about the subject he'd refused to discuss for the last few days. Sitting down in one of the comfortable chairs, he motioned for her to do the same.

"You'd better sit down," Trevor conceded. "This is going to be a long night."

Looking somewhat mollified, Judy sat on the couch facing him. "I have as long as you need."

Hearing those words, and knowing how true they really were, gave Trevor the incentive to continue. "Do you remember, when you visited several years ago, the girl Jamie brought home on the last night you were here?"

Judy hadn't forgotten the young woman who'd piqued her curiosity back then. "Yes, she was quite beautiful and somewhat drunk if I recall correctly."

Trevor's lips compressed into a hard, narrow line. "You're too kind. She was bombed out of her skull that night."

"I also recall you didn't like her very much," Judy reminded him.

"Hated her is a better word. She turned out to be a real loser. She really messed up Jamie's head for awhile. Jamie and I had made a pact before coming out here that neither one of us was going to fall prey to the pressures of what we called the head case scene. Jamie swore his whole life he would never get involved with drugs and alcohol after living with his father, who was a real bad ass."

Back then, Judy had assumed Jamie had some baggage, but when she'd raised the subject with Trevor he politely refused to discuss Jamie's home situation with her or anyone else. The bond between the two boys was impenetrable and she knew Trevor would never break a confidence, just as she herself never would.

"I didn't know much about Jamie's home situation, but sensed it wasn't that pleasant. Why didn't you or he ever come to me about it?"

"Jamie never talked much about it," Trevor said. "But a few times, usually when he was pissed off at his mom, he would tell me stories about the hell his life was like before his mom had the guts to kick his dad out of the house. Sometimes his dad just verbally abused them, calling her a whore and the kids all losers. When the abuse became more physical, his mom finally called the cops and had him arrested. He sort of disappeared after that and only came around a few times more before he was never heard from again."

"When you met him was his dad already gone?"

Trevor nodded. "Yeah! He hadn't seen his dad in about two years."

Judy drew a deep breath. "I'm glad Jamie had you."

"Back then, if you remember, I needed him just as much as he needed me. I felt abandoned by my own father and was headed in the wrong direction. Jamie wanted a better life and I needed to feel part of something. I remember us pricking our fingers and holding them so tightly together, somehow wishing the act would turn us into blood brothers."

He quickly turned his head away, fighting back the tears that threatened to fall.

"Trevor," Judy said, fearing his withdrawal, "Jamie *was* a brother to you. And the loss of a best friend, brother, or anyone close to you is one of the most painful experiences we can have. There is no magical solution to dealing with this kind of pain."

"When will the pain in my chest go away, and when will my throat stop constricting every time I think of him?" he asked solemnly, his face agonized.

"Only time will tell, darling. Talking it out sometimes helps, but most of all...it's time."

Leaning forward, Judy took Trevor's hands in her own and gently rubbed the tight fists, somehow hoping he would loosen his grip not only on his hands but on his heart as well.

"Why don't we go into the kitchen and make a fresh pot of coffee since I'm sure neither one of us is going to be able to sleep tonight? We can also polish off the rest of the apple cake Mrs. Ramirez was kind enough to bake. What do you say?"

Raising one eyebrow, an involuntary gesture he sometimes made when he thought someone was trying to best him, Trevor silently agreed, knowing in his heart that he had to talk this thing through before he went insane.

Chapter Four

Lana left Judy's office feeling drained of all emotion. She'd never expected that reaction from her best friend and couldn't assuage the guilt she felt about being partly responsible for her anguish. Trying to rationalize in her own mind that she wasn't accountable only made matters worse.

She decided to leave work early and head straight to the gym. Getting in a strong workout usually cleansed her mind, and she prayed it would have that effect today.

The workout at the gym, her dinner of delicious sautéed beef over noodles, and the scrumptious chocolate mousse cake she bought at the bakery did nothing to relieve her guilt. Taking two Tylenol PMs before bed allowed the necessary eight hours' sleep but did nothing for the gloomy way she still felt the next morning.

While getting dressed for work, she forced her mind to concentrate on all the things that needed to get done at the office, temporarily forgetting the dark mood overshadowing her.

By noon, Lana could stand it no longer. She couldn't concentrate on anything, not even the simplest of tasks. She had to see Judy and straighten things out if she planned to get anything accomplished today. Judy had tried yesterday to smooth matters over, saying she was sorry for even coming up with such an absurd suggestion. So why did she still feel so unsettled?

She knew the answer but was too scared to even think in that direction. Her alter ego, the one that sat in judgment, was warning that Judy was probably right. It was time. Time for her to regain some of what she'd lost. In all the years she'd known Judy, she'd admired the way she'd never pushed or even once mouthed the words "I told you so." She'd learned to trust Judy more than herself, except this time.

She'd convinced her parents, coworkers, and few remaining friends that things were going extremely well for her, when in fact she still felt like someone else was living inside her body. She knew Judy could see right through her but respected her enough to let matters lie. The few times Judy had broached the subject, Lana quickly turned the discussion around, letting her know, in no uncertain terms, that she was not going to talk about it.

She knew Judy had her best interest at heart and was probably correct in her assessment of the situation. When she really thought about what Judy had asked, she had to admit that for a millisecond she felt some excitement. But that excitement was quickly extinguished as her mind shifted back to cruise control.

There was a problem, though. The tingle she'd felt, for the briefest instant, had entered her gray matter and stuck. A picture had formed in her mind of a person buried deep in a tunnel, almost giving up on life, when out of nowhere a small ray of light appeared. Was this her ray of light, calling her to scratch her way out of this tunnel? Was she strong enough, or would she get halfway there and force a cave-in? Should she take that chance?

Then there were her parents. She'd come to rely pretty heavily on them and was afraid of how they'd react if she somehow got lost again. Once again the words "no man is an island" came to mind. Her parents had put their own lives on hold to help her get over this tragedy and she owed it to them to stay on course. Then she remembered how much better she'd felt after writing the letter to her in-laws. Her mom had quickly phoned after hearing from the Turnwells. Kate had been proud that day—proud that her lost child had emerged enough to carry through with what she'd referred to as the "right thing." Kate always was a proponent of doing the right thing.

Would saying yes to Judy be the "right thing"?

Was she ready?

She had to see Judy today and talk this through with a level head. Picking up the phone, she dialed Judy's extension and wondered what she was going to say. As Ellie transferred the call, Lana wiped her sweating hands on her pants.

Finally, Judy came on the line and said, "I thought about you all last night and was going to call, but I was afraid I was the last person you'd want to hear from. How are you?"

"Honestly, I'm terrible. I've done nothing but think about our discussion and I'm more confused than ever. Do you think we can have dinner tonight?"

"I'd love nothing better," Judy said, feeling relieved. "Do you want to go out or eat in?"

"I'd prefer to eat at my house. What if I pick something up on my way home and you come by about seven?"

"Sounds great," Judy said happily. "I'll get some of that gooey chocolate stuff we like so much for dessert. I'll also pick up a bottle of cabernet."

"Sounds good to me," Lana replied, feeling more at ease. "See you at seven."

"Oh, and Lana?"

"Yes."

"I'm so glad you called."

"Me too," Lana agreed.

The doorbell rang at seven sharp.

Lana had left work a little early to prepare for the evening and was surprised at how fast the time had gone by. During the last hour she'd been busy sautéing lemon chicken, chopping vegetables for the tossed salad, and boiling wild rice, including dried cranberries for some added flavor and color.

After talking to Judy that afternoon, a strange calmness had settled over her. She'd done nothing but think about Judy's proposal for the last few days. After she'd been able to sift through all the reasons why she couldn't possibly do what her friend had asked, a simple question still prevailed: why not?

What did she have to lose? If she hadn't lost her sanity by now, she doubted she ever would. What was the worst that could happen? She'd never shied away from a challenge before—before she'd become the person she hardly recognized anymore.

Just like old times, Judy came sauntering in bearing all kinds of goodies. Feeling the apprehension in the air, Judy walked over and hugged her good friend, immediately putting both women at ease.

Lana realized then that nothing Judy had said or done could extinguish the bond that had been cemented over the years.

When they sat for dinner, the initial conversation was kept to niceties, never once touching on the topic that neither was eager to bring up. Eventually, over dessert, Judy mentioned her proposal, once again apologizing, as she had done before, for bringing up a situation she should have known Lana wasn't ready for.

"Judy, you don't have to apologize for anything," Lana responded. "I overreacted and should have taken your feelings into account instead of just worrying about me. You've been so kind to me and the least I could've done would have been to take your advice and think about it before I went off like that."

"Please don't apologize for the way you reacted," Judy interjected. "I've been trying to get you to react for the past three years. I was proud of the way you let your emotions dictate what you were going to say. It was the first time in a long time I felt the real you emerge and say, 'To heck with decorum. I'm going to say what I feel.' I'm just sorry it wasn't over something exciting rather than painful. I never wanted to cause you any pain and I should've known better."

"I admit I was angry at first," Lana said, pouring the last of the wine into their glasses. "I couldn't believe you would ask me to deal with something so close to home. But after thinking about it for a few days, I realized you had my best interest at heart and would never consider asking me for something you didn't think I'd be able to handle."

Judy shook her head. "You're giving me too much credit. I think my love for Trevor and my feelings of helplessness clouded my judgment. In my heart I'm not sure you're up to the task and I never should have asked you. I'd like to forget this ever happened. Can we do that?"

With remarkable calm, Lana replied, "Your nephew is an important part of your life. And his world has just been turned upside down. You can't forget that any more than I can. I remember reading about the tragedy several months ago, but it didn't register that the Trevor Collins in the news was your nephew. It finally clicked when you flew out to

L.A. on short notice and had to cancel dinner plans. Then when you didn't mention anything when you came back I..."

Judy set her glass down. "I worried about telling you too much. I wasn't sure you'd want to hear about someone else's tragedy."

"I'll probably regret saying this, but I'm really glad you did."

"You are?" Judy's eyes were wide with surprise.

"I overreacted when I first heard what you had to say," Lana went on. "I was nervous before I entered your office that day. I don't know—I just knew something was up. I can't explain it but I feel different about the situation today. I've done nothing but think about what Trevor must be feeling and what's in store for him down the road. For the first time in a long time I've actually thought about someone else's problems. And guess what?"

"What?"

"It actually feels good. I can't seem to get him out of my mind, and that confuses the heck out of me. I've never met the man, I don't even really like his music, but I feel a certain kinship with him."

Judy knew exactly what she was talking about. "I can understand that. People who experience similar tragedies often find solace in each other's grief. Group therapy—something I know you were vehemently opposed to—can usually help most people deal with their pain."

"Back then I couldn't even mention the tragedy aloud, never mind listen to other people's grief," Lana reminded her. "I did what I could handle, and I guess you could say I live my life according to that principle now."

"Taking chances is what makes life so exciting. If life becomes too stale you only exist—you don't really live. We're put on this earth to live. Plants exist, people live. We humans are blessed with brains and the wherewithal to test not only ourselves but also everything around us. What would our world be like if everyone lived a safe existence, never venturing past what they know or can deal with?"

Lana remembered a time when she'd felt the same way about life. "I used to be that way but it all changed when Tom and Jessica were taken away. Existing was the only way I could go on."

"I know that," Judy said softly. "I worry about that kind of existence, though. If something bad were to happen again, say, one of your parents gets ill or something happens to me, I'm afraid of how you'd handle it. Since you're not regaining emotional strength, I worry that if something catastrophic were to happen we might lose you even more then we did before."

"I worry about that very same thing," Lana replied, frowning. "Sometimes I feel like I'm walking a tightrope and it's just a matter of time before I fall off."

"You need to be true to yourself regardless of the pain it takes to get there." Judy gazed at her friend, her expression thoughtful and caring. "You've already dealt with the worst part. In both my professional and personal opinion, I believe you're ready to embark on living life again."

"How can I be sure?"

"By putting yourself out there in both mind and body. Things you can handle, you'll revel in. Things you can't, you'll learn to live with, like the rest of us. But at least you will have tried!"

The leave of absence was approved within days, and Lana suspected that Judy had something to do with the quick turnaround. She gave her boss a two-week notice, promising to fill her staff in on any important issues which might come up during her absence, and reviewed in detail all the outstanding projects she'd be leaving behind.

A week and a half later, standing in the middle of a sea of clothes, anxiety threatened to halt Lana's life-altering mission. *How do I prepare for the unknown?* she wondered, amidst all the paraphernalia covering her bedroom floor. Her thoughts were like waves crashing in, eroding the foundation she'd fought so hard to establish. Was she doing the right thing? Was she doing this to help Judy out at the expense of losing her sanity? Her mom's overprotective words, which had boomeranged in and out of her mind, surfaced once again, making her question her decision.

"Are you crazy?" Kate Webber had cried when Lana announced the unexpected news. Knowing her father would not yet be home from work, she chose that time of the day to drop by to run her decision by her mom first.

Kate couldn't believe her ears when she heard her daughter's shaky voice explain her plans.

"Listen, Lana. I think you are making the biggest mistake of your life."

Chapter Four

"Mom, can't you let me be the judge of that?"

"No, not when I wonder where your head is. I can't believe Judy asked this of you. Has she forgotten what happened to you?"

"Mom, Judy is my friend. She helped me get through a terrible time and was instrumental in getting me my job. Something, I might add, which kept me out of the poorhouse. I could have lost everything a few years back and she stood by me, helping any way she could."

"I'm just afraid for you, darling," Kate admitted.

"I'm a little afraid myself, but down deep I feel the need to do this."

"But at what cost to you?" Kate questioned, not giving up. "Your father and I have also stuck by you through this horrible time and watched your world crumble around you. I don't think we could go through that again!"

"Mom, you and Dad have been wonderful. I couldn't have gotten through this without your support. I promise you I will not let this thing get out of hand. The minute I sense I can't handle it, I'll pack my bags and return home. One thing I've learned is my threshold for coping. Please trust me on that score."

"I don't like it, Lana," Kate persisted. "I've always followed my gut and I don't feel right about this."

"This is something I have to do. Can't you understand that?"

"Not really. But it isn't my life and I won't stand in your way. I just worry about you!"

"I worry about me also," Lana conceded. "But this feels right and I have to start trusting my instincts again. Please accept what I need to do and continue to support me like you've always done."

In a voice laced with uncertainty, Lana's mom murmured, "I'll try."

That evening, Lana received a call from her dad. She'd anticipated this call, picturing her mom waiting anxiously at the front door, bursting to tell him the news. Their conversation would consist of her mom laying out all the problems and her dad agreeing with her assessment and offering to call Lana to put some sense in her head.

What she hadn't expected were the comforting words her father shared that evening. He asked if she'd truly thought the matter through and when she replied yes, he promised to work it through with her mom. He went on to say how caring and nurturing she had always been and how this trip would bring out what he'd always thought was the best in her. She truly had never loved him more and had a hard time stanching the stream of tears rolling down her face. And after receiving his thumbs up, she knew in her heart that she was doing the right thing.

So why, tonight, was she allowing all kinds of negative vibes to take over her thoughts?

She needed to pack up her stuff and get going. Maybe she wasn't as ready as she thought. Panic started to seep in when she heard the doorbell.

Looking through the peephole she saw a smiling Judy, Chinese take-out bag in hand, waiting for the door to open.

"Thought you might be packing and feeling a bit out of sorts," Judy explained, "so I decided to surprise you with some dinner and company."

Judy followed Lana into the kitchen and started rummaging through the cabinets, as she'd done so many times before, grabbing a couple of plates and wineglasses. She pulled hard on the drawer that always seemed to stick and lifted two forks and spoons out, then began setting the table. "I had a premonition you might need some help. Was I right?"

"As usual," Lana laughed. "You'd better be careful, though. If you start reading people's minds, you might be accused of being a witch. And we know what they used to do to witches in Salem!"

Judy could only stare in wonder at the change that had taken place in Lana since she had agreed to undertake the task of helping out her nephew. This was more like the Lana of old. There was still a reserve to her that Judy suspected would always be there, but just seeing a seemingly happier Lana brought joy to her heart.

The night continued with both women talking nonstop. After they'd eaten and polished off the bottle of red wine, they ventured upstairs to finish packing. They'd decided that both would drive to meet Trevor on Saturday, allowing Judy to make the necessary introductions. Coincidentally, Judy had been asked to attend a series of lectures in Portland, Maine, the following week. Lana was happy to have her friend around even for just a day or two to help smooth the waters for her.

Saturday morning arrived much too quickly for Lana. By nine fifteen she was pacing a path down the middle of the living room rug.

Where is Judy? she worried. *We agreed on nine, or at least I thought we did...*

Opening the front door and breathing in the fresh air seemed to calm her beating heart. She heard the sound of a car coming down the street, and as soon as she recognized it, excitement and nervous energy took over. She quickly grabbed the bags she'd left by the door and carried them outside.

Seeing her friend standing next to her luggage, knowing that she hadn't chickened out, warmed Judy's heart. Lana had made the right decision—she was sure of it.

Judy didn't try to hide her excitement as she got out of the car and walked over to greet her friend. "I'm so looking forward to this trip. Are you nervous?"

"Honestly, not as much as I thought I'd be," Lana answered.

"That's what I like to hear! Let's pack up your stuff. The trunk is already pretty full with my bags, so these big ones will have to go in the back seat."

"Sounds good to me," Lana said as she began shoving the first of the two larger pieces into the back. "Something smells awfully good in here, Judy," she added.

Hearing the delight in Lana's voice brought a smile to Judy's face. She knew stopping at the bakery this morning would delay her a little, but Lana's love of fresh baked pastries made it worthwhile. "Why do you think I was a little late?" she asked.

"Let me guess, you picked up our favorite scones and that tea I love so much?"

"Close enough! Two cranberry-walnut scones, two apple-raisin turnovers and a couple of piping-hot cinnamon spiced teas for the ride north," Judy announced.

The bowl of cold cereal she'd wolfed down just an hour before had quickly been forgotten. The delicious aroma in the car had set her stomach juices churning. "Let's hurry so we can dig in," Lana said jokingly.

"Well, I'm all set on this end," Judy responded as she walked around the car and climbed into the passenger seat.

Somewhere between the bottle of wine and the chocolate mousse cake, they'd decided Lana would drive for the first part of the trip and

Judy would finish it off since she knew exactly how to get to Trevor's haunt. Buckling her seatbelt and taking a quick sip of tea, Lana put the car in reverse and backed out of the driveway.

"It's really a beautiful day," Lana remarked as she shifted the car into drive.

"It's that and more," Judy replied.

For the next hour, the two women delighted in carefree conversation and the succulent treats from the bakery, avoiding altogether any discussion of the reason for the trip.

Chapter Five

Trevor awoke feeling very tired and restless. He'd tossed and turned the entire night, thinking about his aunt's arrival that day. When she had phoned a few weeks earlier with what she'd called a marvelous idea, he had stood speechlessly staring at the receiver, wondering how she'd concocted such a notion. He had tried to tell her he wasn't interested, but trying to tell Aunt Judy something when she was sold on an idea was like using your finger to cork the leak in a dam.

She had asked that he trust her and—God help him—he had agreed. After he'd hung up, he chastised himself for being so weak, and several times over the last few weeks he'd dialed her number to cancel. Stabs of conscience would force him to disconnect the line before she'd had a chance to answer.

When rational thought fought its way to the surface, Trevor was willing to admit to himself that maybe Judy was right. He needed some help with what he was going through, and the secrets he'd been harboring were beginning to eat away at him.

Here now, sitting on his front porch, a mug of strong black coffee warming his fingers, he thought back to the weeks right after the funeral when everything had come unglued. Back then he couldn't get a handle on his emotions, which left him feeling helpless and depressed. Resentment was filtering into his attitude, overpowering his otherwise tactful nature when friends, business associates, and band members called or stopped by. Several large mail pouches containing thousands of letters and cards stood ignored in the spacious foyer. The outpouring of love and sympathy should have made him thankful that so many people cared, but just the opposite was true. He didn't want anyone's sympathy or pity.

Never one to be out-and-out rude, he found himself feeling extremely irritated by the constant interruptions. Unable to control what was now turning into anger, he needed to escape to a place where he'd be left alone to let loose the pent-up emotions he'd held inside since hearing the devastating news.

That place was Vermont.

Several years earlier when he needed some much-needed solitude and a break from touring, he'd bought a Vermont hideaway from one of his touring buddies, John Hunter.

Trevor could still remember the first time he flew back East to the place John referred to as God's country. He'd heard John was selling his retreat to buy a spread a little closer to his home in Wyoming, so he called John to let him know he was interested. Hearing this, John quickly offered to accompany his friend to Vermont and show him around.

Trevor recalled thinking he had died and gone to heaven as he and John wended their way through the countryside. The mountainous terrain and winding roads were a welcome change from the sterile freeways of modern L.A. life. Trevor sensed that time had stood still here, freezing out the wonders of big business. Rolling down the window, the scent of pine wafted through the stale air in the truck and overtook his senses, reminding him of Christmases past.

Totally absorbed by the landscape, Trevor was amazed when—after what seemed just a few minutes but was really an hour—John pulled off the main road onto a barely visible dirt lane. The four-by-four pickup truck was the perfect vehicle for this terrain. Knowing John came here only once every few months, Trevor asked if there were any problems with security. He was quickly told that security wasn't even a thought in these parts. His friend hardly ever locked his doors when staying here and had never had a problem with unwanted visitors, with the exception of a moose or deer sauntering through the yard.

Hearing this, Trevor let out a short laugh as he thought about the sizeable check he'd written for a top-of-the-line security system for his home in L.A. The monthly bill to maintain that system was probably more than some folks' mortgage payment, he said to his amused friend. As soon as those words escaped from his lips, he was reminded of why he'd really come to this place.

His life had become so different from that of most people. He couldn't walk down the streets of L.A. without people vying for autographs or snapping pictures. He'd never grown accustomed to the constant attention and more recently had tried to keep a very low profile. Sometimes he likened himself to an inmate at the state penitentiary. Every night he would set the alarm system to keep intruders out, but in reality it was he who was locked in with nowhere to go. He wasn't safe out on the streets and only felt secure when he was behind locked doors. This was a part of being successful in the music business, but as much as he tried to accept it, he couldn't.

The driveway seemed to go on forever as it wound around a magnificent sparkling body of water. The thick forest bordering the lake almost refused to let the light in, and when they neared a clearing it was as if someone had turned on a lamp. Right in the middle of this forest stood an oversized log cabin sporting a huge front porch, with a screened-in gazebo off to the side overlooking the lake.

Entering the house, Trevor felt right at home. The chestnut stained oak floors were covered with several large braided rugs. The twelve-foot-high stone fireplace that took up most of the front wall in the living room was the focal point, making one feel warm and welcome in this place filled with old-fashioned collectibles.

The coffee tables, end tables, and dining set looked as if they'd been hand-carved back in the days when furniture making was a necessity rather than a billion-dollar business. Slipcovers in shades of taupe, blue, and cranberry were draped on the oversized couch and matching chairs, and a large rocking chair stood next to the fireplace.

Behind the living and dining rooms was the kitchen, which blended the old with the new. Mahogany cabinets, adorned with antique pewter handles, some with beveled glass panels, warmed the spacious area, while granite countertops and stainless steel appliances modernized the overall look and feel of this open space. Trevor followed his friend up the open staircase, which led to three spacious bedrooms, all with balconies. His favorite, and the one he ended up staying in, was the bed-room his friend referred to as Daniel Boone's, decorated in flannels and plaids of varying shades of red and green.

After the tour, they spent the remainder of the day sitting on the front porch, taking in the scenery and hardly saying a word. That night they dined at a restaurant in town. The food was plain and plentiful—a contrast to the haute cuisine Trevor had become used to in Los Ange-les.

After returning home from dinner, Trevor immediately fell asleep within the confines of the queen-sized four-poster bed, with its soft flannel sheets and warm goose-down comforter. When he awoke the next morning, after sleeping for ten hours straight, something he hadn't done since he was a boy, he knew he would buy this house.

Watching the sun rise and brighten the dusky sky, Trevor was thankful he'd had the foresight to buy this place. Leaving L.A.—for God only knows how long—and flying to Vermont was one of the hardest things he'd ever done.

He remembered the excitement he and Jamie had felt twenty-two years earlier as they prepared for a new life. They had truly lived out their dream and, in the process, developed one of the deepest friend-ships two people could share.

All that was gone now, leaving him to wonder what life would be like without Jamie.

Leaving L.A. had brought home the realization that Jamie was really gone and life would never be the same. By letting go of Jamie, he was letting go of more than his best friend. The music, if he ever felt the need to compose again, would be different. The L.A. house wouldn't be the same without Jamie bouncing in and out whenever he felt like it, and the circle of friends they'd shared together would bring constant reminders of life before.

In his heart, at this moment in time, Trevor didn't care if he ever went back.

Vermont proved to be the perfect sedative. Tall evergreens, stretch-ing as far as the eye could see, stood over him, whispering soothing sounds, while views of the lake and mountainside eased the darkness of his soul. Time was slow to heal; he accepted that now, but there was a sorrow he couldn't seem to shake.

Over the last few months, he had ventured out a couple of times and introduced himself to some of the townspeople. Most of the people he encountered were retired or working part-time jobs in the local establishments. Not many had recognized him and that suited him just fine.

Mrs. Haversham, the town busybody, tried a few times to finagle information out of him, but Trevor remained tightlipped, not ready to share his life. The only two people he trusted with any information were Ben and Irma Smythe. Ben and Irma lived close by and had done some work around the house when John owned the place. After Trevor bought the house, they came by one day asking if he needed their help.

Ben and Irma looked like they belonged in this part of the country. Ben, tall and lean, had a weathered face, indicating that he'd been working out in the elements most of his life. He was a man of few words, but when he did decide to speak up, Trevor suspected, people listened. By contrast, Irma was a short, slightly round woman, with graying hair, cropped very short. Trevor could tell that Irma was tough yet kindhearted.

Not being able to turn them away, Trevor said he would love to have them continue what they had been doing for John. And so it was agreed that Ben would continue to care for the grounds and provide any snowplowing needed during the winter months, and Irma would get the house ready whenever he came back East.

Over the last few years, Trevor had only used the place a few times, so it came as quite a shock to Ben and Irma when he phoned to say he was coming out for an extended visit and asked that two bedrooms be readied for his arrival. He'd never brought anyone up to the house, so they wondered about the second party. Trevor didn't give much detail, but Irma could sense something was very wrong.

When Trevor arrived a few days later, Ben and Irma were busily preparing for his arrival. Ben was clearing fallen branches from a storm the night before, while Irma swept scattered debris off the front porch. Seeing the two of them so comfortable in these surroundings warmed Trevor's soul. For just a second, the loneliness he had felt during the last few weeks left his body.

True to her word, Irma had readied the house for his arrival, adding the usual special touches he appreciated so much. Two major senses worked overtime as Trevor's eyes caught the beautiful bouquet of colorful flowers sitting atop the dining room table, while the scent of home cooking started his salivary glands working.

Ben and Irma silently watched a haggard-looking Trevor carry a small child up the stairs to one of the spare bedrooms. When Trevor didn't offer any explanations, Ben and Irma politely welcomed him and vanished before he had the opportunity to thank them.

Irma fell in love with the child, and came by every day to help Trevor with whatever he needed. Watching Ben and Irma with this small creature brought back fond memories of living at his grandparents' house as a child. Recalling those times almost made him feel human again...

The sound of running footsteps advancing down the stairs brought Trevor back to the present. "Honey, I'm out here," he called.

A small child with a face that would light up a dark, starless night appeared within seconds on the front porch. Opening his arms wide, Trevor reached for the little girl and softly cradled her in his arms.

Clad in just a nightgown, she wiggled her way closer, clinging to the warmth of his body.

"Why you out here?" she asked, staring into his loving eyes.

"Just enjoying the scenery. Why are you up so early?"

"I not up early. Not dark anymore."

He wrapped his arms tightly around her and tickled her under the chin. "Lily, are you excited about Aunt Judy's visit this weekend?"

Letting out a squeal of delight, she answered, "Yeah! How many more minutes?"

"We have a few hours yet," Trevor said soothingly. "You know Aunt Judy's bringing a friend this time. Did you remember?"

"Uh-huh! You told me zillion times."

"I don't think that many," Trevor jokingly corrected. "Maybe a few hundred, though."

For the next several minutes, neither said a word. When Trevor's stomach grumbled, he asked, "How about we go in and have some breakfast?"

Lily quickly jumped off his lap. "Pancakes?"

Chapter Five

"Whatever your little heart desires," Trevor gladly promised.

The first hour of their trip had gone smoothly. Fortunately, the weather had cooperated nicely. The temperature promised to reach the low sixties by midday, and the few clouds speckling the sky were the non-threatening kind, confirming that no rain was in sight.

Coming upon the "Welcome to Massachusetts" sign brought the realization that Vermont was just a state away and the subject of Trevor and Lily—the two names Lana and Judy had avoided since the beginning of this trip—needed to surface.

The conversation up until then had been much like the weather, breezy and mild, with the two women talking about heart-smart recipes, the commitment of growing one's own vegetables for those dishes, and a bit of gossip regarding people at work.

Very safe topics, just like old times, Judy thought as she glanced over at the sign. Her never-ending patience, a trait all who knew her envied, kept her from being the first to bring up Trevor and Lily.

For Lana, the landmark registering that they were getting closer was like a slap in the face, causing the nervousness she'd held in check for so long to rise to the surface. Time was running out.

"Do you want me to take over?" Judy asked. "You've been driving almost an hour and you could probably use a break."

"No, I'm fine," Lana said cheerfully, trying to mask her uneasiness.

Several minutes passed, then Lana voiced aloud what had been on her mind. "How does Trevor really feel about me coming up? And please don't say, 'Just trust me, Lana.' I need to know what to expect."

This one question lifted a heavy weight that had been sitting on Judy's chest since she'd arrived at Lana's that morning. Finally, Lana was ready to address the issues Judy had desperately wanted to talk about.

When she'd proposed the idea of bringing Lana, Trevor initially rejected it, saying that no one could ever know Lily existed. But Judy, being tenacious as always, had finally worn him down. However, with his acceptance came a condition he wouldn't back down on. The secrets he'd learned after Jamie's death could never be uncovered, and he made Judy vow she would provide Lana with only the sketchiest of details regarding Lily.

"That's a good question," Judy said, finally responding to Lana's concern about Trevor. "I'm not sure I can accurately answer it. He wasn't sold on the idea initially. You have to know Trevor, though. He's a very private person and he becomes very defensive when he thinks anyone's interfering in his life."

"Well, isn't that what we're doing?" Lana countered.

"It depends on how you look at it. I've never really meddled in Trevor's life even though there were times I felt he needed a kick in the pants. This time, though, it's different. I don't think he has the mindset to really see things clearly."

"I'm not sure anyone would, so soon after losing his best friend and business partner."

"I know you can't put a time limit on grief, but I'm worried more about his ability to care for Lily than anything else right now. As I've told you, she was born with fetal alcohol syndrome and although Trevor assures me she doesn't have any long-lasting effects, I can't be so sure. You and I both know there are many hidden facets to this syndrome."

"Yes, I know," Lana nodded. "I was really surprised when you told me he had a child. The only thing I knew about your famous nephew was that he was one of the most eligible bachelors around. I'd never heard any mention of his having a child."

Silence filled the car for the first time since they'd driven off that morning. Then Judy explained, "No one knows Lily exists. That's why I swore you to secrecy when I first told you. Trevor is constantly under public scrutiny and he doesn't want Lily to endure that same fate. If people knew about her, life would never be the same for Lily."

"What about her mother?" Lana asked, confused by the mystery of it all. "Is she part of their lives or does Trevor have sole custody?"

Judy sighed. "I don't mean to sound like a broken record, but you know I can't really get into that with you."

Lana's fingers tightened on the steering wheel. "I can understand him wanting to protect this little girl, but he's going to have to trust me."

Although it was barely noticeable, Judy heard the irritation in Lana's voice. "Trusting people is something Trevor has a hard time doing. He knows he needs help with Lily. I'm sure when he gets to know you better he'll come forth with all the answers you need."

Didn't Trevor know she wouldn't judge him or Lily's mother? Lana wondered, as her thoughts went back to the time she had worked on the pediatric ward, where she had nursed to health many children born to alcoholics or crack addicts.

In her early nursing days, when she thought she knew all there was to know, she had judged these women, calling them weak and stupid. But as she matured and opened her eyes to the horrors of addiction, she realized how powerless these people felt under the grip of their chemical dependency. She was one of the few nurses on her floor who went beyond the call of duty, attending AA meetings with some of the mothers and volunteering time at the local women's shelter, showing new mothers how to care for their babies.

This side of Lana was something her husband had never understood. Tom didn't have any tolerance for what he called the dregs of society and more than once lectured her about getting too involved. After trying several times to soften his views on codependent victims, she'd listen to his chiding, closing off the part of her he'd never understand, and pretend to perceive where he was coming from. In her heart, she knew they would never agree on this topic, and on more than one occasion she resorted to telling little white lies to keep the peace.

Returning to the present, Lana decided to respect Judy's devotion to her nephew and changed direction. "Okay, let's talk about Lily. Does she know I'm coming?"

"Yes, I believe Trevor's told her," Judy said, happy that Lana had backed off.

"You mentioned earlier that she was small for her age, but did you notice if she had some of the other features common to children born with this syndrome—like a small head or eyes, a pug nose, flattened cheekbones, or anything else which would make her appearance different?"

"Not that I could tell," Judy said, relieved that the nurse in Lana was coming to life again. "Other than being small, Lily's appearance is normal."

"How about her behavior?" Lana asked.

Judy knew well enough that children born with fetal alcohol syndrome often have behavioral problems, which is one of the reasons it is so hard to diagnose until later. "Lily seems a little hyper," Judy ventured, "always interrupting, trying to get Trevor's full attention. I chalked it up to her new environment, hoping in time she'd settle down. I wasn't with her long enough to really make an assessment, and with all that Trevor's had to deal with, I didn't want our visit to be clinical in any way. I only wish I had more time with Lily. Don't forget I just learned of her existence a short while ago."

"Why do you think Trevor didn't tell you about her until now?"

"I've asked myself that same question. I'm not really sure why he felt he couldn't tell me. I'd always considered ours to be a special relationship and thought he knew he could come to me with anything."

"Did you ask him why he never said anything?" Lana persisted.

"Yes, and all he said was he'd made a promise that her birth would remain a secret. I suspect the mother would not fare too well, bearing a child with complications resulting from alcohol abuse, especially if this information was exploited on every newsstand in the country. Knowing Trevor the way I do, I believe that if he made a promise to someone he would go to his grave with it."

"Weren't you hurt that he didn't tell you sooner?"

"Yes and no," Judy admitted. "Yes, because in my heart I thought Trevor and I had a bond that went beyond promises. And no, because I understand his commitment to Lily and know that deep in his heart he thought he was doing the best thing for her."

"Without breaking any confidences, can I assume the mother is no longer a part of Lily's life?"

"I'd rather you ask Trevor that question," Judy answered as her attention turned toward the speeding traffic. "I can't believe how fast these people are driving," Judy pointed out.

"I know. I put the cruise control on sixty-eight a while back, and next to these other drivers I feel like I'm creeping along."

Lana then focused on Judy's earlier comment. "Why the mystery about Lily's mother?"

Judy settled back into her seat, remembering her promise to Trevor. "You have to understand that the constant scrutiny by the media makes Trevor wary of imparting any more information than he has to. It's funny, but many years ago when Trevor's name was starting to surface on every teen's lips and his letters home became practically nonexistent, I resorted to reading the tabloids to gain any information I could on his life. The trash that I read in those rag sheets didn't in any way resemble the young man I'd helped raise. Knowing in my heart that Trevor hadn't become the womanizing, jet-setting punk depicted in those articles, I learned to decode, if you will, the information, storing only what I needed to know—where he was touring and that he was alive and well."

Judy's explanation put things into perspective for Lana. "I never really paid attention to all the garbage written about superstars. Training to be a nurse made me look at life very differently from most. I learned early on that happiness comes from following your heart, and if you can wake up every day and feel you've done something good for mankind, you'll be the richest person in the world."

She paused a moment to pass an elderly couple going even slower than she was. She then quickly glanced over at her friend's face and finished her thought. "Money and fame are typically rewards given to those who jump through hoops for others and usually lose themselves in the process."

Judy could see bits of the old Lana coming back. She was delighted to hear her friend refer to herself as a nurse and not as some administrative guru. Happily, she said, "I couldn't agree with you more."

"From what you've told me, Trevor never adjusted to the notoriety associated with being a star," Lana mused. "How has he been able to stand it all these years?"

"Early on, I think he enjoyed the attention. His music was playing on every radio station in the country, his albums were topping the charts, and his concerts were sold out. Trevor was elated that his talents had been recognized and that he'd experienced financial success doing something he absolutely loved." Judy's voice then became solemn. "Unfortunately, there was a price he paid for all that popularity. I know this seems harsh, but maybe Jamie's death was his wake-up call."

Lana gazed over at her friend and noticed the sad, faraway look in her eyes. She changed the subject by saying, "Forgetting all the music and the stardom, what's he really like?"

"Well, I have to admit I'm a tad biased about my nephew," Judy answered with the start of a smile. "When I look into his eyes, I still see the warm, caring boy I've always known. On the outside he's become a little hardened—I suspect from the vultures he's met in the business—and to those who don't really know him I imagine he seems pretty aloof. But I can tell you he's one of the most loyal people you'll ever meet. He has a strong will and, like me, when his mind is made up there's no stopping him."

"Oh, no! I'm really in for it now," Lana said, shaking her head. "Between the two of you I won't stand a chance!"

"But look how well you and I get along," Judy pointed out. "Trevor's a lot like me in many ways. I think the two of you will get along just fine."

"What are his expectations regarding my visit?" Lana asked with interest.

"Right now, I think he'd like to see Lily in a program that can test her skills to see if she exhibits any of the behavioral signs of the syndrome. I know he's done a lot of research on her condition and is aware that many of the effects won't show up until she's school age. That's why now is so important. She'll hopefully be starting school in the fall, and it's imperative that we know what to expect. Besides her small stature and a slight speech problem, Trevor hasn't noticed any other signs of the syndrome. However, since Lily's been in seclusion most of her life, some of the effects may just not have had the opportunity to show themselves."

"Where's she been?" queried Lana.

Tread carefully, Judy thought before answering. "Trevor and Jamie bought a place together well beyond the reaches of Los Angeles. Lily had a wonderful nanny who took care of her from the day she was born. This woman, who is in her early sixties, had a heart attack a few months ago and had to go live with relatives. Last I heard, she was recovering nicely and Trevor was trying to talk her into coming to Vermont."

"I'm a little worried about testing Lily so close to all this tragedy. Do you think Trevor can handle it?"

"I'm not really sure," Judy said, shrugging her shoulders. "I don't think he has a choice, though. If Lily does have any mental abnormalities like lack of coordination, a lowered IQ, any antisocial behaviors, hyperactivity, or anything else, we need to know as soon as possible so we can figure out how best to move forward. Many of the adults I see in my practice are children of mothers who had addiction problems. I can tell you that if you don't step up to the plate early on, serious problems can result down the road." Judy allowed a moment for that to sink in, and then went on. "There's a patient I've been seeing for the last ten years. He dropped out of school in the eighth grade, was labeled a troublemaker by the local authorities, and ended up in juvie by the time most boys his age were starting to sweat under their armpits. I met his mother first at a group therapy session I used to run at the local shelter. She'd been sober for five years and was well on her way to putting her life back together. After the meeting, she shyly stood in the shadows waiting for me to pass before she asked for my help. At that moment, the face I stared into was different from the strong-willed woman I had just a short time ago heard talk of her sobriety. She seemed broken and lost. She told me about her son and asked—no, more like begged—me to see him.

"When I met him I knew he had fetal alcohol syndrome. He had the facial characteristics—small eyes that looked wide-set, a pug nose, and a small chin. He couldn't sit still the entire time we talked and asked me to repeat myself several times. I knew then that the syndrome didn't just include the physical characteristics but the behavioral as well. I wasn't surprised that he ended up where he did. I can't change what happened to him, but I won't sit back and let Lily suffer the same fate."

Lana nodded in sympathy, knowing only too well the characteristics of someone born with the syndrome. "I know you weren't with Lily that long, but did you notice anything that might lead us to think there's more here than we know about?"

Judy thought for a minute. "Well, when I initially talked to Trevor about Lily he mentioned some things that concerned me. He recalled that Lily was a difficult infant. You know, she didn't sleep through the night for at least six months, cried a lot, and refused to eat. He also mentioned that in her early years she didn't like to be cuddled. When I met her, I did get the impression that Lily wasn't quite up to what other children her age could do."

"Like what?" Lana asked. "Give me an example."

"One thing that stuck out was that Lily didn't speak in full sentences. In fact, I had trouble understanding what she was saying and had to decipher just about everything she said. I would then repeat it the correct way, and I could tell she was frustrated with my teachings. Her attention span was very short when I tried to get her to listen to the right way to speak. She would just turn and walk away like it wasn't important. I didn't want to make a big deal of it at the time, but it caused me to wonder if her attention span was more like that of a two-year-old." Judy sighed, then added, "I brought some easy puzzles—you know, the wooden ones with the plastic handles designed for kids aged two to four. When we dumped the puzzle out and Lily had to place the wooden figures back in their slots, she had trouble identifying the right shape. When I helped her determine the right spot, she had trouble fitting the pieces in. I don't think she had ever done a puzzle before and I could tell she was becoming very frustrated with the task. When she couldn't fit the last piece in, she picked it up and threw it to the ground."

"What did you do then?" Lana asked, surprised.

"I made her pick up the pieces with me and then Trevor took her upstairs for a nap, claiming she was just tired."

"Do you think he has any idea of what's ahead if she does have some of the things we've talked about?"

"I know he's read about it but I'm not so certain he's really thought how it may change his life. Hopefully, we'll be able to help him through the discovery process."

There was a long pause as Lana absorbed all that had been said. "I told my boss I'd be gone for a few weeks. Do you think that's enough time?"

"I think so," Judy answered. "All you need to do is point Trevor in the right direction. He's been getting a lot of help from a couple that oversee the place when he's away. From what Trevor's told me, they've grown pretty fond of Lily and vice versa. I'm sure that once you've paved the way they'll be willing to help in any way they can."

Chapter Six

Trevor and Lily were just finishing up last night's leftovers when they heard the sound of a car in the driveway. Lily jumped up from her seat and ran out the front door, leaving a slightly nervous Trevor to follow in her wake.

Judy had taken over the driving once they'd entered Vermont and was delighted when she remembered the turnoff that led to Trevor's house. Now, pulling up the drive, anticipation overcame her at the thought of seeing her nephew and Lily again.

When she originally thought of this plan, she'd quickly pooh-poohed the notion, saying it would never work. She never believed Lana or Trevor would buy into her idea. When they did finally, she was thrilled at the prospect of what could be. In the back of her mind, she hoped that they would hit it off and become truly great friends. They needed one another, but she didn't tell them that. With Trevor and Lana she'd kept the plan focused entirely on Lily, recognizing that both would want to do the right thing for the child. If either of them suspected any kind of ulterior motive, they'd run in opposite directions and probably never forgive her. She knew she was one of those rare species that didn't need to have a significant other, but she recognized that Trevor and Lana were not of her kind and truly wouldn't find completeness without someone else in their lives.

When Trevor's house came into view, Judy recognized the small child, wearing bibbed jeans and a bright pink turtleneck, standing in the middle of the drive, hands and half her arms hidden in the deep pockets. "Hello, sweetheart. How are you?" she yelled from the open window.

Lily ran up to the driver's side, asking if Judy had brought her present.

When Judy had called the other night to confirm the last-minute details, she'd spoken to Lily and promised she'd bring her a little something from Connecticut. She was happy to see that Lily was excited about her arrival and quickly stepped out of the car, lifting the feather-light child in her arms. "Your present is in my suitcase. I'll get it as soon as I unpack."

Lana sat transfixed, observing the warm embrace between the bookend generations. Throughout the drive, she'd talked about this little girl as if she were a patient, never once feeling any emotional setback at the thought of being with a child again. Here, now, seeing Lily in person, she was frozen in place, unable to move from the car. Maybe if she shifted her eyes, her body would follow suit and allow her to shed the paralysis that had overtaken her.

Her mind made up, Lana forced her eyes to look away. They landed on the figure standing casually by the front entry. Trevor's name immediately formed on her lips and for a brief moment their eyes locked.

Lana felt an immediate connection to the man leaning against the railing on the porch. *Why doesn't he walk over?* she thought as she stared into eyes that mirrored her own. For reasons she couldn't explain, Trevor's presence had an extremely calming effect on her. The panic attack that had started to rear its ugly head just moments before washed back down like a pill riding on a stream of water.

As Lana got out of the car, Trevor couldn't stop himself from staring at the woman he'd been reluctant to meet. She was very beautiful in an understated way. Her honey-colored shoulder-length hair moved freely in the breeze and the urge to capture a few of those wisps between his fingertips became ever so strong. Her outfit wasn't anything out of the ordinary—khaki pants and an olive-tinted knit shirt—but the way her clothes hugged her slender body seemed to add to this woman's beauty.

Trevor watched Lana stretch her limbs in an attempt to work out the kinks of sitting too long. The tension he'd felt awaiting their arrival eased a bit, and a smile started to form on his pursed lips. Maybe this wasn't going to be so bad after all.

Feelings he'd thought lost forever began stirring in him. He hadn't viewed the world in the same way since Jamie had died, and, until now, the thought of being with a woman had been the farthest thing from his mind. What was it about this woman that captivated him so? He'd been with plenty of women in the past and no one had ever had this effect on him. He thought back to what Judy had shared with him about Lana's past and suspected the overwhelming feelings were due in part to a sort of kinship they shared. When Judy had first mentioned her plan, he'd listened halfheartedly as she explained Lana's tragic loss. Judy didn't get into too much detail but briefly touched on the accident, the depression that followed, and what had become of Lana's life since. Trevor wasn't much interested at the time, but now, seeing her in the flesh, all those details he thought hadn't sunk in came flashing into his mind.

Even though they'd never met, he felt Lana's sorrow. Traces of it were still there; he could feel it. She looked so innocent and lovely standing just fifteen or so feet from him. He felt this strange impulse to take her in his arms and protect her.

He didn't like feeling this emotionally naked and closed his eyes in an attempt to blacken out the sight of the woman who had stirred up thoughts he'd best put to rest. His rational side chalked the response up to his abstinence during the last several months, but the other side—the one he normally relied upon—knew it was much more than that.

Lana stood in the background while Judy and Lily renewed their relationship, hoping the unsteadiness she felt was not showing outwardly. It took all of her strength to leave the car and walk toward the pair who were kissing and hugging, obviously happy to see one another. She was determined to overcome her uneasiness. After all, she'd committed herself to this and nothing was as good as her word.

Judy realized she'd momentarily forgotten about Lana and told the child, "Lily, I have someone here I want you to meet."

Lily stuck like glue to Judy's leg and shyly looked away.

"Come on, darling. Say hello to my friend Lana," Judy said, turning the little girl to face Lana.

Lana was momentarily frozen in place. She'd avoided contact with children since her daughter's death, and here she was face to face with one.

Judy sensed that Lana was uncomfortable and immediately grabbed for her friend's hand. "Lana, this is Lily."

The warmth of Judy's hand in her own thawed her mind enough to allow her to greet the small child. "Hi, Lily. Nice to meet you."

Without saying a word, Lily turned and ran to the front steps, using Trevor's leg to hide from the stranger she'd been forced to meet. The tugging on his leg caused Trevor to instantly snap out of his reverie. Looking down at the small child clutching his leg, he whispered, "Everything's going to be all right, sweetheart. Just come with me."

Walking slowly down the steps, dragging a reluctant Lily behind him, Trevor opened his arms and welcomed Judy into his embrace. "Lily and I have really missed you. I'm so happy to see you."

Judy loved being in those strong arms. She'd longed to be near Trevor again ever since they had rekindled their relationship after Jamie's death. Maybe she was getting on in years or maybe she needed to feel connected to family—she couldn't be sure.

"How are you and Lily getting along?" Judy asked. But before he could answer she realized she hadn't introduced Lana to Trevor. "Oh, I'm so sorry! Trevor, this is Lana, and Lana, this is Trevor."

Trevor turned from his embrace with Judy and extended his hand before his eyes settled on the deepest blue instruments of vision he'd ever seen. He couldn't stop himself from staring into the pools that matched in color and depth the waters in the Caribbean Sea. Clearing his throat in an attempt to mask his nervousness, he continued to extend his hand, and in a voice as smooth as silk said, "Hello. I've been looking forward to meeting you."

Lana stood speechless as she stared into the eyes that were magnets to her own. When she tried to respond and nothing came forth, heat started to rise in her body. She knew her face resembled a ripe tomato and the embarrassment she felt was almost more than she could bear. What was even more shocking was her inability to move her right hand. Her brain had registered that he wanted to shake her hand, but the signal to move her own must have shorted out. Her eyes seemed to be the only thing working, and when she looked down for a moment, breaking the spell Trevor seemed to have over her, she felt a soft warm hand enfold her own. This small act of kindness gave her the strength she needed, and in a voice barely above a whisper, she responded, "I'm glad to meet you as well."

Trevor felt a tug on his left leg and knew Lily was going to explode if he didn't give her his undivided attention. She liked being the center of his life, as she'd been of late, and for the past month had resorted to using tantrums as a means of keeping him focused on her needs.

Trevor reluctantly released Lana's hand and knelt down to face Lily, wanting to keep the peace and eliminate the histrionics he knew were forthcoming. "Please don't act this way, honey. Lana is a good friend of Aunt Judy's, and we want her to feel comfortable here. Please be nice!"

While Lily was glad to see Aunt Judy, it was obvious she wasn't happy with the woman who'd accompanied her. In a voice loud enough for Lana to hear, Lily responded, "I no like her. She go home!"

"Come with me, Lily," Judy said, taking the child's hand. "I want you to show me the robin's nest you told me about on the phone. Will you take me to it?"

Lily couldn't wait to show off her find and pulled Judy's hand, leading her to the back of the house and momentarily forgetting the experience, or lack thereof, of meeting Lana.

Lana watched the pair disappear behind the house. In a way she was glad Lily hadn't warmed right up to her, thinking that if she had, it might have been harder to quell the turbulent emotions that were running through her. This petulant child reminded her more of the kids she used to nurse back to health than the loving daughter she'd lost. She felt her heartbeat slow and was almost glad the first step of her journey had been accomplished with just a modicum of hysteria.

Trevor was embarrassed by Lily's behavior and started to apologize. "I'm sorry about that...she's..."

His eyes were so mesmerizing that Lana had to look away for a second to collect her thoughts. "You have nothing to apologize for," she finally managed. "She's just a child and I'm a stranger. She'll come around."

"I'm sure you're right. Um, I'll get the bags and show you to your room?"

The minute Lana crossed the threshold into the house, a warm cozy feeling washed over her. This place reminded her of a storybook setting: the fireplace, the rocker, the colorful braided rugs and comfortable furniture.

"I love your place," she remarked candidly, the tension she'd felt moments ago temporarily forgotten.

"Thanks," Trevor responded. He smiled and motioned with a tilt of his head for Lana to follow. "Come on upstairs. We only have three bedrooms in this house, so I hope you don't mind sharing a room with Judy."

Lana followed right on his heels. "Oh, I don't mind at all. It'll be like having a sister."

"Don't you have a sister?"

"No, just a brother. You?"

"Neither," Trevor breathlessly responded as he reached the landing. "Your room is down here."

Entering what was to be her room for the next few weeks, Lana smiled to see that the space had been set up to look like two rooms instead of one. On one side of the room were a bed, dresser, and desk, and directly across was a mirror image.

Each of the pieces looked as if they'd been hand-carved, like the furniture she'd briefly noticed downstairs. The matching sleigh beds were old-fashioned and inviting. Both had similar—albeit not perfectly matched—quilts lying on top, which gave her the impression that they were hand-sewn. The walls were painted a light peach color, and a minimalist floral print was stenciled in a darker version of peach and various shades of green around the ceiling and bare window frames. Each end of the room boasted two large windows, allowing breathtaking views of the beautiful countryside and leaving no need to adorn the walls with pictures.

This room reminded Lana of the one she had occupied for most of her childhood. Back then, she'd slept in a twin bed much like the ones here, and many nights she had relied on the warmth of the hand-stitched quilt her grandmother had bequeathed to her. She knew it was impossible to go back in time, but stepping into this room brought her the closest she'd ever felt to that time in her life.

Chapter Six

Trevor had carried the last of the suitcases up before she realized she'd been standing there staring into space. "I'm sorry, Trevor! This room just looks so much like the one I grew up in. I didn't mean for you to carry everything else up by yourself."

"No problem." Trevor found himself staring into her clear blue eyes. "I...I don't know whose is whose, so I'll just put everything on one side." He moved away, putting some distance between them. "What the hell do you women pack in these things anyway?"

Lana watched the strong muscular form easily lift the overstuffed bags as if they had been filled with feathers instead of all the paraphernalia she'd emptied from her drawers. "I can't speak for Judy," she told him, "but I carry just about everything but the kitchen sink when I go away."

"Are you sure you didn't forget and pack the sink in this one?" he joked.

Laughing, she answered, "Believe me when I tell you I have everything but that." She hesitated then, letting the convivial moment pass. She still wasn't comfortable with the sound of her own laughter. In a more serious tone, she added, "I didn't know quite what to bring since the weather can be so iffy this time of year."

"Good thing! Yesterday the temperature got up into the mid-seventies but dropped to almost freezing during the night. Well...I'll leave you to unpack."

"I can do that later," Lana said, unwilling for him to leave. "Should we go outside and find Judy and Lily?"

As they walked toward the door, Trevor lightly touched her arm. "Lily has a hard time meeting new people. I hope you don't..."

Lana stopped him before he could continue. "She's not the only one. We'll be just fine. I promise."

He turned then and walked away, leaving her staring at the place on her arm where he'd left an indelible mark. He'd just touched her, yet the minute their bodies met, it was as if an electric current had raced through her system.

Whoa, she thought. *Get a hold of yourself.* Sensations she'd long thought dead were starting to appear. She had to quash them before they overtook her. She had made a vow after she'd lost her husband that she would never expose herself to that kind of hurt again. That kind of thinking gave her the strength to move forward and she wasn't about to do anything that would unravel the thin thread that held her together.

"Wait up," she called from the doorway.

Walking behind Trevor, she measured him to be about six foot two, one hundred and eighty-five pounds, give or take a few. She liked the hint of ruggedness in his tall, slender frame. His hair was dark, almost long enough to pull back into a short ponytail. She'd seen him before on videos and covers of magazines, and realized the cameras hadn't lied—he was striking. But most of all, she liked the warmth that emanated from his body when he spoke to her. He had an aura about him that was indescribable.

The logical part of her consciousness reminded Lana that she was here on a professional basis. But it seemed her heart was leaning in a different direction. She knew her limitations, though. The life she'd chosen might not have been the best for most, but it was the one that kept her sane. Even if she'd taken temporary leave of her senses, she knew deep in her heart that this man could hurt her, and that was enough to eliminate any feelings or desires that threatened to surface.

That being silently said, she knew what she had to do. She'd be polite and keep conversations strictly focused on Lily. Anyway, she doubted Trevor had designs on her other than using her experience to help diagnose Lily, so she might as well stop worrying and get down to business.

Lana felt more in control as she wended her way around the back of the house. Trevor had already reached the pair and was holding Lily's waist as she stood on a deck chair looking into the bird's nest.

Judy was the first to spot Lana. "Hey, come see what Lily and Trevor have here!"

As Lana walked over, Trevor moved aside so she could squeeze in and get a glimpse. "Oh, look! Robin eggs. When do you think they'll hatch?"

Lily just shrugged her shoulders and looked away.

Lana tried again. "They're such a pretty color. I can't wait till they hatch, can you?"

Lily remained silent.

Chapter Six

Trevor felt a little embarrassed by Lily's reaction and tried to lighten up the mood. "We're not really sure when the eggs were laid. We check the nest several times a day to see if anything's happened. Right, honey?"

Lily ignored Trevor as well, and jumped down off the chair. It was obvious she didn't want to share her discovery with Lana. "Come," she said to Trevor, pulling his arm in the direction of the house.

Trevor looked at Lana and silently apologized. He didn't want to make a scene by scolding Lily in front of her, so he allowed himself to be guided into the house. When they'd reached the kitchen he took the lead, carefully directing the child to her bedroom.

"Stop!" she wailed, trying to wriggle out of his grasp. "No want to go to room!"

Trevor didn't let go. "You'll follow me to your room so we can talk."

"No!" snapped Lily.

That was it! Trevor picked her up and carried her to her room. All the squirming in the world wasn't going to change his mind.

As soon as they reached her room, Lily buried her face in the sea of pillows decorating the white-canopied bed.

"Lily, please look at me," Trevor said finally.

Nothing happened.

Trevor tried again. "Lily, I won't have you treating our guest the way you've been doing. You're being mean!"

"No!" Lily shouted. "I no like her. Tell her to go away!"

He sat on the bed and tried to cuddle her into seeing reason. "Come on, Lily. Lana is Aunt Judy's very special friend and I'm sure if you give her a chance, you'll really like her. Will you do that for me?"

Normally she loved being in his arms, but nothing was going to make her like that woman. "No!" came the muffled scream. Then she wiggled out of his arms and turned away from him.

"Okay then, why don't you stay in your room until you can agree to be nice to our guest. I'm not kidding, Lily. This is not a game." Her attitude told him she probably needed to take a nap, and he decided to leave her alone so she'd be able to do just that. He didn't like leaving Lily stewing but understood her enough to know that when she got into one of these states there was no reaching her. He left the room, shutting the door quietly behind him.

Judy and Lana had entered the house shortly after Trevor and Lily had gone off. Judy began filling the teapot and pointed to the cupboard just above the dishwasher. "Why don't you grab a couple of mugs? We'll have some tea."

Lana took two earthenware mugs off the shelf. "I could use some."

"Please don't be discouraged," Judy urged. "It's obvious Lily feels a little threatened by your visit and we'll have to work on changing her attitude. Are you okay?"

Lana nodded. "Better than I thought I'd be. Don't worry."

"I want this to work out so badly that I'm nervous you'll get discouraged and run for the hills," Judy admitted. "It took Lily a while to warm up to me, and I'm sure the same will be true for you."

Lana was quiet for a moment, then said, "There are some who believe kids can read people better than anyone—you know, kind of possess a sixth sense about things. I'm pretty sure Lily could feel my apprehension...I guess I'm a little rusty around children."

"Children haven't learned the art of disguise and tend to see things as they are," Judy said. "The most important thing right now is to get the both of you comfortable around each other. Any ideas?"

"I'm not sure. I think it's best to allow it to happen naturally. I learned years ago that manipulating children doesn't work. They're a lot smarter than we give them credit for."

"I'm in total agreement with you on that point," Judy added. "Waiting it out might work for Lily, but what about you?"

"As I told you before, I'm committed to doing this," Lana assured her. "I'll figure out some way to deal with all of it...I usually do."

Right then, Trevor walked into the kitchen. He didn't say what had transpired upstairs; he just announced that he had some errands to run and asked if Judy could keep an eye on Lily for a few hours. As Judy nodded her head, he mentioned that he wanted Lily to sleep a bit to stave off her moodiness. Then he walked out the door without saying anything to Lana.

"Did he seem upset to you?" Lana asked.

"I'm not quite sure. He's a hard read. I'm sure he's upset about the way Lily's behaving. You know, it's funny—when we discussed this plan I worried more about how you and Trevor were going to react. I never even gave a thought to Lily's response…"

The shrill sound of the teakettle interrupted her. Judy handed Lana the tea bags and went to get the kettle. As she poured the steaming liquid into the cups, she looked at Lana's downcast face and said, "Oh, come on, Lana. We've been through worse than this. Why don't we check out the fridge and see what we can make for supper. Sound good?"

"You know the thought of food always takes my mind off of things," Lana guiltily admitted. "It's a wonder I'm not three hundred pounds."

Judy's eyes skidded over Lana's body. "With all that exercise you do, I can't believe you aren't skin and bones."

Lana laughed and said, "Speaking of refrigerators, I read in *McCall's* that you can tell a lot about a person by looking in his refrigerator." Lowering her voice she added, "I feel kind of funny, almost as if Trevor should be present."

"Nonsense," Judy snorted. "I'm sure Irma does all the shopping, so the only thing we'd be able to tell is what she likes to cook. We'll have to find some other way to read Trevor."

As they sipped their tea the women rummaged through the kitchen. Judy practically cleaned out the produce bins, grabbing everything colorful for the salad she was going to prepare.

Lana noticed a package of lemon-pepper flavored chicken breasts sitting on the second shelf in the refrigerator. "Looks like we'll be barbecuing these for dinner," she said to Judy. "Do you know if Trevor has any rice?"

"I'm sure he does since it's one of Lily's favorite dishes. Look there in the cabinet above the stove," Judy said, pointing. "Last time I was here, Trevor and I went to the grocery store and bought a half dozen boxes of Uncle Ben's just for Lily. Maybe there are some boxes left."

Lana shut the refrigerator door and went to look. Sure enough, there were two boxes. Looking over at Judy, she commented, "Maybe this will bring Lily around."

As she watched Lana search the cabinets for what she suspected were any clues about Trevor, Judy felt a sense of pride in the woman who was taking control of her life. Lana had come a long way over the last few years, and sitting here now, Judy felt she'd made the right decision. Even if Lily was going to be difficult, she had all the faith in the world that Lana could break through the child's barrier.

Trevor's foot didn't feel comfortable on the pedal until it was almost hitting the well-worn mat. He desperately needed to escape the place he'd normally found so tranquil. "Jesus Christ," he groaned as he raked his fingers through his chestnut hair in an attempt to flatten down the windblown mess. He had known from the start that this wasn't a good idea. Why did he let his aunt convince him to do this?

"Dammit," he yelled to no one in particular.

He knew the minute he'd first gotten a glimpse of Lana from the porch that she was not at all what he'd expected. He hadn't given much thought to her physical appearance beforehand, but if he had, he probably would have pictured a small, slightly overweight woman in her mid-thirties, dressed in white, with her name carefully embroidered on the upper breast pocket of her uniform. What he'd seen instead was a beautiful, elegant woman who'd carried herself with the grace of a gazelle. She had a shy quality he found so rare in women these days and was instantly attracted to her, which is probably what elicited such a strong response from Lily.

He could tell Lana was nervous around the small child and, after what his aunt had told him, he could understand why. He felt horrible for the way Lily had treated her and couldn't seem to assuage his guilt for the part he'd played. The way he'd acted toward Lana must have threatened Lily in some way. What was it about this woman that had affected him? He'd been with supermodels and business executives, and even dabbled with a few actresses, and no one had struck this kind of chord in him. How was he going to live under the same roof with her?

Thinking along these lines was not helping matters, he decided as he wended his way past town. He had to stay away just long enough to get his bearings straight. Maybe if he dropped in to visit Irma and Ben things would quiet down in his head. He'd lied when he said he had errands to run, so before he returned home he'd have to stop and pick up something to bring home.

Chapter Six

Ben and Irma were in the kitchen cleaning up the lunch dishes when they heard the crunching sound of gravel, their doorbell of sorts. Ben was first to spot Trevor's truck.

"Looks like Trevor's here and he doesn't look too happy."

Irma quickly ran to the window and watched as Trevor walked up to the front door, the usual smile absent from his face. She could tell something was wrong and immediately went to the front door to greet her unexpected guest. "Hi, Trevor. Thought ya'd be home visitin' with yar guests."

An exasperated sigh escaped his lips. "I was. I just had to get out of there." He walked over to the table and sat down. "I've been driving around for awhile and wasn't quite ready to head back. You mind a little company?"

Over the last several months, Trevor had grown close to Irma, sharing more with her than he had with any other person, with the exception of his aunt and Jamie. Irma asked for nothing from him, making her all the more special in his book. He considered Ben and Irma family, and sharing Lily with these two warm souls was like giving the child a set of grandparents she'd likely never know.

Ben and Irma had welcomed their new family, which seemed to fill the void that had been left when their own two children had defected from Vermont shortly after graduating from college. Both had moved to Atlanta, the mecca for young urban adults, married within two years of each other, and were now raising their own families on Southern land. Ben was a Yankee through and through and never could understand how the children he'd raised and nurtured on Green Mountain soil could have moved to a place filled with mountains erected from steel and concrete, and air so thick in the summer that breathing was a chore.

The distance, however, was not a stumbling block for Ben and Irma. They were proficient in the art of e-mail, possessing the latest computer equipment, and sent daily messages to both children. They knew more about what was going on in Georgia than some parents knew about what was happening within their own town.

"Ya know ya're welcome here anytime," Irma assured Trevor. "What's eatin' away at ya?"

Trevor didn't know where to begin. He sat silently, watching Irma fish out a plate from the cabinet and then move toward the lattice-topped cherry pie sitting on the counter. He looked around for Ben and sensed he'd made himself scarce, knowing this was a matter for Irma and not him. Trevor appreciated that about Ben. He always knew the right thing to do, whether it came to fixing something or just knowing when to butt out.

Irma's patience was a close match to his Aunt Judy's. She waited him out by busying herself serving him a slice of pie he wasn't really hungry for and swiping away remnants of the flaky crust she'd won accolades for at the local bakeoff.

After forcing down a few mouthfuls of pie, he began slowly, "I'm not sure this plan of Aunt Judy's is going to work. As we speak, Lily is holed up in her bedroom refusing to accept Lana's presence in the house. That little one really tests my patience, and it takes all the strength I possess not to shake her into seeing reason. Some days when she acts this way, I feel totally defeated. You know, like I'm not equipped to handle a small child. I question myself constantly, wondering whether or not I'm doing the right thing by trying to raise her on my own. When my aunt thought up this crazy idea, I was totally opposed to it at first, but when I thought about it rationally, I realized I was in dire need of some guidance in handling Lily's obstinate ways. It's just I'm…I'm so afraid I'm going to screw up."

"We all worry about screwin' up when it comes to raisin' kids," Irma confessed. "Why should ya be any different?"

"I guess I'm not any different. I just worry, that's all."

"We all worry, Trevor." She threw up her hands and said, "Heck, I still worry about my kids. And now I even worry about my grandkids."

Trevor smiled for the first time. Irma always made him feel better.

"Then there's the woman my aunt brought along. You know the one I told you about?"

"The one Lily doesn't seem to like?"

"Yeah! What am I supposed to do now?"

Irma shook her head. "Absolutely nothin'! She's the professional and I'm sure she knows how to deal with kids like Lily. If ya remember, Lily didn't take to me right away."

"I know, it's just…"

"Just what, Trevor? Yar aunt's a smart lady. I think she knows what's best for that little girl. Ya told me a little about this woman's past and I think it's gonna take a few days for her to get comfortable with ya folks as well."

"You didn't see how Lily reacted to her, though. She was really mean. She didn't just shy away like she did with you."

"Well, why do ya think she reacted that way?" Irma asked, genuinely concerned.

"I'm not sure. I guess…"

"What is it, boy? What aren't ya telling me?"

Running his fingers through his hair, Trevor showed signs of discomfort. "I just wonder if Lily picked up on the way I reacted to her. She wasn't at all what I expected."

Now she was getting somewhere. "What did ya expect?"

"Not her, I can tell you."

"What's wrong with her?" Irma persisted.

"Nothing. That's the problem," Trevor almost shouted. "She's a beautiful woman and…it's just not going to work."

"Why, because she's beautiful? Is that the problem?"

"I think maybe I've been away too long," Trevor said with a sigh. "You know what I mean?"

"Maybe. But I think it's a little more complicated than that. Ya've just lost yar best friend and ya're extremely vulnerable right now. Maybe ya're not so much drawn to her, but more to the idea of allowin' someone into yar life to fill the void."

He understood where she was coming from and realized he'd wondered the same thing. Was his reaction to Lana based more on his loneliness than some weird spell she'd cast over him?

During the last few months he'd begun to depend on Irma's wisdom and instincts, and today was no exception. Even though she'd only completed the eleventh grade, Trevor was convinced she possessed the wisdom of a tenured professor.

One night as they sat up late nursing Lily, who was running a 102-degree fever, Irma told Trevor why she'd been forced to quit school. Tears formed in her eyes, all these years later, when she described her father's tragic death at the lumberyard. Irma had been close to seventeen when she was forced to enter the working world. Her aspirations of going to college and becoming a teacher were banished when the tragedy hit. She was the oldest of six in the family and was expected to pick up where her father had left off. Just a day after the funeral, not wanting to get behind on the mortgage, she'd hit the pavement looking for work.

When she finally landed a position at the local dairy, bottling fresh milk, she worked herself to the bone in an attempt to overcome the despair that hung over her like a noose. Almost single-handedly, with her mom taking in some washing and ironing for a few of the privileged in town, she was able to cover all the bills with a little left over for a picture show on the one day she was off a week.

Fate had played a hand in her life when she met and fell in love with her supervisor, Ben. After they married a few years later, Ben moved in with the family. He and Irma moved into the large bedroom—her parents' old room—and they still lived in the same house today.

Reflecting on Irma's courage and strength, Trevor admitted what he'd been afraid to say. "My reaction to Lana was so strong that I'm pretty sure Lily picked up on it. I guess in some way she felt a little threatened. I've got to convince Lily that Lana means nothing more to me than someone I've hired to help out. I'm just not sure how I'm going to do that when I can't stop thinking about her…"

"Ya know what I do when I can't get something out of my mind?" Irma challenged.

"What?"

"I face it head on." Irma wagged a finger at him. "Ya have feelin's for the little filly who's entered yar stable. After all, ya're a man, and one I'm sure that hasn't felt a woman by his side for some time now. I'm not a man so I can't tell ya how to deal with those urges, but I can tell ya that if ya focus on why Lana came in the first place ya'll be able to get through this. Lily has to come first and ya have to find a way to make her feel secure in all this."

"I get your point." Trevor paused for a moment, and then added, "Oh, and by the way, us men usually take a cold shower to curtail any urges we can't control."

Laughing, Irma tousled his already windblown hair and asked if he wanted more pie.

Chapter Six

"No, thanks! I'd better head back and try to make things right. You coming by tomorrow as planned?"

"I wouldn't miss it for the world," Irma said as she stood up and kissed Trevor on the forehead, a gesture so natural to her and one to which he'd grown quite accustomed.

Chapter Seven

"Wake up, sunshine," Sam whispered as he leaned over his wife's sleeping form. He couldn't help himself when he placed soft feathery kisses around her lips, swollen from hours of lovemaking the night before.

Cindy instinctively opened her mouth, allowing his tongue to gently slide past the velvety surface. The flavor of peppermint tasted so good in her dry mouth that she responded with fervor, deepening the kiss even further.

"Mmmmm...you taste good! I don't want to get up right now. Please come back to bed and make love to me again."

"Hell, I'm not sure I have the strength after last night. Besides, you have to get up now. Did you forget I'm giving you a lift in to work?"

"Oh, yeah. I forgot that my car is in the shop. What time is it anyway?"

"It's already seven thirty, and if I'm going to make it to the office by nine we have to leave in exactly forty-seven minutes."

"Only you would say forty-seven instead of forty-five or three-quarters of an hour. Your anal retentiveness is starting to show itself again, darlin'."

"I know. I just don't want to be late. Please get up. I'll even start the shower for you."

The sound of the running water snapped Cindy out of her slumber. The steam drifting from the bathroom formed a path, showing her the way.

A short time later, dressed and ready to go, Cindy walked into the kitchen and announced that she'd pick up breakfast at the coffee shop across the street from the clinic. Sam loved the idea since it was already forty-two minutes till nine, and he would be at least five minutes late for work.

Clutching the dash as if it were the brake, Cindy pleaded, "Honey, slow down a bit. You're driving too fast and I'm afraid you'll get a ticket—or worse, get us into an accident."

"I just hate being late for work," Sam reminded her. "I expect my people to be there on time, and when I'm late they look at me like I'm the biggest hypocrite in the world. And I don't blame them."

"You're hardly ever late. You usually get to work at least half an hour early, so stop your complaining," she scolded lightly.

"You're right," Sam replied, easing up on the gas. "It won't be the end of the world if I'm a little late once or twice a year. I guess that's why I married you. You make me put things in perspective—something I need to offset my rigid ways. Just one more thing I really love about you. You know that?"

"Yes, I do, but I love to be reminded. Can you believe that tomorrow will mark our one-month anniversary?"

"I know," Sam said, smiling. "I'm still amazed we did it. I always thought that if I ever tied the knot—which, I might add, I truly believed would never happen—my family would throw the biggest and grandest wedding of all. You know they do things in a big way, and with me being the only son in the Stewart clan, they'd want to make it the event of the year."

"Are you disappointed that didn't happen?" she asked, feeling guilty.

"Cindy, I've told you over and over it doesn't matter to me. Keeping our wedding private was what you wanted and I couldn't have cared less one way or another." He hesitated for a second, then added, "We are going to have to come clean pretty soon, however."

She turned away to look out the window, thinking about how his family was going to react to the news. When she felt Sam's fingers reach over to caress her shoulder, she swallowed past the lump in her throat. "I have a feeling your parents will never speak to us again when they find out. Your mom sent a pretty clear message that she didn't really like me. I'm sure she's just waiting for you to come to your senses. If she knew we were married, I'm sure she'd blame me for luring you down the aisle—or, in our case, to the local justice of the peace—and hate me even more."

"First, she doesn't hate you," Sam protested. "My mom has a picture in her mind of what my better half should act and look like, and I can tell you you're the farthest thing from that person. 'Miss Right' in dear old Mom's vision is some insipid, sensibly shod Stepford wife. I love my mother and appreciate everything she's done for me, but in picking a mate we couldn't be more opposite. This is the one area where she really pisses me off, and I actually look forward to reciprocating in kind."

"Please don't say that," Cindy said, looking down at the band of gold around her ring finger. "It makes it seem like you married me to spite your mother."

"If that were the case, I would've married long before this. No one I've brought home to date—and trust me, there haven't been many who've crossed that threshold—has passed her highness's scrutiny." He leaned over then and gently rubbed Cindy's cheek with his thumb, while watching the road out of the corner of his eye. "You know why I married you. I couldn't live without you."

"I know." Cindy nodded happily. "I feel the same way." Her smile faded as she once again thought of his family. "I'm just so afraid they'll figure out a way to erase all we have and kidnap you like they do to those kids who fall prey to some weird cult that brainwashes innocent victims."

Sam laughed. "My mom's a little overbearing, but I don't think she'd go that far. I'm sure she'll be pretty upset when she hears, but eventually she'll come around and accept the situation." He straightened in his seat and put both hands on the wheel. In a firm voice, he said, "She'll have no choice. Don't worry; I'll make that quite clear. As far as my dad goes, who knows how he'll react. I haven't seen any kind of reaction from him my whole life. If it doesn't affect the stock market, he couldn't care less."

She turned to stare at his profile. She believed him. He would make everything right. Feeling more at ease now, she said, "In a way, you and I are so different yet so much alike. You know, I never thought I'd ever marry either. We were like two misfits when we first met. Do you remember?"

"I sure do."

"It was one of the happiest days of my life," Cindy recalled. "You had just committed your friend to rehab and got lost trying to find your way out of the center. The minute I saw you, I felt something here." She pointed to her heart. "At first, I noticed this very handsome, preppy sort of guy—which, I might add, wasn't the type I normally fell for— but more than that, I was taken by how gentle and kind you were to your friend. He was nervous and shaking pretty badly, and you held him close, offering soothing words to try to calm him. You looked so sad as they escorted him away. I wanted to take you in my arms then and tell you everything would be all right."

"So why didn't you?"

"Yeah, right. Go up to a complete stranger and put my arms around him. What would the girls in the office say?"

"They'd probably give you a standing ovation," Sam declared. "If I remember correctly, a few of those same women had been trying to fix you up for some time."

"Don't remind me," Cindy chuckled, then grew serious again. "I remember thinking how compassionate you were to your friend that day, and how I had to meet you. I followed you from a distance and when you seemed to be going in circles, it was my sign to gather enough courage to approach you. Do you remember what you said to me that day?"

"I'm not sure. If you recall, I was pretty smitten myself. I remember you took my hand and showed me the way out."

"That I did. But when we stood outside and you called me your angel, I was hooked. I knew you must have felt the same way I did when you asked if I was real or just a figment of your imagination. Then you touched my face and my hair, examining me to reassure yourself that I was, in fact, a living human being. I think I fell in love with you at that moment."

Chapter Seven

One of Sam's hands let go of the steering wheel to grasp Cindy's fingers. "I'd never believed in love at first sight until then. I didn't want the moment to end. I can still remember fumbling in my back pocket for my wallet so I could hand you my business card. I asked with my voice, yet pleaded with my heart, that you call me to let me know how my friend was doing, when, in fact, all I really wanted was to hear your voice again."

"I still get goose pimples when I think about the first time we met." Cindy shivered, enclosing her fingers around his. "I carried your card around with me all day, running my fingers over the letters of your name. I couldn't wait to call you when I got home that night. I remember we talked for hours on the phone. Do you know we haven't let a day go by since then without touching base with one another?"

"I know. I really do need you in my life." Sam raised their entwined fingers and kissed the center of her hand. "Please don't let my parents' reaction spoil what we have. I'm totally prepared for whatever they may do. Okay?"

Cindy scooted closer and placed a light kiss on his cheek. "I'm sorry if I'm a bit insecure. Let's forget about all this and focus on what we're going to do this weekend. Got any ideas?"

At that point, Sam pulled into the diner's parking lot. "We're going to have to table this until later. I've got exactly twelve minutes to get to work."

Cindy wasn't ready to let him go. But before she could mouth any kind of retort, he kissed her quickly and gently pushed her toward the passenger door.

"Are you trying to get rid of me?"

"Honey, you know I hate to be late."

"Oh, all right." She flung open the door and stepped out.

He leaned over and looked up through the open door. "I'll call you later and we can talk to your heart's content."

"You mean you promise not to look at the clock even once?" Cindy teased.

"Cross my heart," he promised.

"You got a deal." She shut the door and blew him a kiss.

As Cindy opened the door to the diner, she recognized the voice of her friend Sally almost immediately. The place was packed, with not an empty booth in sight. Luckily, one seat remained at the counter. She quickly grabbed the available stool and waited for her friend to notice her.

Sally was about forty years old, single, and, as was evident to all that knew her, loved life. The size eighteen pink uniform she always wore was usually stained with the day's special, and although she was considered large for her five-foot-six frame, she never missed a beat handling the hundreds of orders she delivered throughout the day.

People loved coming to the diner because of Sally. The food was a little better than decent, but nowhere else could you get warmth and friendship from a person like her. She could swap stories with truckers, sharing tales of growing up with a father who practically lived on the road, or talk with some of the common people who just wanted some friendly conversation. Sally was well read and always got the place hopping talking about the day's events. The TV in the corner, permanently tuned to CNN, was the first thing turned on and the last thing turned off each day.

Sally had just finished giving change when she noticed Cindy sitting at the counter. "Hey, doll, where've you been? I haven't seen you in over a month. Whatcha do? Go off and get married or something?"

Cindy hadn't told anyone she and Sam had eloped, and she wanted to keep it a secret until his parents heard the news. Even though she trusted Sally with her life, she didn't feel right talking about it yet. "Sam and I were away on vacation for a few weeks, and when we got back I had a ton of things to catch up on. But now I'm back and hungry as a bear that's been hibernating too long. How about the usual?"

The usual was one scrambled egg with a slice of cheese, accompanied by two pieces of rye toast, barely buttered. Sally quickly wrote down the order, left it on the stainless steel shelf separating the kitchen from the counter space, and filled a mug full of steaming coffee, never once missing a beat.

"You got it! Where'd you go anyway?"

"Cancun," Cindy replied. "It was one of the most romantic places I've ever seen. It looked just like the pictures you see in magazines— the crystal clear water and beautiful white sandy beaches."

Chapter Seven

"I've never been there, but a few of the regulars rave about the place. I understand that tourism has dropped off some in Mexico because of the crime rate. Did you have any trouble?"

"Not a bit," Cindy said as she rifled through a stack of magazines sitting on top of the counter. Between working and being away, she hadn't had much time to keep up on current events. Since she didn't need to be at the office until ten, she had some time to browse.

Sally refilled her coffee and went to answer the bell the cook had just rung to let her know that breakfast orders were ready to be delivered. "Be back in a flash," Sally said, as she hurried to the counter, which was now covered with several steaming plates.

As Sally walked away, Cindy continued leafing through the magazines, looking for one that would be interesting to read. She'd gone through about half of the pile when she came across a headline that more than caught her eye.

Her throat constricted as she read: *"ROCK STAR JAMIE MCKEE DIES IN PLANE CRASH."* Tears welled in her eyes and she began to shake uncontrollably.

She felt as if the walls were beginning to close in around her, and the need to escape was urgent. Clutching the magazine, Cindy ran out of the diner as if it were on fire.

Standing in the middle of the parking lot, she realized she had nowhere to go. She was slowly unraveling and there was nowhere to turn. Her car was in the shop and she couldn't show up at work in this condition. Her legs were just about to give way when she felt an arm on her shoulder.

"Was my coffee that bad?" Sally asked just as she noticed the magazine gripped tightly beneath Cindy's taut fingers. "What's wrong, sweetie?"

Trying to regain her composure as tears streamed down her face, Cindy couldn't find the strength to overcome her despair and respond.

Sally guided her through the back door of the diner and into a small office. "Stay here. I've got to get back out there and deliver a few more plates, but the place is starting to clear out and I'll have Betty handle the rest. I'll be back in a few minutes and we can talk. Okay?"

Cindy was unable to form any audible words but nodded her assent. As soon as Sally left and closed the door behind her, Cindy found the solitude she'd been seeking. Her hands were clenched so tightly around the magazine that she had trouble releasing her hold. She desperately needed to find out what had happened.

By the time Sally returned, Cindy had read the grisly details of the plane crash and was sitting in a catatonic state, staring at the wall opposite the desk. Sally noticed that the magazine she'd clutched to her chest was now rolled up in her hand.

It had been a little more than three years ago that Sally first noticed the petite frail woman who had begun to frequent the diner. She knew right away this doe-eyed beauty was in need of a friend and was more than happy to oblige. She'd missed her calling of becoming a social worker when she'd dropped out of school in her senior year to run away with Junior, who'd turned out to be a real loser. She never did go back and finish school, but instead used her God-given talent of helping people right in the diner.

Sally suspected Cindy had a past but made it a point never to nose into anyone's business. There was no better way of loosening the tongue than serving the stomach. Bartenders and waitresses were the world's lowest-paid mental health specialists, she'd always said.

Although they became fast friends, Cindy had kept her past separate from their friendship. Sally knew her to be a caring and giving person, and she didn't give a fig about her life before. Sally sensed that Cindy's life had not been easy, but whenever the conversation delved too deep, Cindy would always change the subject, using the excuse that she lived for the day.

During the last three years, Sally had seen quite a transformation in her friend. Cindy had put on some weight, received a promotion at the rehab center, and met a wonderful man, whom she never stopped talking about.

Cindy's spirits had been soaring for more than a year now, and Sally was tickled pink that her good friend had finally gotten her life in order.

Leaning down next to the chair, she gently placed her hand on Cindy's arm and whispered, "What's wrong, darlin'? You look like a fawn in the middle of the street right before the headlights go out."

Chapter Seven

Hearing her friend's voice, Cindy began to unfold the fingers that clutched the slightly torn publication. Not saying a word, she pointed to the headline and began to sob uncontrollably.

"Did you know this guy? Is he related to you or something?"

Cindy took a couple of deep breaths. "I…I was once very much in love with him. It seems like a lifetime ago, but it's only been about four years. When it was over, I packed away the memories and swore I'd never look back."

"Why? What happened back then? Did he beat you or something?"

Staring straight ahead, Cindy continued, "No, he never did that. In a way, he was my savior. I know I've never mentioned anything about my past to you, or for that matter to anyone else. Don't get me wrong—I knew it would surface one day, but I was hoping that when it did I'd be strong enough to deal with it. I just didn't know it would be this soon or in this way." She couldn't stop the tears from falling.

"Will it help for you to talk to me or do you want me to call Sam?"

"No," Cindy almost shouted. "You can't call Sam. He can't know anything about this."

"You mean you've never told him anything about your past either?"

"I told him some things, but nothing about Jamie."

"Tell you what: I'm going to tell Betty that I got me some errands to run and you and I are going to head somewhere private and have us a good long talk. Seems to me you've been keeping too much locked inside and it's eating away at you. You just wait here and I'll get my stuff. Why don't you call across the street and tell them something's come up and you won't be in today?"

Not even waiting for an answer, Sally left, leaving Cindy alone to make the call.

The ride to Sally's was short, and the only sound filling the air was the twangy voice of a country singer belting out lyrics that seemed almost to fit how Cindy was feeling at the moment.

Cindy had calmed down quite a bit by the time they reached the small ranch house just ten minutes from the diner. As soon as Sally had unlocked the front door, she ushered Cindy into the kitchen and put a pot of water on the stove. Looking over at her friend's ravaged face, she decided to make chamomile tea, hoping the herbal liquid would soothe whatever it was that ailed her.

Cindy sat at the small butcher-block table and noticed for the first time her surroundings. The kitchen resembled something out of the late fifties. The red and white gingham curtains matched the cushions on the chairs. The sand-speckled linoleum on the floor matched in design and color the Formica countertop. The refrigerator had rounded edges, similar to the one she'd seen on the *Happy Days* show. Even though the kitchen was quite dated, it sparkled clean. Not a speck of dust or dirt could be seen anywhere. This place felt more like home to her than any other place she'd ever been.

As soon as the teakettle whistled and Sally had filled the mugs, the two women sat staring at each other. When Sally couldn't stand the silence any longer, she looked into her friend's eyes and pleaded, "You're gonna have to deal with whatever's bothering you sometime. You'd best start now before it eats a hole in your gut."

During the drive over, Cindy had thought about how she would explain all that had happened to her back then. *How*, she wondered, *can I talk about something that I haven't yet come to terms with myself?* She looked at Sally and felt so much compassion emanating from her. Even though they didn't socialize outside the diner, she still considered Sally one of her good friends. At least once or twice a week she'd stop by the diner for either breakfast or lunch, and she and Sally would talk about everything under the sun. Cindy could always count on Sally to update her on current events, and when she'd met Sam, it was Sally she went to first with the news. She knew she could trust this woman with her life and decided it was time to share what had haunted her for so long.

"Several years back, I started modeling in California. Growing up in my household was pretty depressing. After I graduated from high school I took off for California. I'm not sure my parents cared. I was never good enough for them. But that's a different story altogether. I'd saved exactly three thousand dollars working at a retail store in the mall, and the day after I got my diploma I cleaned out my bank account and boarded a bus for Los Angeles."

Cindy frowned and grimly continued, "Life in tinsel town didn't turn out to be so great. It wasn't long before all my money was gone. I roomed with a girl who was a waitress at a fairly posh café, and when she helped me get a job there I thought things were starting to look up. I met lots of jerks, but one night I met this guy who changed my life forever. He introduced me to the world of modeling, and I was actually earning a decent wage and having one hell of a time for a while. The lane I was traveling in was so fast it made my head spin. Fashion shows always ended with major blow-out parties, and I quickly became addicted to alcohol and drugs."

Sally reached over to put an arm around Cindy's trembling shoulders. "For a while," Cindy continued, "I kept up the facade, but eventually the chemicals took over. It was during this time I met Jamie McKee, the famous musician. I immediately fell for him. He was one of the handsomest men I had ever met and a real gentleman to boot. I met him at a party given by one of the fashion designers I'd been modeling for. It was instant love for both of us. Jamie was warm and generous and had a good head on his shoulders. He treated me with nothing but respect and truly loved me. That was a first for me. I never had anyone to love and I couldn't understand why anyone famous and handsome would want to love me. I think I was so afraid of being hurt that I unconsciously did things to destroy our relationship. I continued to drink too much and dabble in drugs, which Jamie was totally opposed to. It almost became a game with me—you know, seeing how much this guy was willing to take."

No longer able to mask the pain, Cindy allowed fresh tears to fall. Several minutes of silence passed before Sally spoke up and asked if she wanted fresh tea. Neither had taken a sip since Cindy had begun her painful story.

"Yes, please," Cindy responded as she wiped the tears on her sleeve.

"Darlin', I know this is hard for you, but believe me when I tell you shedding this poison will bring you some relief." Sally kept talking as she refilled the mugs. "There are some things that need to be said aloud, and I think it's time you address all this stuff you've hidden away for so long. Seems to me you've found happiness now, and if your past threatens to destroy it, you need to tackle it head on."

"It's just hard, you know," Cindy managed, fighting back the tears that refused to subside. "I really screwed up my life back then and it took all I had in me to let it go. I've finally found some peace in my life, and now I read one friggin' news article and all the ghosts I thought I'd buried came billowing around me."

"You've got me and Sam to help you through whatever it is you can't deal with. I'd say that's a step up from where you were back then."

"I know. I've just never been able to rely on anyone and I guess I've had a hard time trusting people."

"You need to trust Sam and me," Sally insisted. "Me, I hope you know you can trust, and Sam—why, he's truly in love with you and I'm sure there is nothing in your past that will change that."

"I'm not so sure. You haven't heard the worst part."

"Well, drink some of your tea and lay it all out. I'm all ears."

Sipping the warm liquid helped ease the tightness in Cindy's throat, allowing her to finally say aloud what she'd hidden away for so long. "Jamie was getting pretty fed up with my antics and was on the brink of leaving me when I found out I was pregnant. When he heard the news he began to take over my life. He moved me out to a remote place in the valley and didn't care that I was bored out of my skull. He seemed really angry with me all the time, and as hard as I tried, nothing I said or did took away the tension between us. He told me his father was an alcoholic and used to beat his mother. I think Jamie transferred a lot of his hate for his father onto me.

"After a few months when I hadn't had a drop of liquor or any other substances, I convinced Jamie to trust me. He loosened the reins a bit, and that was all I needed to resort to my old life. I became very clever. On days he was at the recording studio he wouldn't be home till late, so I got plastered early knowing by the time he came home I'd be in bed asleep. I was able to curb the drugs I was taking but couldn't kick my habit completely. The strange part was, I was concentrating so much on hiding my addiction that I never gave any thought to what I was doing to the child growing inside me.

"As the pregnancy advanced, so did my depression. I started getting sloppy with my addiction guise. Jamie became totally exasperated with me and eventually, when I'm sure he thought he could no longer help me, he left me alone. He didn't leave me totally helpless. He hired a midwife to live with me during my last trimester. I'm sure he paid her a pretty penny, too.

"My water broke during my eighth month and Jamie came running back. I'd managed to sneak a few drinks earlier that morning—I can't even remember how many—and went into labor drunk. When I came to, the midwife told me my baby was stillborn. I remember screaming at the top of my lungs and then blackness enveloped me."

Cindy's palms felt damp and she couldn't stop her involuntary shaking. "When I awoke, Jamie was sitting by the side of my bed. He held his anger in check and told me he'd taken care of all the details and added that he never wanted to see me again. I could see the hatred in his face and could tell I'd lost him forever. He was truly a good person, far better than I could ever have been. He arranged for me to come back East to the rehab center where I now work. He set up a generous bank account and made me promise to never see him again. I willingly left, feeling nothing but shame. I was filled with such self-loathing over my part in my child's death that at one point in my recovery I tried to commit suicide. I didn't want to live knowing what I'd done. I still haven't completely forgiven myself."

She looked her friend square in the eyes and asked, "Well, what do you think of me now, Sally?"

Chapter Eight

It had been almost two hours since Trevor had walked out the door. As hard as she tried, Judy was unable to quell her feelings of annoyance—at Lily for the nasty way she had treated Lana, and at her nephew for his ultimate defection from the entire situation.

Shortly after Trevor had vanished, Judy had gone upstairs to look in on the petulant child. The minute she saw Lily's small frame soundly sleeping amidst a sea of pillows, her slight displeasure dissipated. How could she be upset with this child who'd never asked to be enshrouded in secrets and seclusion? She didn't know that her whole life hung in the balance, waiting for Trevor to do the right thing. This secret Trevor kept hidden away was eating away at him, whether he acknowledged it or not, and would someday do the same to this innocent child.

The information contained in the hand-delivered letter marked "Confidential for Trevor Collins," which Trevor received shortly after Jamie's death, was almost his undoing. The death of his best friend was nearly too much for Trevor to bear. Learning that his dearest friend had withheld—or, more accurately, lied about—several things concerning Lily was the final blow. In the letter, Jamie had begged for Trevor's forgiveness and asked for him to honor his death by remaining silent about the information he'd shared.

Judy could tell how much this news devastated him. She remembered reading and rereading the single-page document that would change Trevor's life forever. Now that Jamie was gone, the burden fell to the unsuspecting trusting half of the pair. Though not agreeing with the path Jamie had taken, she understood why he had chosen it. His motives, although hidden behind a wall of deception, were what he considered justifiable under the complicated circumstances. Judy knew it would be a while before Trevor saw any just reason for his blood brother's mendacity. Trevor was experiencing a plethora of emotions the night he handed her the envelope, and she knew he needed to stabilize the battle raging in his head before he would open his mind enough to accept any advice in support of or against Jamie's wishes.

That had been several months ago. Since that night, Trevor had refused to discuss any options with her. His first and only concern was Lily. Anything beyond that had been safely tucked away, compartmentalized in his mind for a time when he was strong enough to tackle the issues.

After Judy made sure Lily was sleeping soundly, she helped Lana unpack her bags. When they were finished, Lana announced, "I think I'll change into my running clothes and go for a jog around the lake. Do you know if there's a trail I can follow?"

"Yes. In fact, the original homeowner was big on jogging and had a trail cleared halfway around the lake. Just follow it around that way," Judy said, as she pointed north. "It will end right across from where we are now. I'd guess the whole route might be about two miles."

"Sounds great to me. After sitting in the car for so long, I could use the exercise. Do you mind if I go now?"

"Not at all," Judy said, shaking her head. "I'm going to head down to the kitchen and finish cutting up the vegetables for the salad. I also have to go over some papers for the conference. Take your time."

Lana quickly changed into her running clothes, looking forward to a little solitude. Judy had been great company during their ride this morning, but Lana had to admit she had a lot of deep-rooted anxiety about being alone with Trevor and Lily. Lily, she was sure she could handle and eventually grow very fond of, but Trevor was a different story. She'd been attracted to men before, but never to the degree she'd felt earlier today.

As she began her stretching routine out on the front porch, she let her mind wander back to the day she met Tom. She was almost thirty years old and content working as a pediatric nurse at one of the largest hospitals in the city. She loved her work and didn't mind the fact that she was still single. Her good friend and coworker Emily had coerced her into accepting a blind date with a friend of hers from college. Lana remembered stalling for the longest time, not being particularly fond of blind dates. She finally acquiesced when it seemed like Emily wasn't going to let up. She was sure Emily was doing the same thing to Tom, and at least they could laugh at their friend's tenacity over dinner. They were to meet at Scarlett's, a chic place downtown. Emily had shown them each a picture of one another beforehand, so they knew what the other looked like.

As soon as Lana walked through the doors, she recognized Tom. He was tall, about six feet, give or take an inch, and had a nice face. He also recognized Lana and walked toward her, extending his hand in one of the warmest welcomes she'd ever received. Something about the way he looked into her eyes and held her hand a little longer than necessary spoke volumes about the type of man he was. It felt right. Not the cannons and fireworks she'd always dreamed about, but more a deep sense of belonging.

That night had sealed their fate. True to her friend's word, Tom was genuine and kind, and drinks turned into dinner and later coffee and cannolis at an intimate place in the south end of the city. When he walked her to her car, way past her bedtime, he kissed her softly, whispering how much he wanted to see her again.

Throughout dinner, Lana had wondered how the night would end. Tom hadn't let her pay for anything, and she was praying he wasn't the type to expect something in return. She didn't think so, but then she had been wrong before. She was kind of a prude when it came to sex and had limited experience in that area. She'd only slept with two men in her twenty-nine years.

Her first was Steve, whom she was madly in love with at college. She was sure they would marry right after graduation—until she caught him fooling around with his high-school sweetheart. Heartbroken, Lana hadn't gotten involved with anyone else until she was almost twenty-five. Brian was an intern at the hospital and courted her like a school-boy. She wasn't interested at first, but after he followed her around like a puppy for nearly six months, she relented and accepted a date. They went out for a little over two years, and when he asked her to marry him, she broke his heart. She hated saying the words that seemed so trite and unfeeling but were, nonetheless, true. She loved him dearly but wasn't *in* love with him. She hated more than anything else in the world to have caused him such pain, but she would have hurt him more if they'd married and found themselves living like brother and sister a few years down the road.

Lana had long ago made up her mind that when she married she wanted to be madly in love. It bothered her friends, more than it did her, that she was flying solo those days. But she didn't care. She wasn't going to settle for second best.

Her instincts had been right about Tom. He was a true gentleman. As soon as she had closed her car door that night, he had tapped on the window to make sure she'd locked all the doors. Then he had followed her to the interstate, making sure she found the on ramp. She'd driven home in a daze that night.

They were married almost a year to the day after they met. Theirs was a solid marriage. Tom was employed by one of the big accounting firms in Hartford, and she was content working on the pediatric ward. When Jessica was born almost two years later, their life seemed complete.

Then, in an instant, it was all gone.

Stop thinking negative thoughts, Lana reminded herself as she stepped off the front porch. She breathed deeply the crisp clean air and felt instantly renewed. *This is just what the doctor ordered,* she thought as she began her trek into the forest.

Running alongside the crystal clear water, she marveled at the beautiful topography. The lake itself was mesmerizing enough, but together with the elegance of the tall pine trees and millions of tiny buds emerging on the tips of all the bare branches, she found herself surrounded by absolute beauty.

She felt truly at one with the land and was comfortable being here alone in the woods. She normally didn't feel that way walking in the woods back home. She chose to jog on busy streets instead. A few years back, a jogger's dead body had been found in a wooded area not far from her house. Since then, she'd changed her route, preferring pavement and noise to hardened dirt and solitude. This place was different, though. She felt totally secluded and safe amidst the trees that loomed over her.

Just as Judy had said, the trail ended when she reached a clearing on the other side of the lake. She guessed it was a little more than a mile, and even though she needed to keep the aerobic part of her workout at its peak, she couldn't help but stop to enjoy the magnificent view from this side of the lake.

Looking across the body of water, she could barely make out Trevor's home. She suspected that when the trees were in full foliage, one wouldn't even know it was there. But what captured her attention the most were the mountains. There had to be at least ten peaks sticking up through the trees. Those peaks, some still painted white, reminded her of when she'd watched *The Sound of Music* as a child. Something about this place—its quietness and serenity—cradled her in its embrace, and for the first time in as long as she could remember, she felt at peace.

Lana was so taken in by the magnificent scenery that she decided to sit by the lake and enjoy the view a little while longer. After all, there was no rush to go back. Trevor had bolted as soon as he'd put Lily down for a nap, and she couldn't help but feel partially responsible for the way everything had turned out.

What was it about him that had affected her so? Maybe it was his fame that turned her insides to mush. Or could it have been his unbelievable good looks and lean, hard body? Was it the way he looked at her or touched her hand that rendered her unable to move a muscle? Or was it their shared tragedies that had pulled her toward him, making them sort of kindred spirits?

Yes, that was it, she decided. She'd connected with him on a deeper level—one that she'd never been on before. The loss of her family and the death of his best friend had bonded them in some intangible way.

Lana was starting to feel more in control. *Yes, I can do this.*

Her thoughts then turned to Lily. How was she going to get this little girl to respond positively to her? She'd never had any trouble in her past life working with the kids on her floor, and she tried to remember the little tricks she'd used back then. Laughter was the method that always seemed to work. The problem was, laughter was not really a part of her life now. She liked to keep her ups and downs to a minimum. If she didn't allow herself to feel total happiness, the lows in her life wouldn't seem so bad

For the next hour she sat by the water, trying to come up with some ideas on how to befriend Lily. She had to find a common ground that both could share. In order to learn Lily's likes and dislikes she had to talk to Trevor. It was important that they form some sort of relationship that would not threaten the child, but rather show her a mutual respect between two adults.

How she was going to accomplish that feat she wasn't quite sure. After Lily's reaction, she doubted that it would be easy. But then again, what in life was easy anymore? *I'll just work at keeping things totally professional. That way Lily won't be threatened by the idea that I might be horning in on her territory. Only then will I stand a chance with her,* she decided as she began the jog back.

Right before Lily awoke, Judy had heard the back door open, and, since she hadn't heard Trevor's truck, she knew Lana had returned from her jog. As soon as Lana entered the living room Judy could see that the run had done her some good. Lana looked refreshed; bits of red speckled her cheeks, and the lines that formed around her forehead when she was stressed had been filled in.

"Hi! Sorry I was gone so long. Is Lily still sleeping?"

"Yes. She must have been really tired. How was your jog?"

"Oh, Judy, it was one of the best runs I've ever had. It's just beautiful around here. Did Trevor get back?"

"No, I'm afraid not."

"I'm sure he'll be back pretty soon. I'm going to jump in the shower. When I'm done drying my hair I'll set the table for dinner. Sound okay?"

"Sounds good to me. Take your time," Judy responded as she watched Lana climb the staircase.

Trevor sat in the driveway a few minutes before he entered the house. The lights were on in the living room and he could see Judy over by the fireplace with a fidgety Lily perched atop her lap, reading from a picture book.

He'd stopped at the Dairy Mart on his way home and picked up some cookie-dough ice cream for Lily. Hopefully the sundaes he was going to make for dessert would cheer her up. He glanced up and noticed the spare bedroom was illuminated and guessed that Lana was probably there unpacking. For a minute he sat watching, hoping to catch a glimpse of her lithe form. Something about the way she carried herself made him want to take her in his arms, gently press her body against his, and sway to the rhythm of their beating hearts. "Oh, Christ," he murmured, "I have to get hold of myself and focus on Lily's needs—not my own!" With that said, he opened the truck door, grabbed the cold bag, and proceeded to the front door.

Judy sat by the fire, trying to read a book to Lily. The child had woken up about fifteen minutes earlier and wasn't happy that Trevor hadn't been there to wash away the cobwebs. Judy didn't know how much longer she could answer the girl's repeated questions about Trevor's whereabouts. Since she didn't know herself, she'd given the same excuse he'd given her.

Then she heard the most wonderful sound—the crunching of gravel. "Shh, listen. I think I hear Trevor's truck," Judy said, as she tried to hold back the squirming child.

Lily had heard the same noise and immediately wanted to run outside.

Judy held her back, fearing she'd run right into the truck's path. "Hold on, sweetie. He'll be right in."

As soon as Trevor stepped through the door, Lily jumped off Judy's lap and ran into his outstretched arms. "Hey, sweetie! Did you have a nice long nap?"

"Where you been?" she asked.

"Oh, I had to stop off at Aunt Irma's for awhile. I picked you up a treat for tonight. You want to see what it is?"

"Kay!" Lily said, grabbing the bag from Trevor's hand. As soon as she felt its coldness and recognized its shape she squealed in delight, knowing it was probably her favorite ice cream.

"I thought we'd make Aunt Judy and Lana some of our famous sundaes tonight. Will you help me?"

As soon as she heard Lana's name mentioned, Lily's smile disappeared. "No! Her go home!"

Trevor looked over at Judy for some help. He'd always been able to cajole Lily into seeing reason, but this time was different. Maybe Lily had sensed what he'd been feeling all along and was doing them both a favor.

Judy just shrugged her shoulders. She was leaving this one up to him.

Trevor set Lily down and knelt beside her. Looking her directly in the eyes, he began slowly, "I don't want to fight about this, Lily. Lana is a very good friend of Aunt Judy's and is going to be staying with us for a while. In fact, she's going to give us some help around here. We've been asking so much of Aunt Irma lately, and even though she loves us a bunch, I think she's getting a little tired. You know how you get when we do too much in a day? We don't want to hurt Lana's feelings by being mean to her. Do we?"

"I no care! Want her go home!"

"Lily, look at me," Trevor said as she started to turn away. "You have to stop this behavior. Please tell me what it is about Lana that makes you not like her."

"She stupid!"

"Lily, stop that. We don't say those kinds of things about people. You know better." Changing tactics a little, he went on, "Did you know Lana is a nurse? You know, like Kathy at Dr. John's office."

"I no care," Lily said as she stuck her nose up in the air.

Keeping his anger in check, Trevor deepened his voice to the lowest level and gently scolded, "Okay, Lily, if you can't say anything nice, then don't say anything at all. I mean it this time! If you say anything to hurt Lana's feelings, I will put you in your room until you can be nice. Do you understand?"

Lily could tell by the tone of his voice and by the look in his eyes that she wasn't going to win this one, so she sheepishly nodded her downcast head in understanding.

Lana sat at the top of the stairs and heard the last bit of Trevor's conversation with Lily. She was proud of the way Trevor had stood up for her but wondered if he'd widened the gap even further between her and Lily. She didn't want the small child to tolerate her; she wanted Lily to like her.

Oh, well, she thought. *I'd best get down there. I'm never going to make things happen sitting on the fringes.*

Judy was the first to notice Lana walking down the staircase and wondered if she'd heard the exchange between Trevor and Lily. She didn't notice the deep lines that furrowed Lana's forehead whenever she was nervous, and assumed she hadn't. "Hi, Lana. Look who's up from her nap."

Lana looked over at Lily, who'd moved once again to the protection of Trevor's long legs. "Oh, good! I was hoping you'd be awake. I didn't want to check the bird's nest without you. Will you come with me to see if any of the eggs have hatched?"

Lily clung to the back of Trevor's Levi's like a burr on a wool sock. When no answer was forthcoming, Trevor knelt to face the obstinate child. "Lily, why don't you go with Lana and see for yourself if the birds have hatched?"

Lily had let go of Trevor's legs and was now hitched to his chest. Lana didn't like seeing the unhappy look on both of their faces and wished, for just a split second, that she'd never entered their lair. "It's all right," she told them. "I'll just go check on the nest myself and call out if there's anything happening."

As soon as she left the house and was alone on the back deck, Lana took several deep breaths. *You can do this,* she reminded herself. *You've dealt with children like Lily before and managed to turn things around.* But then, it wasn't so much the child that had unnerved her so. It was Trevor!

Watching Trevor with Lily was like nothing she'd ever witnessed. Not even with Tom. When Trevor looked at her, it was as if she were the only person in the room. His gentle nature and soothing voice were like the love songs she'd listened to over and over as a teenager.

It was a lifetime ago that she'd spent nights alone in her room, playing Barry Manilow and Bee Gee records, memorizing every word. Why now were those memories so vivid?

She had a crush. A good old-fashioned crush.

I have to stop thinking like this, she thought. *Things happened, terrible things that I can't forget.* She wanted to remember that feeling of devastation right now. Only then would it remind her of reality and why she couldn't allow her mind to feel free again.

Lana was so lost in her thoughts she didn't hear Judy walk up behind her.

"Why don't we start supper?" Judy suggested.

"Sounds like a good plan." She then examined the nest, remembering why she'd come out in the first place. "Looks like the chicks aren't ready to face the cold hard world yet. Sort of like Lily with me."

"She'll come around, just as I'm sure those eggs are going to hatch. Patience! That's the key to all things wonderful," Judy reminded her.

When Trevor entered the kitchen and placed the partially thawed ice cream in the freezer, he didn't apologize for Lily's behavior. In fact, he said nothing at all until he noticed the chicken sitting on the counter. He announced to no one in particular that he'd start the grill and was gone as quickly as he'd come in.

Lana felt responsible for the tension that enveloped the household and quickly searched for a way to dispel some of the anxiety everyone was feeling. With Judy busy tossing the salad and Trevor out on the back deck, Lana took the opportunity to seek out Lily. Maybe without the security of Trevor she'd stand a chance, one on one, with this little girl.

Lily was sitting in the rocker turning the pages of the book Judy had left unfinished when Lana walked in. Before Lily could scoot away, Lana moved to stand before her, partially blocking the way to the kitchen. "Can you help me with something, Lily?"

Lily just stood there, staring into her face.

She had to think of something quick. By appearing needy, maybe Lily would respond to her. "Um...I can't find the napkins anywhere in the kitchen and I need to finish setting the table. Can you help me find them?"

When Lily didn't respond, Lana continued, "I just have to have a napkin when I eat. Sometimes I am so sloppy when I drink milk I get a milk mustache. I wipe it off quickly so no one sees but once in a while I get caught. Can you please help me? I don't want everyone to think I have a mustache."

As she said this, she rolled her eyes and made a funny face. She saw the start of a smile begin to form on Lily's face and felt a fleeting moment of triumph before she heard Trevor call out Lily's name. Before she had a chance to watch the completion of that smile, Lily shot past her and ran to the kitchen.

She'd made an inroad, even for the briefest of moments, and that was something to celebrate. *Humor*, she thought, *always did work on the kids.*

Lily stayed on the back deck with Trevor until it was time to bring the slightly charred chicken in from the grill. By that time, Judy had put together a masterpiece salad, mixing red and green peppers, red leaf lettuce, thin slices of purple onion, matchstick-sized carrots, and vine-ripened tomatoes. Lana had kept busy preparing wild rice and setting the table, and was in the process of symmetrically arranging thick slices of Italian bread in what looked to be a hand-woven basket when Trevor and Lily came in through the back door. Lana deliberately hadn't put napkins on the table, hoping Lily would take notice.

Trevor, with Lily on his heels, brought the platter of chicken directly to the table and sat down to eat. Lily took her usual spot, right next to Trevor. Judy sat opposite Lily, and Lana occupied the only space left—the one directly across from Trevor.

They were all so famished hardly any words were spoken for the first five minutes. Lana and Lily remained silent, cautiously studying one another. Lana tried to avoid the hazel eyes that pierced through her and caused her mind to tread on dangerous territory. She focused instead on the little girl, looking for a sign that maybe she was starting to warm up to her. *Now is the time*, Lana thought as she drank greedily from her glass of milk. Gulping a bit too loudly, she could feel the other diners' eyes on her. When she placed the empty glass on the table, she knew she had created a serious-looking milk mustache—one that would have made the milk industry advertisers proud. In that instant, Lily started to giggle. She stepped down from her chair and pulled out a drawer in the sideboard. Grabbing a napkin, she rushed it over to Lana. Trevor and Judy stared in wonder—not so much at the grown woman sitting there with milk all over her upper lip but more at the reaction from the little girl who, not so long ago, hadn't given this woman the time of day.

Lana took the napkin from Lily, winked her left eye, and immediately swiped at the remnants of milk.

After dinner, Judy offered to do the dishes and shooed everyone out, insisting on doing the job herself. Lana suspected there was a reason why Judy wanted the three of them to be on their own and didn't put up a fight.

As she entered the living room, Lana noticed that Trevor had added some logs to the fire, increasing its intensity so that it almost roared, and was seated in the rocking chair alongside the hearth. Lily was playing quietly, over by the toy chest, with some dolls.

The setting reminded Lana of a Hallmark card, it looked so perfect. She knew it wasn't, but a peacefulness did seem to have settled in the room. Lily may not have totally warmed up to her, but at least she wasn't hiding behind Trevor anymore. As for him, well, that was a different story. Lana suspected it would take some time before either of them was comfortable with the other.

The tranquility of the room nearly caused her to retreat to her bedroom so as not to upset the harmony, but the willfulness of her nature led her to the couch. Out of the corner of her eye she watched Trevor as he slowly rocked back and forth. She couldn't tell if his eyes were open or closed but knew he was deep in thought. She wanted desperately to break the silence and start asking the many questions she'd wondered about since Judy had asked for her help. Why the big secret regarding Lily? Where was her mother? How long had he had custody? When, if ever, would he return to California? There was so much she wanted to know but she couldn't just ask. Not yet anyway.

Patience. That word kept echoing in her mind.

In the meantime, Lana decided she could begin her research on Lily. She observed the little girl as she played with her dolls, looking for any signs of FAS. So far, she hadn't noticed any blatant abnormalities. As Judy had previously mentioned, Lily was an adorable little girl with no physical signs of the disorder, with the exception of her being a little smaller than other children her age. Her broken speech pattern was a concern, but without knowing all the details of this little girl's life, Lana was hard pressed to make any determinations as yet. She did notice how focused Lily was playing with her dolls, and quickly dispelled any notion that she might be hyperactive.

Lana wondered about the height of Lily's mother. Was Lily small because of FAS, or was she petite because of genetics? Was Lily's mother beautiful as she suspected Lily would be? Did Trevor really love her? Was he heartbroken when they were no longer together? Once again her mind had drifted to Trevor. *Stop!* she chided herself. *Why must I keep going back to him? Keep focused on the child.*

Judy had wiped every available surface at least three times before she entered the quiet zone. During the twenty or so minutes it took her to clean up the kitchen she had strained her ears for any sound coming from the living room. She stayed in the kitchen a while longer, expecting someone to break the ice, and when that didn't happen she threw in the dishtowel and went to the rescue. "Well, the dishes are done and I could use a good game of Go Fish. Does anyone want to play with me?"

Lily immediately vacated her spot and came to stand beside Judy. "Yeah, me."

"Count me in too," Trevor offered.

Judy immediately added, "Well, come on, Lana. We might as well make it a foursome."

Trevor retrieved the cards, Judy pulled a pad and pencil out of the top drawer in the hutch, and Lily went to take her seat at the dining room table. Lana waited until everyone had sat down before she joined the group.

Lana watched as Trevor wrote all four names down on the pad. Her name was last and as she watched him write the four letters—L A N A—a chill went up her spine. For a brief moment she felt like she was back in middle school, where she'd found solace in writing her latest crush's name, a few dozen or more times, in her notebook.

"Lana, it's your turn," Judy instructed. "Earth to Lana!"

"Oh, I'm sorry," Lana answered, embarrassed. "What card did you ask for again?"

"A six. Do you have any sixes?"

"Go fish!" Lana replied, forcing herself to focus on the game.

During the next hour they played three rounds of Go Fish and, according to the score pad, Trevor and Lily were the big winners. Judy was her usual casual self, making everyone in the room comfortable with her carefully constructed conversation. They talked about Vermont, the weather, who had what pairs, who was going to deal next, and what they'd do the next day.

Both Trevor and Judy decided it would be great to take Lana into town. Lily was quiet when they talked about how they would all have breakfast at Stokey's and afterward show Lana around the quaint village. Trevor was proud Lily didn't put up a fuss, even though he could tell she was very uncomfortable with the situation.

Lana sensed the same thing and quickly turned the focus away from her and onto Lily. "Lily, since you're ahead with two wins, I think you should get a prize for beating the big people. How about tomorrow right after breakfast we'll take you to the store and buy your favorite candy?"

Lily loved candy almost as much as she loved her Beanie Babies. Though Irma and Trevor indulged her with lots of things, Irma felt that sugar made children hyper and hard to manage, so candy had not been a staple in the Vermont home.

Lily was so excited at the prospect of sweet delights that she jumped up and down, practically knocking herself off the chair. "Oh, goody, goody! Can I get M&Ms 'n' Skittles, Trevor?"

Trevor looked over at Lana—more like through her, she thought— before he looked back at Lily. "Now that would be up to the lady doing the offering, sweetheart. Why don't you ask Lana?"

"Can I?" Lily asked, forgetting that the woman doing the offering was not her favorite.

"If it's okay with…um…Trevor." Slightly embarrassed, Lana didn't know how to refer to Trevor. She was surprised Lily hadn't called him Dad. Why hadn't she done that? Was this one of those Hollywood things where kids called their parents by their first name?

Trevor watched as confusion spread across Lana's face. It was obvious Lana knew only the sketchiest details about their situation, and he was sure that when they were alone she'd be asking numerous questions. He wasn't looking forward to that, since he wasn't going to divulge any more information than he had to. Lily was his responsibility and he was going to protect her at all costs.

Then, remembering the question he'd been asked, Trevor said, "I guess a little candy would be okay, but just a few things, though. You know how Aunt Irma feels about too many sweets. In fact, Ben and Irma are coming over for lunch tomorrow, so we need to make sure we're back by twelve or so."

"Oh, wonderful!" Judy exclaimed. Ben and Irma had made quite an impression the first time that she'd met them. It was obvious they had taken good care of her nephew and that pleased her to no end, especially since Trevor and his mother had grown further apart over the years. And although Judy could understand why, with both their careers positively soaring, it still didn't sit well with her.

Carol had never remarried and, from the little Judy knew, had never even dated. Instead of allowing herself to heal and fall in love with someone else, she focused all her energy and passion on climbing the corporate ladder. Judy had tried to persuade her sister to open up and discuss her personal life, but some subjects were closed for discussion as far as Carol was concerned. Judy had never been close with her sister, and watching her nephew fall into that same pattern bothered her more than she was willing to admit. Carol had always pushed people away, and as hard as she'd tried, Judy had been unable to alter her sister's behavior in this regard.

The few times they had been together during the last several years, conversations had been confined to news about Trevor, tidbits about Judy's practice, and the world of big business. Judy noticed the change in her sister when she talked about the latest merger or buyout. Carol actually came alive when she talked of negotiations between what she referred to as the "big boys" and "little old me." Judy could tell her sister had become a hardened woman over the years and couldn't help but feel sorry for the person who shared the same bloodline.

Since Trevor and his mom hadn't been close for some time, Judy had willingly accepted the role of surrogate parent. She loved her nephew more than anyone else in her life and was happy to fill her sister's shoes.

Trevor and Lily had gone up to bed shortly after the card game was over. Trevor announced he'd been up quite early that morning and was having trouble keeping his eyes open. Both women knew better but decided it was best to let the day fade away on a good note. Lily bounced happily up the stairs when Trevor promised to read "Little Red Riding Hood," one of her favorite tales.

Once again, Judy and Lana found themselves alone.

"I think Lily warmed up to me a bit," Lana began. "What do you think?"

"I think you handled her like a pro. It was great the way you diverted the conversation away from you and onto her earlier when we were talking about showing you the sights."

"I could tell by the look on her face that she was feeling threatened again. I could sense she was working up to one of her tantrums and wanted to stop it before it began."

"Good thinking," Judy declared. "All in all, I didn't think the day was that bad. We had a delicious dinner, played a mean game of Go Fish, and ended on what I'd say was a good note. Lily even looked you in the eyes when she said good night. I know it's not much, but it's a start."

"I couldn't agree with you more." Lana hesitated a minute before she went on, choosing her words very carefully. "I still don't think Trevor's comfortable with me. I think he puts on a good show, but I get the feeling that he's not convinced this is a good thing. I want you to be really honest with me now. How much did you have to threaten Trevor before he gave you the okay to implement your plan? Please tell me. I promise I won't turn and run away."

Judy thought for a few minutes before answering Lana's question. She realized that Lana wasn't going to be placated anymore and she felt guilty that she'd allowed it to go on this long. "Okay, so he wasn't that excited about my idea. In fact, it took some convincing on my part for him to even think about the possibility. Like you, he didn't cotton to it right away. I think he's keeping his distance for a reason. I suspect it has to do more with his ability—or rather inability—to trust people. I would never have involved you in this if I didn't think you were trustworthy. We just have to convince Trevor of that fact."

"At dinner Lily called Trevor by his name instead of Dad. Can I ask why?"

Judy shook her head. "I think that's a question better asked of Trevor. I don't mean to sound so mysterious, but I don't want to lose his confidence now. He has to be the one to answer all the personal questions surrounding Lily. Believe me when I tell you that just your being here is a big step for him."

"I just don't think he's comfortable around me," Lana said, sounding a bit defeated. "And for me to start asking the questions I've been bugging you about…well, I just can't see it. He barely looks at me."

"Patience, Lana. You must give him time to adjust to the whole thing. He's just buried his best friend, moved out to another coast, and has Lily to worry about—certainly a lot to handle in a short period of time. Then I go and persuade him to let us help with Lily—another change in his already tumultuous life. Give him time. Become his friend first, then focus on helping Lily."

"Time? I know it works in everyone's best interest, but I just don't think it's going to happen that fast with Trevor. I can't stay away from the hospital for more than two or three weeks and I can't imagine Trevor opening up that soon. He seems a million miles away. Even when we were playing cards tonight, I tried to engage him in conversation. If you noticed, I barely got a response."

"A lot of that had to do with Lily's constant interruptions," Judy pointed out. "As I'm sure you could tell, he simply coddles that child."

"Well, tonight I think he was actually happy for the diversion. I thought I would be the one to clam up after our first introduction, but something happened after my jog around the lake. It sort of revived me. It's like I'm on some sort of mission."

"I'm glad you feel that way. Trust me, Lana. Trevor will come around." She started to rise, a little slower than usual. "Well, these tired bones are going to climb those stairs and get ready for bed. It's been a long day."

"You go on ahead," Lana told her. "I'm going to sit here a little while longer and enjoy the remains of the fire. It's been so long since I've enjoyed the smell of burning logs. It sort of takes me back to when I was a little girl and on Sunday evenings we'd sit around the fireplace and play Monopoly or checkers. Life was so uncomplicated then."

Judy leaned over and hugged her good friend. "I couldn't agree with you more. It's a shame we couldn't stay young longer. It's funny, you know—when we're young all we want to do is get older, yet when we get older all we want to do is recapture our youth. Go figure."

After Judy had gone upstairs, Lana nestled into the far corner of the couch and pulled the handmade quilt over her chilled legs and feet. Nights in Vermont were a bit cooler than in Connecticut and the dying fire exuded little warmth. She wondered if Trevor had turned on the heat. Before he took Lily upstairs, he had made sure all the windows and doors were shut, but she hadn't noticed if he checked the thermostat.

Trevor had lain with Lily for over an hour, reading and cajoling her into sleep. When he was convinced she was in a deep slumber, he picked her up and carried her to her room. He carefully laid her in the center of her bed and tucked the covers just under her chin. He loved the way she looked when she slept—so peaceful and angelic. He cared for this little creature more than life itself, and was still baffled by the way she touched his heart.

Lately, he'd been thinking about his mother and wondering what she would have been like had his dad been around. It was obvious that her heartbreak over the loss of her husband had killed something within her, and it had made loving him unnatural. He'd always felt it.

His dad never returned to meet the son he sired, and that hurt more than the coldness Trevor felt around his mother. Thoughts of loving someone enough to partner for a lifetime were so foreign to him that it became a non-issue.

He spelled this out, up front, to women who seemed to linger too long—usually causing them to give up and walk away. Only a couple of times did their walking away truly affect him. Both were with women who said they didn't need a commitment and hung on longer than he'd been used to. Eventually, though, when it became apparent that he wasn't going to change his mind, they left him. He knew it wasn't fair to prolong something that would never be, but he was unable to hurt them outright by breaking the relationship off first.

Now, here he was looking in on a four-year-old doll that had stolen his heart. He gently closed the door and headed for his room. He was tired but still felt a modicum of restlessness. Today had not quite gone as he'd expected. *Oh, well,* he thought. *Tomorrow is a new day. I'll wake up refreshed and, hopefully, in a better frame of mind.*

While crossing the balcony to his room, Trevor realized a light had been left on downstairs. As he looked over the railing he noticed someone asleep on the couch. Although the room was dimly lit he could tell almost immediately who it was. *Do I go down there and wake her up or should I adjust the automatic thermostat on the first floor so the heat doesn't click off at midnight? Why,* he questioned himself, *am I worrying over this shit? Just grab a goddamn blanket so she'll be nice and warm and adjust the heat so it stays on through the night.*

Anxious to get some sleep, Trevor quickly disengaged the automatic timer and walked over to the couch to lay the blanket over Lana's sleeping form. Even though she had the quilt covering her legs and feet, she'd need something a little larger if she were going to stay warm through the night.

He stood there watching the rise and fall of her chest, and followed suit with his own breathing, matching her rhythm almost exactly. The small lamp on the table behind her sleeping form cast a warm glow over her face. Her skin was perfect. With the exception of a few faint freckles on her nose, not a blemish marred her alabaster skin. He desperately wanted to run his fingers along the contours of her face. Her cheekbones were high and delicately carved and her chin had a small cleft. Her lips were the color of vintage rose and her brows were a shade darker than her honey-colored hair. A few wisps fell gently over her forehead and the urge to feel the tendrils between his fingertips was almost too much to bear.

Softly he placed his thumb and forefinger over the fallen pieces and moved them away from her eyes. Just as he was about to pull back his hand she awoke with a start.

"Oh, you scared me, Trevor."

Quickly backing away, he practically fell over the hand-embroidered stool that Irma had given to him just a few weeks ago.

"I'm sorry if I frightened you. I was leaving Lily's room and noticed you'd fallen asleep down here. It can get pretty cold here at night, so I wanted to give you an extra blanket. I didn't mean to wake you."

Rising to a sitting position, Lana said, "Please don't apologize. I didn't mean to fall asleep down here. What time is it?"

"I'd guess around ten thirty or so."

"I can't believe I'm this tired so early. It must be all the fresh air." Wanting to take this opportunity to get to know Trevor better, Lana asked, "Do you have any chamomile tea?"

"I'm sure we do. I know Irma sometimes prefers it to coffee so there might be some in the cupboards."

Lana watched as he dropped the extra blanket on the side chair and walked toward the kitchen. He moved swiftly, almost reaching the other room before she had a chance to untangle herself from the quilt that had become wrapped around her legs.

By the time she reached the kitchen he was already in the process of filling the teakettle. A box of tea was sitting atop the counter.

"You don't have to do that, Trevor. I can get my own tea."

"It's no problem," he assured her. "Filling a teakettle full of water is about the extent of my culinary skills, though."

"How can you say that? Tonight you grilled the chicken to perfection."

"You are too kind, madam. Standing by the fire, turning marinated chicken every five minutes or so doesn't really qualify me as a chef. I'm more of an order-in type of person."

"I bet there aren't as many order-in places here as you've got in California." The minute she said those words, she realized she'd made a mistake. Trevor's face immediately changed and the easy banter of a few minutes ago disappeared.

Trevor hesitated a minute before he responded, "Not many at all. Well, if you don't need anything else, I think I'll go on up to bed."

"I'm just fine, thank you. Sleep well and I'll see you in the morning."

Without even a backward glance, Trevor walked out of the kitchen.

Why did I do that? she chided herself. She knew there probably weren't any delivery places in remote areas like this, so why had she asked that stupid question?

Chapter Nine

Cindy had been home a couple of hours before she decided to book a flight out to L.A. that night.

Sally had been wonderful, listening to the details of her life and holding back any judgment she may have felt. At the end of her long, complicated story, the only comment Sally made was that Cindy should have been more truthful with Sam. She didn't even know they had married, and Cindy guessed that if Sally had known that fact she would have been really disappointed in her. Cindy knew that Sam loved her and would probably understand, but she didn't trust that things would stay the same after he found out the truth. It had taken her a good long time and a great deal of counseling before she had been able to forgive herself. How could she ever expect Sam to do the same?

She was scheduled to fly out at five o'clock that evening. That didn't leave much time to pack, call Sam, and get to the airport. She had just called work and explained that someone had died and she needed a few days' leave. That was the easy call.

As she dialed Sam's number, Cindy felt sweat beading on her upper lip. How was she going to explain where she was going and why? She had never lied to Sam and she didn't want to start now. She'd hoped her past would stay buried along with her child, but deep in her heart she knew that someday it would surface. She just didn't think it would be this soon.

Just then she heard his familiar voice. "Sam Stewart."

"Hi, honey. It's me."

"Oh, thank God it's you. I called your office an hour ago and they said you didn't come in today. I've been so worried. What happened?"

This was not the time to divulge the past she'd hidden for so long. She knew she had to be as vague as possible and hoped Sam would trust her enough to let it go at that.

"I just learned this morning that a friend of mine from California passed away. I'm flying out tonight."

"Tonight! Who died? I didn't even know you had a good friend in California. Why didn't you call me earlier?"

"I knew you had meetings all morning."

"For something like this, you could have interrupted me." Trying hard to calm himself down, Sam softened his voice a bit. "You know nothing is more important than you. I'm just sorry you didn't call me sooner. Where've you been all day?"

"At Sally's. "

"Who died?"

"An old friend." She couldn't say Jamie's name aloud and didn't want to explain how she'd learned of his death. If Sam knew that Jamie died months ago he would wonder why she felt the need to fly out immediately. How could she offer up an explanation when she herself didn't fully understand why the urge was so strong?

Sam was starting to get upset with the way Cindy was answering his questions. "What old friend?"

The tone of his voice unsettled her even further. She was far too emotional to get into this with him right now, and she had to convince him that all would be better when she returned. "It's someone I used to know when I lived in California," Cindy managed. "Please don't press me on this. I'll explain everything when I get home in a few days."

This must be the other shoe that had been bound to drop sooner or later according to his mother. She had warned him about Cindy—said she could tell by the lines in her face that she'd been around the block a few times. Oh, how those words haunted him right now.

"Please, honey, talk to me. What's going on?"

"Nothing I can go into right now. Please don't worry, though. Trust me."

Those last two words were his undoing. "Trust you? What the hell is going on here? You won't tell me who died, what this person meant to you, or why you feel the need to fly three thousand miles at the drop of a hat. I'm your husband and I deserve better than this."

He'd never used this angry tone with her before and she could hear fear laced within his retort.

"Honey, I know you do," she affirmed. "I just can't go into it right now. Just know that it has nothing to do with our life together. That isn't going to change. Please, I have to leave for the airport. I'll call you tonight or first thing in the morning. I promise."

With that said, Cindy hung up the phone before he could ask any more questions. In all their time together, she had never once thought of recounting her nightmare to him. Her relationship with Sam was pure and untainted and she didn't want to do anything to dampen the feeling she had when she was with him. Through counseling she had learned that her life had begun the day she entered rehab. She believed that wholeheartedly.

Landing in L.A. brought back a host of buried memories. Life in this town had not been good to her. She felt foreign and small in the huge airport and quickly ran to escape the throngs of people pushing and scurrying around her.

Alone in her hotel room that night, she sat by the window staring at the twinkling lights of the city. It wasn't so long ago that these same lights had danced around her partying life. Things had truly changed since then. Nothing about the city's brightness, busy streets, or star-studded sidewalks appealed to her any longer. Now she yearned for quiet, starlit nights in the arms of her husband.

Back then she wanted the fast lane—she actually thought it was the road to happiness. She couldn't have been more wrong. What she found instead was a land paved in drugs, alcohol, sex, and hopelessness.

As for Jamie, he was one of the good ones. She'd loved him with all her heart back then. She still loved him and always would. She loved him through suffering the effects of the DTs, loved him more when she was on road to recovery, and loved him when she stood in front of the justice of the peace vowing to be with Sam forever. She'd loved him enough to keep her promise. Although she'd never contacted him after that fateful day, he was still in her heart every waking hour.

Over the last few years, Cindy had privately kept up with Jamie by reading anything and everything about him. True to his word, nothing ever came out about their stillborn child and she was grateful for that. She'd always hoped that someday they would meet by chance and he would look at her and be proud of what she had done with her life. She wanted so much to show him that the good he'd always seen in her had risen to the top. Now she'd never get that chance.

Exhaustion overcame her and Cindy fell fast asleep, fully clothed, on top of the floral bedspread. She hadn't called Sam as she'd promised—in fact, she hadn't even thought about their conversation since she'd boarded the plane. It was as if the plane had become a time machine and she had been transported back four years ago.

Cindy awoke the next morning to bright sunshine streaming through the picture window. She'd been so tired she'd forgotten to close the blinds. It took her quite a while to build up enough courage to dial the number she had kept hidden in her wallet for so long. It was Trevor's personal line. Jamie had given her this number as a second place to call if he wasn't home. Since he was at Trevor's more often than not, she had used it quite a lot back then.

A heavily accented voice answered the call after the fifth ring. In broken English the woman explained that Trevor wasn't home and wouldn't be expected for some time. Cindy carefully spelled out her name and phone number and asked that he get in touch with her as soon as he could. She could barely understand the woman and prayed that she'd written down the information correctly. *Why*, she thought, *didn't I take Spanish in school, instead of French*? French had seemed so sexy and daring, but—like most of the things she'd done back then—so useless now.

She then placed a call to Jamie's manager and was surprised when Dorie, the young receptionist she used to party with, answered the phone. Trying to sound more sophisticated than in year's back, she now used her birth name, Doreen, in her greeting.

"Hi, Dorie. It's me, Cindy. You know, Jamie's Cindy from years ago."

"Oh, my gawd, Cindy. What the hell happened to you?"

"Too much, I'm afraid. How are you?"

"Oh, you know me—still trying to make it big. I've had a few bit parts over the years but nothin' major. Gotta pay the rent so I'm still here. Whatcha doin' back here?"

"Just visiting. As you know, things didn't work out for me here and I needed to break away."

They'd formed a sort of friendship back then, and, more than once, Cindy had crashed on Dorie's couch when she was too stoned to drive. Dorie had tried to help her, but nothing and no one back then could get her to see the light.

"When I didn't see you around anymore, I asked Jamie what had happened and all he would say was you went back home. He wouldn't even give me your address. Said you needed to put this place behind you."

"Terrible thing, that plane crash," Dorie continued. "I thought maybe I'd see you at the funeral."

"Well, that's why I'm calling. I just heard about it. Can you tell me where's he's buried? I'd like to put flowers on his grave."

It took Dorie a few minutes to remember the cemetery, and when she mentioned the location Cindy knew exactly where it was. She and Jamie had attended another rock star's funeral just a year before she'd left.

"Oh, do you have any idea where Trevor is? I tried his number and the housekeeper wasn't much help."

"I think he's staying at his place in Vermont," Dorie replied. "Word is no one can call him unless he calls first. I haven't seen him since the memorial service and even then he kept his distance from everyone. I heard he's not doin' so good."

"I can imagine. Trevor and Jamie were like brothers. Um...I don't seem to have the Vermont number. Would you mind giving it to me?"

"No can do. I'm not supposed to give that number to anyone. Strict orders from the boss!"

"Dorie, it's me," Cindy cried. "You're not giving it to just anyone, but...me. I'm sure Trevor won't mind. Anyway, I promise I won't say where I got the number. In fact, I'm sure Jamie gave me the number but I've misplaced it. Please, Dorie, I need to speak to Trevor. I feel terrible that I wasn't at the service. He and Jamie did so much for me and I want to pay my respects. Please…"

There was a moment of indecision. Then Dorie capitulated. "Oh, alright. But promise me you won't say where you got the number."

"You have my word."

Cindy was glad she'd rented a car. The streets had not changed much in the four years she'd been gone. She went to a florist shop on Van Nuys and purchased a small flowering azalea bush to plant at the gravesite. Then working her way out of the city, she stopped at a hardware store for a folding shovel, the kind people used at the beach to dig holes for sun umbrellas. *If only I were buying it for that reason,* she thought as she paid the man behind the counter. Walking out to her car, tears began flowing freely.

She sat in the strip mall's parking lot for what seemed to be hours before she was able to start the car. Forty-five minutes later she pulled into the cemetery where Jamie was buried. It was sort of weird, but she drove to the exact spot where he was buried. Maybe it was seeing his headstone in *People* magazine that drew her to the specific location— she couldn't be sure. She preferred to believe it was the connection that she'd always felt with him, even after they'd broken contact.

For several minutes she couldn't move. This was too real for her. Seeing Jamie's name, dates of birth and death, and his favorite saying, "You and me, Bro," pierced her heart. When Jamie had told her their baby was dead, she'd felt pain like no other. That same horrid feeling came back, sweeping through her so fast she felt paralyzed behind the wheel. She desperately wanted to get out of the car and run her fingers along his name and lie on the green carpet over his body. She wanted just once more to feel his closeness and pray for his forgiveness.

Cindy looked over and noticed a small gray bird with a yellow beak perched atop Jamie's headstone. The bird just sat there, staring at her, as if willing her to emerge from the car. It was a sign she would never forget nor ever really be able to explain. She got out of the car, opened the back door, and grabbed the shovel and flowering bush. The bird didn't move—just watched her gather her things. When she was almost within touching distance, her feathered friend decided to leave its perch, its job done. She watched it, soaring through the sky, and peacefulness settled over her. Jamie was free. Free like that bird. Free to be with their child.

Her tears had come and gone and she quietly dug a small hole next to where she thought Jamie's heart would be. She carefully placed the plant in the freshly dug earth and refilled the area around its base. She sat Indian-style between her gift and the cold hard stone, unconsciously rocking back and forth. She talked to Jamie as if he were standing right in front of her.

"There is so much I've wanted to say to you over the years. I'm so very sorry I lost our child. It has taken me a long time to come to terms with what I did, but through years of therapy and a lot of soul-searching I can finally say that I've forgiven myself. When you sent me away, I was so ashamed of what I had done. I will never forget the look on your face when you told me you never wanted to see me again. I knew then that it was over between the two of us. I mourned for our child and the love we had together. When all that was gone, I truly believed I wasn't worthy of that kind of love again.

"The woman I have become is someone you'd be proud of. I owe it all to you. Although I'm sure you felt nothing but disgust for me, the goodness in you showed through, as I always knew it would. What you did for me was over and above what I deserved. Through my journey, I kept you close to my heart. Knowing you were there gave me the strength to succeed. I kept my word and stayed out of your life, even though I desperately yearned to call you. First to hear your voice and beg your forgiveness, and later to tell you how I'd turned my life around and found the true person that only you could see."

Cindy sat at the grave for the rest of the day, sharing stories of her recovery and her life now with Sam. Afternoon turned into dusk and dusk into night before she realized that the day was coming to an end. She hadn't noticed the time and the grumbling in her stomach reminded her that she hadn't eaten all day. As she stood to leave, she once again traced her finger along Jamie's name, savoring the warm feeling that washed over her. She was finally at peace with Jamie. She'd felt his spirit the minute she pulled up to his grave and believed he'd heard every word she'd said today.

As she drove away, Cindy didn't need to look back. That chapter in her life was truly closed and her future now hung in the balance. She needed to get back home to Sam and explain the whole story. She had the strength and will to do that now.

Knowing she had enough time to catch a red-eye, she rushed back to the hotel to gather her things. She needed to flee the place she'd once called home and return to Sam, her home now.

Sam had fallen into a deep slumber and almost missed picking up the shrilling phone. He'd been up most of the night before waiting for her call, and at five in the morning, when she still hadn't phoned, he showered and dressed for work.

After their conversation the day before, he hadn't been able to concentrate on anything. He'd finally given up and gone home early. Today had been a different story. There were reports due by the end of the day, so he buried himself in work and was actually happy for the diversion. If it had been a weekend, he simply would have gone crazy with too much free time to think.

That night, once again, he sat by the phone, feeling more worried than angry. His body had finally given in to the fatigue and he'd fallen asleep.

He didn't know how long the phone had been ringing but was grateful when he heard Cindy's voice on the other end. The minute he recognized who was on the line the tenseness he'd felt in his chest subsided.

"Hi, darling," he heard her say. Before he could get a word out, she started, "Please, before you say anything, I want you to know that I'm at the airport and am catching the red-eye in about ten minutes. I should be home around nine tomorrow morning."

He was relieved she'd called but still bewildered about the entire affair. He didn't want to start anything but couldn't help saying, "Cindy, can you tell me what the hell has happened? I left you at the diner happy as a lark and several hours later I felt like my life had turned upside down. You said to trust you, hung up the phone before I could convince you to confide in me, and then flew across the country for who knows what. I've been a wreck for the past day and a half."

"I know it wasn't fair to leave you hanging. I wasn't in the right frame of mind to go into it. I love you very much and hope you'll forgive me for running out like I did. It was something I just had to do."

Chapter Nine

"Why couldn't you have explained what was going on?" he demanded. "Why didn't you at least call me last night? You can't believe
all the things that went through my head. Thoughts of you never coming back kept filtering through my mind. It nearly drove me nuts."

"Sweetheart, I told you it had nothing to do with us. I love you and
nothing is going to change that. I'll explain everything when I get
home. Can you go in late tomorrow? I need to tell you everything. I
need to be with you."

Hearing her plea, Sam couldn't help but feel sorry for what she
must have gone through. He knew now that Cindy hadn't intended to
leave him and that he'd let his imagination get the better of him. He
was still very concerned about what had made her react the way she
did, but was relieved she was coming home. She had always been
pretty tight lipped about her past, and even though he wondered about
her life before it wasn't enough of a worry to interfere with how he felt
about her. She had shared bits of information about her stay at the rehab center years before, and he'd chalked that up to a young girl's fool-
ishness.

Their life together had been wonderful and he wasn't going to let
anything that happened in her past upset what they'd built together.

"I need to be with you also," he told her. "I'll see what I can do
about going in late. And Cindy?"

"What?" she asked in a worried tone.

"I love you."

"Me too," she answered, relieved. "I've gotta run. They're announcing the last boarding call. I can't wait to be with you."

Chapter Ten

Judy was fast asleep when Lana quietly changed into her night-gown. She knew it was late and decided to skip her nightly rituals so as not to wake anyone. *Already things are changing*, she thought. *My routine is slipping away and I don't seem to care.*

Sleep did not come easily and she found herself tossing and turning. Her mind was racing with unanswered questions, keeping sleep just out of reach. She hadn't slept much the night before in anticipation of the trip, and she started to panic when she realized that, once again, sleep was eluding her.

She tried every remedy she could think of—meditation, counting back from one hundred, remembering favorite times—and was just about to get up and go back downstairs when she heard Judy's voice.

"Can't get to sleep, Lana?"

"No! I've tried everything but nothing seems to be working. Sorry if I woke you."

In the darkness, Lana heard Judy shuffle off her covers and walk across the room. Judy turned on the light as soon as she reached the dresser and began rummaging through her cosmetic case. "I have a couple of sleeping pills in here somewhere. Oh, good, I found them."

She walked over and handed Lana a tablet. "I know you don't like to take pills, but take this one. It will help you fall asleep. Today was a rough one and you need your rest."

Without giving it another thought, Lana gratefully took the pill and swallowed without the benefit of water. "Thanks."

"No thanks needed. Just try to clear your mind and relax. Good night."

The sun hadn't fully risen when Lana awoke the next morning. The pill Judy had given her had done its job. She had fallen asleep within fifteen minutes and had slept soundly, albeit not the usual eight hours she was used to, but just enough to rejuvenate her body and spirit.

She could hear Judy's rhythmic breathing and knew she was still sleeping soundly. Knowing how much Judy enjoyed her weekend sleep-ins, Lana did not want to wake her.

Hardly making a sound, Lana crept out of bed, pulled on a pair of sweats, and fished under the bed for her slippers before she quietly left the room. The hallway was chilly and she realized that she'd left behind the sweatshirt that hung on the occasional chair next to her bed. She could turn around and retrieve it, but decided against it as she did not want to wake Judy. *Oh, well*, she thought. *I'll just brave the cold.*

The open floor plan of the house allowed the light she'd left on over the stove to cast a warm glow throughout the first floor, illuminating things enough so she wouldn't trip on any furniture. As she tiptoed down the stairs, she noticed how still everything was. Even when she perked her ears to listen for any sounds outside, nothing could be heard.

This was her favorite time of the day. She guessed it stemmed from all of those mornings she'd woken up before her mom and enjoyed some time alone with her dad. He'd always enjoyed rising at the crack of dawn, and even though she didn't get up for another hour, he would always wait to have his morning coffee with her. Their ritual was always the same. He would start the pot but wait to drink until she'd risen. The aroma of just-perked coffee usually woke her, and by the time she'd made it down the stairs he'd have a tall glass of orange juice waiting for her.

Those were special times.

The temperature on the first floor seemed a bit colder than upstairs, and Lana was glad she'd donned her slippers and sweatpants. She gently rubbed her arms in an attempt to get her blood flowing and headed for the kitchen. She lit the burner under the freshly filled teakettle and was just about to clean the mug she'd left in the sink the night before when she heard the sound of someone coming down the stairs.

For a fleeting second she hoped it was Judy.

It wasn't.

He stood in the doorway looking as disheveled as she felt—hair out of place, jeans unbuttoned at the top, opened flannel shirt, and bare feet. She'd never seen anyone look better.

"Good morning," she heard herself say. "Would you like some tea?" She turned away then, as she feared his piercing stare was memorizing every inch of her body. A body that right now was quivering all over.

She was sure he'd noticed that she wasn't wearing a bra, hadn't washed her face and had traces of mascara bleeding under her eyes, and her hair was a total rat's nest.

When he didn't answer right away, she continued, more nervously than before, "I'm sorry if I woke you. I was trying to be quiet so as not to disturb anybody. All my rattling about didn't wake you, did it?"

She was babbling and knew it.

The restlessness he'd felt during the night didn't compare to what Trevor was feeling at this moment. Lana looked so soft and fresh standing by the sink with strands of light filtering through her hair. He stood silent for a minute, taking in her baggy sweats, oversized T-shirt, and fluffy slippers. Most of the women he'd woken up with were either in a state of undress or in something lacy and seductive. Lana looked comfortable and at home in his kitchen, and he found himself yearning to bury himself within her softness and feel something for the first time since Jamie's death. But the rational side of him, the one that usually won out in the end, reminded him to ignore those feelings and remain detached.

Clearing his throat, Trevor finally answered, "Don't worry; you didn't wake me. I'm going to brew some coffee. Would you care for some?"

"No, thanks. I feel like tea this morning." Lana removed one tea bag from the box she'd left on the counter the night before. She wrapped its string around the handle of the cup and asked, "How'd you sleep?"

"Just okay. How about you?"

"I had trouble falling asleep, so Judy ended up giving me something."

Right then, she felt him come up beside her and for a brief moment, when he reached for the Maxwell House tin, their shoulders touched. His closeness unnerved her and she moved away, babbling something about giving him more room, but they both knew better.

She had to get a hold of herself.

"I'm sorry if I said anything to offend you last night," she commented. She had to get this situation on neutral ground.

"Don't worry; you didn't. I was just tired and a bit out of sorts."

"I'm sorry about your friend, Trevor," she said honestly. "I know how difficult losing someone you love can be."

Trevor could see, as he looked at her, that she meant every word. "Thanks. Judy told me about your own loss. Boy, I can't even imagine dealing with something like that."

Lana didn't respond. She opened her mouth to speak but found she didn't know how to casually talk about what she'd gone through. Trevor was still a stranger to her and she wasn't prepared to talk about the two people she'd loved more than anyone in the world. She had only talked about them to her parents and Judy. Everyone else steered clear of mentioning Tom and Jessica.

Trevor watched as her body tensed and her lower lip quivered a little. He could tell he'd struck a raw nerve and that the wound had not fully closed.

"I'm sorry, Lana. I shouldn't have gone there."

"It…it's just I don't like to think about that time." Lana moved to the stove and waited for the water to boil. For several minutes neither of them said a word. As soon as the teakettle whistled, Lana offered, "Why don't we take our drinks out on the front porch and watch the sunrise? Do you have something I can throw on to keep off the chill?"

How about my arms? He wanted to say. But he knew better. "Sure! I'll go get it."

While Trevor was gone, Lana took a minute to collect her thoughts. She wanted her past kept separate from what she hoped to accomplish here and wanted Trevor to understand that. *But how,* she thought, *am I going to befriend him if I'm not willing to expose any parts of myself? Friendships operate on a two-way basis, and if I'm going to be successful with getting him to open up, I'm going to have to reciprocate. Only then will he be able to trust me.*

She'd known it was time to let go of the past, but that meant she'd have to move forward with her life. A life she'd grown rather fond of. So it wasn't perfect—so what! She didn't need anyone to make her feel whole. She was as whole as she was going to be. She still kept Tom and Jessica near. They were just ghosts—she knew that—but it was enough. So why didn't Judy believe that?

"Here you go," Trevor said, sauntering into the room with a gray hooded sweatshirt slung over his arm. She noticed he'd buttoned his flannel shirt, had stepped into a pair of Docksiders, and had grabbed a light windbreaker for himself.

Her thoughts quickly shifted back to the present. Trevor had a way of grabbing her full attention. She couldn't deny that she liked the way he looked. The light stubble splattered across his chin and upper lip completed his rugged, mountain look. It was funny—she had pictured a rock and roll icon as having teased hair and tight-fitting leather clothes. Trevor was just the opposite. His appearance was closer to that of someone who swung an axe rather than a guitar.

She quickly pulled the fleece-lined sweatshirt over her head and realized the sleeves were twice as long as her arms. She rolled up the sleeves to free her hands so she'd be able to carry her mug of tea.

"I poured you some coffee. I didn't know if you took cream or sugar."

"Thanks. I drink it black." He grabbed the steaming mug off of the counter and led the way to the front door.

Just like my dad, she thought as she followed on his heels.

The chill in the air was enough to chase away any cobwebs either of them may have felt this early in the morning. Turning one of the rocking chairs to face east, Trevor positioned himself to fully catch the first glimpse of the sun. Following his lead, Lana did the same, leaving about a foot between the two chairs.

The steaming brew in her hands kept the chill off her exposed fingers, but the male scent emanating from his sweatshirt did more than warm her heart. It brought back a plethora of memories, not so much of her life with Tom, but more her life growing up.

It wasn't unusual for her to snatch her father's or her brother's sweatshirt and head out either to get the mail or play flashlight tag after dark. She always liked wearing oversized clothing. Since her mom only bought stuff that fit, she'd sneak her dad's or her brother's clothing instead. Her brother always had a conniption but her father didn't seem to mind at all. As long as she hung it back on the hook in the mudroom, he couldn't have cared less.

Trevor remained quiet as he stared out across the lake. Lana was the first to break the long silence. "It's so peaceful here. Do you do this often?"

"Not as often as I'd like to," he answered.

Silence again.

She tried to stay still and enjoy the first rays of light peeking over the ridge, but felt uncomfortable with the quietness between them. "I think Lily actually warmed up to me a little last night."

"She'll come around. Just give it some time."

"Judy said the same thing to me yesterday. It's just that I want to begin working with Lily so badly, and I can't if she doesn't accept me."

"She will before you know it," Trevor assured her. "She did the same thing to Judy when they first met. A couple of days later they were best friends."

"You mentioned friends coming over for lunch today."

"Ben and Irma. They're good people."

"Have you known them for long?"

"Quite awhile now."

He was being very polite and cordial answering her questions. The trouble was, she was doing most of the talking and was nearly out of what she considered safe topics. He wasn't making things easy for her. She was afraid to talk about anything that might bring up his past life. Discussions about music, California, and Lily all seemed to be out of the question.

"Judy tells me you two have always been close. You're lucky; she's a great person."

Trevor nodded. "I've been fortunate to have her in my life. She's someone you can always count on to give it to you straight."

"You can say that again. She definitely has a way with words."

Silence again. She waited a few minutes to see if Trevor had any additional comments or possibly a few questions of his own to ask. When none came, she tried one more time to light a fire under their dying conversation. "What time does Lily usually rise?"

"About eight or so. She didn't get to bed until late last night, though, so she might sleep in a little longer."

"This place Stoker's we're going to for breakfast—what's their specialty?"

"You mean Stokey's? Well, let's see…they make a mean western omelet and the best cinnamon raisin bread you've ever tasted."

"Sounds good to me. I can't believe how hungry this fresh air makes me. I ate more last night than I think I ever have at one sitting."

When Trevor didn't respond right away, she turned to look at him and noticed his eyes were shut. He looked serene sitting next to her in the warm glow of dawn. She suspected he wasn't quite asleep but knew conversation had ceased on his part. He'd looked tired this morning and she knew before she'd even asked that he hadn't slept much the night before. If Judy hadn't given her the sleeping aid she would have felt the same way this morning.

Lana found herself staring at his profile, studying every detail of his face. His eyebrow was thick and dark, an exact match to both the color and texture of his hair. His eye, though closed, was deep set with a crop of thick lashes extending past his lower lid. The shape of his nose was almost too perfect—straight and evenly sized. His bottom lip was a little fuller than the top and seemed to soften the angular bone structure of his jaw and chin. She noticed his hands were large and his fingers long and lean. His legs extended far past hers, almost reaching the railing on the opposite side of the porch. She guessed he was about five inches taller than she was and, by the look of it, most of the difference was in the legs.

She was so intrigued by his physique that she hadn't noticed his eyes were now open and he'd been watching her.

"The sun's over that way," he said, pointing east.

She reddened at hearing his words. "I was just seeing if you'd fallen asleep."

She couldn't help but notice the slight tilt to his lips, almost reaching a smile, when she tried to worm her way out of being caught studying him.

"No such luck. I was just resting my eyes." Reaching down, he picked up the mug of tepid coffee and took a drink. "I'm going in for a refill. Can I warm up your tea?"

Still reeling from her embarrassment, Lana declined, saying she'd already had enough.

As soon as he went into the house, she stood and began pacing the front porch. Why did his presence do this to her? She didn't want to look at him as a man but as the father of Lily. She wasn't ready for any kind of attraction. He was so different from Tom. Tom had been an accountant and looked the part to a tee. He wore suits to work, went to the barber every five weeks for a trim, and wore chinos on the weekends. He'd never have been caught dead in a pair of worn-out slim-fitting jeans. So why did she find Trevor's look so appealing? Closing her eyes, she tried to picture Tom in his conservative attire, carrying a briefcase and coming home exactly at 6:00 P.M.

No such luck.

When times were really tough after the accident, she'd go to a place in her mind, remembering their first kiss, the wedding, the birth of their child, and anything else that would shut out the depression that threatened her at every turn. Why were those happy thoughts miles away?

Calm down, she chided herself. *Stop getting yourself all worked up. Focus on Lily and the job you're here to do.*

Trevor stood at the door for a few minutes and watched Lana pace back and forth. He could tell by the stiffness in her stance, the angle of her head, and the way her hands were gesticulating that she was wrestling with something in her mind. He was pretty sure it had to do with him. After all, he'd not made it easy for her this morning. It was obvious she wanted to talk and start a friendship but he was still on the fence where she was concerned. From what his aunt had told him she was very trustworthy, but he still wasn't ready to divulge much about Lily. He'd been deeply hurt by what Jamie had done. In fact, he was still in shock that the person he trusted most in the world could have lied to him. Trusting someone he'd never even met before was totally out of the question.

Since Judy had suggested her plan, he'd done nothing but think about what information he would be willing to share with Lana. So much had to be kept secret, and he struggled with his final decision to let her into their lives. Lily came first. More than anything in the world he wanted to help her, but not at the cost of losing her.

Chapter Ten

He was also troubled with his inability to keep thoughts of Lana at bay. All through the night he'd thought about her. He knew he was vulnerable now, guessed he would be for some time to come, and, therefore, wasn't ready to get entangled with anyone. Before he had strolled downstairs, Trevor had convinced himself to keep their relationship strictly on a professional basis. Lily and Judy were too important in his life to screw this up by getting involved with a woman he knew he'd one day hurt. In his heart he also knew that Lana was too fragile to mess with and he didn't want to be responsible for causing her any more pain than she'd already gone through.

But seeing her by the sink this morning, looking so sexy with her hair tangled every which way, her face so perfectly sculpted, and her eyes sparkling like the lake outside on a cloudless day, he could only wonder how he was going to keep his resolve. Since meeting her yesterday, he'd done nothing but try to clear his mind of what it would be like to make love to her.

He thought of how gallantly she had tried to break through his hardened shell this morning. Maybe he should be honest with her. Get it out in the open. There was chemistry between them. He felt it and could tell by her reaction to him yesterday that she'd felt it too.

No, he thought, *I couldn't come right out and tell her I'm attracted to her. What would be the point? I won't allow myself to start anything with her. Besides, from everything my aunt's told me, she's never even had a date since her husband died. I'll just have to get a grip on my libido and curb any further ideas of being with her in anything other than a professional way.*

He watched her a few minutes longer before he made his presence known. "Looks like it's going to be a clear day," he announced.

Lana watched as he returned to his rocker, steam rising from his freshly filled mug. "I think I need to take a run," she declared, then asked, "Do you jog?"

"No, I never really had the time," he answered without so much as a glance her way. "But please go ahead. I suspect our two ladies of leisure will not be waking anytime soon."

He closed his eyes once again as if to say the conversation was over, and irritation rose up her spine. *Screw the jog,* she thought. *I'm not going to let him get away with ignoring me this time. Yesterday he van-*

153

ished, leaving Judy and me to wonder what had gone wrong, and now he's trying to do the same thing. Time is of the essence, based on what I observed yesterday with Lily. She doesn't speak in full sentences, hasn't gained any kind of social skills, and from what Judy had said, has never had any formal schooling. That would have been fine fifteen to twenty years ago, but today, by the age of four, if you haven't been involved in playgroups or attended any kind of nursery school, you're behind the eight ball. If Lily was going to start school in the fall, it didn't leave much time to get her on the right track.

For the first time since they'd met yesterday, she realized that a friendship was probably not in the cards for her and Trevor. His presence stirred emotions deep within her, resurrecting feelings that were best left alone. Becoming a nurse again was one thing, but allowing herself to form a relationship with a member of the opposite sex was quite out of the question. Never again would she enter into an arrangement where she could be broken again. Her shell had already been cracked and she feared that if she fell again, she would truly be gone forever. She couldn't do that to herself or her parents.

By keeping things strictly professional, Lana hoped to gain his confidence. For once, she disagreed with her mentor, Judy. Judy had wanted her to develop a friendship with Trevor first, with the hope that he would eventually open up. That couldn't happen because she didn't trust herself where he was concerned. She thought it best to keep things more professional, while trying to convince him that nothing he said would ever pass her lips.

Lana hadn't realized how long she had stood before him, but at some point during her analysis his eyes had opened and he'd begun watching her. Instead of looking away, she decided to end the game of chicken he seemed to be playing, waiting for her to make the first move.

"What's going on?" she demanded. "I'm here to help you and Lily." She sat next to him, knees almost touching, and gloved her hands gently around his free one.

Pulling his hand out of her grasp, Trevor stood up and began to pace the front porch. "I'm just not ready to get into all this right now. I thought I was, but trust me when I tell you I'm not."

Seeing his anguish, Lana jumped up and placed her hands on his shoulders. "Listen, Trevor. I know what you're going through—probably better than anyone—and believe me when I tell you it's not easy and probably won't be for some time. The difference here is Lily! She needs to be evaluated and put on the right course. If we don't do that now, it will only hurt her more. I don't think you want to risk her future. Do you?"

"Of course not! I'm not some kind of monster. It's just..." he backed away then, out of her reach. "I'm not sure I'm ready to talk about Lily and what problems may lie ahead. My aunt may have jumped the gun on this one."

Lana watched as Trevor struggled with his emotions. She could tell he wasn't comfortable talking about this with her. It might be too soon to talk about his friend's death, but they had to focus on Lily right away.

"Trevor, you know the more we prolong getting the proper help and guidance for Lily, the worse it will be. From what Judy's told me, Lily has never had any formal schooling and hasn't been around any other children. She should be starting preschool this fall and if we don't recognize her shortcomings now, I'm afraid of how she'll react."

Trevor knew Lana was right and that she was probably the best person to handle Lily. He couldn't find the words to express how painful this situation was, and started to turn away from her when she forced him to once again look her in the eyes.

"Tell you what," Lana offered, gently taking hold of his arm. "What if I do all the asking and you answer only the stuff you're comfortable with. I promise I won't push you on anything. I'm not some reporter trying to get a juicy story. I'm only here to help. Please give me that chance."

At that moment, Trevor's thoughts shifted to Lily. In his heart, he knew Lana was right. Sheltering Lily was no longer an option. It had been easy up till now. Consuela had been the perfect nanny, treating Lily as if she were one of her own. But he knew the time had come for change. "Okay," he replied, eyeing her carefully as he crossed his arms and leaned against the rail, "where do you want to start?"

Lana knew she needed to go slowly. Asking who Lily's mother was and why the child didn't call him Dad were questions she wanted to know but was afraid to ask this early on. "When Lily was born, how did the doctors know she might have fetal alcohol syndrome?"

"Because her mother was drunk at the time of delivery and had been drinking and doing drugs throughout her pregnancy. Also, Lily was born three weeks early and was very small even for that time."

Lana had worked with mothers with addiction problems long enough to know that carrying a child only added to the burden of their alcoholism. As she'd promised, she didn't judge Lily's mother, but she couldn't help feeling a tremendous sadness for the woman who had endangered not only her own life but the one she carried in her womb.

"Did the doctors mention if anything was physically wrong with Lily at the time of birth?"

"No. They tested her for everything and she received a clean bill of health. She's been for checkups on a regular basis and, with the exception of minor earaches, colds, teething problems—you know, the things kids get—she's been okay."

"Have you noticed any attention problems? For instance, can she sit still for extended periods of time and focus on one thing?"

Trevor nodded emphatically. "Yeah. She can play for hours with her kitchen set and dolls. When she gets tired at night she usually sits in my arms and listens while I read to her. Some nights we may even read three or four short books."

"Does she understand what you read to her?"

"I know what you're getting at. I've done my homework on FAS, and other than her small size and extreme stubbornness I haven't noticed anything else out of the ordinary. Lily can write her letters, understand the stories I read to her, and count to twenty."

Lana could tell he was getting a little defensive and she'd have to proceed very carefully. "How does she react when she's around kids her own age?"

Trevor shrugged. "I don't know. She hasn't been around many kids her own age."

"Do you mind if I ask what happened to her mother?" Lana knew she was venturing into the danger zone, but decided to try anyway.

"Her mother split right after she was born."

"You've had full custody the whole time?"

"Why is that necessary to know?" Trevor shot back. "Just know that Lily's been well cared for since she came home from the hospital."

Well, she'd struck a nerve. What happened to this little girl after she was born? Did the state take her into custody until a full investigation could be done? Was Trevor involved with drugs at the time? She'd gathered from Judy that Trevor had never been involved with any of that stuff and hardly ever drank, but was that entirely true? Were there things he hadn't confided in his aunt? Those questions were best left unasked for now.

"Did you have help with her?" Lana asked instead.

"Yes. A nanny was hired when Lily arrived home from the hospital and has been with her up until a few months ago when she became ill."

So, Lily was released into his custody. "What kind of illness?"

"Consuela needed to have bypass surgery last month."

"What a pretty name. Was she Mexican?"

"Yes, she's from Mexico City. Came to the U.S. to be with her children, and when she found they all had lives of their own she applied for the job. She's a wonderful lady. Lily calls her Grandma."

This little bit of information told Lana a lot. She now knew the likely reason Lily spoke in broken sentences. Consuela probably spoke in broken English, and since she was the primary caregiver it would make sense that Lily would mirror her speech pattern. "Trevor, how was Consuela's English?"

"Okay, I guess. While her grammar wasn't perfect, we never had a problem understanding her."

"Where is Consuela now?"

"She's recuperating with her eldest son in Oxnard, California."

"When she's well enough, will you bring her out here?"

"I'm not sure," Trevor answered honestly. "I don't think she'd like the cold."

"Was Lily living in California the whole time?"

"Yes. I brought her out here a few months ago when Consuela got sick."

"Do you plan on keeping Lily here in Vermont?"

"I'm not sure. Why?"

The conversation was flowing so easily, Lana made herself comfortable by leaning on the railing next to Trevor. She half-turned her body so she could still face him while they continued their discussion. "If you were going to keep her here, I'd suggest we visit the local elementary school to see if they have a preschool program. We should enroll Lily, so she can start interacting with kids her age. Also, they will test her to see if she is on a par with others her same age."

"Lily will not be attending public schools wherever we decide to live." Trevor was adamant.

"Okay then, we'll have to see what private schools are around here."

"I've already looked into it. We're out of luck. There is no private school within driving distance, and there's only one elementary school for this district. Since she's only four, I'm leaning more to hiring a private tutor."

"I'm not sure that's the best route," Lana objected. "She needs to start interacting with other children."

"You don't get it, do you?" Trevor snapped. "My celebrity status makes her an easy mark for the bloodhounds they call journalists. I can't expose Lily to that kind of life."

"Lots of famous people send their children to school, Trevor."

"Well, I'm not one those people."

There it was again, that defensive cap he donned whenever he considered a subject closed. She thought it best to ignore his obvious annoyance and continue.

"For this year, at least, we might be able to find a local church or daycare center that runs a preschool program a few mornings a week. She'd be sheltered from most of the public, and if the teachers running the program think she needs any extra help you can look into hiring a tutor. You don't have to cross the bridge of elementary school until next year."

Surprisingly, Trevor concurred. "Fine. Would you mind looking into it this week?"

"Not at all," Lana said with a relieved smile. "Do you want to come along?"

"No, thanks. I trust you'll make the right choice." With that said, Trevor pushed off the railing and started to walk into the house. The conversation was over as far as he was concerned. He felt more exhausted than he had an hour ago.

Chapter Ten

"Trevor, wait a minute please."

"What is it, Lana?" came his exasperated reply.

"I just wanted you to know that I appreciate your talking to me. I know how hard all this is for you, and...well, I'm just happy that we're off to a good start."

Chapter Eleven

An unspoken truce had been reached between Lana and Trevor, and the rest of the day went off without a hitch. Judy and Lily woke shortly before nine and the breakfast at Stokey's was plentiful and delicious. Lana had taken Lily into the general store, as promised, and had purchased the M&Ms and Skittles Lily had repeatedly talked about during their morning meal. Lily had brought along Ziggy, the bean-stuffed animal Judy had tucked away in her suitcase. It was obvious the candy and the stuffed toy had lightened Lily's mood considerably, and any signs of animosity she may have had toward Lana seemed to have disappeared.

Lunch with Ben and Irma was great fun. Irma brought a huge tureen of homemade chicken noodle soup, some fresh-baked bread, and delicious chocolate-chip cookies. Irma was warm and friendly and welcomed Lana as if she were one of the family. Ben was on the quieter side but made Lana feel right at home when he beat her two games to one at checkers.

The afternoon went by far too fast, and when Ben and Irma stood up to leave Lana felt a flash of melancholy. She couldn't remember a time when she'd felt so comfortable in a family setting. It warmed her heart to see Trevor enjoying himself too.

Shortly after Ben and Irma left, Judy announced that she had to get going as well. As she walked toward the staircase, she heard Lana's footsteps fall in right behind her.

"I thought I'd help you gather your things."

"Sounds good to me," Judy replied.

Once inside the bedroom, Lana blurted out, "Judy, I feel kind of funny about you leaving. I'm not sure I'm ready to handle all this on my own."

"Oh, nonsense! You've been doing a fine job. Looks like you won over Lily. You're going to have to concentrate on Trevor now."

"I'm not sure that's going to be so easy. He isn't a man who trusts very easily."

Judy sighed. "No, he's not. But I have all the confidence in the world that you'll have a great effect on him. In fact, if I were a betting person, I'd bet money on it. Since I'm not, I'll just let it go at that."

A short while later, Trevor called upstairs to let Judy know it was time to go. Before coming to Vermont, Judy had checked the bus routes to make sure she'd be able to get to the seminar from the bus depot in town. Leaving Lana without a car would have made her too nervous, and Judy actually looked forward to some time alone in which she could familiarize herself with the agenda for the coming week.

Lana waved good-bye from the end of the drive as Trevor, Lily, and Judy drove away. Lana opted to stay home, giving her some time to get used to the idea of being alone with Trevor and Lily.

Lana was sitting on the front porch reading a magazine when the truck pulled in an hour later. She chose to stay put, allowing Trevor to make the first move.

To say she was disappointed when he carried a sleeping Lily up the stairs and hardly noticed her would have been an understatement.

Trevor was coming down the stairs half an hour later when he noticed Lana out on the front lawn, pulling up the brown spiritless weeds that threatened to strangle the gas lantern's post.

The large windows in the living room gave him a full view of her every move. She was on her knees, slightly hunched over, as she lifted the dead plants out of the soil. Right next to her was a good-sized mound that she'd already picked. She seemed totally content kneeling on the hardened earth, with no one in sight—just her and Mother Nature.

Most of the women he'd been around needed an audience. They needed to be seen by the right people as well as be seen with the right people.

She was different.

He could tell that Ben and Irma had taken to her as a budding flower takes to sunshine. Although Lily was still adjusting to Lana, she'd done more than just tolerate their guest today. Why couldn't he do the same? What was it about her that cut so deep? No woman had ever had this effect on him. He shook his head, attempting to clear his thoughts. No way was he going to allow himself to get involved with this person.

He started to back away from the window when Lana turned around and saw him standing there. "Hey, Trevor, you mind giving me a hand?"

The day was fairly mild and he'd left the living room window open a little to let in some fresh air. There was no way he could turn and walk away and pretend he hadn't heard her.

"Oh, hell," he mumbled. "Sure, I'll be right out."

Lana could tell by the tone of his voice that Trevor wasn't very happy about helping her, but she wasn't in the mood to tolerate his aloofness anymore. If they were going to work together with Lily, she had to form a partnership with him as soon as possible.

Being in the woods amidst all the rich soil brought back a flood of memories for Lana. When she was a young girl she had helped her mother tend all their gardens—the oversized vegetable one out back, the perennial display along the western side of the house, and the grouping of annuals they'd planted every spring around the mailbox. Just sitting here pulling weeds brought back thoughts of happier times growing up. This house seemed to do that to her.

Lana was so lost in thought she didn't notice Trevor come up behind her. "So what do you need me to do?" he asked.

"Oh, hi! I didn't hear you. Do you have a compost pile out back for these weeds?"

"No. Just leave them and I'll have Ben take care of it."

"I'd rather not leave them. I'm afraid if we leave this pile of weeds sitting here it will kill the grass. All I need is a plastic bag. I'll get rid of them myself."

"Lana, Ben takes care of the grounds here," Trevor said a little more strongly. "I don't need you working like this."

"But I enjoy doing this kind of thing," Lana protested, "and it makes me feel kind of useful."

"Well, okay. Do what you want. I'll go get a plastic bag from the garage."

"Thanks."

He hadn't tried to hide the fact that her presence here was like a burr under a saddle. What had happened since this morning when they'd talked out on the front porch? She knew from the little Judy had imparted that he was a very complicated man, and she didn't want to lose the headway she'd made earlier. Someway, somehow, she needed to keep the momentum going.

Just then Trevor returned carrying a black garbage bag.

"Would you mind holding it open for me?" she asked, leaning over to pick up some of the pile.

The last thing Trevor wanted to do was brush up against this woman. Working side by side was not something he looked forward to. How was he going to restrain the impulse to take her right here on the front lawn? The smell of her subtle perfume, coupled with her lithe movements and full lips, was almost too much to take. He had to get the hell away from her—and fast—before he lost control.

Quickly opening the top of the bag, he watched as she shifted toward him and dropped in the first handful. He couldn't help but notice the way her shirt hiked up in the back, exposing her creamy white skin. He had to fight back the urge to drop the bag and run his aching fingers up and down her soft flesh.

Lana was totally oblivious to the war raging in Trevor's head. "Would you mind opening it a little wider?" she asked.

He hadn't noticed that he'd let the bag slightly close. "Oh, sorry. My mind's not on this, I guess."

"Don't you like to garden?"

Never in his life had he met someone as naive as she. Here he stood, emotionally naked, trying desperately to get a grip on his wandering, lustful mind when all she could think about was pulling those damn weeds.

"Trevor, don't you?"

Clearing his throat he rasped, "Not really."

"That's too bad. I haven't done it for awhile and it feels good. Kind of soothes what ails ya."

Man, he thought, *I can think of a hundred and one ways that could soothe me right now, and not a one comes close to gardening.*

She was so caught up in what she was doing she didn't realize that Trevor's mind was a million miles away. "Is there a nursery around here where we could buy some flowers? I think some color would really spruce up the place."

He doubted she was even aware of his shifting feet and uncomfortable stance. For her it was like being six years old again, when girls and boys played together without the sexual innuendoes.

He shifted once more, attempting to put some distance between them. "Yeah, there's one in town."

"Oh, great! When Lily wakes up, do you think we could go?"

"If you'd like," he agreed. "But you know you really don't have to do this. Ben takes care of all the landscaping."

"It's really no problem. I love doing this kind of stuff. Anyway, I think this yard could use a woman's touch. Whadda ya think?"

I could use a woman's touch! He almost blurted out. Aloud he said, "I'm sure Ben wouldn't mind if you added a few flowers. If you want, I can give you directions to the nursery, and you could go while Lily is sleeping."

Those words cut like a knife. Why was he so ambivalent about being together with her? "If you wouldn't mind, I'd prefer we all went together," she stated. "It might be nice if we started operating as a team. Do you agree?"

"I don't know how long Lily's nap will be," Trevor replied. "She seemed pretty tired and could sleep a couple more hours. I just thought it'd give you something to do in that time."

Taking a deep breath, Lana looked him square in the eyes. "I might as well be honest with you. Since Judy left, I've been a little nervous about being here alone with you and Lily. So I came out here to occupy my mind. I don't like feeling this way and I can sense that you feel the same way too."

Acting as though she'd completely read him wrong, he curtly replied, "I'm not uncomfortable."

"Come on, Trevor. Ever since I arrived yesterday you've done everything in your power to avoid me. You hardly even look me in the eyes." She then caught his eyes and softened her harsh tone. "How do you really feel about me being here?"

Wow! Her honesty blew him away. The world he'd been involved with most of his adult life was an intricate web of deception. Most people he'd worked with said what they thought you wanted to hear. Even his best friend, his blood brother, had not been honest with him in the end. Honesty just wasn't something he'd put a lot of stock in over the years.

"I don't know," he finally admitted. "I guess it feels a little weird."

At least she was starting to get somewhere.

"Why?"

"Well, for one, I hardly know you and we're going to be sharing the same space for the next few weeks. Doesn't that seem a little strange to you?"

"Kind of. I feel like there's more to it than that."

If she only knew! How could he relay that almost every waking thought he'd had since they'd met had been about her? He didn't even understand it himself.

"Don't go reading more into this," he protested. "I'm sure we'll do just fine. It's just going to take a little getting used to."

"If we don't start being honest with each other this tension will keep us from getting used to anything," Lana insisted.

"So what do you want me to do?"

"How about being honest with me? Do you think you can trust me?"

"You sound more like my aunt now than a pediatric nurse," Trevor charged. "Don't try to get into my head. This honesty crap isn't all it's chalked up to be."

"I've always believed that honesty truly is the best policy. Even though the truth hurts sometimes, it's still better to know where we stand. Don't you agree?"

"No," he insisted. "Some things are better left unsaid. Let people go on believing what they want."

"Well, I guess we can agree to disagree. I don't pretend to know what your world is all about. I'd guess it's a little like make-believe. Young girls wallpaper their rooms with your posters and struggling musicians want the chance to walk in your wake. I've never understood the power famous people have over the average guy. In all my life, I've never wanted to be anyone else but me."

"Then I'd say you're one of the lucky ones. I never thought of myself as powerful. I just believe people need to escape the daily grind, and the best way to do that is to imagine a life completely different from their own."

Lana nodded. "Do you like being on display all the time?"

"No. In fact, that's the one part of the business I've hated the most." He paused to take a breath. "In the beginning, it was a mixture of scariness and euphoria. Then, I became content with all the notoriety and even accepted the fact that I'd never be able to live a normal life. But over the last five or six years, I've grown to loathe all the trappings of stardom."

"Have you done anything to change it?" she asked. "You know, to find some peace."

What the hell was peace? His first thought was Haight-Ashbury or Woodstock, when the youth of America made a V with their first two fingers and walked around as if that gesture alone denoted a peaceful world. He'd never been at peace with either his music or himself.

Lana shifted a little and he could tell she'd been straining her neck to look up at him. He knelt down next to her, the fear of being close now absent from his thoughts. He was actually enjoying their conversation.

"The one saving grace about my business is that it's very fickle," he went on. "If you move yourself out of the public eye, you're as good as yesterday's news. I started to write music for others rather than myself, which allowed me to keep my hand in the business without being in the forefront. I also bought this place here. No one around here seems to care who I am. You don't know how much that means to me."

"I can't exactly imagine what you feel," Lana said slowly, "but I know I couldn't handle everyone knowing my business. I didn't realize just how much I needed my privacy until the…" She couldn't continue, and started to turn away when Trevor lightly took hold of her shoulder.

"Until the accident," he added. She looked so fragile he couldn't help but pull her into his arms.

It felt so right to be in his arms. It had been so long since anyone had held her like that. Other than with her parents and Judy, she hadn't discussed the tragedy with anyone. She'd neatly tucked away all the memories of her past life, both good and bad, and had moved on.

It had not been an easy journey. She wasn't about to let all those hidden emotions rise to the surface again. Pulling away from him, she spoke in a voice barely above a whisper. "I'm sorry about that. I don't like to talk about that time."

Clearing her throat to gain the full strength of her voice, she continued as though the last few minutes had never happened. "Has it worked? You know, backing away from the public."

Her about-face surprised him. One minute she'd almost lost it and the next she'd fast-forwarded to complete their conversation. For the briefest of moments he had felt contentment holding her in his arms. The few minutes she'd allowed him to embrace her reinforced in his mind what a stick of dynamite this situation was. Her demeanor appeared calm and cool, but when he'd held her and felt her vulnerability he knew better. He knew only too well the masks people wore. He'd been wearing one for most of his life. Trouble was, he wanted her to shed hers while he kept his firmly in place.

"Lana, why do you hide from what you feel? How can you talk about me being honest with you when you can't be honest with me?"

"Because I'm not here to talk about me," she pointed out. "My life is just fine. I'm here to help you and Lily."

"Really now, is your life just fine?"

Gathering all the courage she could muster, she answered, "Yes. I found a way to deal with my tragedy and I live a good and decent life. I have my work, my family, and a good friend in Judy."

Shaking his head as though he didn't believe a word she'd said, he added, "Is that enough for you?"

"Please don't go there, Trevor. I've made peace with the way I live my life."

"It just seems a little hypocritical to me. You can peel back my reserve but I'm not allowed to get anywhere near yours."

"This is not about me, Trevor. I'm here to help Lily. In order for me to do that, I think it's best to find out about what her life's been like. But no one is willing to share any of that with me. Judy claims you won't let her say anything more than she already has. And you—you give me little bits of information and clam up any time I try to dig a little further. Don't you get it? I'm not the bad guy. I'm one of the good guys."

Her frustration made him back down. "I know you're not here to hurt either Lily or me. It's just I'm very overprotective when it comes to her. I never want to see her hurt."

"Do you think I do?"

"Of course not! But I don't think you understand what it's like to walk in my shoes. I have to watch every step I make now with Lily. Her birth has been kept a secret so every photographer out there isn't sitting in treetops or waiting in bushes for the opportunity to snap a few pictures. I absolutely won't allow her life to be turned into a three-ring circus!"

His voice had risen and he paused to calm himself down. "Lana, the more attention I get, the more these vultures sniff me out. I've had to lay pretty low when I'm with Lily, and having you here just adds to the drama of the whole situation. I don't want these low-lifes finding out about you and camping out on your doorstep for a story."

She witnessed the defeated look in his eyes and knew he meant business.

Ah, she thought, that must be why Lily didn't call him Daddy. If she referred to him as Trevor, people wouldn't think he was her father. She now realized what he'd gone through to protect Lily, and to some degree she knew he was probably doing the same for her.

"I don't know what to say to make you understand that I would never do anything to hurt either you or Lily. I promise you that whatever I see or hear will never pass my lips."

"You may not mean to say anything, but stranger things have been known to happen. I live in a different world and you have to trust that I know what I'm doing. Do you think you can do that?"

"I guess I'm going to have to."

Silence prevailed as Lana continued to fill the bag. What else could be said? She hadn't stood in his shoes, couldn't even begin to understand what his life had been like. Maybe Judy was right after all. The only way she was going to get Trevor to trust her was to prove that she was trustworthy. How she was going to do that she didn't quite know.

Trevor continued to hold the bag open until she'd obliterated the mound of the cold winter's remnants. For the first time since he'd met her, he didn't want to run away. He had actually enjoyed their brief sparring and looked forward to further go-rounds.

"How about something to drink?" he asked, seeming genuinely interested in continuing their discussion.

She looked up into his eyes that seemed to change color by the minute. They weren't so green as before; rather, they looked a little grayish now. His tone had softened and she was glad they'd reached a sort of understanding. Most of the understanding was on her part, but she decided she could live with that.

"Sounds good to me."

"Why don't I tie up this bag and meet you in the kitchen in a few minutes," Trevor offered.

"Okay. How about some iced tea?" she asked.

"Sure!" He then closed the bag, spun it around a few times, and placed a tie around the top, without taking his eyes off of her retreating form.

The next hour went by without a hitch. Their conversation flowed easily as they enjoyed the iced drinks and homemade cookies Irma had been kind enough to drop by earlier. Talk of food, weather, and Judy kept the conversation light and manageable. Not once did either of them tread on unsafe territory.

The sound of Lily's voice calling Trevor put an end to their conversation. In just that hour Lana had learned so much about him. He loved barbecues, Chinese food, and any kind of pasta dish. She laughed when he mentioned that though his heritage was mainly Irish, he was sure some distant relative had jumped the fence and procreated with an Italian. He had a keen sense of humor and she found herself amused at so many things he said. She couldn't remember a time when she'd had so much fun.

His brief absence from the kitchen made her realize how comfortable she'd become in his company.

By the time Trevor and Lily descended the stairs, Lana had already washed the glasses and changed into a clean pair of pants.

"Hi, Lily. Looks like you took a nice long nap. How about we check the nest to see if the babies have broken through their shells?"

Lily ran to the back of the house with both Trevor and Lana following close behind. Her sleepiness had been replaced with anticipation at seeing the eggs.

Trevor lifted Lily up as soon as they reached the deck and by the expression on her face Lana knew that nothing had happened as yet.

"No babies," said a disappointed Lily.

Then Trevor pretended to drop her out of his hands, and before Lana could gasp in horror she heard the young girl's giggle.

"Oh, Trevor, you scared me half to death."

Lily was tickled pink that they'd pulled one over on Lana, but Trevor was contrite. "I'm sorry, Lana. I didn't mean to scare you."

"It's just she could get hurt," Lana answered.

He didn't know what to say. He'd been insensitive and felt bad for causing her to react that way.

Lana knew what he was thinking and tried to lighten the mood a little. "Trevor, do you think we could go to the nursery now to pick out some flowers?"

"I think we can manage that. What do you say, Lily? Want to help Lana pick out some flowers for the front yard?"

"Yeah. Me wanna help!"

The momentary fear she'd felt had been quickly forgotten and she was actually excited about the three of them going on their first outing. A feeling of déjà vu lightened her mood. The last time she'd been part of a threesome was with Tom and Jessica. The memory didn't bring a flood of tears as she anticipated, but rather hope. She hadn't really been part of anything since that awful night. She was amazed at how quickly she'd adapted to life here in Vermont. It had only been a few days but in some inexplicable way she felt a sense of belonging.

Life dealt her a harsh blow several years earlier, and for the first time in as long as she could remember, she was hopeful.

Chapter Twelve

Cindy slept the entire ride home from California. The short stop at O'Hare airport woke her briefly, but the minute they were airborne again she fell back asleep almost immediately. When the plane caught a tailwind and landed twenty minutes earlier than expected, she was delighted to be back home.

The past few days had represented a milestone for her as all the baggage she'd tucked away over the last few years had been partially incinerated. There'd always be a place in her heart for the child she'd lost, but the guilt and sorrow had been replaced with a respect for living a healthy life.

On the drive home, she contemplated how she was going to explain everything to Sam. Honesty was what he deserved and honesty was what he was going to get.

She decided against sugarcoating any of it. It'd been a horrible time for her and she was going to spell it out—letting Sam decide their fate. She dreaded the thought of him leaving her, but after what she'd been through over the last four years she had the confidence that she could handle just about anything. She remembered her therapist saying, "What doesn't kill you makes you stronger." For the first time, Cindy truly believed those words.

Sam was sitting on the sofa, looking as if he hadn't slept for days, when Cindy came through the door

Cindy dropped her overnight bag and went to sit next to him. Wanting to break the silence that had filled the room since she'd entered, Cindy said, "Sam, I don't know where to begin."

He didn't move a muscle as she sat down—nor did he even try to comfort her. "Why don't you start at the beginning?" he asked coldly.

"I'm afraid you'll want to leave and I couldn't bear that," she replied as her voice cracked.

Sam had never seen her like this. She'd always been so fun loving and carefree. He hardly recognized this person sitting next to him. He wanted things to be back to normal.

"What have you done with my wife?" Sam asked, trying to lighten the mood.

"She's back and feeling pretty horrible. Sam, I love you." She had to say it. Had to make him understand that nothing she'd done these last two days had anything to do with them.

He couldn't stay mad at her, looking the way she did. He knew he looked like hell but she looked even worse. "Sweetheart, I love you too. Please tell me what's going on."

She knew the time had come to share with him what she had kept hidden for so long.

"Remember when you dropped me off at the diner the other morning?"

"Yeah?"

"Well, I started going through some old magazines and spotted a headline that brought back a time in my life that I'd hoped to forget."

"You've really lost me here, Cindy. What headline?"

"The one about Jamie McKee, the singer, and his death."

"You knew him?"

"Yes. A lifetime ago."

"Why don't you start from the beginning?"

Cindy nodded. "I guess you could say it all began when I left home right after high school graduation…"

Cindy was emotionally drained by the time she had imparted all the ugly details of her past. She hadn't left anything out. Sam sat and listened quietly, offering whatever physical comfort he could during the times when crying left her unable to continue. His soothing hands and gentle fingers had brought her back around so she could finish.

After all had been said, she searched his face for a hint of what he was thinking. "I'll understand if you don't want to have anything to do with me."

Brushing away the tears that once again fell, he softly whispered, "Now why would I want to do that? When I married you I knew you had a past. Hell, I had a past. There are a lot of things I've done that I'm not too proud of, but if you found out some of those things I'd at least hope you wouldn't give up on us. I'm sorry for your pain, even sorrier for what you had to go through, but all of that made you the person you are today. I fell in love with that person and nothing you said today is going to change that."

"Oh, Sam," she cried, as she fell into his open arms. "I was so afraid of losing you. I love you so much."

"I love you too. I'm just surprised that you didn't come to me first, before you flew across the country."

"I couldn't. I hadn't been completely up front with you and I was afraid. I had to face this alone. Knowing you were back here waiting for me helped me get through it."

Holding her even tighter, he whispered, "Don't ever leave me like that again." Then grabbing her face and pulling it up to his own, he said in the sternest voice he could muster, "Look me right in the eyes and tell me there is nothing else in your past that will come between us."

"Isn't that enough?"

"I'm serious, honey. I don't want anything else to pull us apart. I want our marriage to be open and honest. If this is going to work out, we need to have faith in each other. Don't ever put me through what you did the last few days."

"I promise. God has truly blessed me with a second chance and having you in my life is a constant reminder of how lucky I am."

"I'm also very lucky. I fell head over heels in love with you from the first time I saw you and I don't ever want you to doubt my love or commitment again. Okay?"

"Okay," Cindy murmured.

"Alright now, I think you have some making up to do for all the sleep I've missed."

"And what do you suggest?"

"Follow me and I'll show you," Sam said as he led her into the bedroom.

Cindy couldn't remember a time in her life when she'd been so content. Sam's parents weren't entirely pleased about the elopement, but they were slowly warming up to the idea of having a new daughter-in-law. News of Sam and Cindy's marriage spread quickly, and already the girls in Cindy's office, along with Sally and a few of the diner's regulars, had surprised her with a girl's night out and post-wedding shower.

Cindy was riding on a natural high. She was settling in to her new life with Sam and enjoying being back at work. But in all of the excitement, she noticed how tired she felt throughout the day. At first, she'd chalked it up to the stress of dealing with her past and sharing all of those details with Sam, as well as the excitement that came from sharing their wedding news with friends and family. But during the last week she had felt more than just tired. She awoke in the morning with a sour stomach, and the smell of some foods in the afternoon made her feel nauseous. Several times she wondered if she might be pregnant but always disregarded the notion knowing how careful they'd always been.

When her sickness did not dissipate after a couple of days, curiosity finally got the best of Cindy. She waited for Sam to leave the house before she fished out the early pregnancy test kit she'd bought the night before. Since she had never really discussed children with Sam, she decided against saying anything to him. She didn't want to worry him over something that might just be a false alarm, and she wasn't ready to talk to him about something that she herself couldn't bear to think about.

A few minutes later, a stunned Cindy sat staring at the small plastic wand that confirmed what she'd been dreading. She was pregnant. How was she going to handle bringing another baby into the world? What if something terrible happened, like before? How was she going to tell Sam? Did he even want children? She wasn't even sure how she felt about having a baby. Did she deserve to bring another life into the world? She needed to tell Sam. She dressed quickly and called her doctor. She wasn't going to call Sam and get all worked up until she was absolutely certain.

The call the next day confirmed that she was pregnant. Cindy knew there was only one thing to do: call Sam. He'd been her rock since they'd met and she'd been foolish not to involve him in this sooner.

"Hi, sweetheart," he said when he heard her voice.

"Um."

"Honey, what's the matter."

"Sam, I'm pregnant."

"You're what?"

Trying in vain to keep in control, she cried, "We're going to have a baby!"

Cindy's announcement brought on a flood of emotions. He was going to be a father! "That's fantastic, honey," he almost shouted. "I wish I was with you right now so I could feel that precious thing inside you."

The jubilance in his voice rang out loud and clear to the nervous mother-to-be on the other end of the line. His exultation touched her heart as nothing else could. She was relieved by his reaction and knew it was going to be okay. "Do you think you could come home early?"

He looked at the calendar on his desk and saw that his afternoon was free and clear. The heavens were with him on this one, he thought as he looked at his full schedule for the rest of the week. "You bet, darling. I'll leave around four."

As Sam walked through the door, he smelled the aroma of fresh tomato sauce. He hadn't eaten a thing all day, nor had he accomplished anything at work.

Cindy was in the kitchen stirring the splattering red sauce when she heard the door open. He was home. She was glad the morning sickness lasted just that, in the morning. By afternoon she was famished, ready to eat far earlier than normal. She knew making her husband's favorite meal would put him in the right frame of mind for their discussion. She needed for him to understand the myriad of emotions racing through her body. Part of her was totally elated. She loved Sam and the life they shared. Another part of her, however, was filled with trepidation and angst. Memories she'd thought long dead surfaced when the idea of bringing a child into the world became a reality. She'd done that once and failed. She never knew what happened to her stillborn child and, up until now, couldn't bear to know. Was there a service or a burial? What had happened to their baby?

The only one who could answer all of her questions now was Trevor.

In good conscience, she couldn't bring this baby into the world with so much unfinished business. As she'd done with Jamie, she needed to close the door on that part of her life. She needed once and for all to mourn and say good-bye to the child she'd lost. She just hoped Sam would understand her absolute need to go back in time once more.

Rushing up behind her, Sam nuzzled the back of her neck. "Hey, love. Something sure smells great." Placing his hands gently over her abdomen, he whispered, "How's my little guy in there?"

For a minute, Cindy forgot the emotional seesaw she'd been riding most of the day. "Honey, I'm so glad you're home." She dropped the wooden spoon on the stove, placed the lid back on the pot, and turned into his arms, burying her head in the crook between his shoulder and head. "I've been such a mess all day. I don't know whether to be happy or sad about the baby."

Tenderly pulling his wife's face within inches of his own, he asked, "What's this all about, darling? Aren't you happy about the baby?"

Walking away from him to gain some control over her weakening emotions, she responded, "I don't really know how I feel. One minute I'm excited, and then I'm worried something may happen. Then, I just get scared."

"I think that's only natural. Every woman is scared when she's pregnant."

"I know. It's just that every woman hasn't had a stillborn baby. Stillborn because of something she's done." Tears began to roll down her face as she turned away from him.

Sam walked over to her and gathered her fragile body into his arms. "Shh, baby. Don't cry. That was a lifetime ago. Look at this as God's way of giving you a second chance." He lifted her chin and looked directly into her eyes. "You're not that screwed-up kid anymore. You're my wife and together we will bring this baby into the world. I'll be with you every step of the way. And if you think I'm not a little scared, you're wrong. But I have faith that we'll be great parents, and that alone makes this a very exciting time."

His eyes were so sincere and full of love. Cindy had to look away before she explained what else had been troubling her all day. "There's a part of me that believes every word you say. I know I'll be a good mother. It's just that I hadn't realized until I became pregnant that I hadn't dealt with the death of my other child. I was sent away right after she was born and I never really learned anything about her. The midwife told me that my daughter was stillborn and Jamie was taking care of all the arrangements. I was so out of it at the time, I never thought about what happened to her. Did Jamie name her? I mean, I don't even know where she's buried. I need to know exactly what happened after I left."

She was shaking by now, and the desperation in her voice affected him like never before. He wanted to tell her to put it all behind her, but he knew that wasn't an option. She loved deeply and would not be able to get past this until she'd faced it head on. He'd seen it with Jamie's death and knew she had to perform the same personal exorcism with her daughter.

"Honey, look at me," he finally said as he pushed back the sodden hair from her eyes. "I'm glad you didn't run off this time. Together we'll find the answers you need. I'm here to help you! So let me."

She stared into his eyes and knew he meant it. "Did I ever tell you how lucky I am? You are so wonderful, and God knows I don't know what I ever did to deserve you."

He felt the tension in her body begin to ease. "Okay, so where do we go from here?" he asked as he tightened his embrace.

"Do you really mean it?"

"Of course I do. I don't want anything hanging over your head when our baby comes. I want you to feel like this is the start of a new life for our family. If that means taking a step back into your past and clearing up a few issues, then I'm all for it. Where do we start?"

Knowing she wasn't alone gave Cindy the strength to face the last bitter piece of her past.

"Um...I guess with Jamie's partner, Trevor. You know who he is, don't you?

"Of course. Doesn't everyone know about those two?"

"Yeah, I guess they do. It just seems like such a lifetime ago—you know, that world…that scene." Hesitating a little, she let her mind wander back to the days she'd put behind her. "Trevor and Jamie were more like brothers than friends. Jamie told Trevor everything. I used to get so upset because I always felt Jamie cared more about Trevor than me. Needless to say, Trevor and I didn't get along very well and eventually Jamie stopped bringing me around the studio or Trevor's house. When our paths did cross, Trevor hardly gave me the time of day. I ignored it back then, but it really hurt."

"Would you rather I call him and explain?"

"Thanks, sweetheart, but this is really something I have to do. When I was in L.A. after Jamie died, I thought about calling Trevor. I even managed to get his number but I never followed through. Let me get it now."

Chapter Thirteen

The week was almost over and everything had gone smoothly since Trevor and Lana had reached their unspoken truce out on the lawn. Judy had called mid-week, happily reporting that the seminar was going better than expected and she'd be back Friday afternoon. By the tone of her friend's voice, Judy sensed that life at the house was going well.

Within days of Judy's departure, Lily and Lana had become inseparable, which couldn't have pleased Trevor more. After their trip to the nursery when Lana had purchased just about every type of flowing plant and bush that would fit in the back of the truck, both woman and child spent a good portion of each day planting the colorful gems in various spots around the house.

Lily delighted in the task of digging holes, fertilizing the earth, and assisting Lana as they set the delicate stems in each of the holes. Watering each evening was essential, and Lily took great pride in carrying around the heavy watering can, sometimes dousing the plants a little more than necessary.

The robin eggs still hadn't hatched, and at least five times a day Lily made it a point to wander out to the back deck to have a look. She'd already decided that as soon as the babies were born she was going to celebrate with a tea party.

Lana had driven into town one afternoon to visit the Children's Learning Center. She'd stumbled across the center when she had gone in search of a day-care facility the day before. The large playground had caught her eye, before she read the sign on the building. Unfortunately, the facility had already closed for the day, so she made it a point to return the following day.

Lana was quite impressed with the staff and its curriculum. Marge Conlon, the director of the facility and a retired pediatric nurse, gave her a complete tour and sat for over an hour discussing various options for Lily. Marge was warm, witty, and full of piss and vinegar—traits absolutely necessary in successfully handling children. Since Marge was still connected with the hospital, she gave Lana the name of a child psychologist who could also be helpful in diagnosing Lily.

After their meeting, Lana felt confident that she'd found the perfect environment for Lily. Not only was Marge qualified to handle a child like her, the facility itself offered a tremendous number of growth opportunities. Lana couldn't contain her amazement during the tour when Marge showed her all the advancements made in the center over the last year. It seemed funny that in such a remote place, in a part of the country that appeared unchanged for decades, state-of-the-art facilities such as this could be found. First was the computer room which housed several of the latest-model PCs and printers, then the library which was stocked with books that people from all over the state had donated, and the finale, a playground that was one of the grandest Lana had ever come across.

That night after Lily had gone to bed, Lana excitedly told Trevor about the center. It took a bit of convincing, but she got the impression he was warming up to the idea of Lily attending the preschool. Lana stressed how important it was for Lily to be with other children her own age, and she suspected he knew the same. He was still a little gun-shy when it came to Lily interacting with the public, and she knew it was going to take some time to convince him.

Lana had also called the child psychologist Marge had mentioned, and an appointment had been made for later that week. When she broached the subject with Trevor, she sensed he was more nervous about this than anything else. She wondered whether he was up to the challenge if they did find evidence of FAS. She tried to sound positive, telling him how normal Lily seemed, but she still sensed a hesitation on his part. Although he agreed with everything she'd done, he still remained very detached, waiting for everything to be investigated before he made any decisions.

After their discussion about the psychologist, he'd gone to bed early, ending their nightly ritual of hot chocolate around the fireplace. She cherished those evenings alone with Trevor. Although he still seemed somewhat aloof when they were alone, she nevertheless enjoyed his keen sense of humor. She kept the conversations focused on Lily and was content with how their relationship was forming.

When she was alone, thoughts of Trevor frequently crept into her consciousness. As hard as she tried to quash those images, they were beginning to appear more and more often. Finally, she stopped fighting with herself and let them come. What was the harm? She'd convinced herself that she'd never act on them, so why not allow her mind to wander?

More than once she'd wondered what would it be like to lie in his arms and feel the touch of his lips against her flesh, or how his skin would feel beneath her wandering fingertips. Sometimes when he was near she had to clench her hands to ease the ache of wanting to touch him.

Too tired to think anymore, Lana finally allowed sleep to come.

The evenings were the hardest for Trevor. He found it was getting more and more difficult to be alone with Lana after Lily was safely tucked in for the night. True to her word, Lana had kept their conversations strictly focused on Lily. But every time she opened her mouth to speak, all he could think about was enclosing her soft, full lips inside his own and losing himself, if for only a moment, in her sweet scent. So many times he had to stop himself from leaning over to brush a strand of her golden hair away from those cerulean eyes that had a way of melting his resolve.

His only defense was his offense. Most nights Trevor kept aloof, adding a little here and there to the conversation but never really venturing into anything too personal. He didn't trust himself. It was all he could do to just sit there without taking her right on the sofa.

When she had mentioned the psychologist, it wasn't so much that he was apprehensive about meeting the doctor; he was more nervous about spending another minute alone with Lana. He'd tried valiantly over the last several days to keep his distance, but it was getting harder by the minute.

Earlier that morning Lana had gone to town for her meeting with Susan Lake, the child psychologist. Lily begged to go along and when Lana explained that she was going to a meeting where only adults were allowed, Lily started to cry. Trevor had felt totally helpless when several attempts to calm her had failed. Finally, the idea of visiting Ben and Irma sprang to his mind and the petite child's tantrum vanished as soon as she heard the couple's names.

Ben and Irma had been scarce most of the week, and Trevor really missed the pair who'd been his lifeline over the last several months.

As soon as he pulled into the driveway he spotted Ben out back chopping some wood and Irma coming down the drive carrying a handful of fresh flowers to plant around the mailbox.

The minute Lily spotted Irma, she began jumping around the front seat, trying to gain some freedom from the stubborn seatbelt. "Me go see Aunt Irma. Help plant flowers."

Trevor stopped the truck and leaned over to help the struggling child. "Hold on a minute. Let me help you get this thing unbuckled."

Lily was too anxious to stop her squirming.

"Lily, please stop wiggling. I can't get the blasted thing undone."

She ceased then, seeing that he was getting nowhere. When he'd successfully released the belt, he held her arm a moment longer. "Lily, listen. Say, 'I want to go see Aunt Irma,' not 'me want to.' Okay?"

She nodded her head and repeated the phrase. Lana had made it a point to correct her speech and Trevor had taken her lead. He hadn't seen much improvement, but Lana promised that over time Lily would catch on.

"Hi, sweetie," Irma cheerfully said as she opened the door. "I've really missed ya. I'm so glad ya came to visit."

"Me too! Me want to...oh, I mean...I want to help you plant flowers."

A large smile crossed Trevor's face. Lana was right after all.

Irma, sensing that Trevor needed to talk, knelt down by Lily and whispered, "I think Uncle Ben needs some help over by the woodpile. Why don't ya give him a hand and when I'm ready to plant these I'll give ya a holler?"

Lily took the bait and skipped out to the backyard. Irma then walked over to Trevor's side of the truck and gave him a warm motherly hug. "I've missed ya, big fella," she said, tousling the windblown mass on the top of his head.

"Well, we've been sort of busy this week." Trevor avoided her eyes, fearing she'd see right through him. "Lily and Lana have planted flowers all over the yard and I just wanted to let Ben know that things look a little different. Seems like Lana's hobby is gardening, and she's planted and transplanted so many things I hardly recognize the place myself."

Irma noticed the deep lines in his forehead, and guessed there was more to why he'd come to visit. She never let on, though. "Ya don't need an excuse to come by here, son. We've stayed away to let ya get settled in with Lana. Felt like if we came by too much, we'd be interferin'."

"That's nonsense." He looked her directly in the eyes then. "We love seeing you and Ben. Lana really enjoyed your visit on Sunday. In fact, Aunt Judy's due back tomorrow, so why don't you and Ben join us for dinner tomorrow night? I'll stop at the store and pick up a few steaks and we'll have a barbecue."

"Sounds like a great idea. Why don't I bring the salad and my famous chocolate cake?"

"That's great. I know Lily has really missed you and it'll be fun to get everyone together."

Taking his arm, Irma led him toward the house. "Let's go inside and I'll fix us some lemonade."

Trevor was happy to follow. There was so much he needed to get off his chest, and, besides his aunt, Irma was the best listener he'd ever met.

The warmth of the kitchen, coupled with his growing anxiety about Lana, caused Trevor to easily blurt out his troubling thoughts. "Irma, I need to talk to you about something."

Taking a pitcher of lemonade from the refrigerator, Irma turned to face him and asked, "What is it, son?"

"I don't know where to start."

Irma filled two glasses and headed for the chair opposite him. "Why not at the beginnin'. What's happened since we last saw each other?"

Trevor ran his fingers through his hair. "Nothing and everything," he answered. "I mean, Lana's been wonderful with Lily and she's taken to her like a bee to nectar. She's found a great place where Lily can interact with other kids and learn all the things a preschooler needs to know. That in itself scares the living shit out of me."

Irma looked confused. "Why?"

"You know how I feel about taking Lily out in public. I'm petrified that her life will become a circus. Lana doesn't seem to understand that side of my life. She tells me how important it is for me to mainstream Lily, but I'm not convinced that can happen."

"I understand where ya're comin' from, but I tend to agree with Lana. That little girl needs to be with other kids her own age. I don't think enrollin' her in a local preschool will cause a big ruckus. Ya've lived here for the past several months and, to my knowledge, ya haven't been bugged by anyone. Have ya?"

Trevor shrugged. "Well, not so far. But eventually I'm going to have to get back into the swing of things. I'm afraid the minute I come out of hiding, the press will be all over me. I can't chance having Lily be the center of attention."

"Why do ya think the focus will be on her?"

"I'm not sure it would be. I just can't take that chance."

"Would it be so bad if people knew ya had a daughter?"

He hadn't shared anything about Lily's parentage with Irma or Ben and was careful with how he answered her question. "I'd prefer that Lily be kept out of the picture entirely. I don't want her to grow up with people hounding her all the time."

"I don't understand, Trevor. Ya can't keep her hidden away forever. That wouldn't be fair to the child."

Trevor started to squirm in his chair. He didn't like treading this close to the secret he'd harbored since Jamie died. He trusted Irma and Ben with his life, but he couldn't bear to tell them about his best friend's deception. There was so much at stake. He couldn't tell anyone for fear he'd lose Lily forever.

"I hear what you're saying," he finally said. "I just haven't thought the whole thing through yet. She's still so young and I want to protect her as long as possible."

Irma had suspected there was some mystery behind Lily's appearance, but never felt it was her place to probe for the truth. "Until that time comes," she proposed, "when ya return to yar music, I don't think there'd be any harm in lettin' Lily attend the preschool. I think ya should trust Lana's judgment. After all, isn't that why she's here?"

"I guess. It's just I'm a little afraid to let go."

"Ya won't be lettin' go, just sort of lendin' her out a few hours a day."

Laughing a little, he agreed she was probably right.

"So what else is ailin' ya?" Irma questioned. "That look on your face tells me there's more."

The words almost came, then stopped. "I can't talk about it."

"It's Lana, isn't it? You're startin' to care for her."

Trevor hesitated, not really knowing how to react to her assessment. Was he starting to care? Was it that noticeable? He couldn't trust his feelings at this stage in his life. Was it his loneliness that made her so damn attractive or was he truly falling for her? He couldn't be sure.

"I don't know what to think," he managed. "Christ, it's been so long since I've been with anyone I wonder if I'm just, well, you know!"

"Look, I'm no Dr. Ruth but I think ya probably feel more for this girl than ya're willin' to admit. I mean, look at her. She's not only beautiful but has a kind spirit to boot. Ya don't find that combination too often."

Trevor pushed back his chair and stood facing the window to the backyard. Lily was helping Ben stack all the wood he'd chopped earlier that morning. He sat watching for several minutes, his thoughts drifting to what Irma had said. Gone was the excuse that he was just vulnerable and needed a warm body in his bed. Lana had become so much more to him. Still, he was scared—afraid of falling for anyone. He'd gone this long in his life without a soul mate; why did she have to walk into his life now? He wasn't prepared to fall in love. He'd promised himself long ago that he wouldn't end up like his mom, bitter and alone. Why now, when things were so confused and complicated?

He turned toward Irma, who'd been silent, waiting for him to gather his thoughts. Leave it to Irma to wait him out until he was ready to admit what she'd guessed all along. Dragging his hands through his hair, he finally found the words to express the tumultuous emotions swirling inside his head. "I don't know what the hell is happening to me. As much as I try to control my thoughts, I find it impossible to do so. I go to bed thinking about her and when I wake in the morning her face appears before me."

"Have ya told her?"

"Are you nuts? She'd freak if she knew what was on my mind. She made it quite clear from the beginning that she wasn't interested."

"Maybe she's as afraid of fallin' in love as ya are," Irma ventured. "From the little I know about her, I would guess she's built taller walls than ya have. But I ask ya, are ya goin' to let an opportunity like this pass without even tryin'?"

"Christ, Irma, I don't know. The last thing I need right now is another complication in my life. Even if I was ready to start a relationship, I can't promise that it would go anywhere. I mean, she's different from the women I've gone out with...you know...kind of old-fashioned and all. I wouldn't ever want to hurt her."

"Why do ya think ya'd hurt her?"

"I'm not the settling-down kind. Never was and never will be! A person like Lana needs a commitment, and that word just isn't in my vocabulary."

"Bah!" Irma barked. "How can ya say that? Ya've just never been in love. That's what's drivin' ya so nuts about her. I think ya're probably fallin' in love. Oh, I know it can be a bit dauntin' at first, but ya'd be surprised at how wonderful it can be. Look at Ben and me. We fell in love when we were just kids. Fell hard, too. At first I tried to run— told Ben I was too young to get mixed up in a serious relationship. He didn't back off, though. Told me he'd hang around till I came to my senses. It didn't take long for me to realize what a fool I was bein'. One of the most liberatin' days of my life was the day I told him I wasn't goin' to run no more."

"It's just not that easy for me."

"Love ain't easy, darlin'. Think about when ya sit down to write a song—does it take an hour, a day, a week, or a month? Are the lyrics correct the first time or do ya write and rewrite until ya get it absolutely perfect? Do ya spend hours and hours in the studio runnin' all kinds of mixes to get the sound just right?"

"Okay, I get where you're coming from. It's just that I'm not any good at this kind of stuff. Look at my family. My dad left when I was just a kid, and to this day I don't know if the bastard's alive or dead. And my mom, well, she handled the breakup by burying her head so far in the sand that even I couldn't reach her. My dad's name was never mentioned around her and I'm not even sure I understand why he left."

"Didn't yar aunt talk to ya about it?"

"A little bit. But I'm not sure she knows why he walked. I love my aunt and all, but look at her. She's virtually alone. I can't remember a time when she even dated. Her profession always came first. And for that matter so did my mom's. I guess the apple hasn't fallen far from the tree."

"Yeah, but do ya think they're really happy?"

He'd never really contemplated whether or not his mom or aunt was happy. "I'm not really sure. If I'd have to venture a guess, I think my mom is probably the least happy. Aunt Judy loves her work and I think she's content with her life. On the other hand, my mom also loves her work but I don't get the impression she's really fulfilled. I don't think she ever got over my dad's leaving, and because she never really dealt with what had happened, just sort of pushed forward like it didn't matter, a stream of bitterness runs through her veins."

Irma nodded. "I can understand how that could happen. Let me ask ya—do ya see yarself growin' old alone?"

"I've never really thought about it."

"Okay. Let me ask ya: do ya want to grow old alone?"

Trevor began pacing the kitchen. Up until Jamie died, he'd always thought of the two of them growing old together. His music and Jamie had been enough. Getting married, raising kids, and having grandchildren had never been on his agenda. "I don't think anyone wants to grow old alone. But that doesn't mean you have to be married or be with one specific person."

Irma couldn't reconcile his thinking in her mind. "Well, ya may be right about that, but it sure as hell is nice to be with someone ya've had a lot of history with—a person that really knows who ya are and what ya're made of."

Her last comment cut deep. Here he was facing middle age and the only person he'd shared a history with was dead. Most of his friendships, if you could call them that, were superficial—and that, in part, was due to his inability to trust others. "I can't talk about this anymore," he muttered in a voice choked with emotion.

Irma walked over to him and put her hands on either side of his face. She looked directly into his eyes and felt his anguish. "Trevor, don't run away from what ya're feeling. Don't be like yar mom and bury all yar pain. Face it and get on with yar life. Ya have a little girl to build a history with and a woman who's pullin' at yar heartstrings. Let Lana inside. Let her help heal yar wounds."

Just then the door burst open and Lily came running in. "Me wanna drink!"

Irma moved away from Trevor and took the thirsty child in her arms. "Come on, love. I'll get ya somethin'."

Trevor stood motionless, watching the scene before him. Ben had just come through the door, wiping his hands with the handkerchief he always kept in his back pocket, while Irma poured two more glasses of chilled lemonade. The three of them sat down at the table and Ben proudly told of the work Lily and he had done on the woodpile.

How had this happened? Trevor wondered as he watched the others. He'd lost his only true friend but in the meantime had formed deep friendships with both Ben and Irma, had a child to raise, and was living with a woman who'd stolen his heart. Unknowingly, his wall had cracked and love had begun seeping through the crevices. It took a moment for it to settle in, but as soon as it did, he knew what he had to do. He was going to stop fighting all these emotions and start living again!

It was late afternoon by the time they returned home, and Trevor was glad to see the car parked in the driveway. During the drive home, he'd thought about what he was going to do about Lana, and decided to let nature take its course. He wasn't going to fight this battle any longer. He sensed she felt the same way about him and someway, somehow, he was going to break through her veneer.

As soon as Trevor stopped the truck, Lily jumped out and ran up to the porch into Lana's open arms. This petite child had somehow erased all Lana's fears about caring for children, and the desire to return to her former craft had never been stronger. Trevor had come up behind Lily and, for a brief moment, Lana felt the strangest sensation that something had changed.

Trevor wished those open arms were for him, but knew better than to test the waters just now. "Hi, Lana! How'd the meeting go?"

For a moment, she just stared at his handsome face. Sometimes when they were together she became engrossed with all the things she loved about his face—his ever-changing gray-green eyes, the masculine angles of his chin, and the sensual way his mouth moved when he spoke. She'd really missed him this morning.

Lana forced her thoughts to return to his query. "It went really well. I can't wait to tell you about it."

"Good. Tonight we'll go over everything. But for now, what do you say we go for a drive? It's such a beautiful day and I feel like being outside."

Yes, Lana thought, *something had definitely changed since last night. He seemed more at ease with her today. This might be the perfect opportunity to bring him over to the learning center. After all, he seemed to be in an amiable mood and Lily would love the playscape.* "Why don't we go over to the Children's Learning Center? Lily can play outside while I show you around."

When Lily heard this she tugged on his leg. "Me…I mean…I wanna go. Pleeeease!"

As far as he was concerned, the decision had already been made.

Later that night, Trevor tucked Lily into bed after a day filled with excitement and adventure, and then he joined Lana on the couch in the living room.

The day had been a milestone for the trio. After touring the facility, Trevor had actually welcomed the idea of Lily attending the center. During the tour, Lily played outside with a dozen other children, and when Trevor announced it was time to leave she started to cry. It was glaringly apparent how desperate she'd been for the companionship of others her age, so he happily obliged. He let her play a little longer while Lana introduced him to Marge. He immediately liked the woman he'd heard so much about from Lana.

Lily was so excited about the prospect of attending school that she could hardly eat when they stopped at Stokey's for dinner. The day had been long and eventful and she fell asleep on the ride home. As soon as they arrived, Trevor carried her up to bed.

Lana was delighted when he came back down quickly. She was even more elated when he chose to sit on the opposite end of the couch rather than in the rocker across the room. They'd had such a wonderful day that she was reluctant for it to end so soon.

When he was first to start the conversation, she knew something had changed between them. "Thank you for today," Trevor said, turning to face her.

She was moved by his sincerity. "You're welcome. Lily really did love the place. She'll do just fine."

"I know that now. Seeing her with all those other kids made me feel a little guilty that I hadn't done it sooner."

"You can't think like that," Lana protested. "You've only been here a little while and you both needed to get comfortable with the environment before you ventured out. Oh, that reminds me—let me tell you about my meeting with Dr. Lake. She's spent the last twenty years working with children and she's seen just about everything imaginable. Apparently, they've made great strides over the last few years in diagnosing fetal alcohol syndrome. She's involved in a study right now that encompasses people of all ages who have been affected in one way or another by FAS. She explained how they've tailored programs that can test IQs, determine if there are any problems with cause and effect, check for memory deficits or the inability to think in abstract terms…"

"Whoa. Wait a minute. You're going too fast."

"I'm sorry. I guess involving myself in the clinical aspect of this has struck a nerve. Even though I haven't really noticed any of the emotional or academic signs of the syndrome in Lily, it still would be wise to investigate further. So many of the signs don't show up until later, and I think it's just something we need to stay on top of. Don't you agree?"

Trevor held up his hands. "Let's take this one step at a time. I've agreed to enroll Lily in the learning center, and I think it's best to let her get used to that environment first before we introduce her into this other program."

"But if Dr. Lake runs a series of tests, she'll be able to work with Marge to tailor an educational program for Lily—if, in fact, she finds any abnormalities. I really think the two have to run concurrently."

"I just don't want to do it all at once," Trevor stated. "Can't we wait this out a little longer? Let her get used to the center first and then start the other testing down the road."

Lana couldn't fathom why he was being so stubborn on this point. She'd learned not to push with him, though, and remained silent, hoping he'd come around.

He didn't relish that she gave up so easily. It wasn't like her. "Look, Lana. I promise I'll think about it. We've had such a good day and I don't want to spoil it."

She couldn't have agreed with him more. Their afternoon had been just about perfect and she didn't want to mar the remainder of the evening sparring with him.

"Will you at least meet with Dr. Lake and talk about the program?"

"Christ, Lana, you don't give up do you?"

"Not when I think something's this important."

He noticed her bottom lip had protruded just a little in what he guessed was a pout. "You're not going to pull that on me."

"Pull what?" she asked innocently.

"That pouting routine."

"I'm not pouting."

"You certainly are. Here, let me show you." He moved closer and gently rubbed the pad of his index finger over her bottom lip. "See, this here is a pout."

She was startled by his touch but found her body had frozen in place.

Without saying a word, he continued his exploration, first touching her soft lips, and then moving to feel the contours of her cheeks, and then ever so softly he placed his hand around the nape of her neck and pulled her closer.

Too stunned to do anything but follow his lead, Lana leaned in and felt his warm breath mingle with her own.

He was so close now he couldn't have stopped himself even if he'd wanted to. He was desperate to feel her lips against his own. He searched her eyes for some kind of sign, but found they only drugged him further. He gently kissed each side of her mouth before he placed his lips directly over hers, urging the meeting flesh to part. Her lips quivered slightly, which gave him the opportunity to slip his tongue into the warm recesses of her mouth. At first his tongue did a slow dance, sliding this way, then that, urging her to match his rhythm. He could feel her hesitancy, her confusion, and her denial. That didn't stop him, though. He loved the taste of her mouth and the feel of its silky contents. He pushed on, luring her mouth to tango with his own.

She was falling deeper and deeper and knew she should back off, apologize for allowing it to go this far, and walk away. But she couldn't. All her life she'd dreamt of being kissed like this. His mouth fit perfectly over hers. His velvety lips continued to caress hers until she became devoid of rational thought.

Just let yourself go, cried the little voice inside her heart, but the louder one inside her head screamed, *Run—you're not ready for all this*. Unable to decide which course to take, she sat unmoving as he devoured her mouth. Her reflexes, however, had a mind of their own. Before she knew what was happening her hands were around his face and her lips and tongue danced alongside his.

As soon as Trevor felt her submission he deepened the kiss, exploring not only with his mouth but with his hands as well. He molded her body against his while he ran his deft fingers up and down her curved sides and muscular back, and then up to her smooth, unblemished face. Her skin was the silkiest he'd ever felt. He couldn't get enough. Carefully, he pulled her beneath him, never once letting up on the searing kiss.

She could feel herself slipping under him and was powerless to do anything but be led by his masterful mouth and hands. His kiss was intoxicating, bringing her to the brink of oblivion. In all of her life, she'd never felt so sensual or desired. It was as if he were the master and she his willing slave, following his lead all the way.

He wasn't surprised that there was so much passion under her hardened facade. All week the sexual tension had been building and now neither one of them could stop the dance. The need to feel her skin against his own was so strong he had to control the impulse to tear her clothing away. Without breaking their kiss, he lifted his chest a little, slid his hands between them and attempted to unbutton her blouse. He had to still his shaking fingers before he could work the small buttons through the even smaller holes. Finally, the first one sprang free, and the rest followed suit.

Their mouths were fused together as if nothing could pry them apart. Nothing, until they heard the shrill sound of the phone. He didn't want this interlude to end, and he knew that if he answered the phone the moment would be lost.

After the devastating call that had told her the fate of her husband and daughter, Lana couldn't stand the sound of a ringing telephone. Hearing it now reminded her of that time. As swift as a lightning bolt, she tore away from his mouth and tried to sit up. But Trevor's weight made it impossible.

"Just let it ring," Trevor pleaded. Trying to find her lips again, he felt her resistance. "Come on, Lana. I don't want to stop."

"Please, Trevor, it could be important."

"Dammit, who could be calling now?" he growled as he reluctantly rolled off of her and went to answer the phone.

Lana felt like a schoolgirl who'd just been caught in the backseat of her father's car. Never in her life had she acted so wantonly. She quickly tried to erase the memory of what just happened by attempting to fix her disheveled hair with one hand while working the buttons on her blouse with the other. But all the fussing in the world couldn't relieve her memory of that kiss. She wasn't sure of much at that moment, but one thing was certain: never in her life had she been kissed liked that.

Chapter Fourteen

When Trevor reached the shrilling phone, he grabbed the receiver with such a force that he practically pulled the cradle off the wall. Trying to still his beating heart, he breathlessly said, "Hello."

As soon as she heard the familiar voice, Cindy's heart skipped a beat. That voice, that inflection—it took her back to a time she'd rather have forgotten. *Just one more chapter to close,* she silently vowed, *and then it will be all behind me.*

Frustrated that no one was answering, Trevor yelled, "Hello? Is anyone there?"

Sam watched as the blood drained from his wife's face. He noticed that her left eye had begun to twitch and her lips were quivering. He wanted so desperately to still those lips with his own and take her pain away, but he knew he couldn't. Instead, he placed his hand on her shoulder and gently squeezed.

Feeling her husband's touch gave Cindy the courage to respond. "Trevor, it's Cindy."

It felt like the earth had just opened up and sucked him into its core. He sat down on one of the kitchen chairs and raked his free hand through his hair.

When no response came, Cindy felt more at a loss than before. *Doesn't he remember me?* she wondered. Feeling her husband's stare, she knew she had to continue. "Do you remember me?"

Why had he answered the damn phone? Just a moment ago the world had seemed so full of opportunities and promises, and now this.

"Trevor, are you there?"

"Yes, Cindy, I am."

He was getting angry now. How could this woman come back into his life? Hadn't she wreaked enough havoc four years ago?

Her hands were shaking so badly now that Sam leaned over and took one between his palms. His powerful grasp gave her the strength to go on. "I know I'm probably the last person you'd ever have expected to hear from."

"You could say that again," Trevor said, not hiding his disgust.

"I'm really sorry about Jamie, Trevor. I know how much you loved him."

"Gee, thanks for the condolences. I've gotta run..."

"No, please wait, Trevor," Cindy pleaded.

"What is it?"

"Please hear me out. After this, I promise to never call you again."

"I don't have the time for this now, Cindy," Trevor barked.

"Please, Trevor, there's so much I need to explain." She didn't give him a chance to respond before she added, "I've gotten my life back together. I'm married now and I'm going to have a baby. I've been clean now for a few years, and I owe so much of my recovery to Jamie."

"That's great, Cindy. I've really gotta go."

"Please don't hang up. I've got something to ask you."

All he wanted was to get off the phone and forget she'd ever called. She'd ruined his friend's life and he wasn't about to let her ruin his. "What is it?"

Choking back her sobs she said, "I need to know where my baby is buried. Can you at least find it in your heart to tell me that?"

Dammit! Why was this happening to him?

He needed time. Time to sort out what the hell he was going to say. "Look, Cindy, I don't remember."

"That's okay, Trevor. I'm sorry I bothered you." Her hopes faded then. Feeling defeated, she said, "Before I started making a bunch of phone calls, I thought I'd give you a try. Again, I'm sorry I bothered you."

Fear gripped his entire body. He knew she was probably going to start searching for her daughter's death certificate and that just couldn't happen. "Um, Cindy, give me a few days and I'll try and find that information for you. Give me your number and I'll call you back."

She never even wondered why the about-face—she was just glad that he was willing to help her.

"Thanks so much, Trevor. I really appreciate this. My number is…"

He wanted to die. Never in his wildest dreams had he thought she'd one day come back into his life. What the hell was he supposed to do now?

When Lana heard the back door open and close, she guessed Trevor had gone out to get some air. Who could have been on the phone? Why was he turning away from her? Maybe he was embarrassed by what had just happened? God knows, she certainly was. Should she just sit and wait him out? *No*, she thought. *I need to see him and talk this through.*

The night was dark but the crescent moon lit up the sky enough to give her a glimpse of his silhouette on the top step. She knew he had heard her, but he didn't make a sound. She couldn't fathom how one minute he couldn't get enough of her, and the next he seemed to want her gone. She wished she had the strength to say *the hell with it* and walk away, but she knew that wasn't in her character. She'd grown very fond of him, probably had fallen in love with him, and wasn't about to let him shut her out of his life. Not like this.

She walked up behind him and when he didn't acknowledge her presence, she asked, "Trevor, what's wrong? Is it me? What just happened?"

Trevor shook his head. "Please, Lana, just go on up to bed."

"I won't be able to sleep until I know what's going on," she said, looking at him miserably. "Is it about before?"

"No. This has nothing to do with you." He forced himself to stay calm.

"Then it's about the phone call. Has something happened?"

"Dammit, Lana! Please just leave it alone and leave me alone!"

She couldn't have hurt more if she'd stepped on a hive full of swarming bees. His rejection sent her running into the house and up the stairs. Part of her wanted to be more understanding of what he was going through, whatever that was, and the other part wanted to hate him.

For the first time since the death of her husband and daughter, she'd opened her heart up to the possibility of actually finding love again. *Ha! What was I thinking?* She flopped down on the bed and buried her face in the pillow. Tears of pain, humiliation, and then anger dampened the crisp white pillowcase. *How dare he lure me into his arms one minute and toss me aside like day-old bread the next!*

Trevor knew he'd hurt her, but there was so much more at stake now. He couldn't keep a straight thought. How could his world have turned upside down once again? Why had he let things go this far with her? He wanted to call his aunt but didn't have her number. He was relieved that she would be returning the next day. She'd know what to do. He suddenly felt very tired and longed for a good night's sleep. *Maybe*, he thought, *in the morning things won't be so bleak.*

He quietly let himself into the house, being careful not to awaken anyone. He wasn't in the mood to face either Lily or Lana right now.

As he climbed the stairs, Trevor heard the sound of muffled sobs coming from Lana's room. It was as if a knife had been plunged into his heart. He'd gone and done what he swore he wouldn't do—he'd hurt her.

He had to make it right. He cared too much for her.

Silently, he opened the guest room door and by the light of the moon saw her curled-up form in the center of the sleigh bed, her face buried in the pillow.

Sensing his presence, Lana lifted her head and saw him standing there. Turning away, she whispered, "Please leave, Trevor."

He walked over and sat down by the foot of her bed. At that moment, she shifted her body as far from him as possible, drawing her legs up to her chest, making sure there was no physical contact. She looked so small and fragile curled up in a ball; it pained him to see her like this. He wanted so much to take her in his arms, rewind everything from the phone call on, and repeat what had happened on the couch earlier.

Trevor sat for several minutes, and when he couldn't stand the silence any longer, he said, "Lana, please don't cry. I'm sorry about before."

Holding back her sobs, she pleaded, "Please just leave."

"I can't leave you like this," Trevor said, worried about what all this was doing to her.

"I'm begging you. I'll be alright by morning."

"You and I both know that's not true."

He heard her sniffle and knew the tears had not yet abated. "Lana, what happened before—me leaving and not coming back—had nothing to do with what happened between us. That was wonderful. It's the phone call that turned me upside down."

This news should have made her elated—to know that he'd not regretted what had happened—but it didn't. All week she'd jumped through hoops trying to get him to open up and today had been the first day he'd reciprocated. And tonight, after he'd put Lily to bed, he'd proven to her that she was a desirable woman who could love and in return be loved.

She heard his words and sensed they were true, but still couldn't change the terrible despair that racked her body. "It doesn't matter!" she cried out.

Trevor raked his fingers through his hair. "Of course it matters. You matter! This has nothing to do with us." He leaned over to rub his fingers down the length of her leg, and the minute she felt the slightest physical contact she retreated even farther away from him. "Come on, Lana. Please don't do this."

She didn't care that he sounded truly sorry and a little desperate. He'd shut her out one too many times, and after what had happened between them she couldn't forgive him. He'd taken advantage of her vulnerability and proved that their brief moment of intimacy hadn't changed a thing. He still didn't trust her. "I don't want to talk about this right now."

Jesus Christ, he thought. *I have this huge dilemma hanging over my head and I have to deal with this! I should just walk out, say 'the hell with it,' and move on!*

But he couldn't.

"If we don't at least talk, neither of us is going to be able to sleep tonight. Will you please look at me? I promise not to touch you." He stood then and backed away from the bed.

The pleading in his voice disarmed her. He seemed genuinely concerned about her state of mind. She owed it not only to him, but to herself, to see if he'd at least open up and tell her what had abruptly changed his mood. She needed to know if he was ready to trust her enough to explain what had happened.

Trevor then saw her turn toward him. She looked pitiful lying there all scrunched up, her face ravaged by tears. He actually felt physically ill seeing what his actions had caused. He walked toward her, knelt down beside her, and gently pulled her face so that it was within inches of his own. Her traitorous body responded to his touch and she had to quell the urge to wrap her arms around his broad shoulders.

Although it was dark, the moon's rays and the faint glow of the hallway night-light illuminated her face enough to show him how selfish he'd been. He bent a little lower then and kissed the salty tears from her eyes, following the path of her fallen tears. When he reached her mouth he delicately kissed around its perimeter.

She wanted more than anything to forget what had happened and surrender to his lips. But her head refused. Pushing him gently away, she whispered, "Trevor, please stop. Don't do this to me. It's not fair."

"I know it isn't but I just can't stop." He ignored her plea. This time when he went for her mouth, it wasn't as gentle, but more demanding and persistent. He captured her lips in his own and when she went to protest he slipped his tongue into her generous mouth and sped up the tempo.

This kiss was different from the tender exploration he'd made before. His mouth was ravenous, his tongue exploring every inch of her mouth. After he'd devoured the warm cavern, he moved down to her neck and over to her ear, where he changed tactics and lightly nipped at her soft flesh. As he traced the contours of her ear with his tongue, he whispered, "I need you, Lana. Oh, if you only knew how much."

She needed him too in ways even she didn't understand. She'd always been in complete control when making love and couldn't conceive what was happening to her. Her head was telling her to put a stop to this and rewind the clock, erasing any intimacies they'd shared. But every other inch of her body was screaming for it to continue, for it had been far too long since her nerve endings had danced this way.

Tomorrow she'd have to deal with the consequences, but for tonight, she was totally in his hands. As soon as her mind relented to the needs of her body, her mouth and hands took control.

Chapter Fourteen

In their hunger, neither spoke; they just used their body language to do the talking. By the time he'd removed her blouse, his lips and tongue had touched every inch of her upper torso. Then he moved downward, continuing his exploration, savoring the softness of her skin. He kissed, stroked, nipped, and aroused her to distraction. When he started to undo the intrusive belt buckle that stood in the way of deepening their union, Lana's mind opened up the floodgates of doubt she'd suffered earlier. Where was this going? What would a man like him see in an ordinary person like her? Panic replaced the euphoria she had felt just seconds ago, bringing her back to the realization that this couldn't continue. She couldn't lose herself in the moment—there'd be no going back if she did, and for Lily's sake, she had to keep things professional.

Wrapping her hands around his in a viselike grip, she wordlessly let him know that it was time to stop. He didn't fight back, just ceased any further exploration and held still, waiting for her to make the next move.

She released his hands and gently pushed him away, breathlessly saying, "I can't do this, Trevor."

He moved up her body, trying, without words, to show her how much he needed to be with her. This time, though, she refused to meet his demands. As soon as he tried to capture her lips, she escaped and moved away from his searching hands and mouth. "Trevor, please stop. I don't want this to go any further. It's already gone too far."

He took a deep breath, trying to still his pulsating heart. "Honey, please don't stop. We both need this right now." Once again, he tried to pull her close and she retreated farther toward the wall.

"No, Trevor. What we need is to trust each other."

"I trust you."

"No, I don't think you do. If you did you would have told me about the phone call."

Hearing that was like getting hit in the face with a glass of cold water. He immediately sat up and turned away from her, placing his elbows on his knees and his face in his hands. How could he respond to that remark? She was right. He was annoyed at himself for letting it go this far. Christ, what had he been thinking? He knew she wasn't the kind of woman who fell into anyone's bed, but it would have taken a man with Herculean strength to walk away from a person like her. He was just a man after all—a man who hadn't been with a woman in a long time.

"You're right, Lana," he gave in. "We shouldn't have let it go this far. I'm sorry!"

As Trevor stood to leave, she was aghast at his effrontery. To think, just minutes ago, the two of them had almost shared the most intimate of moments, and then, to have him just walk away, was too much to bear. Her head was telling her to calm down and talk this out rationally but her heart felt betrayed and angry. "That's it then. Just walk away like nothing happened!"

"What do you want from me, Lana? You wanted me to stop and I did."

"I want you to be honest with me," she said, feeling around for her blouse. "I want you to tell me what happened before."

Trevor shook his head. "I can't, Lana. There are some things I can't share with you or anyone else. But that doesn't diminish what I feel for you."

"If I don't have your total trust, then this can't happen. Making love is something I take seriously. And, believe me, I was willing to risk it all just a moment ago. Why can't you do the same for me?"

"I just can't," he murmured.

There, she'd heard it. His feelings didn't match her own. If they did, he would have thrown caution to the wind, trusted her, and told her everything. Coming to this conclusion hurt, but at least she knew where she stood. "I'm sorry you feel that way," she told him. "Let's forget this ever happened."

He was frustrated that she could so calmly put aside the depth of their feelings. He hadn't just wanted a warm body tonight—he wanted her! "Do you think you can do that, forget what happened between us?" he demanded.

By now, she'd buttoned her blouse for the second time that night and had moved to a sitting position at the edge of the bed. She watched him pace the room and could tell he was as confused and annoyed with the situation as she was. "I'm certainly going to try. We let this thing between us go too far, and I can't allow my feelings for you...or for this...to interrupt what needs to be done for Lily."

"Well, at least we have that in common. Lily is the most important part of this equation and someday you'll realize why I couldn't tell you everything."

"Someday will probably be too late, Trevor. I'm just sorry that I wasn't able to gain your trust. I was willing to sacrifice everything I believe in tonight, and you weren't." Before the tears fell again she pleaded, "Now will you go?"

He knew he wasn't going to convince her that his feelings were as strong as hers. She'd been right. She'd been willing to risk it all and he hadn't met her challenge. "I don't want to lose you over this, Lana. You mean too much to me."

"I'm not sure you know what that means. People who really care for one another develop a bond that extends beyond the measurement of trust. You haven't given an inch in the trust department."

"There's just too much at stake here, Lana. Can't you just let it go?"

"I'm afraid not." She shook her head. "It's too important to me— like fidelity, honesty, moral code—you know, all the things two people need to be considered compatible."

"I'm sorry then. My feelings for you go deeper than you think, and if you're going to let this stand in our way, then there's nothing more for me to say...except good night." He turned then and walked toward the door, never once looking back.

Friday morning came far too quickly for Trevor. Last night had been one of the worst of his life, and today didn't hold much hope either. So many times during the night he'd almost stormed into Lana's room and relieved himself of the haunting details of Lily's birth, Jamie's pronouncement from the grave, and the unexpected phone call that threatened to destroy everything he'd built around him. All of it was too much for him to think about, never mind burdening her with all the ugly truths. All night, he'd thought about ways of making it up to her. But he knew the only thing that could do that was the truth.

He awoke earlier than expected, surprised that he'd finally been able to fall asleep. He couldn't wait to have some coffee, hoping that the warm strong liquid would soothe his aching soul. He started the coffeepot and was grabbing a mug from the cabinet when he heard the front door open and close. He quickly ran to the living room, hoping to glimpse Lana's slender form, but was disappointed to see she'd already left. She must have gone for a jog, he thought, as he walked back to the kitchen.

An hour later, when Lana still hadn't returned, Trevor's thoughts ran wild. What's happened to her? Did she fall and hurt herself? Does she just need some time alone, away from the house, to think things through? Has some weirdo abducted her? He couldn't stand it any longer. He went upstairs to make sure Lily was asleep before he set out to find her.

He slipped into his Docksiders and grabbed the sweatshirt he'd lent her earlier in the week, taking a moment to breathe in her scent. God, she smelled good, he thought as he pulled the fleece-lined top over his head.

As soon as he reached the trail he began calling her name. When he didn't hear a response, he ran deeper and deeper into the forest, fearing the worst. Where the hell could she be? He raised his voice so that anyone within a half mile could hear him, and still no response. Panic set in and he didn't know where to turn. Should he continue on the path and run the risk of Lily waking, or go back to the house and trust that Lana knew what she was doing? Where had she gone?

Just then he heard the familiar sound of her voice and followed its pitch to a clearing just around the bend. He saw her sitting on a fallen tree, rubbing her right ankle, which, he then noticed, had started to swell.

In all the years since she'd taken up jogging, Lana had never once even pulled a muscle. Her ankle was smarting but not nearly as much as her pride.

She had arisen early that morning, feeling much better than she had the night before. It was during the long dark hours of the night that she'd resolved the dilemma swirling around in her head. Okay, so she'd acted on her sexual desires and things didn't quite work out as she'd expected. At least it proved her theory that men were not going to be a part of her life. Yes, she truly cared for Trevor, but the rational side of her brain had sent warning signals from the very beginning that he was off limits. She'd gone through hell and back over the last four years, and she wasn't about to let a failed romance take her down now. Trevor did look adorable though, all disheveled and worried about her.

"What happened to you?" he asked, rushing to her side. Bending down to examine the damage, he gently reached out to touch the swollen area.

"I tripped on something and twisted my ankle," she told him, trying hard not to show him how much pain she was in. "Thanks for coming to rescue me. I tried to make it back, but couldn't walk on this foot any longer."

"We have to get you back," he said, standing up to survey the area. "Do you want me to carry you?"

"No! I mean, I think if I lean on you, I'll be able to hop on one foot."

"Okay, then let me help you stand." As he lifted her up he could tell she was in a lot of pain. She tried hard not to show it but it was clear that between the ache in her foot and the close proximity of her rescuer she was probably suffering a lot more than the pain in her ankle.

No words were spoken as the two worked their way back to the house. By the time they reached the end of the trail, Lana was out of breath and had been clenching her teeth so tightly that her jaws ached.

Trevor admired her strength, but decided enough was enough. He scooped her into his arms and, despite her protests, carried her into the house. He then placed her on the sofa and began to remove her sneaker and sock to investigate her injury.

She leaned back against the soft pillows, too sore and tired to protest. He was trying to be so careful, but every time he tugged on the stretched sock, cries of pain escaped her lips. Finally, he reached into the drawer of the coffee table, pulled out a pair of scissors, and began cutting away at the white cotton material. "Don't worry. I don't think we'll have to amputate," he said, trying to lighten her mood.

"Thank God for small miracles," she weakly responded.

"I'm not sure what to do here. Do we get ice, heat, both or what? Should we go have an X-ray to see if anything's broken?"

"It's okay, Trevor. I'm pretty sure nothing's broken. We'll just follow the RICE procedure."

"What on earth is a RICE procedure?"

"It's an acronym for rest, ice, compression, and elevation."

Before she even got the word elevation past her lips, he shot into the kitchen, and she could hear the sound of ice trays being emptied. He came back into the room, carrying a plastic bag full of ice in one hand and a blanket in the other. Before she could say a word, he began administering first aid to the ankle.

First, he positioned a few more pillows beneath her foot and then he gently placed the plastic bag around her ankle. After he was sure her foot was elevated enough and the ice was resting on the right spot, he covered her with a blanket. While he'd been getting the ice, he'd lit a fire under the teakettle and the shrill sound now coming from the kitchen let him know the water was ready.

When he came back a few minutes later, carrying a tray with steaming tea, a slice of lemon, and a couple of pieces of toast slathered with the peach jam she loved so much, she could have cried. He was being so wonderful and generous that it was hard to hate him at that moment. Not that she'd ever really hated him, but after last night she'd wanted to.

"You needn't have done all this," she said, slightly embarrassed.

"Why not? I'm paying you back for taking such good care of Lily and me."

"I can't believe this happened to me. I came up here to help you with Lily and I end up being the one who needs help."

"So what?" he shrugged. "You've been great with Lily and I'm sure a little sprained ankle isn't going to change that much around here."

"Yes, it will," she countered. "How am I supposed to drive her to the Children's Learning Center and then to Dr. Lake's for testing?"

He could tell she was becoming frustrated. "Don't go getting all worked up about this. I can drive Lily over to school, and when I think she's ready to be tested by Dr. Lake, I can do that too. I'm not an invalid, you know."

His words had a calming effect. "I didn't mean it that way. I just want to make sure that Lily follows this thing through."

"You don't think I'll do that?" he asked, surprised.

"I don't know. You were so against the idea of Lily attending the school in the first place, and I'm not sure that at the first sign of trouble—and believe me, she'll have some issues in the beginning—you'll be able to see through the tangle. Even though she's excited about attending, there will be times when she'll refuse to share something, or another child will pick a fight for no other reason than he or she woke up on the wrong side of the bed. Because Lily's never been with other kids her own age, she'll have some difficulties with the various moods and personalities of the group. It's important to stick it out and allow her to learn to accept and deal with those kinds of issues."

"I'm not sure I'm ready for all this," Trevor admitted.

"I know that. That's why I wanted to get her started as soon as possible so I'd be around to help both of you adjust."

He thought about what Lana had just said and realized that this arrangement would be ending soon. Lana had done her homework, had met with the appropriate people, and had set a course for Lily. She'd also taken a more personal interest in the child and had worked wonders on her language skills, her alphabet and number recognition, and her stubborn streak. During the week Lily had tried to get away with her usual tantrums, but Lana ignored them as if they weren't happening. The minute Lily saw that they weren't gaining the desired effect, they'd stopped. In just a week's time, Lana had managed to touch their hearts, and he couldn't even fathom what life would be like without her cheerful smile.

He didn't want to think about that right now. He had to focus on Cindy and what he was going to do about that situation. Aunt Judy was expected a little later and he couldn't wait to unleash the latest developments. She'd know how to handle this—he was sure of it!

Lana observed the deep creases in his forehead and knew he carried a lot on his mind. Whatever news he'd heard last night, coupled with their estrangement, had obviously taken its toll on him today. She had to do something to ease some of his tension.

"Trevor, thank you for all you've done. I hope we can get past what happened last night."

"We can talk about all that later. Right now, I want you to get some rest. Lily will be getting up soon, so I think it's best if I leave you alone so you can relax."

With that, he walked away, leaving her to wonder how she could have gotten herself into such a mess.

Chapter Fifteen

Lily heard the crunching gravel sound and knew Aunt Judy had arrived. Before anyone could stop her, she shot out the door ready to share the news of Lana's injury. Lily had been playing Go Fish and Chutes and Ladders with Lana and was beginning to get bored with the games. As for Trevor, he had made himself scarce after fixing Lily a late breakfast and hadn't shown his face since.

Judy came running in after hearing that Lana had been hurt, and expressed sympathy for her friend's plight, offering to do whatever she could to make her comfortable.

Judy was a perceptive old coot, as she liked to say, and sensed that all was not right in the house. Trevor briefly came inside to welcome his aunt, and from the look on his face and the slump to his shoulders, she knew something was terribly wrong. Lana was still hurting from her fall, but Judy knew her well enough to know that there was more going on than just a sprained ankle. She'd called just the other night to let Trevor know that she wouldn't need to be picked up at the bus station because a colleague who lived in the next town over had offered her a ride. During the brief call she had sensed that the week had gone better than expected. So what could have happened in just a day and a half?

Lily, however, was her same charming self, and Judy relished the hours she'd spent in the early afternoon with the child. She had taken

Lily out for a walk, skipped rocks by the lake, and received the grand tour of the newly flowered grounds by the excited child.

With Lily safely tucked in her bed for a nap and Lana fast asleep on the sofa, Judy sought out her nephew. She happened upon him over by the woodpile. *If he cuts any more wood*, she thought, *he'll have to clear the lot next door to stack it all*. She noticed Trevor's face and neck were streaked with a combination of dirt and perspiration, and he looked positively fatigued. "What's troubling you, Trev?"

He quit swinging the axe and wiped the sweat from his brow. "Oh, just about everything in my life."

"What's happened?"

"The worst. Guess who called me last night?"

When Judy didn't reply right away, he answered himself. "No idea? Well, it was Cindy!"

She remembered the doe-eyed beauty and immediately knew what was going through his head. "What did she want?"

"She wanted to know where her baby girl was buried. Apparently she's married now and expecting a kid and wants to finalize what she'd been too strung out to do back then."

Judy had known in her heart that someday Jamie's secret would come back to haunt all of them. She'd held back those thoughts from Trevor the night he shared what had been bothering him after his friend's death, not wanting to add to his already immense burden.

"What did you tell her?"

"I didn't know what to say. She shocked the hell out of me." He put the axe down and led his aunt over to two Adirondack chairs that sat in the middle of the backyard.

"Well, what did you two talk about?" she gently probed, knowing this was a delicate situation that needed to be handled carefully.

"Not much. I said I'd get back to her." Trevor half turned in his seat and stared at his aunt, looking for any sign of what he should do. His mind, though, was too absorbed with what he'd already decided. Taking a deep breath, he added, "I've been struggling with this since I read Jamie's letter, and since the call last night, I've done nothing but think about what would be the best thing for Lily. She loves it here, and Lana's done a lot of research on schools and programs in the area. In fact, we just enrolled her at the Children's Learning Center and she's supposed to start on Monday. Her life's been disrupted one too many times and I refuse to uproot her again so soon."

"Sounds like your mind's made up then. What will you tell Cindy?"

"I'll just tell her Jamie donated her body to science or some hogwash."

Raising her eyebrows, Judy asked, "Do you think she'll believe you?"

"I don't think she'll have much choice."

Judy sat for a moment without saying a word. After Trevor had shared the document left behind by Jamie, she'd held back any words of advice. At the time, Trevor had been far too upset for her to say what was really on her mind. Her first order of business had been to get Trevor back on track. She'd always planned on broaching the subject of Lily's birth when he was strong enough to handle the consequences.

"Could you live with yourself if you lied to Cindy?" Judy asked.

"Christ, I don't know." Then he thought for a minute and added, "Yes, if I thought I was doing the best thing for Lily."

"Don't you think one day she'll want to know the truth?"

"I haven't thought that far ahead," he admitted.

"Well, wouldn't you want to know the truth?"

Trevor's thick eyebrows met in a dark frown. "You're asking the wrong person. I'm forty years old and I still don't know why my dad left."

"Have you ever searched for him?"

"Absolutely not!" Trevor fumed. "What kind of person leaves his wife and a small child?"

"I suspect a very troubled person," Judy said softly. "Have you ever forgiven him?"

"Since when did this become about my father and me?"

"I bring it up because only you can guess what that child will feel later on in life. If Lily finds out that you withheld certain information from her, you could lose her forever. Are you willing to risk that?"

"If I tell certain people the truth now, I could lose her forever anyway."

"Yes, you could. But the way you've been living, sort of hiding out, isn't fair to either you or Lily. Believe me, someday this will all come out, and it's better to face it head on."

Trevor shook his head. "I can't understand how you think I'd will-ingly give up Lily. I love her like she's my own." His throat started to constrict as his voice became heavy with emotion.

Judy leaned forward and took his callused hands in her own. These were painful times for him, and they were going to get worse before they got better.

"Have you talked to Lana about this?" she asked.

"Of course not. This has nothing to do with her."

"Maybe you should get her perspective. She was once a mother and knows how it feels to lose a child. Maybe it's time to forgive Cindy and see things from her point of view."

Pulling his hand out of Judy's grasp, Trevor stood up and began pacing. "Are you nuts? Do you realize the implications of Cindy find-ing out the truth? That can't happen. There's too much at stake."

Judy took a deep breath before she responded. Trevor wasn't going to like what she had to say, but she had to say it. "I disagree. There's far more at stake if the truth doesn't come out. Jamie took on the role of judge and jury when he denied a mother her rights. While I can under-stand his reasons, I can't condone what he did. Can you?"

"I'm not about to judge my best friend. He had his reasons and that's good enough for me. Cindy was a user of not only drugs and al-cohol back then, but of people too. She sucked Jamie in and damn near destroyed him!"

"Is your hatred of her tainting your decision to do the right thing?"

"How could it not? She wasn't a good person."

"Don't you think you owe it to Lily to find out what kind of person Cindy's become?"

"How do I know she's not just sniffing around trying to get some of Jamie's money?"

"You don't know that until you talk to her. You have to have more faith in people, Trevor. The only people you've really let into your life have been Jamie and me. Now Jamie's gone and God knows I'm not getting any younger. I'm so worried that when I'm not around you'll be all alone in this world. I don't want to see that happen. People make mistakes, and who are we to judge them? You have to learn to forgive and have faith in mankind. Cindy was young and foolish back then. Don't immediately think the worst of her now." Judy stood now and took his face in her hands. "I don't want to see you alone anymore. You need to put the past behind you and move forward as well."

"Is that the real reason you brought Lana here?" Trevor asked, drawing away from her.

Judy couldn't tap dance around this one. "In some ways, yes, and in some, no. I knew she'd be right for Lily, but I can't deny that a part of me hoped that the two of you could form some sort of bond. Both of you have suffered loss and I hoped that your shared tragedies would bring you together." Judy hesitated for a moment, then asked, "Did that happen?"

He'd suspected all along that there was more to Lana's appearance than his aunt had let on. As much as he wanted to be angry with her, he found it impossible. Lana had filled a very empty void, even for just a time, and he had her to thank for it.

"Briefly," Trevor reluctantly answered. "Then Cindy called and shot that to hell. I was so devastated after that, all I wanted was to be alone."

Why does that not surprise me? Judy thought. Then she took a small step forward and wrapped her fingers around her nephew's hand. "Trevor, I've never interfered in your life before and I don't intend to start now. You were raised with strong moral values and I know you'll eventually do what is best for everyone involved. I will give you one piece of advice, though. Don't let this situation thwart any chance you have to find happiness. The eventual pain will pass and it makes a whole lot of sense to build on something in the meantime."

Her words of wisdom rang loud and clear in his mind. He wasn't certain if he'd heed her advice, but he sure as hell would give it some thought.

Without another word, Judy left him standing where she'd found him. He had a lot of soul-searching to do, and he needed to do it alone.

Lana was wide-awake when Judy returned to the house. "Hi, Judy. Guess I fell asleep for awhile."

Judy sat in the rocker by the fireplace, gently swaying back and forth. For several minutes she didn't say a word; she just sat peacefully staring into space.

"Judy, is anything wrong?" Lana asked.

"Oh, I'm sorry. I must have been someplace else. I'm just enjoying the peace and quiet. The seminar was very interesting but was packed with people and very noisy. How are you feeling?"

"Oh, much better." Looking down at her ankle, she said, "It looks like the swelling's gone down. In a few days I'm sure I'll be walking like normal. Did I hear you talking to Trevor?"

"Yes. We were out back. Why?"

"I think something happened to really upset him and I was hoping he'd talk to you about it."

"He did," Judy confirmed.

"Is everything all right?"

"I'm not really sure. He has to work it all out."

Lana knew Judy would never divulge anything personal about Trevor, but her vagueness spoke a thousand words. Whatever the call was about, it was something pretty serious. She only wished Trevor trusted her more.

"Did Trevor mention that Irma and Ben are coming for dinner?" Lana asked, trying to change the subject.

"No, he didn't. But it'll be nice to see them. Is there anything we need at the store?"

"As a matter of fact, we need butter."

"I'll just run out and pick some up." Judy stood then and asked, "Anything else you need?"

"Well, if you wouldn't mind, I could use an Ace bandage."

"I'm sure the drugstore will have one," Judy said as she picked up her pocketbook. "I'll be back in a little while. I'll tell Trevor where I'm going on my way out."

"If you can find him," Lana mumbled to herself. She knew he'd been avoiding her since this morning, and although she could understand why, it still hurt. When she'd gone jogging that morning, she'd felt rejuvenated and in control of her life. The minute she'd fallen, though, everything from the night before came charging back. Why didn't he trust her? How could he kiss her like that and then turn away so quickly? Why had she let herself become so involved? She couldn't wait to finish up here. She needed to be back home to follow her carefully woven regimen. Then everything would be back to normal.

Chapter Fifteen

She'd talk to Trevor tonight about when she would leave. She had planned on staying another two weeks until she was sure Lily had adjusted to her new routine. She knew that planning her departure would help her to stay focused.

The evening went by in the blink of an eye. Irma and Ben came for dinner, bringing an assortment of homemade goodies and the finest looking salad Lana had ever had the pleasure of eating. Trevor fired up steaks on the grill, and everyone gathered around the picnic table for the feast.

When the meal was about to be served, Lana hobbled from her post to the back deck, refusing help from anyone. When Trevor appeared ready to carry her out, she snapped that she could make it herself. She immediately regretted the way she sounded and tried to apologize, but he had turned away so fast she doubted he'd even heard her.

After supper Irma and Ben stayed for a few hours, playing with Lily while Judy entertained the group with funny stories about her stay with a bunch of Freudian wannabes.

As soon as the dinner guests had gone, Trevor took a sleepy Lily up to bed and Judy followed suit, claiming she hadn't had a good night's sleep all week. She offered to help Lana climb the stairs but Lana declined, saying she'd slept all day and wanted to sit by the fire. Secretly, Lana hoped that Trevor would come back downstairs and they could clear the air.

That didn't happen.

The minute Lily was asleep Trevor tiptoed out of her bedroom and went directly into his room. He didn't want to face Judy or Lana this evening. He had so much on his mind he wouldn't have been good company anyway.

Lana waited a good long time before realizing he wasn't coming back down. She guessed their nightly conversations by the fireplace had come to an end, and she was surprised at how empty she felt inside. Even if they couldn't have a romantic relationship, which was now out of the question, she had hoped that they could at least go back to the way things had been before. She had enjoyed their light-hearted banter and missed the friendship that had developed.

Finally giving up, Lana rose from the couch and hobbled to the stairs. She had a lot of trouble maneuvering the steps and tried to be as quiet as possible so as not to wake anyone. By the time she'd climbed halfway up, she had to sit down to catch her breath. As she pulled herself up to finish the task, she noticed Trevor standing at the top of the landing.

"Oh, Trevor! I'm sorry if I woke you."

Dammit, why did she have to look so precious sitting there? He could tell she was hurting and hated the thought that she hadn't called for help. Why did she have to be so damn independent?

"Don't worry. I wasn't sleeping. Can I help you the rest of the way?"

Oh, sure, she thought, *avoid me all day long and when I'm at my lowest point, ride in on your white horse.* Aloud she said, "No, thanks, I can handle it."

He watched her struggle, and when it looked as if she was about to take a tumble, he swept down and scooped her up. The minute he picked her up she started to wriggle free from his arms. Gritting his teeth, he muttered, "Don't be so damn stubborn!"

Trevor's strength more than overpowered her own, and Lana ceased flailing her arms but continued protesting, "Let me go! I can do this myself. I don't need your help!"

Trevor could feel her frustration and could see the anger and hurt in her darker-than-usual blue eyes. "Stop this! You need my help and I intend to give it to you."

She felt so helpless in his arms, a feeling she wasn't accustomed to. She wanted to talk to him but not like this. She wanted to be the one in control, and right now she felt about three feet tall. "I don't need anything from you."

He stopped in his tracks. "Why are you so angry with me? All I'm trying to do is help you."

"I don't need your help, nor do I want it!"

Her attitude obviously baffled him. "What's the matter with you?"

"With me?" Lana hissed. "What about you? All day long you've ignored me and now you want to be my knight in shining armor. No way. I'm not some damsel in distress and I don't relish the thought of playing any more games with you."

Instead of carrying her up the stairs, he headed back down.

"Where are you taking me? I want to go to bed."

"Shh, you'll wake the whole house," Trevor said firmly. "We obviously need to talk."

"Well, that would be a first for you!"

"Why are you being so nasty?" he demanded, plunking her down on the sofa.

Before she could struggle to her feet, he sat alongside her and gently eased her back down.

"Please don't touch me," she said. "I'm very tired. Tired of all the secrets, the games, and your moods. Need I go on?"

"Okay!" he conceded. "I'll admit I did try to avoid you all day."

His honesty dissipated some of her pent-up anger and Lana was curious to hear if he was going to elaborate. When he left it at that, the hairs on the back of her neck again stood erect and she had trouble keeping calm. "That's all you have to say? No apology or explanation? Either you have an ego the size of Texas or you just don't get it!" She softened her tone, too tired and sick of everything to fight any longer. "Do you know how that made me feel? Do you even care?"

"I never meant to hurt you, Lana," he said softly. "I just had a lot on my mind and needed some space."

"I'm just having a hard time understanding what's happening here," she replied. "These ever-changing moods of yours are driving me insane. I just wish you could trust me."

"It's not you I can't trust; it's the whole messed-up situation," Trevor corrected. "I just don't want to get you involved."

"Don't you think I'm already involved to some extent? Did what happened between us last night mean nothing to you?"

"Of course it meant something to me," he almost shouted. "What's between you and me has nothing to do with the other thing."

"How can you say that?" Lana asked. "I care about you and if something's bothering you I want to try and help."

"Don't you see? You can't help."

"Why don't you let me be the judge of that?"

He stood up now and began his usual pacing. "My whole damn world is falling apart and I have Florence Nightingale here who thinks she can kiss and make it go away."

That was it. She'd heard enough. "If you're going to be that way, we certainly have nothing to talk about."

"Lana, can't you just let it alone?"

"If that's what you really want, I guess I'll have to. It's just so hard for me to know how to act around you. Call it the nurse in me, but whatever it may be that is tearing you up inside is hurting me too. I care about you and want to help."

He knew she meant every word she said. The trouble was, she couldn't solve this problem. No one could. For the first time he saw it from her perspective. She was a nurse, a healer, and treating pain was an innate part of her. He sat down then and gently pulled her sore ankle into his lap. "You should be keeping this elevated. You know, follow the RICE procedure."

She couldn't help but smile. One minute he was wearing a hole in the rug and the next he was calmly joking with her. "Oh, Trevor, you confuse me so."

He began unraveling the Ace bandage, and when he saw the purple and red speckles around her anklebone, he placed feathery light kisses over the tender area. "I don't mean to."

The feel of his warm breath and supple lips on her skin temporarily eased the ache not only in her ankle but also her heart. "But you do anyway."

"Does this hurt?" he asked as he began massaging around her heel, then arch, and then onto her toes.

She loved his gentleness. As angry as she was with him, his touch had a way of melting her defenses. "Trevor, we can't do this. We made a pact last night that we're just friends. We both know that neither one of us is ready for this."

"Oh, Lana, what's wrong with what we're doing? We're not hurting anyone."

If only that were true. Could he be that blind? "We're hurting each other, Trevor."

Still caressing her foot, he asked, "How can you say that?"

For a moment, she was caught up in the pleasure of his touch, but then reality set in, "Because I'm not like the women you're used to. Making love is not something I do casually to pass the time. I'm just not the love 'em and leave 'em type. Never was and, believe me, never want to be."

"Just because I'm not willing to share everything in my life with you, you see me as some kind of womanizer who's just looking for a quick roll in the hay. Is that it?"

"You're oversimplifying it," Lana retorted. "It goes way beyond your not telling me things. You don't have faith in me. How can I share something so precious to me when you can't do the same?"

He'd never really put making love into the same category as trusting someone. Christ, if he had, he'd probably still be a virgin. "Well, that's where we differ. You put too much emphasis on sex. Haven't you ever felt like letting go and being with someone you were just attracted to?"

She didn't know how to answer that question. It had been so long since she'd thought of a sexual relationship that she'd almost forgotten what it felt like. "I'm not really sure. The few men I've been involved with were not only my lovers but also my best friends. For me, sex was not just the act of intercourse, but a whole host of other things."

He had never really talked to a woman about sex before. He wondered whether or not the women he'd slept with over the last two decades had felt the same way. They seemed happy enough after the fact, but were they really satisfied? He'd never really cared enough to find out.

Neither of them said a word for several moments. Trevor hadn't realized how much he respected Lana until just now. He knew the sexual tension between them was stronger than either of them was willing to admit, but she'd had the strength to hold firm, keeping true to her beliefs. When had he stopped doing the same? Even in the state he was in after Jamie died, he knew the minute he'd read the letter what needed to be done. Nothing could change the fact that deep in his heart he knew the right thing to do. Why hadn't he acted on it?

Trevor slowly eased Lana's foot off of his lap and stood up. He walked over to the roll-top desk, pulled something out of his wallet—a key, she noticed—and proceeded to unlock the large bottom drawer. He retrieved a legal-sized envelope, opened it, and pulled out a white sheet of paper. From her vantage point Lana could see that someone had hand-written a letter, and it was obviously very important to him.

Without saying a word, Trevor turned back to her and handed her the letter. She noticed that his eyes had glossed over and he seemed incapable of speech. This simple act on his part showed her the extent of his feelings for her.

As soon as Lana took the letter, Trevor walked over to the rocking chair, where he sat facing the fading flames with his back to her. Her first impulse was to quickly glance over the letter before he changed his mind and took it away. After reading the first few lines, she stopped. This was something between a man and his best friend, and what right did she have to read it? She, more than anyone else, should have understood the need for privacy.

"Trevor, I'm not sure I can read this."

In a monotone voice, with not even a hint of emotion, he responded, "Why not?"

"I'm not sure. Just your trusting me enough to hand it over shows me how much faith you have in me. I don't need to read it to understand how important it is. Here, take it." She neatly folded the letter and held it out for him.

He turned his chair to face her but didn't move to take the piece of paper. He needed her to read it because only then would she truly understand the hell he'd been living through these past months.

"I want you to read it," he said firmly.

"Why?"

"Because I want you to know the whole story. I need for you to understand why I did what I did."

Lana unfolded the piece of paper and began reading, stifling the Pandora's box feeling that came to mind.

Dear Trevor,

If you get your hands on this letter it means that I have departed this world. First, I want to tell you how much our friendship has meant to me. We met as confused young lads in search of our true selves and our journey together was not only filled with success but a brotherhood that I'd never imagined. Though the blood that runs through our veins is different, I've always thought of you as my brother. What I'm about to tell you deeply troubles me, and I hope with all that I am and all that I meant to you that you will one day be able to forgive me. Before you continue, I ask that you keep an open mind and try to understand the road I chose.

I don't like to write, as you know, so I'm going to get to the point. After Lily was born, I felt desperate and out of control. By then my love for Cindy had turned to hatred and when I saw my little girl, born too early and so small, I couldn't find it in my heart to forgive the woman who'd threatened this small innocent child. I paid the midwife a small fortune to tell Cindy that the baby had died, and I used a bogus mother's name and named you as her father on the birth certificate.

Cindy was so distraught by the news that our daughter had been stillborn, she willingly entered a rehab facility back East. Before she left, I opened a bank account in her name and deposited a large sum of money, making her promise that she'd never contact me again. I lied to you when I said that Cindy had abandoned our child. I kept Lily's birth and subsequent life a secret from the outside world for many reasons. You and I both agreed that it was important to keep her out of the public eye, but I had an even more desperate reason—Cindy. If she ever found out that I'd lied she could have had me arrested, gone after any or all of the money I'd put into a trust for Lily, and, worst of all, gained custody.

I know I've put you in a difficult position, and, believe me, I'm sorry. I only did what I thought I had to do. Growing up with an alcoholic father was more than a tough little shit like me could stand and I couldn't willingly hand my sweet innocent daughter over to a woman like my father. I'd rather have died first!

I tell you this now because with me gone, you will have some very difficult decisions to make. I hope and pray with every inch of my soul that you follow the path I've set for Lily. On record she is your daughter and I know you would never do anything to threaten her well being and happiness.

I end this now with a heavy heart. I didn't like deceiving you, brother, but felt I had no other choice. Please try to understand why I kept this from you and know that it tore me up inside to do so. Take care of our little girl and remind her of the man who loved her more than life itself.

Love,
Jamie

Lana didn't know what to say, how to respond, or where to begin. She could only imagine what losing Lily would do to Trevor.

She neatly folded the letter and handed it back to him.

Neither said a word as he took it from her hand and placed it back in the bottom drawer, securing the lock and replacing the key in his wallet.

He stood for a long time watching the last embers die out in the fireplace before he found his voice. "Well, now can you understand why I couldn't trust anyone with this?"

Truth be told, Lana didn't know how to react to this letter. The person he'd trusted most in the world had not only betrayed him but had left him with an enormous burden. "I don't know what to say," she finally managed. "This must have been a shock for you."

"You can say that again. My best friend goes ahead and dies and then from his grave lets me know what an idiot he's been. Not only that, but he expects me to continue this messed-up charade."

Lana wanted to go to him then and kiss away all of his heartache, but she knew he was too distraught for something as simple as that. The best she could offer was her thoughts on why his best friend had betrayed him.

"Jamie had his reasons, Trevor, and although they may not have been what you or I would've done, you have to at least understand where he was coming from."

"What? Playing God? All he had to do was tell me the truth and together we would have worked something out."

"He probably didn't see that as an option," Lana pointed out. "His love for his daughter obviously overrode all rational thought. You have to stop being angry with him, Trevor."

Trevor raked his fingers through his hair. "How can I stop when it consumes me? My best friend lies to me and then leaves me the task of carrying out his master plan—a plan, I might add, that I never would have agreed to in the first place. Jamie knew it and that's why he kept the truth from me."

"But don't you see that letting your anger control you only keeps you from rising above this? I'm telling you this from experience. When my daughter and husband were killed in the car accident, I was so angry I couldn't think or see straight. At first I was angry with Tom, thinking maybe he was driving too fast or not carefully enough. Then that anger shifted over to me. If I hadn't taken that part-time job, they wouldn't have gone to my in-laws that night. Then I just plain became angry at the world. It wasn't until I let go of some of that rage that I started to heal. It took your aunt's help and a whole lot of spiritual healing to come to terms with my loss."

"You sound like my aunt now," Trevor snorted. "Believe me, I do understand why Jamie did what he did. A part of me has already forgiven him. It's just that I don't know where to go from here. I can't lose Lily!"

"Why do you think you'll lose her?"

"Come on, Lana!" he nearly laughed. "If Cindy knew the truth she'd be all over her like white on rice. Even at four years old Lily is a millionaire. Cindy was a gold digger back then, and if she knew there was money involved she'd be here before you could say compound interest."

"Do you know what happened to her?" Lana probed.

Trevor shook his head, not ready to admit what he did know.

"Do you know if she ever tried to contact Jamie?"

"I don't think so."

"Could you hire someone to find her? If you knew what her life was like now you'd be in a better position to know what to do."

"I don't need to hire anyone," Trevor said through clenched teeth. Reluctantly, he added, "She contacted me."

"She did!" Lana gasped. "What for?"

"According to her, she's gotten her life back on track, is about to have a baby, and wanted some closure on this whole nightmare. I'm supposed to be getting back to her with the location of where her daughter's buried."

Suddenly, she remembered the call from the night before. "Cindy," she said aloud. "That's who called when we were…"

"Yeah," Trevor admitted.

"Oh, Trevor, I'm sorry I made such a stink about that. What did you tell her?"

"At first I was too stunned to even move. Never in my life did I expect to hear from her. After I'd gathered my wits, I made something up about not remembering. When she mentioned something about seeking out the answers, I had to think fast. I told her to give me a few days and I'd get back to her."

"What do you think you'll tell her?"

Trevor's voice lowered. "Hell, I don't know."

The defeated look on his face convinced Lana she had to try to make things right. It was in her nature to heal, and more than anything right now, she wanted to see his eyes sparkle again. The truth! That is what would turn this around. He'd been carrying this burden long enough. She wanted to get him to see Cindy's side...

"I can't even imagine what she's had to live with," Lana began. "I know how I felt when my own daughter died, and I didn't have anything to do with her death. It would've killed me if I had."

Trevor's tone was icy as he said, "I've no sympathy for a person like Cindy. She was a user and couldn't have cared less about that baby. All she wanted was her next fix."

"I've spent a great deal of time working with new mothers who've had addiction problems, and trust me, they don't intentionally try to harm their children."

"How can you say that?" he asked incredulously. "Last I knew, taking drugs and drinking were voluntary actions. I don't believe she wanted to stop."

Now he sounded like Tom. "I just don't think you should judge her, that's all. Be mad as hell, yes, but don't assume she could have stopped." The pain in her ankle had moved up her leg, and she shifted slightly to ease some of the pressure before she continued. "Addiction problems are something you and I can't really understand. Unless you're afflicted, it's hard to know how powerful they can be. Look at all the famous athletes, musicians, and even Wall Street jockeys who find themselves addicted to one drug or another. Good rehab clinics all over the country are bursting at the seams with people trying to kick the habit."

Trevor walked to the rocking chair and firmly gripped the back of it. Staring into the dying fire, he said, "Believe me, I've seen more than my fair share of people addicted. Hell, I think half the people in my business have made it part of their daily food group."

"Don't you ever feel sorry for those people?" Lana asked hopefully. "Do you really think they like living that way?"

"No, I don't feel sorry for them," Trevor insisted. "If I knew I had a problem, I'd get my ass into rehab fast."

Lana frowned up at him. "The only reason you can say that is because you have a rational mind, one that hasn't been saturated by God knows what. I used to volunteer at a woman's shelter, and I saw how hard some of those women tried to kick their habit. Every day of their life is a struggle to stay clean, and even though I can't even fathom how hard it is for them to survive, I can at least lend them some sympathy and encouragement."

"I applaud your generosity but I don't share your sympathy," he said after a moment. "I believe everyone in this life makes choices. Taking drugs and imbibing too much are still learned behaviors, and no one's going to convince me otherwise."

So much of what he'd said mirrored how Tom had felt. Both had strong characters and had trouble identifying with those who weren't as stalwart. "Do you think a person can change?"

"Oh, come on, Lana! What the hell does it matter?"

"Just answer me. Can a person change?"

Trevor hesitated a minute. He had to take care that his answer didn't back him into a corner. "Yes and no. I think people can change some of their behaviors. But I don't think a person can change who they really are."

"Okay then, don't you think you owe it to Lily to see if her mother's changed some of her behaviors?"

"At the risk of seeming heartless, no! She gave up her right to mother that child when she repeatedly got high or drunk during her pregnancy."

"You sound like Jamie now," she said in a cool voice that took him by surprise. "Do you really believe that she should live her life thinking she killed her child?"

Trevor walked to the fireplace and leaned his arm on the mantel. Staring at the fading orange glow beneath the ashy logs, he took a moment before responding, "I know the right answer to that. I just can't involve Lily in all this. Her life will be hard enough because of the things her mother did. I can't in good conscience expose her to that all over again."

Face the Music

"I understand that, Trevor. But what if she truly has gotten her life together? Can you deny a mother her own flesh and blood?"

"Christ, Lana, I think you and I both know the answer to that. It's just not that simple. I can't hand over a child I've loved like a daughter to a virtual stranger. Just think how Lily would react if all of a sudden a woman appeared out of nowhere and demanded custody. Because of Jamie's deception, she'd get it, too."

"I'm sure she wouldn't be that heartless. I have a hard time believing any mother would want to emotionally scar her child. Maybe Cindy would work with you on shared custody or something."

"If Cindy knew her child was still alive and there was a fortune at stake, she wouldn't hesitate to pull out all the stops to gain custody. I know her kind, and believe me, Lily's better off not having anything to do with her."

Lana softened her tone in an attempt to cool the heated discussion. "Yes, maybe the old Cindy would have done something like that. I just think you should investigate her further before you make any decisions. If she turns out to be the person you seem to think she is, you have a tough decision to make. On the other hand, if she's cleaned up her life, there's only one solution. And as painful as it may be, you're going to have to do the right thing. Because if you don't, this thing will eat you up inside."

He knew she was right, but he was too emotionally drained to continue. "It's late and I'm not about to make any decisions one way or another tonight. Come on—I'll help you upstairs."

This time when he hoisted her off the sofa they touched as two old friends would. She knew that the conversation was over for tonight and that, more than anything, he needed a friend. Maybe tomorrow, after they'd had a good night's rest, she'd get him to see reason.

Chapter Sixteen

Judy woke up early Saturday morning and was enjoying the peace and quiet of a household still asleep. Last night she'd awoken when she heard her nephew and Lana. Although the voices were muffled, Judy could decipher a few words, and by the tone of Lana's voice, she knew something had happened to make her friend pretty angry. When Lana didn't come to the room right away, she guessed that they'd gone back downstairs to straighten out whatever it was they were arguing about.

Judy heard her nephew's heavy footsteps coming down the stairs before he entered the kitchen, looking disheveled as usual. The puffiness around his eyes and the deep lines running horizontally on his forehead clearly showed that whatever happened last night had not been resolved, at least not on his part.

"Good morning, Trevor. Looks like you could use some coffee."

He was glad it was his aunt sitting at the kitchen table and not Lana. After they'd gone to bed, he had tossed and turned all night thinking about what she'd said. Even though it seemed like she was offering up suggestions, he knew that deep down, she believed that Cindy should know the truth, no matter what. He couldn't help but feel that her white-bread world in some way sheltered her from the realities of dealing with a person like Cindy. He hadn't gotten into it with her last night, but he wondered if Lana knew the success rate of all those women she'd so generously given her time to, or if she'd followed through with their children to see just how their mother's addiction problems affected their lives. Donating a few hours a week to a woman's shelter was in no way the same as living in it.

Trevor was so lost in thought it wasn't until his aunt placed the steaming mug of coffee in front of him that he realized he hadn't answered her. "Thanks. I guess you could tell how much I needed this."

"Care to share what has you looking the way you do?" Judy asked.

"It's this thing with Cindy."

Judy nodded. "Ah, have you made your decision?"

Trevor took a sip of the hot coffee, strong and bitter, just the way he liked it. "I don't think you're going to like what I have to say."

"Try me," Judy offered, taking a seat opposite him.

"I'm not going to tell Cindy the truth. I can't. I'll make up something about her daughter being cremated and Jamie spreading her ashes over the ocean."

When Judy didn't respond, he continued, "I've thought long and hard over this and I can't betray Jamie. I'm not sure what I would have done had I been in his shoes, but I do know that Lily is happy and well adjusted and I'm not going to do anything to change that."

Judy sat silent, watching his eyes betray what his heart had decided. She had also thought a great deal about his situation and knew that whatever he decided could have devastating consequences. If he didn't tell Cindy the truth, he ran the risk of her stumbling over the information one day or, worse yet, Lily finding out someday and never forgiving him. On the other hand, if he told Cindy the truth, he ran the risk of losing Lily altogether.

"You're not saying anything," Trevor remarked.

"What's to say? Sounds to me like you've already made up your mind."

"I know. I was just hoping you'd support me."

"This is a very complicated situation. It's a 'damned if you do and damned if you don't' decision. Can you live with this lie hanging over your head?"

He didn't answer right away. Then, with the ease of a person totally in command of his decision, he answered, "I have to. I'm doing this for Lily."

"I'm not sure I see it so black and white," Judy ventured. "Someday Lily will grow up and want to know all about her mother. What will you tell her?"

"I don't know. I haven't thought that far."

"Don't you think you should consider that before you make a decision to perpetuate the lie?"

"I can't go against Jamie's wishes," Trevor said in a harsher tone than he would have liked. "I'm sorry. I just can't let that woman into Lily's life. You didn't know her like I did. She was really screwed up and there's no way in hell that I'm going to let her near Lily. In time, I'll come up with something to tell Lily, but for now it has to be this way."

"Well, I guess that's the end of it."

"That's it?" Trevor was incredulous. "You're not going to try to change my mind?"

How could she change his mind when she wasn't sure what she would have done in the same situation? Over the last four decades she'd dealt with hundreds of women like Cindy. Although she'd never given up on any one of those patients, the success rate for someone who had suffered with addiction woes and the loss of a child was dismally low. Cindy's lack of a strong support system from her family and close friends made the odds even greater.

"I'm not sure there is a right or wrong answer," Judy said. "I think the moral thing would be to tell Cindy, but I understand why you're afraid. I love Lily too, and don't want to see her hurt any more than you do. I wish I could say that doing the 'right' thing would work in this situation, but I can't."

"Then you're not upset that I've decided to keep this from Cindy?"

Before Judy could answer his question, Lana appeared in the doorway. Though she looked a hair better than Trevor, Judy knew sleep had not come easily for her friend either, so she greeted her with a cheery, "Good morning, dear. I'll put the kettle on for tea."

Lana was happy Judy was there to smooth over the jitters she'd felt at seeing Trevor. After their brief spat and subsequent conversation last night, she was afraid that he would once again retreat into his solitary world.

Face the Music

Trevor watched as Lana sat across from him. God! She looked beautiful hobbling over to the table. Her hair had been neatly pulled back, with a few wisps falling on her face. She'd donned a pair of slim-fitting black jeans that hugged her in all the right places below the waist, but, by contrast, she wore an oversized sweatshirt that concealed her soft curves above the waist.

"Mornin'. How's the ankle?" Trevor inquired.

His voice didn't hold the usual timbre she'd grown so fond of hearing, and she guessed that after their conversation last night sleep had eluded him as well. "It's much better. Thanks for asking."

Judy watched the scene before her and sensed that the previous evening's disagreement still lingered in the air. Thinking it best to leave the pair alone, she quickly thought up a plan. "You know what I feel like?"

Both Trevor and Lana answered in unison. "What?"

"I could really go for some fresh pastries for breakfast. Is there a bakery in town where we could pick some up?"

The thought of eating something gooey and sweet appealed to Lana this morning. Trevor, not being particularly hungry, couldn't have cared less, but decided he'd enjoy the trek into town to clear his head. "Yeah, there's a small bakery over on Vine Street." Standing up, he continued, "I'll go get my wallet and throw on something decent."

With Trevor safely out of earshot, Judy asked Lana the question she'd been itching to know. "I heard you and Trevor arguing last night. Is everything all right?"

"I'm not sure. Trevor pretty much ignored me yesterday and I was kind of upset last night. I guess I let him have it. I'm sorry if we woke you."

"Don't worry about that. Did you work it out?"

"That part, yes. I didn't let up on him, though, until he finally broke down and showed me the letter Jamie had written."

Judy was shocked. "Other than me, he hasn't mentioned that letter to anyone."

"Well, you know how tenacious I can be," Lana reminded her friend. "I think I might've pushed him too far."

"Why do you think that?"

"I gave Trevor my opinion and I don't think he shared my train of thought."

"And what was that?"

"That he should investigate Cindy before making any final decisions. What if she's turned her life around? Should she suffer for the rest of her life?"

"What did he say to that?"

"I could tell he'd tuned me out by then. He listened, or pretended to anyway, and then feigned tiredness. I don't think I got through to him."

After having heard Trevor's admission, Judy knew he hadn't heeded Lana's advice. Just then she heard footsteps on the stairs and knew Trevor was ready to go. He had to come back to the kitchen to pick up his keys, and Judy intended to make sure Lana accompanied him on his trip to town. As soon as he came into the kitchen, she spoke up. "Lana, why don't you go with Trevor? You know what I like and I'm sure he could use the company."

Lana welcomed the suggestion, wanting to spend some time alone with Trevor to finish what they'd started last night. "Trevor, would you mind if I tagged along?"

How could he say no to the woman who had the uncanny knack of unraveling him at the seams? "It's up to you. I'll go warm up the truck while you get ready."

It wasn't the glowing response she had wanted to hear, but it would do. She carefully stood, remembering not to put too much weight on her bad ankle. Last night, she'd lain in bed for several hours berating herself for the righteous part of her nature that surfaced without warning. She should've held back her comments until she knew how Trevor felt. The situation was tenuous enough without her adding fuel to the already out-of-control fire. She wanted a chance to apologize for her insensitivity and become the listener for once.

They had driven a few miles before either said a word. As usual, Lana couldn't stand the silence and began the conversation. "I want to apologize for last night."

"No need."

He wasn't going to make things easy.

"I shouldn't have nosed into your business."

"You didn't! I'm the one who gave you the letter."

"Yes, I know. It's just that I should've kept my comments to my-self."

"Why? You said what was on your mind. I respect that."

"Yeah, but now I'm afraid you won't want to talk to me about it."

"There's really nothing to talk about. I've decided I'm going to let things stand the way they are for now."

She was surprised he'd made a decision so fast. "What will you tell Cindy?"

"I'll just tell her that Jamie had her daughter cremated and that she should get on with her life."

"Do you think she'll be able to do that?"

"I don't know and, quite frankly, I don't really care," Trevor admitted.

Lana knew Trevor to be a caring and sensitive person and couldn't understand his coldness. Trying desperately not to alienate him, but wanting to hear why he had come to this conclusion, Lana admitted, "I'm worried, Trevor."

He wanted this conversation over. He'd made his decision. "Look, don't worry about anything. I know what I'm doing. Can we talk about something else?"

She wasn't going to be placated that easily. "I worry about you and Lily. I can't help it!"

He wasn't going to get into this with her. "I've said all I'm going to say on the matter. Stop worrying about us…okay?"

He was one of the most stubborn people she'd ever met. Sure, he was a big rock star and was used to getting his way, but she couldn't just turn her feelings on and off like he did his electric guitar.

"Maybe it's easy for a person like you to walk away without a care, but that's not me."

Trevor looked over at her, furious. "What do you mean a person like me?"

"Well, someone who is used to walking away."

Why was he letting her get to him like this? He should just cut off this conversation and demand she remain silent for the rest of the trip.

"Lana, you don't know what you're talking about. I don't want to fight with you; I'm not in the mood."

Once again she'd riled his temper. Why did he bring out the worst in her? She knew she couldn't change his mind, and although she didn't agree with the path he'd chosen, it really wasn't any of her business.

"I'm sorry. I didn't mean to get you mad. Can we forget this conversation?"

"I'd like nothing better."

"Just promise me one thing," Lana asked politely.

A little exasperated that she couldn't let it completely drop, he asked, "What is it?"

"Promise me you'll think about it some more?"

Just wanting to forget the whole thing, he promised he would.

The rest of the trip went smoothly, with talk about the weather, what they'd buy at the bakery, and plans for the remainder of the day. Trevor wanted to take everyone to the nearest ski resort, which ran a gondola up the mountain all year long. The walk for Lana would be minimal and, from what he'd witnessed earlier, her ankle seemed better than the day before. They agreed to pack a lunch, picnic on the top of the mountain, and ride back down before it became dark.

Lana and Trevor arrived home with the baked goods to find Lily up and dressed and waiting for them. It appeared to Judy that Trevor and Lana had worked out their issues on their brief trip into town. In fact, she'd never seen her nephew so attentive to anyone as he was to Lana that day. Judy silently observed as he guided Lana into the gondola, then assisted her as she departed the swaying car. During their picnic at the top, he made sure she was comfortable sitting on the plaid woolen blanket covering the hard ground. She noticed Lana wince every now and again when she forgot and stepped too hard on her right foot, but she didn't allow the brief pain to interrupt their fun.

After they'd eaten lunch, Lily wanted to explore a bit and Judy welcomed the idea of some exercise. It also would give two of her favorite people a chance to be alone in this perfect setting.

When they arrived back from their short hike, Trevor had moved next to Lana and was rubbing her tender ankle. Even though Lana hadn't walked that far, the little bit she'd done had obviously caused the muscles to ache. But the tender look Judy saw on her friend's face was not one of pain but of comfort. Lana and Trevor had obviously patched up their disagreement, and Judy couldn't have been happier.

They stayed longer than originally planned and arrived home several hours later than expected. Since they'd packed a weekend's worth of food and had snacked all day long, dinner wasn't even a thought. Lily had fallen asleep on the ride home and Trevor carried her upstairs for the night.

Lana had begun to unload the backpacks when Judy shuffled her into the living room and told her in no uncertain terms to put her foot up. Judy was happy to do the task alone and was more than willing to get it done quickly so she could go soak in the tub. Like Lily, she felt weary after the long day.

Lily had woken up as soon as Trevor placed her on the bed, and she demanded he lie with her until she fell back to sleep. It took Lily about half an hour to finally doze off, and Trevor used the time to think about the call he was going to make later on.

When he came downstairs, Trevor noticed that Lana had fallen asleep on the sofa. Just moments before, Aunt Judy had stuck her head into Lily's room and quietly mouthed that she was taking a bath and going straight to bed.

Trevor stood at the bottom of the stairs and watched Lana's sleeping form. She seemed so content here in his house and he briefly wondered what life was going to be like without her uplifting presence.

She made him smile like no other could. She also pushed buttons he never thought he had. All day long he'd fought the urge to hold her hand, kiss her full lips, or just lie beside her on the blanket. He loved the way she moved her hands when she spoke—speaking more with body language than with words.

The sadness he'd noticed in her demeanor when they'd first met had faded some over the last week, and in its stead emerged the makings of a carefree spirit he'd never have guessed that she possessed. On the outside she tried to appear controlled and thick-skinned, but he knew differently now. This place had done for her what he hoped it would someday do for him—release him from the cocoon he'd woven after Jamie died.

He tiptoed past, making sure he didn't wake her, and headed for the kitchen. The call he was about to make was something he had to do alone. After tonight, he was prepared to put the entire matter at rest and go on with his life.

Chapter Sixteen

He sat at the kitchen table, pulled from his wallet the number Cindy had given him, and dialed.

For the past few days Cindy had waited for Trevor's phone call. Both she and Sam were prepared to fly out to her daughter's gravesite at a moment's notice to finally close the chapter on the part of her life she'd hidden away for so long. Her pregnancy was going well and Sam was ecstatic about starting a family. Although he understood Cindy's need to finally put to rest her stillborn child, he didn't let her past interfere with the joy he felt about becoming a father.

This pregnancy was so different from the one she barely remembered. Different not so much physically but psychologically. When she'd first found out she was pregnant with Jamie's child, she was excited, hoping it would bring them closer together. For quite a while, she'd felt him slipping away. Carrying his child brought some hope that he would once again love her as before.

That didn't happen. Jamie became angry when he heard the news. He tried to talk her into having an abortion. When she wouldn't hear of it, he became angrier and belligerent. She took the verbal abuse, knowing that deep down inside he was as scared as she was. She made promises that day which she fully intended to keep, vowing she'd stay clean throughout the pregnancy if only he'd give her a second chance.

A second chance was not in the cards. Cindy's depression deepened with every day Jamie didn't show up in the godforsaken countryside he'd hidden her away in. It didn't take long before she'd forgotten her oath and started using again.

Being too absorbed in her own world and far too strung out to do anything about it caused her to lose her child. Those memories had haunted her since the moment she was mentally well enough to understand the consequences of her actions. At first she had been in denial, blaming Jamie for not loving her enough. It wasn't until she accepted some responsibility for what had happened that she started to heal.

It was getting late. The dinner dishes had been put away, and Sam was waiting for her in the living room to watch the romantic comedy he'd picked up at Blockbuster on the way home. Sam had been wonderful, trying anything and everything in his power to keep her occupied since she'd called Trevor.

Just as she was about to turn out the overhead light, the phone rang. Before it had a chance to ring again she leapt across the room and grabbed the instrument.

"Hello!"

Trevor recognized the voice immediately and had to take a deep breath before he put the final touches on the web of lies Jamie had started. "Hi, Cindy. It's Trevor."

She was so excited to hear his voice. "Thanks so much for calling me back."

Oh, God, he thought, *she sounds so happy to hear from me*. He replied, "No problem. I've got that information for you."

She couldn't find her voice. Anticipating this moment was one thing, but hearing the truth was something she hadn't known how to prepare for.

"Cindy, are you there?"

Quietly she answered, "Yes, I'm sorry. This is just such an emotional time for me."

He had to get this over with before he lost his nerve. "Well, I can imagine it is. I didn't know how to tell you the other night, but Jamie had the baby's body cremated. He set the ashes free at Bluff's Point."

Bluff's Point had been a favorite spot of theirs, and knowing that Jamie had thought enough of their time together to do such a thing brought Cindy some solace. She didn't try to stop the flow of tears as they fell onto the receiver. In a voice choked with emotion she responded, "I appreciate you telling me the truth. I have a lot to thank Jamie for and I'm just sorry he's not here to hear it."

Before Trevor could say good-bye she made one more request. "Can I ask you one thing, Trevor?"

He didn't want to continue this charade any longer and would have promised her anything just to get off the phone. "Sure."

"Did Jamie ever forgive me?"

Why was she making this so hard? He'd lied before and was able to pull it off, so why not once more? "Yes, I believe over time he did."

"Thanks, Trevor. I owe him so much, you know. I really believe he saved my life back then. I'm so ashamed of what I did. I never thought I'd find my way back to humanity, but with a lot of therapy, a wonderful rehab clinic, and the love of my husband, I've been able to sustain a clean and healthy life. I work at Brayden's Clinic now, doing for others what was so generously done for me."

She was babbling, she knew, but couldn't seem to stop herself.

Dammit, why had he stayed on the phone to hear all this? He wanted so much to believe she was still the junkie Jamie had shipped east four years ago. "I'm happy for you, Cindy," he lied. "I wish you the best."

Cindy knew he hadn't liked her back then and probably still harbored a lot of resentment. She didn't know why it was so important to her that Trevor know how she'd turned out—it just was. But she could tell by the sound of his tone that he wanted to end the call. "I'm sorry, Trevor. I didn't mean to ramble on. Thank you again for finding it in your heart to call me back."

"Good-bye, Cindy."

The sound of the dial tone rang in her ears for several moments before she was able to hang up the phone. Placing the receiver in its cradle not only cut off any further communication but also put an end to the unanswered questions that had been circling like vultures for the past four years. The need to visit her daughter's grave had disappeared the minute she'd heard the body had been cremated. Just knowing that Jamie cared enough to go to a place where they'd shared so many good times released the vise clenched around her heart.

Lana had fallen into a light sleep, and was awakened when she felt Trevor's presence in the room. It wasn't until he walked into the kitchen that she was able to fully rouse herself from her slumber. Anxious to catch him alone, she was hobbling toward the kitchen when she heard his voice. Since his was the only voice she heard, she knew he must be on the phone.

As she turned to walk away, she heard Trevor say, "Jamie had the baby's body cremated." Too stunned to move, she listened as Trevor created a picture of Jamie freeing his daughter's ashes over some place she didn't recognize. She knew then who was on the other line. Lana felt a deep sadness for the woman who would never know the truth. How could Trevor lie like that? Did he hate Lily's mother that much?

She needed to get away from there fast before he spotted her. All the fondness she'd felt for him disappeared the moment she heard him so casually lie about something so critical. Who did he think he was?

In her haste to retreat, Lana momentarily forgot about her ankle, and as soon as she stepped fully on her right foot she fell to the ground, involuntarily screaming out in pain.

Trevor heard her shriek and ran out of the kitchen. He bent to lift her up, but before he could get his hands around her, Lana retreated as if she'd been stung. He knew then that she'd heard every word.

"Come on, Lana. Let me help you up," Trevor offered.

Lana could barely look at the man she had thought she knew. Judy had told her how sensitive and caring he was, and she too had seen that side of him. She'd even started to care more than she ever thought possible. But when she heard him on the phone, that image was replaced by one of a cold, hard soul who wasn't worthy of her respect. "I can get up on my own," Lana snapped.

Trevor backed away. "I guess you heard then."

"I'm sorry to say that I did." Too angry to hold back, she asked, "How could you?"

"I don't expect you to understand. I had to protect Lily."

"Protect Lily from what?" she nearly shouted. "Her own mother?"

"Exactly!" Trevor yelled. "The mother who nearly killed her! The mother who nearly drove my best friend mad! And the mother who was so screwed up and strung out half the time she didn't know which way was up! Don't you dare make me out to be the bad guy!"

Lana realized she had to gain a modicum of control before their shouting match woke the entire household. "I'm trying to understand your side of all this," she said, wanting to reason with him, "but it's difficult knowing that someone is going to suffer the rest of her life for something that didn't happen."

"I couldn't care less about her suffering. Do you realize the hell she's put everyone close to her through? Hell, her parents couldn't even stand her!"

"I see: an eye for an eye!"

"Don't go there, Lana. I won't discuss this with you or anyone else. I made up my mind and that's that!"

Chapter Sixteen

Once again, he was shutting her out. *Why do I care so much? I should finish what I started with Lily and get the hell out of here,* she thought. And with that in mind, she snapped, "Fine! It doesn't seem like you'll listen to what I have to say anyway. I might as well save my breath! Now please get out of my way so I can get up." She tried to stand, but without the help of a chair or table to lean on she was unable to do so. Too stubborn to ask for help, she started to crawl over to the dining room table.

Trevor had to hold back a laugh as he watched her on all fours. Even through all of this—their shouting, her righteousness, his indignation—he still found her so damn attractive. "Please let me help you. You're going to hurt yourself." Then, without waiting for a response, he hoisted her into his arms and carried her over to the sofa.

"Let me down!" Lana demanded.

Trevor ignored her plea and continued to walk toward the couch. When he reached his destination he dumped her gently on the cushions and walked away without a word.

The minute Trevor entered the quiet of his room, he shut the door behind him, stripped off his jeans, and sank down on the bed, drawing one of the down-filled pillows over his face. He didn't want to see or hear from anyone else the rest of the night!

Jesus, why had he gone ahead and lied to Cindy, knowing full well that she wasn't the person he remembered? Never in his wildest dreams would he have imagined her being sober and actually pleasant. That's just what she was tonight—pleasant. Lana had been right. She had asked him to investigate first before he made his decision on whether or not to carry out Jamie's plans. She had faith in mankind—something he'd never possessed—and believed that people could really change. When had he become so cynical about life? Was it early on, after he was old enough to realize that his deadbeat dad was never going to come back, or had it been later on when his life had spiraled out of control with stardom, money, and power?

He shuddered when he replayed the phone call over in his mind. Why hadn't he heeded Lana's advice and at least looked into the matter before he blurted out the lie?

Here, in the confines of his room, with no one looking on, he answered that question. He had lost Jamie and that almost broke him in two, but losing Lily would be the final blow. As small and young as she was, every time he looked into her beautiful eyes, he was reminded of his best friend. His music, his memories, the scrapbooks filled to bursting—showcasing every concert and hundreds of snapshots covering the last two decades—couldn't hold a candle to the way he felt when he held Lily. Lily was a living, breathing reminder of Jamie. Being with her had grown to be enough. Losing her now would be like losing Jamie all over again.

Lana didn't move from the couch for several hours after Trevor had left. She hated that he lied, hated his stubbornness, hated that he refused to discuss why he did what he did, and most of all, she hated that he'd once again shut her out of his life.

So much had changed for her this past week, and instead of being frightened by the changes, she'd unconsciously welcomed them. Now she had trouble picturing herself behind a desk, looking over budgets, arranging schedules, and preparing reports. A seed had sprouted and she longed to be back on the pediatric floor, administering medications and spreading cheer to a group of children who needed her more than some administration department. And most surprising was her desire to feel love again. She'd not only grown fond of Lily and Trevor, she'd fallen in love with them. There, she'd finally admitted it.

Why, then, was she being so hard on Trevor? Why couldn't she have given Trevor the benefit of the doubt? She guessed that being a mother, even for a short time, prevented her from putting herself in Trevor's shoes. To her way of thinking, holding a grudge against Lily's mother for having an illness most people didn't recognize or didn't understand was insane.

But when Lana was able to set aside her maternal instincts and remember the pained look on Trevor's face when he had shown her the letter, she understood why he'd chosen that path. So why was she so angry with him? Maybe it wasn't so much his decision, but more that he hadn't confided in her first. Or maybe it didn't have anything to do with Lily's situation, but rather her fear of loving someone. Had she unconsciously been looking for the perfect excuse to run back into her shell and escape the world she'd adjusted to so easily? Maybe she was more like Trevor than she had thought. He couldn't take another loss, so he lied to save himself the pain all over again. Similarly, she'd con-jured up issues that would keep them apart.

She needed to see him. She needed to make sense of all this. She didn't care what time it was or whether or not he'd fallen asleep; she had to speak to him that night.

Lana carefully maneuvered her way up the stairs, cautiously watch-ing how much pressure she placed on the tender ankle. When she fi-nally made it to the top, she walked toward Trevor's door. She listened for a moment before she mustered up the nerve to lightly knock.

Trevor was awake when he heard a light tap on his door. He had tried to put this night behind him, but had been unsuccessful, which made falling asleep impossible. At first he didn't want to answer, knowing it was Lana. When he heard a slightly louder knock, he knew she wasn't going to go. Still, he didn't answer, wishing she would get the message. When he heard the faint sound of the handle being turned, he wasn't surprised by her tenacity. It was obvious she had something compelling on her mind and, whether he liked it or not, she was going to make him listen.

"Trevor," she whispered, "are you awake?"

Just hearing that voice sent shivers up his spine. As much as he wanted to be angry with her, he found it nearly impossible. "Yeah, come in."

Lana had trouble adjusting her eyes to the darkness. The faint glow from the night-light in the hallway barely reached into the room, and she could only vaguely make out his form lying atop the covers.

"Can I turn on a light?"

"No!" he said gruffly. "What do you want?"

"Um…" Twisting her hands, she felt totally out of place standing in the middle of his room. "I didn't want to go to bed leaving things the way we did."

He could tell by the tone of her voice how uncomfortable she was in his room. "You should be off that ankle," he said. "Here—come sit on the bed. I promise you'll be safe."

She took several steps forward before she hit the mattress with her knee. Feeling around for a place to sit, she perched at the very edge of the bed.

For several minutes no one said a word. Then she broke through the silence and asked, "Why do you do that?"

"Do what?"

"You know, make me start all of our conversations."

"You're the one who came here to talk," he reminded her.

"Believe it or not, I'm not here to fight with you. I came to tell you that I'm sorry about treating you so rudely. I shouldn't have judged you the way I did."

He should have felt better knowing that she'd at least softened a little, but he found it had the opposite effect. He hadn't expected this of her. Deep in his heart he knew he'd chosen the wrong path. He'd known it the minute the words came out of his mouth. But it had been too late. The script had already been written. And now she surprised him with her generosity. Even though his choice went against everything she believed in, she was capable of the kind of compassion that knew no bounds. She truly was remarkable.

"Thanks."

"It's just…"

"Stop while you're ahead," he interrupted. "I don't want to talk about this anymore tonight."

She felt his body roll toward her and knew she should run, but the minute his searching hands found her clammy palms she was lost. With the gentleness of a warm breeze, he placed feathery light kisses in their center. His hands then moved up her arms and lightly pulled her down to meet his hungry lips. He'd missed those lips, her tongue, the smoothness of the inside of her mouth, and her breathless moans.

She felt herself totally slipping away, and though her mind screamed warning signals, her traitorous body ignored all the red flags and responded in kind. Every pore, nerve ending, and erogenous zone—parts she'd never even have guessed existed—ached to be touched this way. The chemistry between them had been so strong it was almost surreal, but lying partially over him now had the most devastating effect on her sensible nature. All she could think about was memorizing with her hands, lips, and mouth every inch of his body.

Neither spoke as clothes were unbuttoned, unzipped, unhooked, and pulled roughly away from burning flesh. There wasn't enough illumination in the room to actually view their nakedness, which only heightened the sense of excitement as they explored each other's bodies.

Their bodies fit perfectly together like cogs in a wheel, and the light sweat that seeped from their pores provided the perfect lubricant, eliminating any friction from their writhing, twisting forms.

Trevor meant to go slowly, to relish every second she was in his arms, but the need to be inside her and feel her soft flesh surround him was more than he could bear. He started to pull away, fearing he was going too fast, when he felt her fingers tighten around the back of his head and pull him closer. His mouth sought her lips, then her throat, and then moved on down to her breasts, where he suckled and teased the round orbs that grew taught under his silent command.

Sometime during the dance, their positions changed and he found himself on top. His knees gently urged her thighs to part and his hands and deft fingers played her like an instrument. Her hips swayed with his, and when he slid his fingers into her soft fold she cried out before he could stifle her gasps with his open mouth. He wanted to taste her release when the time was right, and from the way she was dancing with him now, that time had almost arrived.

Her soft moans inside his mouth told him what she needed, and when he entered her slowly she arched her back for more. Filling her completely, he pushed deeper and deeper until her body began to tremble and she cried out his name. Wanting to share this moment of complete joy, he gave in to his own release, and together they surrendered to the physical demands of their entwined bodies. Moments later, she could feel his warm breath against her hair and his heart beating rapidly against her own. She tasted a salty tear slip between her lips and was surprised at her response. Never in her life had she felt like this. These tears were not of sadness but of wonderment. She'd given herself so completely to Trevor, more than she'd ever done with anyone else, and the aftermath was almost too much to take. Tom had mentioned once that he sensed she was holding something back, but she hadn't realized what he'd been talking about until now.

As soon as Trevor found the strength to lift his head, he started to place butterfly kisses around her face. When he tasted the salty wetness he couldn't believe it. "What's this?" he whispered into her ear. "Did I hurt you?"

"No," she said softly. "I think I'm just a bit overwhelmed, that's all."

He kissed the salty path from her eyes to her swollen lips before he settled once again on her hungry mouth.

The darkness in the room eliminated any chance of seeing her face, and he needed to know that she was going to be all right with what had just happened. Trying desperately to read her expression with his fingertips, he whispered so closely to her mouth that she breathed in his words. "Are you upset?"

She didn't know how to answer that question, since she didn't even know what she was feeling. Although she had faith that these were not tears of sadness, she couldn't explain exactly what they were. "No."

Outlining every inch of her face, memorizing the exact bone structure, he asked, "Talk to me, Lana. What's going on in that pretty head of yours?"

"I don't know," she answered honestly, her tears now flowing freely. "I think I just need to be alone right now."

He pulled away, sensing that his contact with her was scrambling her thoughts. He needed her to be okay with what had just happened. If she in any way felt used by him, he had to do everything in his power to change her thoughts. "Do you really want me to leave you alone for awhile?"

For someone who prided herself on self-control, she wasn't living up to her reputation. She pulled herself up and started feeling around for her clothes. She was glad it was dark so he couldn't see the embarrassment reddening her entire body. Thoughts of what had just happened seeped through every rational fiber of her being and confusion settled over her like a morning fog.

He tried to reach for her again, but the minute she felt his touch she jumped off the bed, ignoring the pain that shot up her leg. "Trevor, I'm sorry. I just have to go." She could make out the doorway and made a mad dash.

Upon reaching her room, she took a deep breath and quietly opened the door, being careful not to wake Judy. Alone in her bed, Lana tried to still the lingering ache in her body. Her trembling fingertips brushed over her swollen lips where his mouth had so skillfully devoured, then over to her still erect breasts, which seemed to have a mind of their own. Her hands continued their exploration down to her stomach and to the area that continued to throb between her legs. She couldn't explain why her body refused to be sated.

Why had she run? Once again, her strong will overrode the needs of her body. She closed her legs tightly, trying to erase the memories from her mind. And when that didn't do the trick she curled up into a ball and silently cursed her traitorous body. *Why did I let it go this far?* she wondered as tears streamed down her face.

She was both exhausted and rejuvenated, and that combination formed a tornado of thoughts swirling in her head. Too spent to make any sense out of the entire night, she gave up and allowed her tiredness to prevail. *Tomorrow*, she thought as sleep came knocking, *I'll sort it all out.*

Chapter Seventeen

Lana awoke the next morning shortly after nine, surprised that after what had happened the night before she'd been able to sleep at all. She looked across the room to see that Judy's bed was empty and was glad she had some time alone to compose herself before facing anyone. Thoughts of the night before came flooding back, and she seriously considered staying in bed the whole day. But since that would raise questions she wasn't prepared to answer, she reluctantly rolled out of bed.

Part of her was happy that last night had happened. She'd let herself go for the first time in her life, and allowed her body to completely respond to the needs of not only herself, but of someone else too.

Throwing caution to the wind brought along certain risks she hadn't thought about the night before. Sleeping with a patient's father went against the professional oath she'd taken, and she didn't even want to think about what it could do to her friendship with Judy.

How will he be this morning? she wondered. *I need to at least explain why I abandoned him and try to make him understand that last night should never have happened. Hopefully, we'll agree that Lily should be our main focus and the incident from the night before should not be discussed or repeated.*

Feeling a little more in control now, Lana decided it was time to face the day. As she walked down the stairs, she heard voices out on the back porch. Her ears strained for Trevor's voice, and when she didn't hear it, she wondered where he was. Her eyes quickly scanned the spot out front where he usually parked his truck, and when she noticed it was vacant, a sinking feeling invaded her heart.

Assuming what she hoped looked like a genuine smile, Lana headed toward the voices. As soon as she walked out back, Lily gestured for her to come over. Lana walked to the chair Lily was standing on and peered into the nest, immediately observing the small crack in the largest of the powder-blue eggs. "Wow! Did you see it crack?" Lana asked as she hugged the little girl's waist, for the moment forgetting Trevor's absence.

"Nah. It already cracked," Lily insisted. "I staying right here till the baby comes out."

Judy watched the way Lana and Lily stood staring into the nest. During the past week, the two had become very close and she briefly wondered if she'd done the right thing after all. She was so sure Trevor and Lana would instantly bond that she had never really considered the downside if things didn't work out.

This morning when she'd walked down the stairs and spotted the note lying on the table, she'd suspected that something wasn't right. The look on Lana's face when she had stepped outside this morning confirmed her fears. At the moment, though, Lana was as mesmerized as Lily, so she'd have to wait until later to find out what had happened.

Lana was so caught up with the happenings in the nest that she had forgotten to acknowledge her friend, who'd been busy watering the red geraniums they had planted during the week. "Oh, I'm sorry, Judy," Lana apologized. "I got so caught up with Lily I forgot to say good morning."

"Don't worry about it," Judy said, smiling.

"I noticed Trevor's truck is gone. Do you know where he went?"

"Well, I'm not quite sure. He left a note this morning saying he'd be gone for a few days. Said something important came up and he had to leave town."

Lana couldn't believe it! How could he have done this to her, knowing the turmoil she was in last night? And as hard as she tried to conceal the hurt she felt, she knew Judy could see right through her.

Judy didn't want Lily to sense that anything was wrong, so she announced, "Lily, darling, Lana and I are just going to check the flowers out front to make sure they have enough water. You call us if anything happens."

"Oooookay, Aunt Judy," the child promised, still glued to the chair.

Judy took Lana's arm and led her away where they could talk without being overheard. As soon as they were out of earshot, Judy leaned in and whispered, "So what's going on?"

Lana didn't know where to begin, and when tears threatened to fall she turned her head away. "I don't even know where to start."

Judy watched Lana's shoulders slump forward and knew it must be pretty bad. "What is it? Did something happen last night after I went to bed?"

Lana nodded her head yes, but couldn't utter a word.

Judy wrapped her arms around Lana's shoulders and pulled her close. "Please don't cry. Tell me what happened and we'll try to sort things out."

Judy's warm, welcoming arms were just what Lana needed. Judy's strength and ability to make logical sense of things always made the valleys seem more like peaks. "I'm so ashamed of the way I acted last night."

Surprised by this admission, Judy asked, "Why? What happened?"

Lana desperately needed to talk to someone but was very apprehensive. "I'm not sure I can talk about this with you."

"Why not?"

"Because it involves Trevor and I don't want to put you in the middle."

"Why don't you let me be the judge of whether or not I'm going to be in the middle of anything?"

As much as she wanted to blurt out that she'd done the unthinkable and fallen in love with her best friend's nephew, Lana knew she would have to keep that information tucked away for now.

"Oh, Judy," she said as tears began to fall, "I'm afraid I made a mess of things yesterday."

Judy let her cry it out before she took her heartbroken friend's tear-stained face in her hands and soothingly asked that she start at the beginning.

It was as if her mouth had a mind of its own when it started telling the story that her heart was too afraid to recount. "I inadvertently eavesdropped on Trevor's phone call to Cindy last night," Lana began, "and I heard him say that her daughter had been cremated. At first I froze, and then when I realized what I was doing—you know, listening in on his conversation—I turned to walk away and stepped too hard on my right foot. Trevor heard me scream and before I knew it, he was by my side. It didn't take him long to figure out that I'd heard every word."

"Ah, I see. So what did he say?"

"It wasn't so much what he said. It's how I reacted. After I heard him lie to Cindy, I got angry that he could let her believe that her child was dead. I know the pain of losing a child, and in that instant, I felt her pain as if it were my own."

"Could you at least understand why Trevor did what he did?"

"At that moment, no. All I could think about was a mother out there living the rest of her life thinking she'd killed her daughter. I tried to explain what I'd felt when my own child died and the guilt I carried around for months afterward. Part of my downward spiral was thinking that I could have prevented their deaths. Oh, I know now that it wasn't true, but the months that I believed it was were the hardest of my life."

Judy nodded sympathetically, recalling those early times. It had taken months to convince Lana that nothing she could have done would have prevented their deaths. "How did Trevor react when you explained your position?"

"How do you think? He'd made up his mind to follow Jamie's wishes and nothing I said was going to change that."

"I understand how you feel, but I also relate to what Trevor's going through. I don't think he'd be able to handle losing Lily, and I do believe that if he'd told Cindy the truth that's exactly what would have happened."

"But can you condone him lying to spare himself the pain of losing Lily at someone else's expense?"

"I didn't say what he did was right," Judy countered. "I just said I could understand it. Now tell me the rest."

"Well, after the initial shock wore off and I'd had some time to think about it, I saw Trevor's side."

"Let me guess: you never had the chance to tell him so."

"Well, not right away."

"But you did tell him, right?"

"Oh, Judy," she cried, "I totally messed up."

"Come on, Lana. Just tell me what happened."

"I went to his room to just tell him that I'd thought more about it and could understand why he lied to Cindy. But the minute I walked into his room, he asked me to sit on the bed. He didn't say much, just let me do most of the talking, and when I was finished and about to leave he pulled my hand toward him." Sobs wracked her body and Lana became too emotional to continue.

Judy held her close. Although she felt great sorrow for her friend's obvious distress, part of her was glad that Lana was finally letting go. It had been a long time coming. Then when it seemed as if Lana had exhausted all her tears, Judy asked what she'd already guessed had occurred. "Did something happen between you and Trevor?"

Lana nodded, still unable to choke out any words.

"Okay, so things got a little out of control," Judy said kindly. "You're only human, you know."

Hearing Judy's matter-of-fact response gave Lana some hope. "You mean you're not mad at me?"

"Mad at you? For what?"

Lana moved out of Judy's embrace before answering, "For sleeping with your nephew."

"Why would I be mad at you for that?"

"Well, it wasn't very professional of me, and now that he's left, I thought you'd blame me."

"Why would I blame you for something Trevor is famous for? All his life, when things have started to heat up, he's gone into hiding. I'm sure he has a lot on his mind and needed some time away to put everything into perspective. Now what about you? How are you feeling about all this?"

"I'm not quite sure," Lana murmured. "I really care for Trevor and Lily, and it scares me a little. You have to know how hard I've tried to fight my feelings for him. From the first day I met him, I felt this deep connection, and every day since, it's been a battle for me. I tried to stay focused on Lily, hoping that I'd be able to keep my feelings for Trevor at bay. Last night, though, I let my guard down—and look what happened."

"What are you going to do about what happened?"

"I don't know. Last night, when it was all over, I was so overwhelmed. I mean, I kept thinking how wonderful I felt inside but another part of me was terrified of experiencing emotions I'd never expected to feel again. Trevor sensed I was upset and when he tried to get me to talk about it, I ran from the room. I couldn't explain to him what I didn't understand myself."

Judy sensed her pain and uncertainty. Finding love again was scary, and she was sure now that it was probably love that both had begun to feel.

"My heart sank when you told me that Trevor had left for a few days. You know me—I haven't allowed my emotions to rule me for several years. I'm not even sure I ever really let myself go, come to think of it."

She plucked a flower from the azalea bush and studied it without really seeing it. "Trevor sparked something in me that made me want to be totally free. Throughout my life, I'd always been afraid of really letting go. In college when all my friends were getting totally wasted, I was always the designated driver. Everyone who knew me could be sure that I'd always stay in control. I guess I inherited that trait from my mother. When I woke up this morning, I realized that the hell I'd been through years ago was by far the worst that could happen to anyone, and look, I survived. Even a broken heart couldn't come close to what I went through when I lost my family. It actually felt wonderful to be close to a man again, and even if nothing comes of it, I'll always cherish the fact that it was Trevor who chiseled away the wall I'd built."

Lana's words meant a great deal to Judy. Throughout the past few years, she'd tried valiantly to open up Lana's heart enough to at least consider the possibility of finding love again. She knew coming here would enlighten her friend but never guessed it would almost cure her broken spirit. She only wished the same were true for her nephew.

The experience Trevor and Lana had shared the night before seemed to have had the opposite effect on him. Lana was prepared to face what had happened and move on, in whatever direction that was, but Trevor had departed, leaving the matter to hang. Avoidance was the way Trevor handled issues that were emotionally painful. Neither he nor his mother had ever really dealt with Rory's abandonment, which subsequently affected their abilities to coexist in a healthy relationship.

Over the years, Judy had tried to intercede and provide guidance, but her assistance was usually met with disdain. Believing she was too close to the situation, she had let the matter drop, hoping that in time each would seek the help they needed and eventually heal.

"I'm so proud of you, Lana," Judy said, hugging her friend once more. "I wish I could tell you that Trevor has come as far as you have, but I'd just be fooling myself."

Lana knew exactly what Judy meant. She'd finally broken through what Judy had called her invisible shield and in the process had been reborn. Although she still felt a modicum of pain when thoughts of her daughter or husband surfaced, she also realized that feeling anything at all was better than feeling nothing. "It's all still new to him," Lana concluded. "Look at how long it took me to get here."

"I know. It's just that I wish Trevor and I were closer. He keeps so much bottled up inside—always has and probably always will. He's so alone now and I worry about him."

Lana nodded. "Me too. There's so much I want to tell him. I want to thank him for giving me back my life, but I want to make it clear that he owes me nothing. In a few weeks I intend to go back home and jumpstart my life. I want to get back into nursing and volunteer at the women's shelter again. I want my life...no, I need my life to have meaning again."

At that moment, they heard Lily's scream and ran to the backyard. Though her ankle was considerably better this morning, Lana trailed slightly behind Judy, cautiously maneuvering each step.

The child was where they'd left her, but instead of just standing on top of the chair, she was jumping up and down. Fearing Lily would hurt herself, Lana walked over and quickly placed her arms around Lily's small waist. She then followed the child's awestruck eyes and saw that a tiny bird was fighting to get out of its shell.

Lily was so excited she had trouble holding back the hand that wanted to help the little creature emerge. Both Trevor and Lana had repeatedly told her that even the slightest touch would turn the mother bird away from the nest.

As soon as the first bird gained its freedom, the others followed suit. It was just a matter of minutes or so before all the birds were opening and shutting their beaks, looking for something to eat.

Lana quickly ushered Lily away, knowing the mother bird would soon return. The minute they backed away, the mother bird came swooping down, giving a very clear warning to the trio to stay away. How long she'd been watching, Lana could only guess, but she knew that any mother—whether beast or fowl—would do anything to protect her young.

She would have done anything to protect her daughter Jessica, even lie, and with that realization came a deep regret that she'd treated Trevor so badly. How could she have judged him so harshly when she herself, given a similar set of circumstances, would probably have done the same thing?

Chapter Eighteen

Trevor drove half the night without paying much attention to where he was going. When he ended up in Westchester County, he knew his subconscious had taken over the wheel sometime during the trek south. He didn't know exactly where he was, but the minute he saw the illuminated motel sign from the parkway, he knew where he was headed.

It was almost sunrise and he prayed that whoever was behind the counter wouldn't recognize him. The motel was a little on the seedy side, but the neon vacancy sign spoke to him like French vanilla ice cream over warm chocolate-chip cookies. He needed some rest before he carried out his plan, and God help him, he wanted to be wide-eyed and mentally strong when he entered the lion's den.

Memories of the night before infiltrated his thoughts. He had been miserable after Lana ran from his bed. How could she just walk out like that? Didn't she know how much it meant to him that she'd shared herself so completely? Why the tears, when all he'd felt was elation? Why had she refused to talk about it? After all, she was the talker, the one who needed to air everything, while he was the one who preferred to let sleeping dogs lie. He had known all week how vulnerable she was. Why did he let it go this far?

He didn't deserve a woman like her. She was good and honest and he'd become the aloof recluse he'd read about in the tabloids. How could he raise Lily, knowing the lies surrounding her birth? What had he been thinking when he perpetuated the lie with Cindy?

He'd immediately known that she was no longer the woman he remembered, and yet he went ahead with the lie anyway. And then to sleep with Lana, knowing full well he was taking advantage of an extremely fragile person. Had he been so caught up in his own world that he'd temporarily taken a vacation from the value system he'd followed his entire life? Had Jamie's death and subsequent deception turned him bitter and merciless? Would Lily grow to hate him when she eventually learned the truth?

He had to make things right.

Maybe his luck was starting to change. The slightly hunched woman with her eyes fixated on the latest copy of *Soap Opera Digest*, perched on a stool behind the cracked linoleum counter, hadn't given a fig who he was or what he did for a living. She took his credit card, swiped it through the register, and charged him for the two nights he'd requested.

Too tired to even notice the tacky decor of his room, Trevor flopped down on the double bed and slept for the next fifteen hours.

Early the next morning, Trevor sat in his car outside Brayden's Clinic. When Cindy had mentioned working at the clinic, the name had seared itself into his brain. Even though he'd never heard of it before, it didn't surprise him that he'd filed it into his memory. Maybe a part of him always knew he would come looking for her.

He had been sitting for about an hour in the employee parking lot, studying every person coming and going through the large front entrance. Unless Cindy had drastically changed her look, none of the people he'd seen had been her.

The coffee and Danish he'd picked up across the street had been devoured almost immediately, and his stomach was starting to rumble again. He could have used a refill, but was afraid that if he left, he'd probably miss her.

Just as he was about to give up and head for the diner, Trevor spotted Cindy. Although he'd never really warmed up to her, he couldn't deny that she was a beautiful woman. The difference today was that instead of looking into the eyes of an out-of-control teen, he saw a self-assured woman walking through the parking lot.

Chapter Eighteen

He noticed that her once small waist had thickened and guessed she probably had a ways to go before she'd be ready to give birth. Her conservative outfit was in no way indicative of the way she used to dress. Back then her clothes looked painted on, the fabrics shiny.

Cindy's face reminded him so much of the doe-eyed child he'd left in Vermont. Lily's resemblance to her mother was startling, and he knew then that it would have been just a matter of time before the truth came out. He wanted so much to start his engine and race out of there, forgetting that Cindy ever existed. But he couldn't.

Before she had a chance to enter the building, Trevor emerged from the truck and shouted her name. She turned then, and even though the rays of sunlight blinded her, she would have recognized his voice anywhere. "Trevor?"

He'd gone over a thousand times what he would say when he finally confronted her. But all that dialogue he had memorized had vanished and he stood agape, not knowing where to begin.

Cindy walked toward the tall form and repeated, "Trevor?"

He took a deep breath then and answered, "Yeah, it's me."

By now she had moved closer and could see that it was really he. "What are you doing here?"

It was too soon to tell her the truth. "I have a friend staying here."

She had no reason not to believe him and never even questioned the coincidence. "It's good to see you again." She shielded her eyes from the sun with her hand and added, "You haven't changed much."

If she only knew, he thought. Aloud he said, "Maybe not on the outside. Anyway, this is where you work?"

"Yeah. I really love it. Come—I'll walk you in."

"Um, no! I mean, I thought I'd run across the street first and grab a cup of coffee before I came in. Would you care to join me?"

Cindy didn't know how to react. Last week she would have jumped at the chance to spend some time with him and finally put to rest her past life, but now she wasn't so sure. After his call the other night, she had mentally buried her daughter and had moved on. Seeing him today was like digging everything up again and she wasn't prepared to go back there.

"I'm not so sure that's a good idea."

He was a little surprised at her reaction. On the phone it had seemed as if she wanted to continue their conversation and talk about Jamie and her new life.

"Oh, I'm sorry to have bothered you then."

As he turned to walk away, she gently touched his arm. "Trevor, wait. I'm sorry! It's just that seeing you now brings back memories I've tried so hard to put behind me. I'm a different person now."

Trevor nodded. "I can see you've changed, and I'm happy for you. Jamie would've been proud."

Her eyes started to mist and it was too late to stop the few tears that descended over her cheeks. "I owe him so much. If he hadn't forced me to come here, I'd probably be dead by now."

Trevor wanted to reach out and comfort her, but he didn't. "Who knows, you might've had the strength to do it on your own."

Looking into his eyes, she was reminded of Jamie. Even though they didn't look alike, many of their mannerisms were the same. "I don't know about that. I was in here a pretty long time before I finally saw the light."

"And your life now—are you happy?"

"Very much. I have a wonderful husband who knows everything and, believe it or not, still loves me." She was crying in earnest then, and began fishing in her purse for some tissues. "I'm sorry about this. It must be my hormones."

He knew better, though. She would never get over the loss of her child, and knowing he had the power to change that made running away at this moment impossible.

"I didn't mean to make you cry. Why don't you let me buy you and your husband dinner tonight?"

"That's not necessary," she managed, wiping the tears away with the tissue.

"No, I mean it. I don't have any plans and I'd really like to take you out."

Why would he want to take her out when four years ago he couldn't stand the sight of her? Cindy's sixth sense told her something wasn't right. Taking a deep breath, she asked, "What is it, Trevor?"

"What do you mean?"

"I get the feeling that something isn't right here," she said, shaking her head.

Trevor cleared his throat. "There's something I'd like to talk to you about but not here or now."

She was more confused than ever now. What could Trevor have to say to her that hadn't already been said on the phone the other night? "Can I at least know what it's about?"

"It's about Jamie."

Cindy's eyes sought his and when she'd captured them, she said, "Okay...now you've really piqued my curiosity. You're not going to tell me he's not really dead, are you?"

"No," Trevor began, "he left a letter after he died, and I think you should read it."

All these years she'd hoped and prayed that Jamie had forgiven her. Now she would at least know the truth. "Why don't you come over for dinner tonight?" she offered. "I remember how hard it was for you to go out in public."

On her way home that evening, Cindy stopped to pick up the chicken and fajita mix she and Sam would be preparing for dinner. The minute she pulled in the driveway and saw Sam's car, much of the trepidation she'd been feeling during the day vanished. Sam had always said that together they could handle just about anything, and seeing his car made those words seem possible.

They worked together on the meal, never once bringing up the subject of Jamie or Trevor, both realizing it was better not to second-guess what was in the letter.

When the bell rang exactly at seven, both went to the door to greet their guest.

Trevor had been driving around for about an hour. He'd practically memorized all the streets in the small town and noticed there wasn't a bad neighborhood in sight. Cindy lived in a townhouse whose parking lot was filled with every foreign luxury car on the market. He found himself looking for schools, playgrounds, and clusters of children. There seemed to be plenty of each.

He glanced at his watch just as he was about to do another loop around the block and realized it was almost seven. His armpits felt wet and his hands were clammy as he parallel parked in front of their unit.

He wanted to turn and run, pretending this was just a bad dream, but the part of him that had forced him to come here in the first place took over and guided him to the front door.

Sam was the first to extend his hand in welcome. He had a nice enough face, some would even say handsome. When he stared into Trevor's eyes with a silent "don't hurt her any more" warning, Trevor's nervousness intensified twofold. His first thought was to stuff the letter deeper into his pocket and make up some story about its contents.

After initial pleasantries were exchanged, they moved to the spacious living room. Cindy had once again surprised him. The masterfully decorated room was filled with expensive casual furnishings. The colors were warm and soothing, with splashes of brightness provided by the many pillows propped on the oversized couch and chairs.

Sam offered their guest wine or beer, and when Trevor requested beer, Sam excused himself to retrieve the drinks. With Sam out of the room, Cindy felt more nervous than ever. All day she wondered what it would be like to have Trevor in her home, and now that he was here, she couldn't think of a single word to say.

Trevor was first to break the silence. "You have a lovely home."

"Thank you. Right after we got married, we splurged and bought all new furniture. In fact, we're in the process of decorating a nursery upstairs."

"Oh. When's the baby due?"

Cindy lowered her gaze and patted her stomach. "Four and a half months."

He stared at her a moment and said, "You look great. Everything going okay with the pregnancy?"

"Well, the first three months were pretty ugly," Cindy said, rolling her eyes. "But now I'm feeling just fine."

"Then I'd say that pregnancy surely agrees with you."

He was being so kind and gentle Cindy didn't know what to think. This was not the person she remembered. "Thanks, Trevor. I'm really glad to see you again. There's so much I have to apologize for. I don't know where to begin." Tears pooled in her eyes and she had trouble keeping herself together. "I'm sorry. I swore I wasn't going to do this."

Cindy then excused herself to help her husband with the drinks. As she entered the kitchen, Sam caught a glimpse of her red-rimmed eyes and suggested, "Honey, why don't you go splash some water on your face and I'll entertain Trevor?"

Leave it to Sam to always protect me, she lovingly thought as she walked toward her husband, who was having a little difficulty balancing the tray of beverages on one hand. With the other hand, he wiped away the last vestige of her tears.

"You're going to be fine," he assured her. "Take your time. I'll keep Trevor company. Just come back when you're ready."

"Thanks, Sam," Cindy said, clearing her throat. "I just need a few minutes."

Sam leaned over and gave her a warm soft kiss. "You'll be fine, darling."

Sam entered the living room carrying two frosted pilsner glasses with just the right size head and a third glass filled with what appeared to be seltzer with a slice of lemon. Trevor gladly accepted one of the ales and immediately downed about a quarter of the liquid, extinguishing the cottonmouth he'd felt the minute he stepped through the door.

Sam felt extremely protective of his wife at the moment. He'd always liked Trevor's music. He probably owned several of his CDs. But right now, he wasn't feeling too friendly. "I'm going to be straight with you, Trevor, and I expect you to be the same," he said, motioning for Trevor to take a seat. "I won't allow you or anyone else to hurt my wife."

Trevor took a seat on the sofa, not at all surprised by Sam's attitude. If he loved someone as much as he guessed Sam loved Cindy, he would have done the same. "I haven't come to hurt her."

Sam sat across from Trevor, leaning slightly forward. "Then do you mind telling me why you're here?"

He knew that imparting this news to Sam first wouldn't relieve him of having to tell Cindy, but at least he might be able to gauge from Sam's reaction how she might respond. "I'm afraid that what I have to tell Cindy will alter your lives forever. I'm just not sure this is the right time—you know, in the condition she's in."

"What are you talking about?" Sam demanded.

Trevor didn't like games himself, and lest he rile Sam any further he thought it best to just show him the letter before Cindy returned. Then it would be up to Sam to determine if his wife was strong enough to handle the truth.

Fishing in his pocket for the letter, he began, "After Jamie died, his lawyer called me into his office. I thought it had to do with Jamie's estate, but when he handed me this," he held up the envelope, "I was shocked."

He handed Sam the crumpled envelope. "Why don't you go ahead and read it yourself? Then maybe you can tell me what the hell I'm supposed to do with this information, because God knows, it's been eating away at me since I read it."

Sam took the once-white envelope and pulled out the letter without an ounce of hesitation. He wanted this thing over and done with before his wife came back into the room. He quickly scanned the letter, then went back over it a second time to fully digest what was written.

Neither said a word for several seconds. Then Sam looked directly at Trevor, his face expressionless, and asked, "Did Jamie hate her that much?"

Trevor didn't know what to say. Even though Cindy had told him that Sam knew everything, he didn't know how much that really meant. "I'm not sure hate is the right word. I'd say overprotective of his daughter would be more accurate."

"But to let someone believe that she'd killed her own daughter, no matter the circumstance, is inhumane," Sam declared.

"I understand how you feel. But I can also understand why Jamie felt he needed to protect his daughter. I don't know how much Cindy's told you, but it wasn't a pretty sight back then. Jamie must have felt he had no alternative."

"I can't think about that now," Sam said, lowering his voice a notch. "I'm more concerned about how Cindy's going to take the news. She's more fragile than we think, and I'm worried how she'll react."

Just then, Cindy walked in and heard her protector's words. "Okay, what's going on? I may seem fragile because my hormones are directly tied to my tear ducts, but trust me, after what I've been through I think I can handle it."

As soon as she saw what her husband was holding, she asked, "Please, Sam, let me have it. It's obvious you've already read it and I think it's only fair that you let me in on whatever it is you think I need protection from."

Sam glanced at the letter, then back at his wife, unsure of what to do. But the expression on Cindy's face clearly showed that she wasn't going to back down. He knew at that point there was no option.

Cindy reached for the envelope, pulled the letter out, and read without interruption. Halfway through, never taking her eyes off the page, she felt around for the chair behind her and sat as if her body had become too heavy for her legs. When she finished reading the letter, she dropped it to the floor, pulled her legs up close to her chest, and stared into space, too shocked to show any emotion at all.

When Sam stood to walk over, she put her hand up to halt any further progress. "Please, Sam, I'm all right."

She looked at Trevor then, and with quivering lips asked the same question he'd heard just moments before. "Did Jamie hate me that much?"

Trevor watched as tears cascaded down her face. "No." He couldn't stop his own tears from forming and had to look away before he lost his composure completely.

A few minutes later, when he had regained some control over his emotions, he took a deep breath and turned back to face her. "You know what Jamie grew up with, and I think he wanted to spare his daughter the same fate. I'm not sure he gave any thought to what it would do to you."

She wrapped her arms around her legs and began gently rocking back and forth. She had heard every word he said, and even understood some of the rationale, but couldn't get past the shock that had momentarily paralyzed her brain.

Sam immediately sat down on the floor by her chair and tried to console her. She was unreachable at this point, and he started to worry. "Cindy, look at me!"

The tone of his voice—one she hadn't heard before—snapped her back to reality, and the minute she saw his worried expression she fell into his arms and sobbed until every drop of water had drained from her tear ducts.

Sam cried alongside his wife, sharing her sorrow, not in the least embarrassed by his actions.

Trevor wanted to leave, thinking it best to give them some time alone, but found he was rooted to the couch. Unable to do anything but feel their despair, he sat in purgatory, doing penance for his part in all this.

When Cindy had exhausted all feelings of distress, new sentiments rose from the ashes. This startling information gave the word "bittersweet" new meaning. She had a daughter. She wasn't responsible for anyone's death. Jamie wasn't perfect after all.

Just then she felt flutters of movement in her swollen belly and gently stroked the area, whispering, "Did you hear that you have a sister?"

Sam backed away then and watched his wife regain her equanimity. Clearing her throat, her voice still a bit raspy, she said, "I know how hard this must have been for you, Trevor. You loved Jamie and went against his dying wish to do the right thing, despite your feelings for me."

"I just wish it was Jamie sitting here today sharing this news with you. He never should've kept her from you."

"No, he shouldn't have. For him to do what he did and let me suffer all these years..." She couldn't continue.

Sam and Trevor sat transfixed, afraid anything they said would seem inappropriately trite. Their pained expressions caused Cindy to quickly pull herself together. What was done was done, and she'd learned only too well to leave the past behind her. Jamie had his reasons for acting the way he had, and nothing could be done about it now. She had to move forward.

"Tell me what she's like," Cindy asked, her voice filled with emotion.

Trevor didn't hesitate; he just let the words flow as if he'd said them a thousand times. "Well, Lily's really beautiful both inside and out. She loves animals, flowers, books, and puzzles. She loves watching Barney and listening to Raffi tapes. Here—let me show you a picture." He extracted from his wallet a small photo and handed it to her.

The little face staring back at her was like looking in the mirror years ago. Cindy's hand shook as she brought the picture closer, memorizing every detail of the child's face. Though Lily's hair, nose, and eyes were exact replicas of her own, the shape of her mouth had a hint of Jamie.

Her eyesight suddenly became blurry, as once again the dam broke, and she let the tears flow freely. "Look, Sam. She has my eyes."

Sam studied the picture, noticing so many of his wife's features—the doe-like eyes, dark hair, and small features. "She's as beautiful as you are, honey."

Unashamed of her raw emotions, she pleaded, "Tell me everything, Trevor. From the minute you saw her, to her first steps, her first words, everything!"

It was almost two in the morning when Trevor unlocked his motel room door and fell onto the faded spread. The gamut of emotions he'd experienced had taken their toll, and he was drained. On the drive back, he had talked to Jamie for the first time since his death. He wasn't a very spiritual person, or so he thought, until this evening when he'd felt Jamie's presence the minute he started driving away.

At some point during the one-way conversation, his initial anger had turned to self-pity when he relived what his life had become since he had been forced into solitude. Even though he'd had Lily's love and company, a part of him had always known it was temporary.

He talked to his brother of the abandonment, anger, and hurt he had felt—the first time when he was old enough to notice his father's absence, and then again after Jamie's death and subsequent deception. He talked aloud of Cindy and what had become of her life. He even admitted to being wrong where she was concerned, and apologized for not trusting him enough all those years ago.

He then spoke of his betrayal and inability to carry out the request written in the letter. When lightning didn't strike, he talked of giving up custody—allowing the bond to form between mother and daughter, which never should have been severed in the first place.

To say he was despondent was too light a word. He'd done the right thing tonight. His conscience was now clear. But the thought of losing Lily had ripped open the wound that had just begun to heal.

They hadn't gotten around to talking about Lily's fate tonight, but they all knew what would eventually happen. She deserved to be with her mother.

He had never felt so alone in his life. Sleep would be his enemy this evening when he needed it most. He wanted to go home to California and immerse himself in his music. For the first time since Jamie's death, he wanted to compose and lose himself in the process. He needed to be lost for a while.

Rolling off the bed, Trevor threw the few clothes lying around into his bag. He left the key on the bureau, shut off the light, and never looked back.

Chapter Nineteen

On Tuesday morning, too early for anyone—including the sun—to be up, Lana sat on the front porch. The past few days had been mentally exhausting for both her and Judy. Trevor had left, leaving behind a note that only told them he'd be gone for a few days, and no one had heard from him since.

Judy had cancelled all her appointments for the week and decided it best to stay on. Both women were concerned that when Lily found out Trevor had gone away for a couple of days she'd throw one of her tantrums. That didn't happen. Surprisingly, Lily hadn't responded to Trevor's absence. She was more excited about the baby birds than anything else and had stayed focused on watching every move they made.

As she sat outside in her usual spot, she gently rocked back and forth, analyzing the events of the last two days. Trevor's disappearance had taken her by surprise. After their night together, she suspected things would be a little uncomfortable, but she never expected that he'd run away. All day Sunday she had waited for him to call, and when midnight rolled around she'd finally given up and gone to bed.

When he still hadn't returned Monday morning, Lana began to worry. It was Lily's first day of school, and if Trevor wasn't lying in some ditch somewhere, he deserved to be. She had understood why he needed some space and actually welcomed the brief respite herself. But the fact that he hadn't even called to make sure everything was all right was frustrating. Luckily, Lily was so excited about school and the babies in the nest that she hardly noticed he wasn't around. Lana's ankle was healing nicely, and she was happy that she'd be able to drive Lily to school without any problem.

On their way to school, Lana had thought about what Trevor had missed. Lily had been so precious getting everything ready for her first day. Filling her backpack with crayons, pencils, and her favorite trinkets was a new experience for the child. She helped Aunt Judy pack her lunch and even added some extra goodies, just in case one of the other kids forgot theirs.

She ate quickly and then went out to the nest to tell her new family why she wouldn't be visiting them until later. She could hardly stand still when Lana posed her for a photo. "Every child needs a picture of their first day of school," Lana said as she quickly took a few shots before Lily dashed out the door.

Lily could barely contain herself when they pulled into the parking lot. A few of the kids she'd met the previous week recognized her and called her over to the playground, and she was off before Lana could kiss her good-bye. Marge was standing in the doorway and made it a point to greet the new child before she joined the others.

On the drive back, Lana prayed that Trevor's truck would be in its usual place. She didn't care why he had left at this point; she just wanted to make sure everything was okay between them. She couldn't wait to share Lily's first day of school with him. Didn't he realize how important this day was to a child? No, how could he? From what she'd learned from Judy and to some extent from Trevor himself, he rarely thought about his childhood. He didn't like talking about his mother and he never spoke of his father. Once, when they were out on the porch, she'd asked if he ever thought about his dad. He didn't hesitate when he answered a flat "No" and changed the subject.

She never brought the topic up again.

When Lana drove in and noticed his parking spot was still empty, her mind started going off in different directions. Why did he leave? Had he gone away because of what happened between them? Did he expect her to be gone by the time he returned? Why hadn't he at least called Lily? Even Judy didn't know where he'd gone or why.

Lana waited up until long past midnight, listening for the familiar sound of Trevor's truck. Uneasiness continued to knot her stomach. All day she had pretended that it didn't matter, but the lateness of the hour weakened her resolve. Eventually, after the fire had died down, she gave up the vigil and headed for the stairs.

The first rays of morning sun were now starting to lighten the darkened sky as Lana sat alone on the front porch. Thoughts of going home crept into her mind. She was homesick. Life had changed for her during the last week, more than she ever thought possible.

The situation with Trevor was far more complex than she would have liked, and as much as she had grown to care for him, she couldn't allow herself to get embroiled in a relationship that was clearly one-sided. She had been the one who had sought him out all week when it seemed all he wanted to do was avoid her. She didn't quite feel as if she'd been used, but damn close.

It was at that moment that Lana decided her job here was really done. She'd stay until Friday, making sure that Lily's first week went well, and then head back to Connecticut. By then she was sure Trevor would have at least called, if not returned, and would have no problem with her departure.

And leave she must before her already splintered heart broke in two. Maybe his departure was a godsend, as it allowed her to get her bearings once again. Her career had been the center of her existence over the past four years, and it was time to get back into focus. She had missed being a nurse, and as soon as she reentered her life, she was going to make some changes. The trip had proven fruitful after all—just as Judy had expected.

For the first time in days, Lana felt in complete control. She was going to move forward with her life and that was something to celebrate.

She then heard Judy stirring upstairs and knew she was getting Lily ready for her second day of school. The minute Lana saw the cheerful child bouncing down the stairs, her mood brightened. Lily was excited about going to school and her enthusiasm was contagious.

The drive home to Vermont had provided Trevor with the time and solitude to think things through. After the dust had settled the night before and Cindy had regained her composure, they'd talked the rest of the evening about Lily. Trevor held nothing back when he told of possible complications from fetal alcohol syndrome, but made a point of mentioning that other than her petite size, which could have been hereditary anyway, nothing had shown up so far.

It was almost too much for Cindy to absorb. Trevor held her hand as he recounted the young girl's past four years. But when he brought up custody and what would happen next, the conversation came to a screeching halt. Cindy couldn't think beyond that point. The remaining issues, including how Lily would be told, where she would eventually live, who would be her primary guardian, and establishing a time frame for deciding these things were left for another day. They all knew their lives would forever be joined, and Trevor promised that he would be in touch.

When he stood to leave, Cindy asked the one question that had been in the back of her mind all evening. She wanted to meet her daughter. Lily didn't have to know who she was yet; Cindy just wanted to meet her.

Watching Cindy's reaction and hearing her plea made Trevor realize that she needed her daughter as much as Lily needed a mother. Both he and Jamie had been denying that fact—first Jamie and now him. It wasn't until Lana came to stay, and he saw how she and Lily responded to one another, that he was reminded of his own childhood. Growing up without a father had created a void no one ever could fill—not his mother, aunt, grandmother, or grandfather.

A voice then rose up from his subconscious and he extended an invitation for Cindy and Sam to come for a visit.

There was no hesitation on Cindy's part as she wrapped her arms around his shoulders and hugged him tightly. "Oh, thank you," she cried, burying her face in his chest.

Trevor stood motionless, not knowing what to say next. He was a little surprised that he'd blurted out the invitation but knew it was too late to withdraw. He left then, promising to call in a day or two.

The drive home had been one of the most painful times in his life. It felt like he was losing Jamie all over again. He knew Lily belonged with her mother, and a part of him had known it all along—it was just hard to finally admit it.

He thought of a hundred ways to break the news to Lily but couldn't come up with a single one that made any sense. Damn Jamie for putting him in this situation. He'd have to talk to his aunt to get her perspective before calling Cindy. She would know how to handle it.

After he had contemplated all the different scenarios with Lily, his mind moved on to Lana. He'd really screwed up on that one. His emotions had been idling on high since Cindy's call, and he hated that Lana had been the one he had turned to. She had been through so much in her life and didn't deserve to be smack-dab in the middle of his problems.

As he came upon the familiar exit, thoughts of Lily lying warm and cozy in her bed came to mind. After she had lost her daddy, Trevor had worried about her. She'd hidden in her room for several days, refusing to talk to anyone, and even though she and Trevor had been close, she'd shut him out as well. Finally, she had given in, and in her broken speech had been able to talk to him about her feelings.

He was surprised that someone her age could share as well as she did the depth of her loss. She pointed to her chest, saying how much it hurt to have a broken heart, and then made him look down her throat to check the burning that persisted. She didn't let him out of her sight after that, and that was fine with him. He needed her as much as she needed him.

It had not been an easy road for either of them, but her youth and exuberance had won out in the end. Even though they often spoke of Jamie when they were alone, Lily had been able to do what he had failed to do—move on. She had accepted life in Vermont, had fallen in love with her surrogate grandparents, and would start school... And then he realized what day it was and that he'd missed her first day. He had been so caught up in his own struggle to make sense of everything that he'd forgotten one of the most important days of her life. How could he have done that?

Trevor was so lost in thought he almost missed the turn onto the narrow dirt road and had to slam on the brakes. The truck careened sideways and almost hit the hundred-year-old oak standing at the end of the driveway. His heart was pounding hard; he sat for a good long time trying to calm his frazzled nerves.

What if I'd killed myself just now? Who would have taken care of Lily? How did I ever think that I could take care of a child on my own? It suddenly became crystal clear that he'd made the right decision. Lily deserved to be part of a family with a mom and a dad, brothers and sisters, cousins, aunts and uncles, and a ton of friends. A family like he'd never known—only fantasized about in his dreams as a young child.

Trevor was sitting in the idling truck, contemplating his next move and feeling pretty sorry for himself, when he glanced up and saw Lana half-running, half-hobbling toward the truck.

Lana had been just about to open the porch door to go inside when she heard the bone-chilling sound of screeching tires. Even though her ankle was still a little tender, it didn't stop her from racing to the end of the drive to see what had happened.

As soon as she saw Trevor's truck, she sped up her pace, being careful not to step fully on her right foot. Once she realized he was okay, her mind allowed the pain shooting up her leg to register. In an effort to ease some of the discomfort, she slowed down and limped the rest of the way.

The minute he saw her wince, he shot out of the truck and ran toward her. "Here. Let me help you."

She allowed his arm to wrap around her shoulders, and for a brief moment leaned into him to take some of the weight off. After she had caught her breath and realized how close they were, she pulled away from the warmth of his body. "I thought there was an accident." For the briefest of moments, Trevor held her body against his and basked in the feel of her in his arms. The instant she moved away he not only felt a deep loss but a distinct distance between them.

"I almost missed the turn," he explained. "I'm sorry to have worried you. Come on. Get in the truck and I'll drive you back up to the house."

Lana wanted to look him in the eye and say, *"To hell with you,"* but since her ankle was hurting so much, she reluctantly accepted the ride.

Neither said a word during the brief ride to the house. She was the first to exit, and when he ran around the front to help her, she kindly told him she didn't need or want his help.

Where had he heard that one before? She had told him the same thing when he had found her on the stairs when she'd almost broken her neck, and then again after she'd overheard his discussion with Cindy. Both times he'd been able to cajole her into accepting his help, but this time she wasn't budging, and he wasn't in the mood to push.

Chapter Nineteen

One last-ditch effort on his part caused her to finally snap, "I don't need your help, Trevor. I might have needed it Sunday or yesterday when I had to take Lily to school. I managed then and I can manage now. Now if you'll excuse me, I think I'll go in."

This time he let her go. He was tired, confused, worried, and far too depressed to argue with her. He needed to be close to Lily right then.

Lily was in the kitchen finishing up a bowl of Frosted Cheerios when Trevor walked through the doorway. The minute Lily saw Trevor she abandoned the remaining sugary oats and jumped into his open arms.

The sadness he felt deep inside his soul went unnoticed by the four-year-old child who couldn't wait to tell him about her first day of school and her new feathered-family. His aunt, though, saw clearly the pained expression hidden behind Trevor's feigned excitement at Lily's news. All through his life she'd been the one to instinctively know when he needed her most, and having her here waiting for him felt so right.

He was grateful Lana was nowhere in sight, as he was anxious to spend some time alone with his aunt. He had always relied on her logical nature and sense of spirit, and now, more than ever, he needed a dose.

Lily was anxious to show him her babies, as she referred to them, and barely had time to identify each of them by name before Aunt Judy whisked her back into the house to prepare her backpack for school.

Trevor was glad to drive Lily to school, selfishly wanting to spend as much time with her as possible. Judy tagged along for the ride, and Trevor was grateful they would have some time alone together. After his brief encounter with Lana earlier, she'd stormed into the house and grabbed the keys to Judy's car. His aunt didn't say anything at the time, but he knew she'd have plenty of questions.

The minute Trevor pulled into a parking space and turned off the engine, Lily shot from the truck to join a group of children playing on the jungle gyms. Watching her face light up the minute she saw her new friends seemed to reinforce how wrong he'd been by keeping her secluded. His intentions were good, as they usually were, but the reality was just the opposite.

On the drive back, Trevor decided to stop at Stokey's for some much-needed sustenance and a heart-to-heart with his aunt. After the waitress had filled two coffee mugs and set them down, he took several gulps before the story flowed from his mouth.

It was a couple of hours later, after a double serving of eggs benedict and half a dozen refills of coffee, when they stood to leave. As usual, Aunt Judy had been his rock. She had listened attentively to the entire story before confirming what she had known all along. She was proud that he'd done the right thing and applauded his sense of duty.

When Trevor hadn't arrived home by Monday morning, Judy had cleared her calendar for the next few weeks, knowing that she would be needed in Vermont. She offered to stay on as long as needed. Trevor gratefully accepted her offer. This next chapter in his life was going to be difficult, at best, and he was smart enough to know that he wasn't prepared to handle it alone.

Even though Judy truly believed Trevor had done what was necessary, it was hard for her to see the anguish written all over his face. She had faith that he would come out of this a better man. It gave her great solace to know that Cindy had turned her life around and that Lily would grow up with a mother and a father. She also knew that Trevor's love for the little girl wouldn't vanish when she went to live with her mother. From what he'd said, Judy understood that Cindy was willing to do whatever was necessary to make sure the transition went smoothly. Trevor also mentioned that Cindy had made it very clear that he would be welcome in their home at any time.

She sensed the depth of his wounds when he talked of moving back to Los Angeles and immersing himself in his music. He'd been doing that his whole life, and the thought of him hiding behind that veil once again bothered her more than she was willing to admit. However, now was not the time to analyze his past behavior. She would wait until he had built up enough of a cushion from his recent pain before she ventured into that area.

He never once mentioned Lana, and Judy had been careful to avoid the topic as well. She knew enough about Trevor to know that he could only deal with one thing at a time. He was an emotional cripple when it came to handling matters of the heart, and this time he was faced with several all at once.

She had guessed where he'd gone when she'd read his note a few days ago, even though she didn't share it with Lana. She was certain that before her nephew could even think about the mess he'd made with Lana, he'd have to first reconcile the situation with Cindy. She'd tried on more than one occasion to convince Lana that Trevor had not left because of what had happened between them, but Lana was hurting too much to listen to reason. Lana had been deeply wounded by Trevor's disappearing act, and nothing Judy said had eased her pain. Judy had worked with Lana enough over the years to know that when Lana wasn't ready to listen to reason, nothing she said or did could change her opinion.

Lana drove for about an hour before her stomach began sending little reminders that she hadn't yet eaten this morning. The neon sign up ahead blinking "Diner" caught her eye almost immediately, and, like Pavlov's dog, she felt her salivary glands come to life.

The parking lot was hardly big enough for the cars already there. She spotted a man leaving the diner, and waited patiently for his tight but open parking space.

The front booth was open, and she guessed the man who'd just left had occupied it since there wasn't another open booth or counter space in the place. As soon as she sat down, she began fumbling with the packets of sugar and rearranging the salt and pepper shakers, doing anything to avoid eye contact. She'd never eaten in a restaurant by herself and was convinced everyone was staring at her.

As soon as the scrambled eggs, bacon, and country home fries were devoured, Lana stood to leave, allowing her eyes to wander now that she was on her way out. It seemed no one had really been interested in her in the first place, and she felt a little silly thinking they had.

Today had been a first for her, and she suspected that from this day forward there would be a lot of them. During the twenty or so minutes she'd sat by herself, she had settled a few issues that had been nagging her since she'd driven out here.

She needed to leave Trevor's place. Today. Seeing him this morning had been much harder than she thought it would be, and putting some distance between them was probably the best for everyone. The strain she was under when Trevor was around wasn't good for anyone, and since Lily had adjusted so well to school yesterday, Lana felt comfortable leaving at this point. She had really done all she could have in regard to establishing a course for Trevor to follow. Judy was well aware of everything she'd accomplished and hopefully wouldn't mind following up to make sure both he and Lily stayed on track.

Lana then realized she'd left her own car back in Connecticut, but rationalized that if she promised to come back on the weekend to pick up Judy, there wouldn't be a problem. If Trevor and Judy weren't home when she got back, which she prayed they wouldn't be, she'd leave a note explaining her plans. She couldn't stay any longer in the house. It hurt too much to be near Trevor. Judy would understand.

As soon as Lana pulled in the driveway and saw that Trevor's truck was gone, she knew what she had to do. As she suspected, the house was empty, giving her the perfect opportunity to pack her things. Knowing she'd be back on the weekend, she didn't fuss over making sure she had everything.

After she had carried her bags to the car, she went back in to write a quick note to both Judy and Lily. Although the impulse was strong to write one to Trevor, she pushed away the thought, remembering that he hadn't bothered to explain his actions to her.

When Trevor and Judy arrived home later that morning, they were surprised to see that Lana still hadn't returned. Judy was the first to say aloud what she knew Trevor was probably thinking: "I wonder where Lana's gone off to." And when he seemed to be ignoring her comment, Judy asked, "Did you talk to her this morning?"

"Just briefly."

"And…"

"And what?"

"Well, did she say where she was off to?"

Shaking his head, Trevor answered, "No. We barely spoke."

"Was that your fault or hers?"

"What difference does it make?" Trevor muttered as he opened his door and started to get out.

Judy was starting to get a little frustrated with his vagueness. Exiting the truck, she practically had to run to catch up with him. "I just wanted to know if she was upset."

They had reached the house, and Trevor held open the front door. "I'm not quite sure what Lana's problem was this morning. She sure wasn't willing to share it with me."

"Well, after what happened between the two of you, can you blame her?" Judy couldn't believe she'd let that slip but was actually glad it had.

Trevor was shocked that his aunt knew what had happened between them. "I can't believe she told you!"

"Unlike you, Lana desperately needed someone to talk to. Since you weren't around, she came to me. At first she just told me about overhearing your conversation with Cindy and how bad she felt afterward when she laid into you. I sort of guessed the other part."

"Great," Trevor said holding up his hands. "Now both of you are mad at me."

"Who said I was mad?"

"Well, aren't you? I've really made a mess of things. How can I expect you not to be mad when I'm pissed at myself?"

"Funny, she said those same words to me, the part about really messing things up. I'm a little disappointed that you ran away before you'd straightened things out, but not angry. As for Lana, I can't speak for how she's feeling, but if I had to venture a guess, I think confused would be a better term."

"Yeah, well, she can join the club," Trevor grunted.

Judy started to walk toward the kitchen and noticed that two envelopes had been left on the dining room table. One was marked *"Judy"* and the other *"Lily."* Trevor spotted them at the same time and felt a pang of disappointment that Lana hadn't left one for him.

Judy quickly tore open hers and read the brief note.

When she didn't offer up any information, Trevor asked, "Well?"

"Looks like you two are more alike than you think. Says she needs some time alone and will be back up either Saturday or Sunday."

"Oh, great! She just ups and leaves Lily. A real professional, that one!"

Judy didn't want to remind him that he'd done the same thing. "She writes that her job here is virtually done. All the preliminary testing she did showed no visible signs of FAS and the school Lily's enrolled in now will monitor her progress. She also asks that I remind you about setting an appointment with Dr. Lake."

"And does she say what we're supposed to tell Lily?"

Judy heard the anger in his voice and had to control a smile. His anger at least meant he cared. "No, she didn't mention what we should say, but I'm sure she explained it in Lily's letter. Why don't you go ahead and open it?"

He grabbed the letter from the table and ripped it open. He read through it quickly and threw it back down on the table.

"Well, did she give a plausible explanation?" Judy asked.

"It's a bunch of crap! She says she left to visit her own family for a few days. Says she felt a little homesick."

"I'm sure she probably was. This is the first time she's been away from her family since the accident."

Trevor frowned. "I'm sure there's more to it than that. But right now I'm falling through my socks, and if I don't catch up on some sleep I'm not going to be good for anyone." He turned then and walked up the stairs.

When it was time to pick up Lily, Judy knocked lightly on Trevor's door, waking him from a dead sleep. She wished she could have driven his truck herself but wasn't comfortable driving a stick shift anymore.

He was very quiet on the way over to the Children's Learning Center and that was just fine with Judy. Lily was playing outside when they pulled in. The minute she recognized the truck, she began waving frantically.

Trevor was just as excited to see her and couldn't get out of the truck fast enough. Marge Conlon met him as he crossed the parking lot, and, extending her hand, she said, "Hello again."

Trevor recognized her immediately and firmly shook her welcoming hand. "Hi!" He couldn't remember her name and wished Lana were there to remind him. "How'd Lily do on her second day?"

"Lily's doing quite well. In fact, better than I expected. She's adapted very nicely to the structure of the classroom and I think she's having a lot of fun."

Trevor watched as his small ward slid down the slide and immediately ran back up for another thrill. "Well, it certainly looks like it to me."

They had established that Lily would be picked up fifteen minutes earlier than everyone else so Trevor could remain as anonymous as possible. This wasn't a problem since the last half- hour of the day was spent either out on the playground or in the library, depending on the weather.

When Trevor spotted a few cars pulling into the parking lot, he called to Lily, "Come on! We have to go now."

"I stay longer to play!" she yelled back.

Marge jumped in then, knowing the petulant child was more likely to respond to a teacher than a parent. "Time to go, Lily."

Lily heard the kind but stern voice and reacted immediately. "Okay! I get my backpack."

"How'd you do that?" asked a surprised Trevor.

Marge lowered her voice so that the other children wouldn't hear her secret. "At this age, most students are a bit intimidated by teachers, even though it isn't our intention. By the fifth grade, kids have learned better and we experience the same problems parents do."

Trevor heard most of what Marge had said but the minute he noticed Lily running toward him, he bent low with open arms. As soon as she jumped into his arms, he whispered, "I missed you today. How was school?"

She hugged him tightly and answered, "Good!" She then whispered, "Me wanna stay."

He knew she had whispered so the teacher couldn't hear her. "Not today, honey. We're going to stop by Aunt Irma's, so we'd better get going."

"Yippee!" Lily hollered as she pulled him toward the truck.

"Hold on, sweetie. Say good-bye to your teacher." Damn! He wished he could remember her name.

Lily then gave a backward wave and yelled, "Bye."

Lily couldn't wait to share all the wonderful tidbits of her day. Billie peed his pants and had to go home. Katie sucked her thumb during story time. And her new best friend, Molly, wanted to know if she could come over someday.

Trevor hadn't given any thought to having Lily play at someone else's house or vice versa. This was all new to him and he wasn't sure he was ready for it. She wasn't demanding an answer right now, so he was momentarily off the hook, but he knew it was only a matter of time before she'd be asking in earnest.

Ben and Irma were working in the yard when they saw the familiar truck pull in. They hadn't seen Lily for a few days and were anxious to hear about her first day of school.

"My, my, what do we have here?" said Irma as she pulled Lily into her arms. "A backpack and everythin'."

"I go school now."

"I heard. How do ya like it?"

"It good! Molly's my best friend."

"Molly ya say. I once had a friend Molly too."

Lily's eyes opened wide. "You did?"

"Yesiree! She moved away when I was ten. I cried for a week." Irma then realized she hadn't acknowledged the others. "Hello, Trevor and Judy. Come on—why don't we sit out back and I'll fix us some lemonade. Ben, you lead the way and I'll bring out a tray."

Most of the conversation that followed focused on Lily's new babies and school. The subject of Lana didn't come up until later when Lily asked to go home to see Lana. Silence filled the air for a moment before Judy spoke up. "Honey, Lana's gone home for a few days."

Sadness washed over Lily's face. "Why?"

Trevor stood up then and walked away.

Judy hesitated a moment as she watched her nephew's retreating form. Sadness filled her heart when she thought of what could have been. She wasn't giving up completely on them working things out, but she wasn't as optimistic as she had been earlier.

She then felt a light tug on her cotton dress and knew Lily was still waiting for an answer. "Oh, sweetie, Lana had to go home to get a few things done. But don't worry, she'll be back in a few days."

Trevor carried his empty glass into the kitchen. The subject of Lana was not up for discussion as far as he was concerned. He wasn't surprised, though, when Irma came up behind him and asked if he wanted a refill.

"No, thanks," Trevor said shaking his head. "I think we'd better get going."

"What?" Irma exclaimed. "Ya just got here. Why don't ya stay for supper? I have a meatloaf in the oven big enough for an army, and we'd love to have ya."

She could see he was a bit jumpy and knew him well enough to know that he carried a heavy heart. Last night when she'd called to see how Lily's first day was, she sensed from Lana that all was not well.

"What's wrong, Trevor?" Irma asked.

He sat then and put his face into his hands. "Too much—that's what!" He waited a minute, then asked, "Did you ever want to just run away?"

Laughing a little, Irma said, "Only about a thousand times. But I can sure tell ya it never solves anythin'."

"Sometimes I think I've been running my whole life."

"Runnin' from what?"

"Oh, I'd say just about everything! I've never really felt...you know...settled."

"And what is settled supposed to feel like?"

Trevor shrugged his shoulders. "I'm not quite sure. I just know I've never felt it."

She sensed what he had meant. "What do ya think would make ya feel settled?"

"I don't know."

"I'm not so sure of that."

Looking at her as if she were a little crazy, he asked, "Now what's that supposed to mean? If I knew, don't you think I'd be going for it?"

"I'm not so sure. I'm beginnin' to think that settlin' down scares ya."

Shaking his head, Trevor took a moment before he responded, "What the hell did you put in your lemonade?"

Laughing, Irma walked over and tousled his already unruly mane. "Ya've been as anxious as a jackrabbit looking down the barrel of a thirty-ought-six since Lana came walkin' through yar door. Maybe ya just better face the truth."

"Oh, yeah, Ms. Freud, and what would that be?"

"Very funny. I may not be schooled in this stuff, but I've been around long enough to know that deep down ya really care for that girl."

Not much got by Irma, and right now she was reading him like a bestseller. "I'm not going to deny that I have feelings for her," Trevor conceded. "Hell, look at her. She's intelligent, compassionate, and very easy on the eyes. Who wouldn't fall for her? It's just not in my nature to let things go too far."

Irma sat down directly across from him and shook her head as if she didn't believe a word he'd said. "Why are ya so afraid of sharin' your life?"

"There's no room in my life for that type of commitment—never was and never will be," he said sharply.

"Why not?" Irma persisted.

"There just isn't!" Trevor said, springing erect. "Look what falling in love did to my mother."

"Look what fallin' in love did for me!" Irma countered. "I think ya're really missin' out on life if ya don't let yarself fall at least once. After that, it's up to ya whether or not ya want to take that chance again, but I, for one, would take it every single time. From what little ya've told me about yar mother, I'd say she stayed bitter all these years not because of what yar father did but because she refused to let love into her life again."

A few weeks ago he would have argued every point Irma had just made, but after meeting Lana he saw things differently. "Maybe you're right. It's just that I've lived this way for so long I'm not sure I can change."

"Oh, horse hooey!" Irma snorted. "I suspect the reason ya've never really felt settled is because ya've lived yar life accordin' to what's in yar head rather than followin' what's in here," she added, pointing to her heart.

Trevor knew too well that what she said was true. He'd always analyzed his relationships to death and the outcome was always the same. When things got too hot and heavy, he walked away without looking back. He'd convinced himself that the brief loneliness he experienced shortly after was a far cry from what it could have been.

"Irma, there's so much going on in my life right now that the last thing I need is to embark on foreign soil."

"Maybe the distraction is just what ya need," she told him.

"You just don't understand."

"Well, sport, the only way I'm gonna understand is if ya tell me."

When he failed to answer, she asked, "Well, how 'bout it?"

What was it with these over-sixty women who could make him sing like a bird? He'd always been completely comfortable discussing just about anything with his aunt, and with Irma it had been the same. But when it came to really sharing his views with a woman near his own age, he'd shut down faster than lights out at boot camp.

Before he knew what was happening, he'd spelled out the entire story. He told her about the letter, the lies, and his eventual trip to Westchester. Unable to stop himself, he went on to explain what had happened between Lana and him and how she'd gone away because of what he'd done.

Having said it all, he searched her face for a response. Her pained expression made him look away, and he glanced out the window to see Lily and Judy, sleeves rolled up to their elbows, assisting Ben with the replanting of some rose bushes. Then he heard Irma sniffle and felt the warmth of her hand on his shoulder.

"I'm not a deeply spiritual person like yar aunt," she began, "and I can't for the life of me figure out why all this is happenin' to ya. But I do believe there's a reason. My mama used to say there was a reason why my papa was taken so tragically. No one ever guessed what that reason was; we just sort of knew one existed. When things became too hard then, I'd pray to my daddy for the strength to go on, and somehow, someway, we all got through it. I believe Jamie's the one who's been guidin' ya through all this. He's workin' through ya what he couldn't do on this earth."

More emphatically she said, "Lily's mama deserved to know about her daughter, and from what ya told me, that little black cloud that left ya the night ya unleashed the truth was yar buddy's soul bein' set free." Irma then lowered her voice. "I never told anyone this before—felt my family would throw me in the loony bin if I'd ever mentioned it—but I too felt that same cloud leave me the day I met Ben."

Trevor then turned and looked her directly in the eyes. "Maybe you're right. In my head I knew Jamie had died, but in my heart I never felt like he'd really gone. It wasn't until I met with Cindy and told her the whole story that I felt him slowly slipping away. I don't feel his presence anymore and it's like I'm reliving his death all over again."

"I don't think ya ever allowed yarself to mourn Jamie's death. That little wonder out there," she said, pointing out the window, "has kept ya so busy ya haven't been able to completely say good-bye and move on. Ya're sort of stuck in third gear."

"I'm not sure I know how to move on."

"Whether or not ya believe it, ya've already started. Ya've righted a wrong and in the process opened yar heart wide enough for Lana to slip in."

Shaking his head in disbelief, Trevor said, "Whoa! Wait a minute here. I'm not sure what my feelings are for Lana. I just know I shouldn't have let things go as far as they did, and I regret involving her in all this. I should've known better."

"Trevor, there are some things we can't control, no matter how hard we try."

Irma watched Trevor grip the back of the chair, his lips now a thin fine line. She placed both her hands over his taut fists and challenged softly, "Ya couldn't protect Jamie from a person like Cindy, nor could ya have saved his life. Just like ya couldn't have survived much longer knowin' that Cindy was out there thinkin' she'd been responsible for her daughter's death. Whether it was Jamie leadin' ya down that path or yar own conscience, we'll never really know. Through all of this yar mind became saturated with the enormous responsibility of handlin' a child and yar guard slipped a little, openin' a small piece of yar heart to feel what it had never felt before—the stirrin's of lovin' someone."

He turned back to the window, slipping his hands from her gentle grasp. The tension he'd felt just moments ago evaporated the second her words registered in his mind. How could he be sure that's what had really happened? He didn't deny needing someone. He'd needed a warm body in his bed many times before and he'd never called it love.

Still, he wasn't about to admit anything, not to himself or to her. "I know that's what you and my aunt would like to believe. I just don't see it that way."

"Oh, and how do ya see it?"

"I'm not really sure, but I know not the way you see it."

"Why are ya so damned stubborn? Why can't ya admit that ya really care for that girl?"

"I never said I didn't care. Just said that I wasn't in love with her."

"Then define love for me," Irma challenged.

A few moments went by and when no words came from his mouth, she asked, "Ya don't know, do ya?"

He was cornered. She'd asked the one question he'd never been really sure of. He knew he'd felt love. Hell, he'd loved his grandparents, his mother, his aunt, Jamie, and Lily. But he'd never felt the kind of love she was talking about.

Trevor turned back to face her. "You want to know what I really believe about love?"

"Yes, I do!"

"Love rips your heart into tiny little pieces, bringing some joy, but mostly pain. It makes you weak and vulnerable. You put up with things you normally wouldn't allow, and most of all, when it goes sour, it shrivels you up inside and slowly takes you down."

Hearing those words saddened Irma. "I'm sorry ya feel that way, Trevor. Love has been just the opposite for me. When I met Ben my shattered heart was miraculously pieced together and I became strong again, lookin' for new challenges. Our union taught us how to compromise and act unselfishly. I didn't lose myself the day we met. Instead, I found out who I really was."

She walked out the back door then, giving him a chance to digest her words. She'd never suspected until now that he'd been so badly hurt. She knew about his father's abandonment, knew his mother never remarried, and hearing now about Jamie's affair, knew how Trevor viewed that relationship as well. It would take one strong lady to break through all that rubble, and right now she didn't know if Wonder Woman existed.

Chapter Twenty

At Irma's insistence they'd stayed for dinner, and when they'd eaten their fill and had almost polished off the pot of decaf, Trevor noticed Lily was having trouble staying awake. Irma spotted the young child about the same time and quickly shooed them away, saying she'd clean up everything since they'd saved her from the laborious task of transferring bushes.

After his conversation with Irma, Trevor had remained fairly subdued for most of the evening. He'd never said aloud his innermost feelings about love, and the minute the words had sprung from his mouth he'd regretted them. Throughout most of his life, he'd never placed any value on the relationship between a man and a woman, and he hadn't realized until today just how tainted his views sounded when spoken aloud.

After tucking Lily in for the night, Trevor and Judy sat by the unlit fireplace, both too exhausted to get a blaze going. Judy's exhaustion was mostly caused by the hours she and Lily had spent helping Ben dig up the old rosebushes, while Trevor's was more the result of an emotional drain.

His home felt empty this evening. Could it be that he was missing her? Irma had struck a nerve earlier when she'd read him so clearly. He saw the disappointment written all over her face when he'd voiced his take on love. The funny thing was, he couldn't be sure those same words rang true anymore.

"I hope Lana got home safely," Judy interrupted his musing. "Do you think we should give her a call?"

No way was he going to admit he'd been thinking about Lana. His conversation with Irma had been enough for one day and he needed a good night's sleep and some time alone to fully recover before he got into this with his aunt. "You do what you'd like."

"I'd sleep better knowing Lana was safe and sound. Would you care to talk to her?"

"No, thanks. I'm pretty tired and I think I'll just go on up to bed."

"But I thought you wanted to talk to me about Cindy's visit and how you're going to handle it with Lily."

"Not tonight," Trevor said, holding back a yawn. "I'm too tired to even think about that right now. Good night."

"Wait, Trev."

"What is it?"

"I'm worried about you."

"Don't be. I'll be fine in the morning."

As soon as he started to get up, she reached over and grabbed his arm. "Please talk to me. I know this is difficult and I'm here to help."

"You have helped," he assured her.

"Then why do I get the feeling you're ready to bolt?"

"Because you've always been able to read me better than anyone else. But don't worry, I'm not going anywhere this time."

"I'm glad to hear that," Judy admitted, patting his hand. "Lily will be fine. I feel it in my bones."

"I know."

Judy frowned. "What about you?"

"I'll be okay," Trevor promised, squeezing her hand.

"You don't have to go through this alone. Whether you like it or not, you have Lana."

"I know. That's the problem. I keep hurting her and I can't seem to stop myself."

Judy nodded. "It's only because you're scared. Letting someone in is risky business."

"Right now the risk is far too high. She deserves a lot more than me."

"You're being too hard on yourself. You're one of the finest people I know."

"In your eyes maybe. But until I believe that myself, I'm no good to anyone." He then started for the stairs. "I'm really tired of thinking about all this. You've always told me about the magic of time and its healing powers. Well, right now I need a good dose of it. I'd like nothing better than to go hibernate for a few months. But for now, I'll just call it a night."

Lana hadn't notified anyone that she had returned home and looked forward to a peaceful night. She had arrived around midday and had spent the remainder of the afternoon weeding her garden. The boy she'd hired to mow the lawn in her absence did only that. She hadn't pulled the weeds before she'd left, and in the week and a half she'd been gone it appeared as if they'd had a party and invited all their relatives. Three hours later, as she soaked in a steamy tub, she realized she hadn't had a thing to eat since breakfast.

Cooking hadn't been a priority since the accident, so when she pulled open the refrigerator door she found only a few paltry items. She was famished. Pulling open the freezer, she was delighted to see a lone Lean Cuisine box nestled in the right-hand corner. Directly opposite, sitting atop the two ice-cube trays, was the last vestige of edible fare, a bag of frozen corn, which would round out the meal perfectly.

As Lana watched the numbers slowly descend on the microwave's clock, she couldn't stave off the unsettled feeling in the pit of her stomach. This was not one of hunger but of something else. She felt like a stranger in her home. For most of the day she'd been a bit edgy, and nothing—not the weeding, which normally soothed her aching soul, or the steamy forty-five-minute soak—could assuage the emptiness.

She had left Vermont before she'd had a chance to settle things. There was something about Trevor's house, his yard, Lily, Ben and Irma, the garden. She had to stop thinking that way. How could ten days turn everything upside down? The lake, the jogging trail, Stokey's...*Oh, God*, she thought, *it must be my low blood sugar.* The timer registered three more minutes and she contemplated, for just a second, eating a half-frozen meal.

Time! All she ever did was wait for it to pass her by. Everything in her life was run by the clock: when she arose from bed, reported to work, took her lunch break, worked out, and even went to bed. Without her watch, the clock on the wall, or the digital timer on the microwave, her life would have held no meaning.

Staring at the red glaring numbers ticking away, she was reminded of a fact she hadn't thought about until now. While in Vermont she'd never noticed the time or, for that matter, followed much of a routine. During the last week and a half, she'd unknowingly reverted back to her old self, the person she'd thought lost forever. A part of her had been awakened from a deep long sleep, but another part, albeit small, felt guilty that she'd been able to recapture the person who was fortunate enough to have survived, when the two people she had loved more than anything on this earth had perished.

She now understood what Judy had tirelessly worked so hard to get her to see. Since the accident, she'd unconsciously punished herself for being the one left behind. The job change, the rigid schedule she'd followed to the letter and the quasi-reclusive lifestyle had been her penance for being alive.

Several times during the evening she thought of calling Judy and sharing what had been so long in coming. But what if Trevor answered? What would she say? She wondered how Lily had fared on her second day and actually started to dial the number twice, hanging up each time before depressing the final number.

The hour was late and her body was lagging far behind her enlightened mind. Just as she was about to turn in for the night, the phone rang. The minute she heard her friend's voice she knew that they'd been on the same wavelength. "Judy, I'm so glad you called. I'm sorry to have left so abruptly but I needed some time to sort things through, and being there made it seem impossible. I've been meaning to call to let you know I got home all right but…"

Lana's hesitation gave Judy the opportunity to cut in. "Lana, dear, slow down a minute. I understand why you left and it's okay. Really it is. I was just calling to make sure you arrived safely and to let you know that, other than missing you, we're doing fine."

Lana took a deep breath in an effort to calm down. "How was Lily's second day?"

"I'd say as good as the first. She seems to be doing nicely."

"That's good. I kept thinking about her all day. I really miss her."

"She was a little upset you'd left, but once I explained that you'd be coming back she seemed to perk right back up. She's really pretty resilient."

"How's Trevor doing?"

"I'm not quite sure," Judy answered honestly. "He's got a lot on his mind."

"Did he tell you where he was the last few days?"

"Yes. We had a nice talk at breakfast after we dropped Lily off."

It wasn't any of her business—she knew that better than anyone—but it still didn't stop her from asking. "Where'd he go?"

"He went to see Cindy."

Nothing Judy could have said would have surprised her more. "You're serious? What happened?"

Judy narrated what Trevor had shared during breakfast.

"Wow! I can't believe it. They're actually coming up this weekend to meet Lily?"

"Yes. I've decided to stay an extra week just in case I'm needed."

"How's Trevor taking all this?" Lana asked, genuinely concerned. "Last I knew he was going to try to bury this whole thing. What changed his mind?"

"I suspect a little of what you said, coupled with the fact that he'd been wrestling with doing the right thing for some time now." In her heart she wished Lana hadn't left, but was wise enough to know that Trevor needed to focus his attention on the situation with Cindy and Lily first before he could "fix" what had happened with Lana. Having Lana in the house would only add tension to an already stressful environment, which wouldn't do either of them any good.

"Is there anything I can do to help?" Lana asked.

"Right now Trevor's up to his eyeballs with putting his life in order. I'm afraid he's not going to be good for anyone or anything until this weekend's over. Since I won't be coming home this weekend, it's probably best that I call you Sunday night and let you know how everything went. Does that sound alright?"

Trying to hide her disappointment, Lana responded, "Okay."

Judy knew her friend only too well. "Lana, please don't think we're shutting you out. Trevor's got to get through this before he can even think about anything else."

"I know. It's just that I wish I could be there for him."

"I'll let him know you are. Anyway, enough of all that. How are you?"

"Based on what Trevor's going through, I'm ashamed to say that tonight I had what you'd call a breakthrough."

"Well, come on—I can't wait to hear."

"I realized what you've been trying to tell me for years. I don't want to live in this cocoon any longer. I want to stop punishing myself for being alive. I want my old job back and to volunteer at the women's shelter again. I want to put myself out there again."

Tears sprang to Judy's eyes, causing her to pause briefly before she let Lana know just how proud she was. "You've made my day. I'll be happy to help you any way I can."

"I don't think my boss will be too happy," Lana speculated, "but I'm sure I can work out an arrangement where I can work part-time both at nursing and in administration until a replacement can be found."

"I wouldn't worry too much about it. It'll all work out. When do you intend to implement this plan?"

"Well, now that I'm not going back to Vermont right away, I'll probably announce it at the office first thing tomorrow. I'll also talk to the head nurse in pediatrics and tell her the good news. Whenever we run into one another, she always lets me know that if I ever want my old job back all I have to do is ask."

"Are you ready for all this?" Judy asked.

"I think so. I won't know if I don't try."

"You know I'm behind you all the way. I'm really proud of you, Lana."

"Thanks! Right now I'm pretty proud of myself. It took me a long time to get here, but I'm so lucky that I had you to keep hammering away at me. You never gave up on me, and I'll never forget all you've done."

By now sniffles could be heard on both ends of the line, and Judy thought it best to end the conversation. There were too many uncertainties looming ahead for both Lana and Trevor, and before reality set in and threatened to destroy the good mood, she said her good-byes with a promise to call on Sunday evening.

Trevor woke Lily extra early, knowing that in a few hours both of their lives would change forever. As promised, he'd called Cindy during the week and arranged for a Saturday afternoon visit. At the time, he wasn't certain what he was going to tell Lily, and when Cindy asked, he honestly admitted that he hadn't quite worked that out. He still couldn't get over Cindy's transformation. When she responded that she trusted his judgment, he felt a pang of guilt that he'd let things go this far.

Even though the hour was early, Lily was excited to spend some time alone with him. Going to school, watching her babies grow bigger by the minute, and having Aunt Judy there had significantly reduced the amount of time she'd spent alone with her surrogate father.

Today when he appeared in her room earlier than usual and asked if she wanted to go for walk along the lake, she was quick to respond. She loved tossing rocks into the lake almost as much as dipping her toes into the icy liquid.

Judy heard the commotion in the next room and decided to stay behind the scenes, fearing that if Trevor saw her he'd change his mind about telling Lily. He'd been vacillating all week about whether or not to tell her right away, and when he'd finally made the decision last night to impart only as much as a four-year-olds mind could handle, she was relieved. She truly believed Lily was young enough to accept her mother coming into her life with the simplest of explanations. From what Trevor had told her, it seemed Jamie had done a good job of skirting the issue when it had come up in the past. When Lily would ask about her mother, Jamie would simply reply that she had become very sick and had to go away.

Judy watched from the window as Lily and Trevor started down the path. Lily was happily skipping alongside Trevor without a care in the world. "Just as a child's life should be," she said to no one in particular.

They'd reached the gently lapping water, and before Lily could pick up her first stone, Trevor gently pulled her toward him and hugged her hard. "Lily, there's something we need to talk about before we start skipping stones."

Lily sensed his apprehension and stood still, awaiting his next words.

"Do you remember when your daddy said your mom was very sick and lived far away?"

She nodded her head and waited for him to continue. "Well, your mom isn't sick anymore and would like to come for a visit."

Bewildered, the small child asked, "My mom?"

"Yes, honey, your mother. She's coming today to see you."

Lily then tore from his grasp and turned to face the opposite direction.

"What's the matter, hon? Don't you want to meet your mom?"

A small barely audible sound could be heard. "No."

Trevor stayed where he was, giving her the space she needed. "Why not?"

"I not know her!"

"Well, don't you want to get to know her?"

"No! I stay here with you."

He then understood her concern. "You're not going anywhere. You're going to stay here for as long as you want. Your mom just wants to meet you, that's all."

Lily turned back then and saw him kneeling, his arms outstretched. Without hesitation she wrapped her arms around his neck and answered, "Okay. Can we throw rocks now?"

As soon as it began, it was over. How wonderful, he thought, to be a child—no analysis, blame, baggage, or judgment. When in a person's life did all that start? All week he'd labored over how she'd react and, as usual, his aunt had been right. She'd assured him that Lily would be able to handle the truth.

He was pleasantly surprised about how well it had gone. Thinking about the actual visit was another story. He had several hours to get used to the idea and decided to stick like glue to Lily in case more of what she'd learned this morning sank in.

For a brief moment, he thought of Lana as they attempted to skip rocks across the dark, seemingly bottomless body of water. A silvery glow shone from various parts of the lake where the sun's rays filtered down through a cloudless sky. The deep azure color had never seemed so brilliant. This shade made him think of Lana's eyes, which had cap-tivated him from the minute he was close enough to be mesmerized.

A light breeze, barely enough to be felt, had little effect on the glasslike surface of the lake, and the peacefulness of the gently lapping water brought back memories of sitting on the front porch. It had felt right sitting next to her on those cool, crisp mornings.

Part of him was still angry that she had left without a word, but he knew why. She had run just as fast and as far as he had been doing for most of his life. Trouble was, the shoe was on the other foot this time and he wasn't sure how to handle it. He'd always been the one to walk away. He just hadn't been ready to let go this soon—and he wasn't sure he would ever have been ready with a person like her. Maybe this was best.

The route Sam had mapped out took about three and a half hours, and for the last two not much was said as the Kenny G CD played for a second time. Neither Sam nor Cindy had spoken more than a few words since their departure.

Cindy blamed herself for the distance between them. She couldn't be sure whether it was the pregnancy or her nerves that had caused her stomach to feel queasy every waking hour all week.

Despite Sam's patience, her disposition over the last few days had caused more than their share of arguments. She was so edgy and nerv-ous about the upcoming trip that nothing could pull her out of her fraz-zled state.

The night before, Sam had brought home long-stemmed roses and even attempted a backrub to soothe her nerves, but neither had any ef-fect on her. Finally, he'd given up and gone to bed alone. This morning they had worked in tandem getting ready for the trip, hardly looking each other in the eyes.

Sam guessed they were more than halfway there and wanted to clear the air before they reached their destination. Without any warning, he asked rather curtly, "Are we going to ignore each other for another hour?"

He was sick of listening to the lonely sounding sax and snapped the player off, displaying the real anger boiling underneath. He had always handled Cindy with kid gloves, fearing she would run when the going got tough. As of now, he wasn't going to be afraid anymore. Keeping the lid on his frustration wasn't working.

Cindy was ashamed of her behavior and knew she'd pushed him to his limit. The last person in the world she wanted to hurt was her husband. As important as Lily was, Sam had stood by her through everything and she owed it to him to let him know how much he meant to her.

As tears began to fall down her cheeks, she cried, "Oh, Sam, I'm so sorry for everything." She couldn't even look at him. Instead, she looked out the window and silently prayed that she hadn't ruined everything.

Sam immediately slowed down and pulled onto the shoulder of the highway. As soon as the car came to a full stop, he turned off the ignition and sat motionless. He wasn't going to coddle her any longer. She needed to make amends and face what had really been bothering her all week.

She hoped Sam would take her in his arms and say everything would be all right, like he'd always done. Today was different. She looked over at his profile and saw the sternness of his jaw. He wasn't giving in this time and fear gripped her.

"Sam, please look at me."

He couldn't just yet. Hearing her pleas nearly broke him in two, but he wanted her to feel, for just a moment longer, the anguish she'd caused.

When he continued to stare straight ahead, ignoring her request, Cindy thought surely she'd lost him. Sam had been her lifeline, and she wondered if she had the tools to fix the torn relationship.

Softly she whispered the words that nearly killed her to say. "I'll understand if after this trip you never want to see me again. I've been a beast all week and I've taken it all out on you. You, who don't deserve any of this." She turned away from him then, too ashamed to face him.

When she felt his strong arms pull her over the console and into his lap, she didn't try to escape. Even though the steering wheel was digging into her ribs she'd never felt more comfortable.

Sam didn't want to punish her any longer but wanted to let her know exactly what was on his mind. "I don't want to hear you ever say that it would be all right if I walked away. I'm not Jamie! I need you to fight for what we have."

"But everything's so screwed up," Cindy cried. "There's a child now! And a past that's been catching up with me ever since we met."

He placed his forefinger gently under her chin and brought her tear-stained face within inches of his own. When she turned to look away, he stiffened his hold and forced her to look him in the eyes. "I'm telling you this one more time and I hope it never needs to be repeated: I want you in my life. I'm not happy about you shutting me out most of the week. When this weekend is over and we're both a little more rational, I hope we can talk it through. We're going to face lots of ups and downs in our life and we need to trust that neither one of us is going to run away."

She had heard the words before, but today they finally sank in. He wasn't the type to run the minute the going got rough. "I wasn't really aware, until now, of how much the past has dictated my life. Jamie was always threatening to leave. I just assumed you'd be the same way."

"Is that what you've felt all week, that I'd leave you over this?" Sam asked incredulously.

"I wasn't really sure. I can't expect you to like what's happened, and you mean so much to me. I would never want to do anything to make you unhappy."

"Well, know this: living without you would make me the unhappiest man in the world." Then to lighten the tension, he remarked, "Let me know now if there are any other children in the wings or dead boy-friends lurking above."

She punched him lightly on the shoulder and promised the book on her past had finally been closed.

Sam's legs started to cramp and he kissed her hard before he lifted her off his lap and guided her back to her seat. Starting the car, he glanced over and noticed that the tightness he'd seen around her mouth for the last week was gone, and in its place was the hint of a smile.

"Okay, now let's get a move on and meet that little girl of yours."

Trevor had paced the living room so many times he could have qualified for a 5K race. Cindy and Sam were due to arrive at any minute and he was having a hard time focusing on anything.

Flashes of images kept creeping into his mind. Would Lily hide behind his leg or run screaming the minute she saw her mother? Or would she take to her as if time had stood still and they'd never been separated? If she did, how would he feel? Would he lose her forever? And how would Cindy react to seeing her daughter for the first time? How would he respond watching the exchange?

Lily was sitting at the dining room table coloring a picture, and Judy had gone into the kitchen to brew a pot of coffee. It surprised him that they were treating this day like any other. How could they be so calm?

Judy hid her trepidation well, not wanting to show her nephew that, like him, she was uneasy about Cindy's visit. Although she was the ultimate optimist, she knew this meeting could go either way. She hoped and prayed that Cindy would, first and foremost, take the child's welfare into account before any decisions were made. Lily had to come first. But did Cindy understand that?

As she came back to the living room, Judy heard a car door slam and knew the moment had come. Trevor's ashen face revealed his apprehension, so she took his hand in her own and led the way to greet their guests.

As they passed the dining room table, Lily stood and immediately grabbed Trevor's leg, impeding his progress toward the door. Maybe she knew more than she'd let on about missing a mother, or maybe it was watching Trevor's meltdown that caused her to hide.

Sam appeared first at the door, and when Judy moved aside to let him in, Trevor saw Cindy lingering behind. Trevor noticed immediately that both mother and daughter were hiding behind the men in their lives, and wondered just how much of a role genetics played in a person's development.

It was Judy who broke the ice and introduced herself to Sam and Cindy. Cindy had a vague recollection of meeting her years ago and said as much. Without any prompting to meet the child peering out from behind Trevor's leg, Cindy knelt down and extended her hand in greeting. The back of her throat had become dry and swallowing was a labored task. Her knees were shaking, and when she noticed her hand doing the same she immediately pulled it back. As soon as the child's eyes met hers, time seemed to stand still. It was as if they were the only two people in the room. Cindy couldn't help but memorize every detail of Lily's face—her dark eyes, a mirror of her own, her nose, an exact replica of her grandmother's, and the perfect shape of her lips, which reminded her of Jamie.

After several minutes had passed and the thickening air began to stifle, Judy knelt down next to Cindy and finished the introductions. Lily moved toward Judy, allowing herself to get closer to Cindy, and uttered a faint hello.

Cindy wanted so much to take her daughter in her arms and tell her how much she loved her. But Lily's barely audible reply was all she was going to get for now, and she had to accept it as enough.

Judy then stood and invited them all into the kitchen for a bite to eat. It was lunchtime and she'd arranged an assortment of cold cuts and cheeses on a platter for sandwiches. She was famished and knew the diversion of food would help to lighten the tension in the room. Sam offered to help and walked two steps behind her into the kitchen.

As soon as Judy walked away, Lily retreated to her spot behind Trevor's leg. She was still unsure of how to act with this woman, and hiding seemed like the best thing to do.

Cindy got to her feet and walked over to the shoulder bag she'd dropped by the door. Like a magician pulling a rabbit out of a hat, she pulled out one of the most elegant-looking dolls Lily had ever seen. As soon as Cindy saw Lily's face light up, she handed her the doll.

"This is a Madam Alexander doll. I had one just like it when I was your age. I used to have tea parties in my room and Lexie—that's what I called her—she came to every party. Do you like tea parties?"

Lily loved dolls. She had a collection of them in her room upstairs, and almost every day she'd play tea party, carefully selecting which dolls would be invited that particular day. Without realizing what she was doing she responded, "Yes. Me have a table and chairs and everything."

"Well, how about that! I did too. My father hand-painted flowers all over it to make it even prettier."

"Where it is?"

"That's a good question. I think they might have given it to another little girl when I left home. Do you think I could see yours and maybe we could have a tea party and invite—Oh, what should we call her?"

Lily thought for a moment then blurted out, "Sarah! That her name."

"Okay then. Can we invite Sarah to the party?"

A common ground had been established, and when Lily ran up the stairs announcing she could come up as soon as everything was set up, Cindy couldn't have been more thrilled. It wasn't important that Lily didn't call her Mom or fall into her arms like she'd dreamed. The truth of the matter was that she hadn't run away crying either. Baby steps. That's what she'd learned to take in rehab, and that's what she'd do now.

Trevor watched the exchange and felt a sense of pride knowing he'd been the one to bring these two together. Instead of feeling intense sadness, as he thought he might, a wave of relief bounded over him—relief at righting a wrong and, more importantly, giving a mother and her daughter a chance to nurture the bond that only they could share.

Within minutes, Lily was calling down that everything was ready. Cindy went up alone. Trevor stayed behind, thinking it best to give them some time alone to get to know each other. As soon as she walked into the little girl's room, Cindy was reminded of the one she'd occupied as a young girl. Everything was delicate, just as it should be.

"Thank you for inviting me, Lily." Cindy said, fighting back tears.

"You sit here," Lily directed, pointing to one of the child-sized chairs. The Madam Alexander doll had been placed on another of the chairs, and directly opposite was another doll.

Cindy sat down and couldn't help but study every movement Lily made. Her fingers were so small and feminine, her hair was dark and thick, and her smile was infectious. Cindy had fallen in love on sight.

All the trepidation and anxiety had faded away the minute their eyes met, and she wanted so much to take her child in her arms and erase the last four years. *Dammit, why had Jamie kept this small wonder from her?* Anger started to rise and she had to swallow it before it threatened to destroy her calm exterior. She couldn't go back in time. She had to move forward.

Just watching her daughter pour the imaginary tea and slice the nonexistent cake reminded her of the only times in her life, before she'd met Sam, worth remembering. Her parents had doted on her when she was Lily's age. It wasn't until she reached adolescence that their relationship had started to deteriorate. She didn't want that to happen with her daughter.

Lily didn't seem in the least concerned about the woman sitting across from her. She talked about the baby birds, her school, and people she referred to as Aunt Irma and Ben, and even mentioned a woman named Lana.

Cindy could have listened to her daughter talk for hours, but when Trevor soon poked his head in to remind them about lunch, the spell was temporarily broken. She could tell how much Lily loved Trevor, and briefly wondered if that same intensity would ever be aimed at her. She hoped so.

Later that night, Trevor sat alone on the porch, wondering about his father for the first time since he was a boy. He wondered if he resembled him in any way or possessed any of his mannerisms. Why hadn't he ever tried to find him and ask the thousands of questions he'd tucked away for so long?

Just watching the way Lily had responded to her mother brought up feelings he had pushed so far back he'd almost forgotten them. There was a definite bond between mother and daughter that was hard to miss. Would it have been the same for him with his father?

His mother's excessive bitterness and absolute silence about his father's absence had stifled any ideas of a search long ago. Now, seeing a mother and daughter reunited unearthed a multitude of emotions he'd quashed from boyhood. So much had happened—had changed—since then. He'd grown into manhood, reached the pinnacle of success, suffered a terrible loss, and somehow been reduced to that boy again, sitting alone on his porch.

Trevor walked into the house several hours later, and even though the hour was late, he picked up the phone and dialed one of the few numbers he'd ever memorized.

When his agent groggily answered on the fourth ring, Trevor felt a little guilty about waking him up. But that unsettled feeling vanished when, as soon as his voice was recognized, the voice perked up and asked how the hell he was doing. Trevor didn't go into too much detail and his agent was smart enough not to ask too many questions. Several minutes later, after he'd hung up, Trevor knew that within a few weeks his life was probably going to be altered once again.

He hadn't written any songs since Jamie's death, and as he walked up the stairs to call it a night his mind wandered back to what had always been his comfort zone—his music. He lay in bed a long time before sleep overtook him. Jamie was gone, and watching Lily respond to her mother this evening only reinforced what he'd known all along—they belonged together.

He loved Lily more than he'd thought possible and giving her up should have been devastating, but the sensation he felt was just the opposite. Lily would eventually go home. Home to where her mother resided, where she'd look up to a man she would call Dad, and where she would share her hopes and dreams with a sister or brother. She'd have the freedom to walk to school, ride her bike through the neighborhood, and have sleepovers on Friday nights. That is what he wished for the child he'd thought of as his own.

Tonight was the first time his body and mind had been at peace since the plane crash. He knew this to be true because sometime during the evening, as he watched Lily grow closer to her mother, he'd heard the tapping of a drum and the strumming of a guitar seep through his consciousness. Jamie had always teased him that most people's minds were filled with words and numbers but his flowed with melodies and lyrics.

After Lily had gone up to bed, they'd talked at length about the inevitable. Trevor reminded Cindy about the possible effects of FAS, which might show up later in life. When he noticed her on the verge of tears, he softened his delivery, saying once again, that so far nothing had shown up. Cindy was familiar with the syndrome from working at the rehab center, and she told Trevor about the programs her facility had in place for both children and adults born with FAS.

They all agreed that the time for any transfer wouldn't be predetermined, but would be decided when Lily was ready. Trevor didn't say it, but from the way Lily had responded to Cindy, he knew it'd be much sooner than he would've liked.

Chapter Twenty-one

The day after Lana arrived home she'd been up at dawn preparing for her first day back at work. She'd been out of the office for more than a week and was a little nervous about telling her boss about her plans. The opportunity he'd given her in administration had been a godsend at the time, but working with Lily had brought her back to her true calling.

That was five weeks ago. For the past two, she'd been working half days in the pediatric ward and the other half helping the new assistant administrator get acclimated.

Lana had been a bundle of nerves that first day back, but seeing some of the old faces cross her path during her shift allayed any fears that she'd made the wrong decision. It had been like riding a bike. Within a few hours she'd changed three bandages, checked five temperatures, administered a dozen medications, and read a short story to a group of kids able enough to walk to the playroom.

She'd also resumed her volunteer work, committing two evenings a week at the women's shelter, teaching young mothers the art of caring for their infants and toddlers. They somehow seemed younger than they had four years ago. She'd been through so much during her absence that she didn't know whether they were actually younger or if she'd aged in more than just years. She guessed the latter.

As promised, Judy had called after Cindy and Sam's visit to fill her in on how everything had gone. The following weekend she had headed north to pick up her friend, and when she'd arrived and learned that Trevor and Lily had driven down to Westchester for an overnight stay with Cindy and Sam, her heart had sunk.

Twice since, she'd conjured up the courage to call Lily, and when Irma answered the first time and Cindy the next, it was all she could do to hide the disappointment in her voice. She'd apologized to Lily both times for not saying good-bye, offering excuses anyone old to enough to know better would have seen right through.

She longed to hear Trevor's voice, but couldn't bring herself to ask for him. The next move would have to be up to him. Judy had mentioned that he'd started writing music again and had plans to produce his first solo album. It seemed that he was getting on with his life, and that knowledge hurt more than if she'd learned that he was sitting alone in Vermont, slowly descending into a deep dark depression.

Tonight she and Judy had plans to meet for dinner. Lana decided it was time to share with her friend just how she'd been feeling. She missed Trevor more than she thought possible and she had to know if he'd mentioned her at all.

She'd been standing at Mario's Restaurant for only a few minutes when she noticed the familiar shape crossing the street. The last time they had really spent some quality time together was when she'd picked Judy up in Vermont. The conversation during the ride home that day had been kept to news about Lily and her mother, and Lana's decision to go back to her old profession. Judy had purposely kept Trevor's name out of the conversation, knowing only too well how much distress it would cause, and Lana had been grateful. There wasn't much Judy could have shared anyway, since Trevor had been pretty tight-lipped whenever talk of Lana surfaced.

As they sipped a delicate merlot and waited for their dinners to arrive, Lana was the first to finally broach the subject.

"What have you heard from Trevor?" she asked, trying to sound calm and indifferent.

"Not much really," Judy answered. "We've been playing phone tag. I've been so busy trying to play catch-up and he's been so busy taxiing Lily back and forth to Westchester that we haven't had much time to talk. I do know he's been logging in time at some studio in New York City when Lily's been with her mother."

Life sure has moved on for Trevor, Lana thought, painting a smile on her face. "How's Lily adjusting?"

"Trevor says he's never seen her happier. Last week she met Sam's family for the first time and was thrilled to learn she has a slew of cousins. Apparently, the Stewarts, Cindy's in-laws, have welcomed Lily with open arms and have invited her to stay with them at their summer place on the Jersey shore for a few weeks in August."

"I'm so happy everything's working out for them. Trevor made the right decision to tell Cindy."

"From what I can tell, Cindy's going to make a fine mother," Judy said as she poured more wine into their glasses. Then as she set the bottle down, she added, "Speaking of mothers, how's yours?"

"Oh, you know—the usual," Lana answered, circling the top of the wineglass with her finger. "She's worried I'm biting off more than I can chew. She now fills my refrigerator with leftovers to make sure I'm eating."

"You're a lucky woman," Judy said, shaking her index finger at Lana. "I wish someone would do that for me."

"I know." Lana sighed. "It's just that she's still trying to control my life. I love her dearly, but sometimes she really drives me nuts."

"A mother's job never ends. To her you'll always be her little girl."

Just then the waiter came over with two steaming plates of pasta. The one with the red meat sauce—Bolognese, they'd called it on the menu—went to Judy, and the other one slathered in alfredo sauce was set in front of Lana.

Lana had eaten half of her meal before she summoned up enough courage to ask the one question that had been haunting her for weeks. "Does he ever ask about me?"

Judy knew exactly who *"he"* was. Although Lana generally put up a good performance and kept her emotions in check, Judy saw the defeated look in her eyes and knew something was bothering her. "He asks about you all the time."

Lana was so flabbergasted she didn't know what to say. "He does?"

It took a minute for Judy to respond. She wasn't sure if the last bite of pasta had stuck in her throat or if she was affected by the sudden sound of hope in Lana's voice. Clearing her throat, she answered, "Yes, he does."

Lana's appetite had just flown out the window. "Why haven't you ever told me?"

Judy set down her fork and took a sip of wine before answering. She'd had a feeling that tonight was going to be the night that Lana would finally need to talk about her relationship with Trevor. Lana couldn't stand to keep things bottled up, and Judy had known it was just a matter of time before she'd be put on the spot. Her nephew, in contrast, couldn't have been more different.

"Honestly, I was afraid to give you false hope."

Lana didn't know how to respond. Did Judy know something?

"What has he asked about me?"

"Mostly he asks how you're doing. I hope you don't mind, but I told him about your job change."

"Not at all. I'm just happy to know that he at least cared enough to ask about me."

"Of course he cares, Lana. I think maybe a little too much, and it's frightening the hell out of him."

"Oh, come on, Judy. Why would caring about me scare him so?"

"After all he's gone through over the past few months, I think it's only natural that he'd retreat a little. He knows he's vulnerable and I don't think that's a comfortable position for him. I also think it goes much deeper. Growing up without a father, coupled with his mother's bitterness and silence about her failed marriage, left some deep wounds."

"Have you ever tried to help him…professionally, I mean?"

"More times than I can count. In fact, the only times I've felt completely at a loss in my profession were when I tried to help Trevor and his mother. My sister thinks what I do is for the weak and helpless, and Trevor…well, he's just a different story. I think fear is what keeps him from any kind of analysis."

"Why do you think that?" Lana asked.

"I'm not sure he's ever really faced his past. When he was a little boy, I tried to fill the gap as much as I could, but having an aunt is not the same as having a father. To Trevor, I was his aunt first and then a psychotherapist. Whenever I'd start to sound like a therapist, he'd kindly remind me that I was his aunt and not some shrink paid to dig inside his head."

Chapter Twenty-one

"I know this sounds silly, but do you think there's any way I can help him?"

"It's just not that easy. Trevor's a grown man, and you know yourself if you're not ready to deal with something, no one can tell you otherwise."

Judy had hit home with that one. "I guess you're right."

Once again she felt defeated.

The disappointment in Lana's voice cut deep. For years Judy had felt helpless when it came to her sister and, to some extent, her nephew. "I'm so sorry, Lana."

Looking somewhat perplexed, Lana asked, "About what?"

"Getting you mixed up in all this. I should've known better. I let my closeness to the situation cloud my judgment, and now…"

"Whoa! Hold on a sec," Lana interrupted. "There's no blame to take. I knew what I was doing. I can't deny that I'm sorry things didn't work out for Trevor and me. But I'm very grateful for the time I spent in Vermont. Even though I left a piece of my heart there, I at least had a piece to leave. I became me again—something I'd given up hope on."

It was close to ten o'clock by the time Lana arrived home. The dinner with Judy had been just what the doctor had ordered. Knowing that Trevor had cared enough to ask about her made her heart soar. Although she knew nothing would ever come of it, she found some comfort in knowing that what they'd shared had meant something to him.

She had finished brushing her teeth and was almost done removing her makeup when the phone rang. Her mom always had a knack for calling when she least felt like talking.

"Hello, Mom!"

"Lana?"

The minute she heard his voice she nearly dropped the receiver.

"Ah…yes. I'm sorry—I almost dropped the phone. Can you hold on a second?"

She needed to catch her breath and quiet her speeding heart. No way in the world did she want him to know how excited she was that he'd called.

Several seconds later, sounding somewhat calm, she said, "I'm sorry! I was right in the middle of…ah…forget it." Her palms were sweating and she cradled the receiver between her shoulder and ear, leaving her hands free to wipe on her pajama bottoms. She then asked, "So, how are you, Trevor?"

Trevor had been home the two times she'd called for Lily, and both times he'd feigned disinterest, when in fact it had taken all his strength not to steal the phone away. Late at night, when everyone was in bed, he'd run his fingers over the keys on the phone, composing her number but never once pressing hard enough for the call to go through. To-night, though, was different—his fingers had a mind of their own.

"I'm doing okay," he told her. "You?"

"Oh, pretty good." Trying to keep it casual, she mentioned, "I had dinner with your aunt tonight."

"Oh, yeah? How's she doing? I haven't talked to her in a while."

"She's great. Says she's pretty busy getting caught up, though."

"I know. We've played phone tag a few times."

"Yeah, she told me." Oops! She'd let slip out that they'd talked about him. "How's Lily?"

"She's doing great. She really appreciated your calls. Things around here have really changed. As I'm sure my aunt's told you, Cindy is now part of her life."

"I heard that. I'm really glad you decided to tell her."

He knew she would be. After all, it was her urging that tipped the scales. "Me too. After seeing the two of them together, it seems right. In fact, Lily's going to be staying with her for a week while I head out to L.A."

Hearing that bit of news deflated some of the excitement she'd felt upon hearing his voice. "You're heading back to L.A.?"

Did he hear disappointment in her voice? "First thing tomorrow. I've got some business to take care of, and I need to catch up with a few people."

He did say that Lily was only going to be staying with Cindy a week. That meant he'd be back—didn't it? "Sounds like everything's going well for the two of them. Are you doing as well?"

"It's hard not to be happy for the two of them when you see them together. As for me, I'm getting back into my music and life goes on."

Trying desperately to hide her disappointment, Lana asked, "Are you moving back to California?"

"Eventually, maybe. I don't like to admit it, but it wouldn't surprise me if by the fall Lily was living full-time with her mother."

She heard a slight catch in his voice and felt his pain. "I'm sorry, Trevor."

He hesitated a moment, raked his fingers through his hair, and then admitted, "You and I both know she belongs there."

Silence filled the air for several seconds before Lana changed direction. "I'd love to see Lily again. Do you think that would be possible?"

What she really wanted to say was Lily *and him.*

Trevor was thankful for the diversion. "I could tell Cindy, and maybe you could meet her halfway," he suggested. "You're only about an hour and a half from each other. I'm sure Lily would love it."

Not quite the answer she was hoping for, but she really did want to see Lily again. "I'd like that, Trevor. You'll give Cindy my number?"

"I'll make sure she gets it," Trevor assured her.

Silence again. This was beginning to remind her of their talks on the front porch. As much as she hated playing games, she went ahead with one anyway. "Well, it's late and…"

"Wait! There's something else."

It had worked!

"Lana, are you still there?"

"Yes."

"I wanted to thank you for all your help. Lily has really come into her own. Without you showing me the way, that wouldn't have happened. You did so much for us and I'd like to at least pay you for all you've done."

She could have spit nails she was so angry! How could he have reduced what they'd had to a financial arrangement? If he'd been standing in front of her she would have slapped his face.

Too stunned to say anything at the moment, Lana actually welcomed the dead air. Then, without caring how angry she sounded, she stormed, "That won't be necessary, Trevor. I offered my services free of charge. It's late, so I'll say good-bye." She hung up the phone so hard it bounced onto the floor.

When the phone rang seconds later, she thought about letting the answering machine take a message. But the sound of a ringing phone was a reminder of that tragic night. Before she even had a chance to say hello she heard his voice.

"Don't hang up."

She wanted to do more than hang up. Hell, she wanted to wrap the cord around his pompous neck!

"Please, Lana. That came out all wrong." The minute the words had come out of his mouth he'd regretted saying them. Lana was different from anyone he'd ever known. She couldn't have cared less about his fame and fortune. In fact, he wondered if his success was more of stumbling block than an asset. Why couldn't he come out and tell her just how he felt?

"Well, what did you really mean to say?" Lana shot back.

"That I'm sorry for running out on you and not getting in touch with you sooner."

If he'd said those words a few minutes ago, she would have been reduced to tears. Now it only mildly lessened the anger boiling inside. "I'm sorry too, Trevor. I thought what we had was special, and when you walked away without a word, it was like a slap in the face."

"It *was* special to me," he declared. "I don't know—I just needed some space to sort everything out. So much was happening I didn't know what to do. I'm sorry you took it personally."

"How was I supposed to take it?" She couldn't control the tartness of her tongue.

"Look, I didn't call to fight with you."

"Well, maybe that's what we need to do. Fight it out!" And she was ready to do just that.

"Hey, don't forget you were the first one to walk away," Trevor reminded her.

She hadn't forgotten that fact. But leaving for a few hours had been a far cry from running away for days. "Did that hurt you enough for you to want to hurt back?" There it was again, that snippiness she tried unsuccessfully to control.

After a pause, he said, "No! It wasn't like that at all. I left for many reasons, none of which was to get back at you. In fact, after you'd left that night, I wasn't sure you'd want to see me again."

Surprised, Lana asked, "Why would you think that?"

"Well, for starters, I know you're not the kind of woman who indulges in casual sex. And I worried that maybe you weren't ready for what had happened and had developed a case of the guilts. Either way, I thought I was doing you a favor by disappearing."

She didn't know how to respond to that one. She'd thought he hadn't wanted to face her or what had happened. She'd never considered the possibility that he'd stayed away for her. The fight left her then and she slumped down on the bed.

"Oh, Trevor, we've really made a mess of things," she said, softening her tone.

"I didn't like the way we ended things and I wanted to make it right."

What did he mean by that? Was he ending this? Never before had her heart been on such a roller coaster.

"I didn't like the way things ended either," she admitted.

"You should have called me," he mildly scolded.

"That goes for you too!" she shot back. "But I thought you knew by now that I'm from the old school." Laughing a little, she added, "My mom always told me never to call boys."

"I haven't been a boy for some time now. Come on, Lana—we're in the twenty-first century!"

"Some things just never change," Lana jokingly responded.

To keep the mood light, he asked, "Can I go on my trip now with a clear conscience?"

She was more confused than ever. What did he mean? Had he needed to end *"it"* with a clear conscience? "I'm not sure what you mean."

Trevor wasn't sure either. He wanted to see her again, but his track record with women scared him. The last thing he wanted to do was start something he couldn't finish, especially with her.

"I'm not sure myself what I mean." After a silent moment, he reluctantly admitted, "I've really missed you, and as much as I want to hold you again in my arms, I know I can't."

She knew in her broken heart why, but had to ask, "Why?"

Distrust and fear of commitment reared their ugly heads again. "Lana, I'm not the settling-down type and I don't want to lead you down a path to nowhere."

"Funny—I don't remember asking you to settle down."

"I know you didn't but…" he paused then, wondering himself why he was letting her go. He needed her, wanted her, and probably loved her. There was still a part of him that wouldn't fully admit what his heart was convinced of. But the one thing he was sure of was that he couldn't involve a person like her in his life right now. He had to make her understand. "A woman like you deserves so much more than I can give."

When she didn't respond he added, "I've started composing again, and there's very little time for…well…you know."

Silence.

Hell, he thought, *she's not making this any easier*. Softly he pleaded, "Talk to me, Lana."

She wasn't about to beg for morsels of his time. She might not be an expert on dating or even love for that matter, but she did know that whomever she fell in love with had to feel the same way.

"What do you want me to say, Trevor?" Completely deflated now, she'd lost any sense of propriety. "Go, Trevor. Run and hide behind your music. You're right. I do deserve better."

For the first time since they'd made love, she saw things clearly. She was a survivor. She'd come back after being lost, allowed herself to feel love again, and now felt deserving of a healthy relationship.

Her tone then softened as she explained this epiphany. "Trevor, after I'd lost everything that was precious to me, it was time that healed most of my wounds, but the one thing I didn't get back, besides the obvious, was being number one in someone's life. From the minute I met my husband, I was number one in his life, and I gladly shared that spot when we had our daughter. Now, I'm number one to no one, and I miss that."

It was about midway through her emotional speech that the floodgates flew open, not so much out of anguish, but enlightenment.

He'd heard every word. He'd never been number one in anyone's life, and, until Lily came along, no one had ever been number one in his. He felt trapped. He didn't want to lose Lana, but he knew better than to string her along. She deserved it all. He couldn't offer that to her now. Deep down he wondered if he ever could.

"I don't know what to say, Lana."

"Please don't say anything." She truly meant it this time. "Just know that I'll be fine. I wish you all the best. Good-bye."

"Wait!" he yelled. But she'd already hung up.

If this was for the best, and he really believed it was, then why did he feel so miserable? He slammed the receiver down into its cradle and started packing for LA. He was going home! The change in surroundings, he convinced himself, would surely get her image out of his mind.

Chapter Twenty-two

Trevor sat in silence as Jack Lerner, the retired sergeant from the L.A.P.D. that his agent had hired, walked out of his house. The thin file, all two pages of facts, sat open atop the coffee table in the living room. He didn't need to read again what had already been emblazoned in his memory bank.

All these years he'd believed his father had been living at large, not giving a damn about him, when in fact he'd been killed in a car accident just a year after he had walked out of their lives.

According to Jack, his mother had never been notified because his father had remarried just a month prior to his death. Jack had even gone so far as to track his second wife down, but she had sworn she'd never known anything about a child.

He'd had many childhood fantasies of his father walking through the door with a bundle of toys for all the birthdays and holidays he'd missed. These fantasies stayed with him well into the teen years. And when he hit the big time, he fantasized about hearing from his dad. He'd even gone over a thousand times in his head what he'd say. He'd be angry and hateful at first. But in his dream his father would persist and he'd eventually soften to the idea of building a relationship with the man who shared the same DNA.

Those dreams had ended when he'd turned twenty-five. The bitterness that had found a home in his mother's heart had unfortunately settled in his, too.

Now he would never know for sure whether or not his father would have one day contacted him, but it was nice to consider the possibility. Trevor's mistrust of people and fear of commitment had been built on feelings of abandonment, which may or may not have been based on reality.

He wondered what his life would have been like had he learned of his father's death long ago. Would he have fled to California? Would he be alone today if he had learned how to trust? Would his mother have shown some emotion when she'd learned of her lost love's death? Would she have shared with his only son some of the redeeming qualities Rory must've possessed for her to love him in the first place?

As he contemplated what might have been, he suddenly experienced an overwhelming urge to put pen to paper. The truth about his father was like a gust of wind pushing away the dark cloud that had found a home in his soul.

Life was definitely going to be different without Jamie. He wasn't even sure he'd ever play again with the band. He was solo now. But for the first time since Jamie's death, he felt hopeful.

Several months had passed since Lana had returned to nursing. In those few months, she'd clocked more overtime than half of the nursing staff combined on the pediatric floor. When she wasn't filling in for someone at the hospital, she was volunteering at the women's shelter. She'd only spoken to Judy a handful of times since their dinner out, and Trevor's name was thankfully never spoken.

Lana had put in another marathon week at work and was relieved she wasn't volunteering at the shelter that night. During her drive home, she could think of nothing else but falling into bed. Work had been her salvation again, keeping at bay the deep sadness in her heart. She missed him. She'd only been with him a week and a half, but it had been enough for her to fall in love.

Every now and then, Lana would let her guard down and wallow in the memories that had altered the course of her life. Tonight would be one of those nights. From her evening of self-pity, she would summon the strength and determination to face life without her husband, her daughter, and now, Trevor. Trevor was gone—just a memory now. She had to face that and get on with her life.

She'd been through hell and back, and had survived. This should've been easy. It wasn't the gut-wrenching pain she'd experienced after the accident, but nonetheless, it hurt. She should have hated him for using her—but she didn't. He was as wounded as she was, so why then was he soaring and she still grounded?

She had read in *USA Today* that he was working on his latest album. Obviously, he'd healed. Why couldn't she? She'd returned to nursing, but her heart remained up north. *Maybe I'll sell the house and get a fresh start,* she pondered. That thought at least steered her mind away from the relationship that would never be.

The streetlight outside her house was out, and it wasn't until she reached her driveway that she noticed the truck parked in the street. Her knees started to shake and she gripped the steering wheel, hoping to regain some stability. She slowly pulled into the driveway, craning her neck to see if he was sitting in the driver's seat. It was too dark to tell. She then turned the ignition switch off and sat for a second in the quiet, watching, wondering, hoping... Her mind raced. *Why is he here? How am I supposed to behave? How can I stop these tears?*

She then noticed a dark form on her front stoop.

His eyes were riveted on the car. For the past few days he'd waited, a few doors down, for her to pull into the driveway. He hadn't had the nerve to approach her the first day. The second, he almost called out her name. This time he'd finally gotten the nerve to pull in front of her house and walk up to her door.

What do you say to the woman you want to spend the rest of your life with? That thought alone, six months ago, would have scared the hell out of him. But now it was the first thing he thought of when he woke up and the last thing he thought of before he closed his eyes. He had been able to temporarily put it out of his mind, during the day at least, but it was becoming harder as time went on.

Memories of Jamie had accompanied him into the studio each morning. Instead of the deep sadness he'd felt for months after his friend's death, he found instead the motivation to write of love, loss, and hope. The writing and composing had once again come naturally. But at night when the moon was high in the sky, and first thing in the morning when the sun inched upward, loneliness wrapped its arms around him.

He needed first to make amends for the way he'd left things. That night on the phone, Lana had struck a nerve when she said she deserved to be number one. He'd never thought about relationships that way, and until she'd mentioned it, he never believed it could happen for him. After all, there was no way in hell he was ever going to let someone in that deep. But in denying himself, he'd been no better than his mother who'd grown old alone. He didn't want to grow old alone. He knew that now. Cindy promised he could always be in Lily's life, and he knew he would. But it wasn't enough.

Before he'd gone in search of Lana's house, he'd sat in his aunt's office for hours, letting her glimpse the man he'd hidden away for so long. He'd always known she'd seen through his facade, and he was now sure that's why he'd stayed away. Up until now he hadn't wanted to face that reality. He was comfortable being alone, and even though a part of him never felt totally fulfilled, he'd learned to live with it.

Now, he sat on Lana's stoop rooted to the spot. He'd resolved so much in his life and couldn't wait to share it with the one person who had been instrumental in changing his life.

Lana took several deep breaths before she had the strength to open the car door. All the hurt and anguish she'd experienced over the last few months were nothing compared to the flood of fear that he'd leave once again. He was here now, and that's all that mattered. Wasn't this what she wanted? One more chance to see, touch, and experience him.

She slowly walked toward the steps, realizing she'd forgotten to leave the front lights on again.

Even though the night sky was black and he could only see a few feet in front of him, thanks to the flickering street light, Trevor could distinguish her form as if the sun were shining. As she came closer, he caught a glimpse of distrust in her demeanor and a knifelike sensation cut through his heart.

He stood then, facing the image that emerged out of the darkness.

"Hi," he said softly.

It was like déjà vu. She couldn't find her voice or move from her spot. She looked down, too fearful and nervous to lose herself in his gaze. She noticed he had a folder in his hand and was holding it out for her to take.

But she couldn't. She was frozen.

He took her hand then as he'd done the first day they'd met. He bent his head slightly as he captured her eyes and mouthed the words she'd thought had chased him away.

"I want to be number one in your life and I need to have you as number one in mine."

As her mouth dropped open he took her in his arms and kissed her long and deeply, taking her breath away in the process.

She momentarily lost herself—giving in to the craving—until fear ran up her spine and jarred her memory. "Trevor, we can't start this again."

She tried to turn away, but he still held her hand. When he gently pulled her back, she snapped her hand from his warmth and pleaded, "Please don't." Her tears flowed freely now and she turned away. "I can't. It's too hard."

His shoulders lifted with his sigh. "I guess I don't blame you, Lana. I never meant to hurt you."

"I know you didn't," she said between sobs.

He had to make things right. No matter what she said, that kiss had proven the depth of her feelings. He couldn't let her walk away! Not when he'd figured out what he'd been missing most of his life. She'd struck a raw nerve when she said she wanted to be number one in someone's life. That's what he'd been missing his whole life. And not being anyone's number one allowed him to avoid having to reciprocate. No one had ever earned that privilege in his life—until now.

He gently lifted her chin so their eyes met. "Hi, I'm Trevor."

She looked at him perplexed. "What are you doing?"

"I want to start over, Lana."

"Oh, great," she said, a little exasperated as she wiped the last vestige of a tear. "What happens when you run away again?"

"That's not going to happen," he said quickly. "My running days are over."

She felt stronger now. She wasn't going to let him deceive her a second time. "That's good for you, Trevor. I'm happy for you." She started to walk around him, but he caught her arm and gently pulled her back.

"Please don't do this to us," he whispered in her ear.

"Us?" she cried, pulling away. "When has there ever been an us?"

"There was and you know it!" He was starting to get scared. She wasn't melting like moments ago. "I know you felt it the minute we met. I admit I wasn't the easiest person to deal with, but believe me when I tell you it's different now."

The streetlight in front of the house stopped flickering and the bulb that had petered out earlier shone brightly once again. Lana could now see the eyes that had caused her so much pain. Those eyes that bore into her soul like a bee into nectar. She had to look away before she lost her nerve. She couldn't let him back into her life, no matter what her heart was telling her. The logical side of her nature demanded that she walk away. Her sanity was far more important than getting mixed up with a man who'd plainly told her that music was his first love. She couldn't be second in anyone's book.

Trevor could practically see the wheels turning inside her head. He knew her inner struggle. He was a risk that a person like her was foolish to take. How could he get her to understand the depth of his feelings?

"Lana, I know what you're thinking. How can I waltz up to your door and expect you to open your heart to me again? You're scared and I don't blame you. But I'm not afraid to say that I need and want you in my life."

His love for her had never felt so strong. He had to make her believe him. "In the past, I avoided commitment like the Asian flu. Whenever I started to care about someone, I ran. I not only hurt them, but myself in the process. Honestly, no one has ever affected me the way you have. You made me want to face my fears and shed all the baggage I've carried around. Honey, I never stopped wanting you in my life."

She turned from him then, too scared to let him see the depth of her feelings. She felt his hands rest on her shoulders, and knew she was losing the battle. The man who'd carefully protected his soul had loosened the string, and it was dangling right there for her to grab onto.

He said he'd changed—but could she take that chance? She was lonely, yes, but she was in complete control and that gave her a great deal of solace.

Trevor felt her tremble and pulled her back against his chest. He couldn't lose her. " Am I right? Are you scared?"

She turned then and met his stare. In a barely audible voice she whispered, "Terrified is a better word."

He cupped her face within his hands and delicately kissed her quivering lower lip. "I don't want you to be afraid of me. I will never hurt you."

"You can't promise me that." She turned away from him then, fighting to hold back tears. Swallowing past the lump in her throat, she added, "No one can."

He swung her around, then gentled his touch as he tilted her face upward. "Sweetheart, you survived the worst and went on with your life. You're a survivor! I love that about you. I love many things about you. I love you."

She hadn't heard those words in so long. Without thinking, she leaned into him and wrapped her arms around his neck. "Just hold me," she cried, pressing her face into his shoulder.

As he pulled her closer, the folder he'd been holding fell to the ground. In tandem, they leaned down to pick up the sheets of paper that spilled onto the porch.

"What's this?" she asked, picking up what looked to be a CD cover. Even though the light was dim she was able to make out the title. "*Face the Music*," she proudly announced. "I like it!"

"You should. You were my inspiration."

"I'm scared, Trevor."

He took her into his arms then and kissed her hard on the mouth. When his lips left hers it was to offer assurance. "I know you are. I promise I'll always be here for you."

Lana gazed up into his eyes, trying desperately to make sense of it all. Drawing a jagged breath, she asked, "What about L.A. and being too busy with your music?"

Trevor caressed her cheek with a forefinger, outlining the delicate curve of her cheekbone. "The only thing I want to be busy doing is making you happy." His voice grew more serious as he added, "I realized after you'd gone how empty my life was. I don't want to live that way anymore. As for L.A, well, they have pediatric hospitals out West, you know."

Fear crept up her spine. "Trevor, I can't leave here."

"Why not?"

"Everything I know is right here. I feel like I've just come home from a very long journey, and I need to feel settled for awhile."

He'd never felt settled in his life until he'd met her. Nuzzling her neck, he whispered, "I know how it is. Being with you makes me feel like I've come home. Looks like that long-term lease I signed earlier today on the studio in New York was a good idea after all."

"Won't you miss L.A.?" she asked softly.

"As long as I have you in my life, I won't miss it at all. We'll be close to Lily, and Aunt Judy will be thrilled. I talked to Irma earlier and told her my intentions, and she couldn't be happier. It will be nice having her within reach, too."

"And then there's my parents," Lana said, rolling her eyes. "My mom takes a little getting used to."

Trevor smiled down at her, and the feeling of contentment fit like a glove. "If she's anything like you, it'll be easy."

She kissed him full on the mouth then, forgetting any of the hesitancy of before. "I love you, Trevor. I think I fell in love the minute our eyes locked."

"Lana, will you be my number one?" he asked.

As tears sprang to her eyes, she whispered, "I'd love nothing better."

END

ABOUT THE AUTHOR

Kerri Malloy's mid-life assessment led her to abandon corporate America after 20 years to follow her true passion for writing. In her first novel, Kerri engages her readers in a powerful tale of people's triumphs over tragedy.

Born and raised in Connecticut and mother of two active boys, Kerri introduces you to three characters whose suffering brings them unexpectedly together. You travel through the closets of her characters where skeletons are skillfully revealed and rediscover the healing powers of love.